UP THE WESTERN TRAIL

Point the Tongue North

BOOK 5
HOME ON THE RANGE SERIES

Rosie Bosse lives and writes on a ranch in northeast Kansas with her sweetheart of many years. She was once told, "If you can't find the books you want to read, then write them." That is what she is doing. May this book be all you hoped it would be, and may the characters become your friends.

UP THE
WESTERN TRAIL

Point the Tongue North

Rosie Bosse

POST ROCK
PUBLISHING

ISBN: Softcover - 978-1-958227-10-7
ISBN: eBook - 978-1-958227-11-4
Second Edition
First printed 2021, Second Edition published 2025

**POST ROCK
PUBLISHING**

Post Rock Publishing
17055 Day Rd.
Onaga, KS 66521

www.rosiebosse.com

Git Along, Little Dogies

As I was a walkin' one mornin' for pleasure,
I spied a cowpuncher all ridin' alone.
His hat was throwed back an' his spurs was a jinglin',
An' as he approached he was singin' this song.

Whoopee Ti Yi Yo! Git along, Little Dogies,
It's yore misfortune an' none of my own.
Whoopee Ti Yi Yo! Git along, Little Dogies,
Ya know that Wyomin' will be yore new home.

American Cowboy Song
Dating back to Trail Drive Days

Montana
Territory

Dakota
Territory

Wyoming
Territory

Nebraska

North Platte R.

CHEYENNE ✳   ✳ OGALLALA

JULESBURG ✳
South Platte R.   *South Platte R.*

Colorado

Kansas

Arkansas R.
Buckner Creek

Cimarron R.   DODGE CITY ✳

Bluff Creek

NO MAN'S LAND   *Beaver R.*
(THE STRIP)   ✳   *Arkansas R.*
                                   Cimarron R.

FORT SUPPLY   *Big Creek*

North Canadian R.

Indian
Territory

New Mexico
Territory

Canadian R.

North Fork
Big Elk Creek
Salt Fork

Brazos R.   *Red R.*

DOAN'S CROSSING ✳

Red R.   *Wichita R.*

Big
Pasture

EAGLE FLAT ✳   ✳ DENISON

✳ SEYMOUR

BUFFALO GAP ✳   *Brazos R.*

Western Trail →

Texas

The Red River
divided Texas
and Indian
Territory

BANDERA ✳

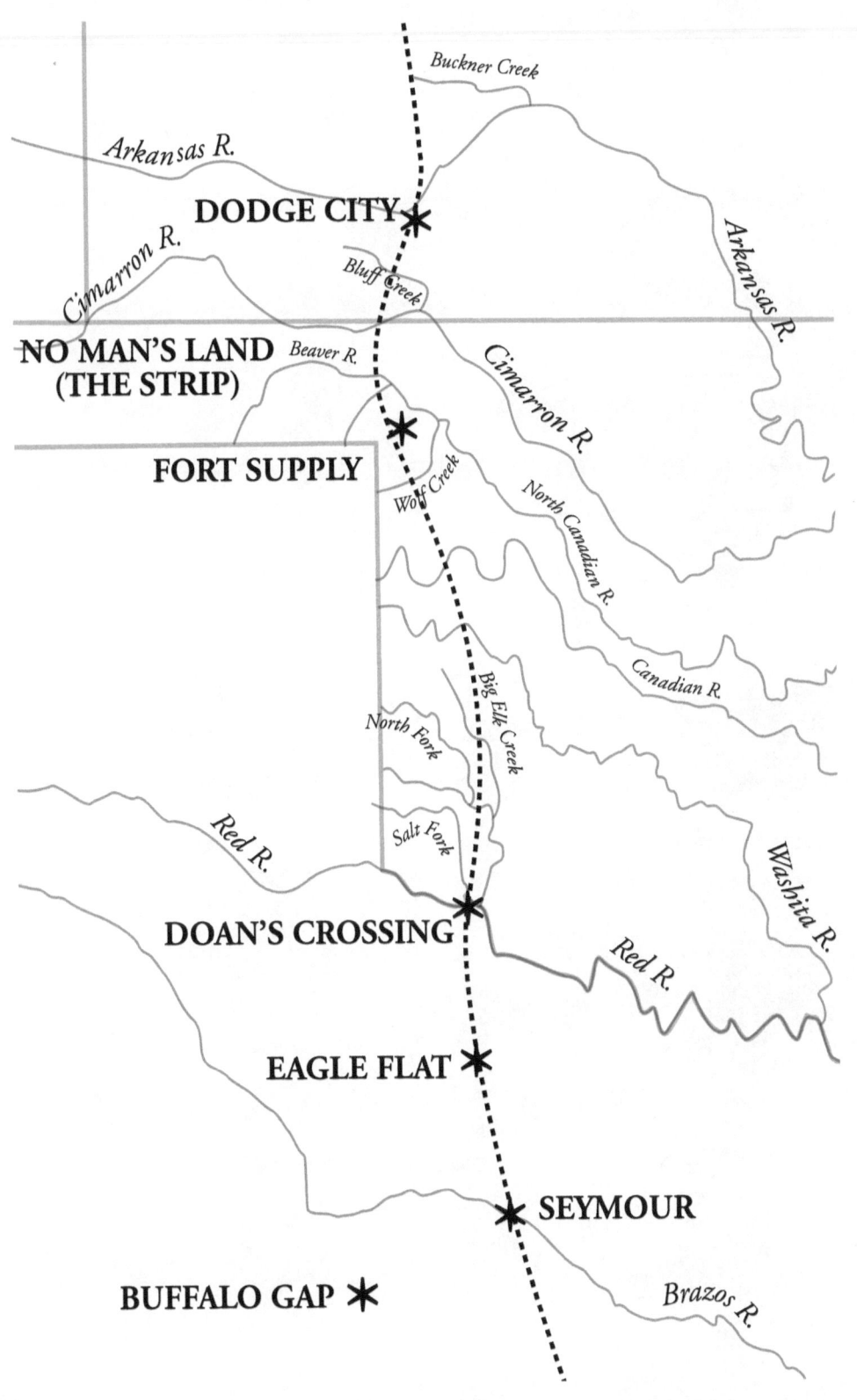

Prologue

Up the Western Trail, Point the Tongue North is the fifth novel in my Home on the Range Series. It is a trail drive along the Western Trail from Vernon, Texas (known in its early days as Eagle Flat), to Dodge City, Kansas. That is a distance of around two hundred seventy-seven miles. The full trail begins deep in southern Texas and runs all the way to Canada.

The cook on a cattle drive pointed the tongue of his chuckwagon north at night. He chose his direction by looking at the North Star. Since there were no roads, the cowboys knew which way to point the cattle in the morning, an important factor if it was cloudy, raining or snowing.

Cattle Trails

Oliver Loving was among the first Texas cattlemen to attempt to drive cattle long distances for a better market. In 1866, he partnered with Charlie Goodnight for a drive to Fort Sumner, New Mexico Territory. Their route through the New Mexico, Colorado, and Wyoming Territories later became known as the Goodnight-Loving Trail. Even after losing nearly four hundred head on their first drive together, the two men still cleared over $12,000. They immediately planned a second drive.

While Loving was scouting the trail ahead of their herd the following year, he was shot by Comanches. His arm wound was not life-threatening. However, it became infected and gangrene set in. The inexperienced army doctor at Fort Sumner refused to amputate his arm and he died on September 25, 1867. The television series, *Lonesome Dove,* loosely follows part of Goodnight and Loving's story.

The Chisholm Trail began as a series of trails connected to ranches around San Antonio, Texas. It crossed the Red River (the dividing line between Texas and Indian Territory) about halfway between Doan's Crossing and Denison. Several branches of that trail split as it went north with ending points in Kansas, first in Abilene and later in Newton, Wichita, and Ellsworth. The Cimmaron Cutoff, a branch of the trail, passed near Dodge City.

In 1874, John T. Lytle and his crew of cowboys left south Texas with thirty-five hundred head of longhorn cattle as well as a remuda of saddle horses. Within five years, the trail that he plotted north to Fort Robinson in Nebraska had become the most heavily traveled cattle trail in use during that time. That trail later became known as the Great Western Trail.

The Western Trail is less well known than the Chisholm Trail. However, it is longer in length and carried cattle for two years longer. It saw over seven million head of cattle and horses pass over it as they moved north through Texas and present-day Oklahoma to the rail heads in Kansas and Nebraska. Some were trailed even farther north. Although the Great Western or Western Trail is what it is most commonly called now, it was also known as the Texas Trail, Fort Griffin Trail, Old Doan Trail, Dodge City Trail, and the Northern Trail. From 1875 to 1884, The Western Trail was the most commonly used cattle trail.

In this book, I refer to this trail as the Texas Trail. Cowhands of the 1870s, many whose roots and pride were steeped in Texas, likely referred to that trail based on where it started.

Longhorn Cattle

The Texas longhorn is a hybrid breed that is drought and stress tolerant. The breed is believed to be a mix of Spanish stock brought to the New Americas and English cattle that frontiersmen brought to Texas in the 1820s. Longhorns are slow to mature and can live in nearly any environment.

By the end of the Civil War, the Texas longhorns with their rangy bodies and large horns that extended up to seven feet were a recognizable breed. Their behavior was wild like Spanish stock, but they did have an appreciable amount of British blood. The cowboys who worked with them said that they had the strength of a bear, the agility of a cat, and the speed of a deer. They were called slab-sided and loose-hided. Longhorn steers were usually three to four years of age before they had enough beef on them for slaughter. Larger animals typically brought more money.

In the late 1800s, ranchers began crossing the longhorns with the shorthorn Durhams and later with Herefords and Angus to create an excellent beef animal. By the 1920s, only a few small herds of longhorns remained. Today, many variations of the breed are sold. Longhorns are desired not only for their lean meat but for their horns and their hides.

The Chuckwagon

Charlie Goodnight, legendary rancher and trail driver, invented the chuckwagon in 1866. It was born of necessity. Top hands were in short supply due to the many herds heading north. To recruit and hold them, Goodnight decided to improve the quality of meals served on the trail.

His first chuckwagon was made from a sturdy war-surplus munitions wagon acquired after the Civil War. It was strong enough to make the journey north of more than a thousand miles along difficult trails in all weather. He outfitted the wagon with a kitchen on the back. His cook helped him to develop an efficient layout. It was soon copied by trail drivers all across the West who called it a "chuckwagon." Was it named for the food it carried or after its founder, Charlie "Chuck" Goodnight? Only history knows.

The chuckwagon carried the food, eating and cooking utensils, and at least one water barrel. It also carried tools and bedrolls for all the cowboys. It was pulled by horses or mules. It was usually around ten feet long and thirty-eight to forty inches wide. The wagon and team could belong to the ranch or to the cook himself.

Supplies for about a month were carried in the chuckwagon and were purchased in large quantities with the bags holding fifty to one hundred pounds. Some of the foods served were beef and buffalo steaks, Son-of-a-Gun Stew, beans, sourdough biscuits, and always Arbuckle coffee. Fruits and vegetables were difficult to carry so prunes, raisins, and other dried fruits were a staple. The approximate provision cost for a thousand-mile trail drive was $1000.

The chuck box held a foldout counter on hinged legs. This was used for food preparation. Drawers and shelves were built into the wagon. Some wagons also had a "boot" or storage compartment beneath the chuck box. A canvas top covered the wagon.

A cowhide cradle was sometimes slung beneath the bottom of the chuckwagon. That "possum belly" was to carry fuel for cooking when traveling through treeless areas. Once wood supplies were depleted, dried cow chips were gathered.

The chuckwagon became the headquarters of the cattle outfit as well as the social center. In addition to long hours and difficult working conditions, the cook was also the barber, the doctor, and the banker. He was usually older and held more seniority, second only to the trail boss. He sometimes served as the referee and mediator if a disagreement erupted among the riders.

A good cook was in high demand as food played a large part in a cowboy's life. Some cowboys took riding jobs based on the food that was supplied.

Mavericks and Branding

Samuel Augustus Maverick was a politician and land baron in early Texas. He was also one of the signers of the Texas Declaration of Independence. Maverick was from South Carolina and moved to Texas in 1835. He stayed about a year and then departed Texas due to illness and pressing family business. Maverick returned to Texas in 1844. Cattle purchased in 1847 were allowed to roam free and unbranded until he gathered them seven years later. The local cowboys began to refer to the unbranded cattle as "Maverick's." The term stuck. To this day in cattle terminology, the name maverick denotes an unbranded calf.

The practice of branding came to the New World with the Spaniards. The first brand used in the Western Hemisphere may have been used by Hernan Cortes in the late sixteenth century. It was three Latin crosses. Spanish brands were typically designed to be beautiful. Additional curves or pendants were added to the original brand with the introduction of each son. This made the brands difficult to interpret if you were unfamiliar with the system or the family.

Many of the early Anglo Texas ranchers were unable to read the Spanish and Mexican brands. They made their brands simpler. Often, they were initials. The brands were clear and could be read with ease by anyone. Richard H. Chisholm may have owned the first recorded brand. It was registered in Gonzales County in Texas in 1832.

As in the past, brands still have their own language. They are read from left to right, top to bottom, and outside to inside.

A leaning letter or character is read as "lazy." The addition of short bars at the bottom make it "walking." If the letter rests on a quarter circle, it is "rocking." These are just a few of the branding options that are possible.

A brand is filed based upon its first letter or character. There are no laws that dictate the exact spot on a cow's hide for branding although many of the first brands were placed on the left side. Some old-time cowboys suggest that cattle typically mill more to the left than to the right, making a left-side brand easier to read.

In the United State, brands must be registered, and those brands are recorded by each state. Brands laws vary from state to state, but location as well as the brand itself is important. The same brand may be repeated within a state, but a different brand location must be used. While the hip brand is common, other locations include the side and the neck.

Tick Fever

Tick-borne splenic fever was first noticed as early as 1796 after cattle from the south were introduced in Pennsylvania. It was identified in Arkansas and Missouri after Texas cattle were moved through there in the 1850s. However, since the Texas cattle remained healthy, their role as a possible carrier was discounted. It was not understood until later that the longhorns were immune to the disease that the ticks carried. When the South Texas cattle passed through, the ticks dropped off. They then found local cattle to feed on, thus transmitting the disease to the northern herds. Farmers and ranchers in Missouri, Arkansas, and southeast Kansas began to protest the large herds that passed through, dropping their deadly ticks in the process.

Northern Texas cattle didn't seem to have a problem with the ticks. Some cattlemen in the Panhandle of Texas even posted armed cowhands at their southern boundaries to keep the tick-infested South Texas cattle out. This came to be known as the "Winchester Quarantine" in honor of the gun used to enforce it. In some cases, this made the North Texas cattle more desirable to buyers.

Luckily for everyone, the ticks were susceptible to cold weather. Some herds were quarantined through the winter before they could be moved to the shipping points.

Missouri was one of the first midwestern states to ban Texas cattle. That ban pushed the movement of the large herds farther west. In 1874, the Kansas government established a north-south quarantine line east of Dodge City. This line effectively ended cattle herds on the more eastern Chisolm Trail making the Western Trail more desirable to all Texas herds. In 1885, the Kansas government moved the quarantine line again. This time, it was moved west to the Colorado border. This was intended to stop all movement of Texas cattle through Kansas.

The new quarantine line obviously caused traffic on the Western Trail to dwindle and eventually halt. Of course, railroads were easier to access diminishing the need to move cattle so far. In addition, homesteaders began using barb wire to prevent the large herds from entering their lands. The last large herd to move up the Western Trail crossed the Red River in 1893, headed for Deadwood, South Dakota.

Cattle Drives

The large cattle drives began at the end of the Civil War. Texas was a Confederate state. At the beginning of the war, they provided beef to the Confederate army. Both sides blockaded and destroyed rail and freight lines whenever they could. However, the Union was effective in cutting off the Texas beef supply. That, along with constant attacks from the Comanches and a lack of cowboys due to all the young men who enlisted to fight, resulted in large Texas cattle herds left unattended.

When the Civil War ended in 1865, Texas had a glut of cattle and no market. Steers in Texas were worth a maximum of $2 per head. In fact, some ranchers said the more cattle you owned, the poorer you were.

Those same steers could bring $30 to $40 per head in Kansas. The cost to trail cattle from Texas to Kansas was estimated at $1 to $2 per head. Money was to be made, and huge herds began to move north.

Cattle drives usually averaged eight to twelve miles per day depending on the terrain and the weather. Of course, the cattle were not actually driven—they were trailed. The cowboys kept them grazing north, following the trail designated by the trail boss. If the longhorns were moved too fast, they walked off the pounds. If they were allowed to graze and the grass was adequate, they could actually gain weight on the drive.

An unwritten rule of trail etiquette was not to pass the herd in front of you. Because of this, many ranchers wanted to be one of the first herds on the trail in the spring. Those herds would have the best grazing and often the best prices, especially if the market became glutted with beef. Available grass was also a consideration so they didn't want to start too early in the spring. Cattle herds moved north from spring through fall and sometimes into the winter.

Trail Bosses, Cooks, and Drovers

The trail boss was the highest-paid position on a trail drive. He was paid $100 to $150 per month. The cook or Cookie as he was often called was the next highest paid. He was often an old cowboy and was paid $60 to $75 per month. The drovers—the cowboys who moved the herd—were paid $30 to $40 per month. The job of horse wrangler was often given to the youngest or least experienced, and he received about $25 each month. Each drover had a position he rode on a cattle drive, and that position gave him a specific job. Drover positions were point, swing, flank, and drag.

The trail boss was in charge. It was his job to find water and to know the trail. He was often away from the herd as he checked the trail before them. He was expected to take a herd through safely with few animals lost. His position required that he be familiar with river crossings as well as be able to foresee and avoid as many problems as possible.

The riders who rode point were usually more experienced and more familiar with the trail they were following. Drives could have one or two point riders depending on the size of the herd. They followed the direction set by the trail boss and controlled the speed of the herd. They also gave the cattle something to follow. The most rambunctious cattle pushed to the front of the herd, so the point riders had to be excellent cowboys.

Swing and flank riders rode alongside the herd. The swing riders were closer to the front and helped the point riders turn the herd. Flank riders rode closer to the back. Both sets of riders tried to keep the herd from fanning out too far. They also made sure no animals broke away from the herd.

Drag riders had the dirtiest job. They rode behind the herd and pushed the slowest animals. Drag position was given to the least-experienced rider. If all the riders were experienced, that position was assigned at the whim of the trail boss or possibly traded around. Neckerchiefs, wild rags, and bandanas were a necessity to somewhat protect the drovers' noses and mouths from the dust.

Wranglers were responsible for the care of the horses including grooming, wound treatment, and shoeing. Riders usually had five to six mounts each, so a drive with fifteen hands or cowboys had a remuda of seventy-five to ninety horses. The wrangler was responsible for moving the extra horses and penning them at night. In addition, he had to learn what mounts each rider chose for his own. The horses usually belonged to the ranch, but the cowboys all had their favorites.

Cowboys often had specific horses they preferred for water crossings. "Water horses" were the mounts that crossed rivers the easiest. Many cowboys didn't know how to swim so a horse that took to water easily was valued. At night, a horse was saddled and ready for each rider in the event of a stampede. While the wrangler was paid less, his job was an important one.

Lead Cattle

When they weren't grazing, groups of cattle on a drive followed in a long line. Once they were trail broke, they assumed the same positions each day.

Lead cattle were often self-appointed. They could be either cows or steers and could be a single animal or a pair. The most famous of these was Charlie Goodnight's "Old Blue." He was a blue or mulberry steer. Old Blue had a cowbell hung around his neck. The cattle soon became used to the sound of his bell and followed him. At night, the bell was tied so it didn't ring. Old Blue was so tame that he often came into camp and ate with the drovers. At the end of the drive, Goodnight took Blue back to Texas, often by train. He was then sent up the trail again with the next herd. Over ten thousand cattle followed the sound of Old Blue's bell up the trail in the eight years he was used.

Deacon Cox of Dodge City also had a well-known cow. He often rented out his Jersey milk cow to lead herds across the Arkansas River.

Mixed herds that consisted of cows and calves were a problem. Calves that were born along the way were usually not strong enough to keep up and there was often no way to haul them. They were either given away or destroyed.

Landmarks and River Crossings

There were many crossings and landmarks that every herd used. Doan's Crossing over the Red River, Mount Tepee, Big Elk Crossing, Soldier Spring, Edwardsville Rock, Deep Hole Crossing on the Cimmaron River, Big Basin, St. Jacob's Well, and finally Bluff Creek were all places where the cowboys crossed, watered, or rested their livestock. The Arkansas River was the last river to be crossed before Dodge City.

Crossing rivers was one of the most difficult parts of cattle drives. Many graves were left on the riverbanks and surrounding areas. The R.I.P. grave that is referred to in this book was an actual grave. Those who came later did not know who was buried there or what the three letters stood for. Was it "Rest in Peace" or was it someone's name? In the 1900s, the name of the man buried there was discovered. It was determined that marker carved in stone did indeed stand for "Rest in Peace."

Markers were usually made in a hurry and were often made from wood. They were susceptible to the weather and erosion as well as those less than concerned travelers scavenging for wood. Most graves would have been lost within several years of burial.

The trail bosses spread their herds out to graze as they trailed north and brought them together to cross rivers at specific locations. If the rivers they needed to cross were high, herds would stack up at the crossing areas as they waited for the water to go down.

For the herds started north of the Brazos River in Texas, the Red River was the first major river to be crossed. The red soil of the region gives the river its reddish color. Salt deposits from many years ago leech through natural seeps and send over three thousand tons of salt per day flowing down the river. The salt gives the water a brackish and unpleasant smell which cattle do not like. It would have been even more difficult to push cattle across when they were not yet trail broke.

The Red River was a terror to trail drivers. Red bluff banks made it difficult for the cattle to clamber out of the water. When the water was high, strong currents ran through the river. In addition, previous flood waters left red sediment and driftwood lodged in the trees and along the high banks. Seeing debris lodged that high would have sent a chill through many a soul.

Low water levels were difficult as well. This meant the quicksands that moved and shifted in the river bottom would be more of a problem.

Other difficult rivers to cross on the Western Trail were the Canadian River in current-day Oklahoma, the Cimarron in both Oklahoma and Kansas, and the Arkansas River just south of Dodge City.

Most cowboys dreaded river crossings, and they were correct to do so.

Cowboy Music and Stampedes

Cowboys rode around their herds at night to keep watch over them. Usually, two nighthawks or nightguards would circle the cattle, riding in opposite directions. They sang as they rode. The cattle became acclimated to the soothing sound of their voices even if the notes were off-key or the words were less than appropriate. Riders took turns and kept this up all night. Many songs were carried north as a result of the cattle drives and the music that was shared.

Stampedes were often deadly for both cattle and cowboys. A stampede could be caused by any unusual sound. Lightning strikes were common and were nearly guaranteed to set a herd running. However, small sounds such as a twig breaking or a match being struck could set them off at night.

Once the cattle started running, the cowboys would try to turn them in a direction away from rivers or cliffs. Then they would keep pushing the leaders to circle them. Once the cattle were circling, they forced the circle smaller and smaller until the cattle began to slow down. As the cattle slowed, the cowboys would once again begin to sing to them.

Shooting in the faces of the cattle was a desperate attempt to turn a running herd. It was not the first choice but sometimes was the only one. If a horse stumbled and went down during a stampede, it was almost certain death to the cowboy and sometimes the horse.

When longhorn cattle were frightened, they ran over or through anything in front of them. The cattle behind followed blindly so stampedes usually meant a loss of livestock even if no cowboys died.

Stampedes also meant money lost. One steer could run off up to fifty pounds of weight in just one stampede on a hot night.

Indian Territory and No Man's Land

Oklahoma in 1879 was known as Indian Territory and was quite lawless. "The Strip" was a strip of land across the top of Texas that belonged to no territory or state. "No Man's Land," as it was sometimes called, was completely without law. This made outlaws prevalent. Cattle drives were a cash business, and outlaws gathered where money was to be had.

The Indians also demanded a fee for crossing their reservation lands. This fee was usually paid in cattle. The huge herds consumed large amounts of grass. Those herds that tried to cross without paying a toll were often stampeded. Some trail bosses paid with healthy animals while others tried to pass off their sick or weak animals. Pregnant cows and pairs were also used as payment. These were sometimes desired by the Indians if they were building herds of their own.

Stand Watie

Stand Watie was born near New Echota, Georgia, in 1806. Encroachment by Whites on Cherokee lands was a constant problem. When gold, already known to the Cherokee people, was discovered in the Appalacian Mountains in 1828, plans for Indian removal came to a head.

In 1835, Stand Watie was part of a small faction of Cherokee leaders who signed the Treaty of New Echota. That treaty agreed to the removal of the Cherokee people from their ancestral homes and ceded all their lands east of the Mississippi River for $5 million. That treaty was rejected by the majority of tribal members and caused internal as well as legal battles.

Even favorable court decisions could not stop the inevitable. In 1838, the Cherokee were forcibly removed from their lands to a reservation in what would become Oklahoma. This exodus is best remembered as the "Trail of Tears." Nearly four thousand Cherokee died on the thousand mile journey during the fall and winter of 1838 and 1839.

As a soldier, Stand Watie raised and commanded the first volunteer Cherokee regiment during the Civil War in 1861. His Confederate cavalry was called the Cherokee Mounted Rifles. In 1864, he was promoted to brigadier general.

Stand Watie was fiercely loyal to the Confederacy even though the majority party of the Cherokee people withdrew their alliance in 1863. During the Civil War, he was the highest-ranking Native American to fight for the South. He was also the last Confederate general in the field to give up his arms. He surrendered on June 23, 1865, nearly six weeks after the surrender of Robert E. Lee.

Denison, Texas

Denison is located four miles south of the Red River on the Texas side. The town was created on February 8, 1873. Within four months, the population had increased by nearly three thousand people. It was the hub for the Missouri, Kansas, and Texas Railroad or the MK&T.

Skiddy Street was one street south of the main street and it soon became the "sin center" with rough saloons, bawdy dance halls, and prostitution.

The street was named after a railroad executive for the MK&T. When it became known as the location for debauchery, Skiddy petitioned the city to change the name of Skiddy Street to Chestnut. The name was finally changed in the 1880s, but until that time, Skiddy Street had a wild reputation that was known far and wide. Interestingly, it was also referred to as Skid Row.

The distance from Denison to Doan's Crossing is about one hundred sixty miles.

Doan's Crossing, Northern Texas Border

Jonathon Doan established a trading post a mile southwest of the Red River in Wilbarger County, Texas, in 1878 to serve the cattle herds headed north on the Western Trail. His nephew, Corwin Doan, joined him a year later. By 1880, besides the trading post, Doan's had a hotel, the Cowboy Saloon, and a school. The popular river ford just north of there on the Red River became known as Doan's Crossing, and the town was called by the same name.

Corwin Doan kept detailed records of the herds that passed through as well as the business that was done through his store. 1881 was the peak of the cattle herds with three hundred one thousand head driven through Doan's Crossing. C.F. Doan, as Corwin was called, kept the names of the trail bosses, the number of cattle, and who they belonged to. It is through his records that we can see an accurate accounting of the numbers of cattle that were moved north.

Quanah Parker was a regular visitor at Doan's Crossing. It is said that the Indians convinced Jonathon Doan to build on the south side of the river. Ammunition and guns could be purchased by the Indians in Texas but could not be purchased on the north side of the Red River since it was reservation land.

In 1885, the Fort Worth and Denver Railway bypassed Doan's Crossing by several miles. Eight years later, the last large herd of cattle passed through Doan's Crossing. Railroads, barb wire, and ticks ended the great cattle drives and determined the demise of Doan's Crossing as well.

C.F. Doan's records show around six million head of cattle, and one million horses crossed the river at Doan's Crossing and moved north up the Western Trail.

Waggoner Ranch

Dan Waggoner started the Waggoner Ranch in 1849. He and his first wife, Nancy Moore, began their ranching operation with 6 horses and 242 longhorn cattle. Their only child, William Thomas or W.T., was born in 1852. Nancy passed away in 1853. About five years later, Dan married Sicily Ann Halsell from Wise County, Texas. Sicily Ann was from a large Texas ranching family. She and Dan had no children.

W.T. knew he wanted to be a cattleman from an early age. Father and son formed their partnership after a successful cattle drive from their ranch in north Texas to Kansas in 1866. W.T. married Ella Halsell, a younger sister to his father's wife. She was seven years younger than W.T.

In 1885, the Waggoners leased six hundred fifty thousand acres of grass in the "Big Pasture." This was in the Indian Territory and was reservation land owned by the Comanche, Apache, and Kiowa.

When open range in Texas ended, W.T. and his father began to buy land along the Red River in north Texas for around $1 per acre. In 1902, W.T. found oil while drilling for water, much to his disgust. By 1903, Waggoner Ranch ran in a continuous line thirty miles east and west by twenty-five miles north and south, encompassing over a million acres. Dan died in 1904.

In 1905, W.T. went wolf-hunting with President Teddy Roosevelt. He, along with rancher Samuel Burk Burnett, had hopes of persuading the president to keep the land in the Big Pasture as open range. The president greatly enjoyed himself, particularly after seeing Jack "Catch 'm Alive" Abernathy catch wolves with his bare hands. Even though he talked highly of his adventure, Roosevelt was not convinced. In 1906, Congress allotted some land to tribal children, but most was sold by sealed bid. The proceeds were placed in the United States Treasury for the tribes. The Big Pasture was the last large land tract opened for settlement in what would become the state of Oklahoma.

The Waggoner Ranch is now over five hundred thousand acres and is known as the largest ranch "under one fence." Although the ranch still spans six counties, most of it is located in Baylor and Wilbarger Counties. It sold in February of 2016 to Stan Kroenke. The asking price was $725 million.

Quanah Parker

Quanah Parker was born in 1845, the son of Peta Nocona, a Comanche warrior and Cynthia Ann Parker, a white woman captured by the Comanches when she was nine years old. She became the wife of Peta and was happy with the Comanche people. Quanah had a younger brother, Pecos, and a sister, Topsana (Prairie Flower).

Nadua or Nautdah as Cynthia Ann was called, was taken by soldiers during a raid on Peta Nocona's village while the warriors were away. Since she was white, it was assumed that she wanted to return to her white family. However, Cynthia Ann did not want to leave her husband and children. She tried to run away numerous times. When her daughter died four years after they were removed from Peta's camp, Cynthia Ann scarred her breasts and offered prayers to the Indian spirits. Some say she starved herself to death. Others believe that she adapted to her old life and lived another ten years. Records of her life are minimal and inconsistent.

Quanah became a great warrior. Through his leadership, his band of warriors were some of the last Comanches to continue fighting the soldiers. In 1875, in a battle with the soldiers, all their horses were captured and their villages were burned. Quanah and the Quahadi band surrendered. They were moved to a reservation in southwestern Oklahoma.

While many Indians found it difficult to adjust to reservation life, Quanah did not. He called on his people to adapt by building houses like the white man. He also leased the grazing rights of the reservation to large cattlemen. This gave him cash that his people needed. In addition, the ranchers had a vested interest in protecting the Comanche grasslands.

Quanah was appointed principal chief of the entire Comanche Nation by the federal government. He was proud to be a friend to the white man including President Teddy Roosevelt. He was a warrior, a rancher, and a businessman. However, he never adapted the white man's belief in monogamy. He had eight wives and twenty-five children, including some children who were adopted. When an Indian agent once suggested that he should only have one wife, Quanah stated, "You tell them."

Quanah eventually became one of the wealthiest Native Americans of his time. He was truly a man to two worlds.

The First Bulldogger

Bill Pickett was born in Williamson County, Texas, around 1870. He was the second of thirteen children born to Thomas Jefferson Pickett, a former slave, and Mary "Janie" Gilbert. Although Pickett is usually identified as African American, he was also part Cherokee. When he became older, Pickett used his Cherokee heritage to enter rodeos where Black cowboys were not allowed.

Pickett dropped out of school in fifth grade. At that time, he went to work on a ranch where he became a valued rider and ranch hand.

Young Pickett developed his method of bulldogging by watching actual bulldogs. They were sometimes used to stop a running animal by clamping their teeth down on the cow or steer's upper lip and nose. Once this sensitive area was bitten, the animal was subdued. Pickett decided if it worked for a bulldog, it would work for him.

He practiced by racing his horse after a steer, jumping from the horse while it was running, grabbing the steer by the horns, and wrestling it to the ground. He then bit the steer's lip until the steer held still. After several exhibitions, he became knowns as a "bulldogger." It is said that

Pickett was five feet, seven inches tall and weighed around one hundred forty-five pounds in his prime.

Pickett's method of bulldogging eventually morphed into modern-day steer wrestling which is still a popular rodeo event. He died on April 2, 1932, after being kicked in the head by a high-strung horse. However, his legacy as the "Dusky Demon" lives on in the sport he helped to create.

Bill Pickett would have been around nine years old at the time of this fictional story, far younger than when he started his bulldogging career. However, I thought it would be fun to make his story part of the campfire talk shared by my lonely cowboys on their cattle drive.

Dodge City, Queen of the Cowtowns

Dodge City was founded in June of 1872, five miles west of Fort Dodge. The original name of the town was going to be Buffalo City, but that name was already in use. Instead, it was named after Fort Dodge. The fort itself was named in honor of General Grenville M. Dodge, a Civil War general and engineer for the railroad. There was one, three-room sod house in the new town. It became a popular stopping place for buffalo hunters and traders. The first commercial business was a whiskey bar built of sod and boards.

The new town quickly became a trade center for travelers on the Santa Fe Trail as well as buffalo hunters. It exploded with growth adding two grocery and general merchandise stores, a dancehall, a restaurant, a barber shop, a blacksmith shop, and a second saloon—all before the arrival of the railroad in September of 1872. The first train was the Atchison, Topeka and Santa Fe Railroad. Dozens of cars each day were loaded with hides and meat while dozens of carloads of grain, flour and other provisions were unloaded. It is believed that the term "red light district" was coined in Dodge when the trainmasters took their red caboose lanterns with them when visiting the town's "soiled doves."

Dodge's early years were wild. There was no local law enforcement, and the military had no jurisdiction over the town.

An estimated eight hundred fifty thousand buffalo hides were shipped from Dodge between 1872 and 1874. By 1875, the buffalo were gone as a source of revenue. However, the herds of longhorns were arriving from Texas.

Chalk Beeson, besides being a cattleman and lawman, was the owner of the original Long Branch Saloon. He also formed the Dodge City Cowboy Band in 1879. It continues today making it the longest-running municipal band west of the Mississippi.

More than three million head of cattle passed through Dodge City or were shipped from there between 1866 and 1878. Dodge City received more cattle than any other cowtown and was used as a shipping point longer as well. It is considered by some to have been the greatest cattle market in the world. By 1877, Dodge City's population was twelve hundred, and nineteen of its first businesses sold liquor.

Robert Wright was an early resident and founder of Dodge City. He grew his general merchandise store to $250,000 in retail sales annually. He also opened a branch store in Fort Griffin, Texas. Wright sent a Texan out to meet the incoming herds to solicit their business, a practice that was common at the time.

Dodge was ten years old before the first bank was organized in 1882. Until that time, mercantile houses such as Wright, Beverley & Co. as well as Hadder and Draper Mercantile Co. handled the banking services. Hundreds of thousands of dollars changed hands in Dodge. The mercantile stores accepted large deposits and allowed the cattlemen to draw on their accounts. Dollar amounts as high as $50,000 were often sent by train to banks in Leavenworth.

Orphan Train

Between 1854 and 1929, around two hundred thousand orphaned, abandoned, and homeless children from crowded eastern cities were moved west. They were placed with families throughout the United States, Canada and even Mexico. However, most were placed in the rural Midwest. It is estimated that New York City alone had thirty thousand abandoned children living on the streets when the movement started in the early 1850s.

Institutional orphanages were uncommon before the early nineteenth century. Until then, relatives or neighbors usually raised abandoned or orphaned children. Around 1830, the number of homeless children in the large Eastern cities exploded. Some of this was due to epidemics while other children were abandoned due to poverty or illnesses, including addiction.

Charles Loring Brace, a young minister, became concerned with the numbers and plight of the street children. In 1853, he founded the Children's Aid Society. This religious shelter and training center eventually became our nation's first runaway shelter. There, vagrant boys were given basic education along with inexpensive room and board. Homes and jobs were sought for the young men they housed. When Brace and his colleagues became overwhelmed by the number needing placement, he conceived the idea of sending groups of children to rural areas for adoption. He believed they would have better lives if they left the poverty and filth of the streets to be raised by morally upright farm families. First the children were sent individually to farms in nearby states. In 1854, the shipment of children to the Midwest was begun.

The children were transported to their new homes in rail cars. These trains later became known as "mercy" or "baby trains." Less than half the children who rode those trains were orphans, and up to twenty-five percent had two living parents. While the intentions were noble, the process was not always pleasant for the children. Some were separated from their siblings and taken advantage of. Still, many did find loving homes. The first Kansas-bound baby train arrived in 1867. In 1930, the last orphan train reached Kansas, spelling the official end of the Orphan Train movement.

Pillsbury Crossing, South of Manhattan, Kansas

Pillsbury Crossing is a natural limestone, slab-bottomed crossing that was used by settlers to cross Deep Creek. It is located seven miles southeast of Manhattan, Kansas. Below the natural ford is a sixty-foot-long ledge that forms a waterfall.

The natural flat rock crossing was named after pioneer J.H. Pillsbury who homesteaded near there in 1855. Mr. Pillsbury was a Free-State settler in the Kansas Territory. He was also a member of the Topeka Constitutional Convention.

The Katy Railroad

The Missouri, Kansas and Texas Railroad was incorporated in May of 1870 in Junction City, Kansas. Its purpose was to build a supply route connecting the frontier military bases of Fort Riley, Fort Gibson, and Fort Scott in Kansas. Fort Worth was eventually added along with connections to other railroads that serviced Fort Leavenworth and Fort Smith. An even loftier ambition was to connect Chicago and New Orleans. The Missouri, Kansas and Texas Railroad's name was shortened to the MK&T.

The MK&T built south as fast as possible. It hoped to be the first rail system to reach the southern Kansas border through the Neosho Valley. The winning rail system was promised federal land grant money.

The MK&T arrived at the border of the Indian Territory in June of 1870, shortly after the competing railroad. However, a technicality caused the MK&T to be declared the winner. While the land grant money was never received, the rails still continued southward. The MK&T reached Denison, Texas, in 1872. Passengers quickly shortened the name of the train to "the Katy."

Diphtheria

Diphtheria is called the strangler. It is characterized by a fever, sore throat, and mucus formation. The disease is an upper respiratory disease caused by a bacteria. That bacteria can produce a toxin which damages the tissue, usually in the nose and throat. This then produces a tough, gray-colored membrane or mucus. Swelling, along with the production of the thick mucus, can block the airways and cause suffocation.

Before the ability to treat or vaccinate for this, diphtheria was often lethal. It is transmitted through the air but can also be passed via contact with infected people. It can attack all ages and is often deadly to children. In advanced cases, the heart, kidneys, and nervous system can be affected.

In June of 1879, Harry Sterrett, a three-year-old boy drowned in a well in Bloom Township in Clay County, Kansas. Also that month, four children in the Mussellman family in neighboring Clay Center Township died of diphtheria. They were Benjamin and Edward, age three; David, age thirteen; and Michael, age eleven. They were the earliest of the twenty-five diphtheria deaths over the next eight months in Clay County.

Five Creeks Township is where the most deaths occurred. Table Mound Cemetery there has a section called Diphtheria Hill and is where most of those who died from the disease are buried. Death was usually rapid, and many deaths were members of the same family.

Did the Sterrett funeral and the logical mingling of people from the neighboring counties have anything to do with this outbreak in 1879? No one knows but I incorporated both of those details in this novel.

A Cowboy Legacy

Today, ruts left by over six million longhorns mark part of the once-great Western Trail. US Highway 283 roughly follows it from northern Texas, through Oklahoma, and into Dodge City, Kansas. Various civic groups have placed markers and monuments along the old trail.

Cattle drives are part of our heritage. However, the long trail drives were mostly over by 1886, twenty years after they began. Still, they left the United States and especially our western states with a cowboy legacy. The cattle drive more than any other western icon creates nostalgia for the cowboy way of life and romanticizes the "Old West." Perhaps that draw to the west is best expressed by this quote from famed western author, Louis L'Amour.

"When a man or woman came West, their past became an unknown and the present became an open book. They soon became known by their actions or lack of. No one cared who your father was or what you had done. The only things that mattered were, that you were honest, had courage and that you did your job."

Thank you for choosing to read my novels. Enjoy the history and may this story become another favorite. Please follow me on Facebook: Rosie Bosse, Author. Your comments and reviews are welcome as well.

Additional novels may be purchased through my website below or through your local bookstore. Paper and digital copies are also available through various online suppliers. My books may be requested at your local library as well. Happy Reading!

Rosie Bosse, Author
Living and Writing in the Middle of Nowhere
rosiebosse.com

Manhattan, Kansas
Tuesday, April 1, 1879

CHAPTER 1

GRACE

THE YOUNG WOMAN SAT IN FRONT OF HER DRESSING table and brushed her hair. Her blue eyes rested for a moment on the tintype that had captured a happy family. The small girl with bright blue eyes was smiling widely as she sat on her father's lap. The man had his arm around a pretty blonde woman who was pregnant, and they were both smiling as well. The young woman picked up the picture and stared at it as tears pooled in the corners of her eyes.

"Mother and Father, how I miss you. I was so small when you died. Had James not taken care of me, I would never have survived."

She kissed the tintype and placed it back on her dressing table.

A woman's voice called up the stairs, "Hurry now, Grace. We need to leave in just a few minutes if we don't want to be late."

Grace answered quickly and began to twist her hair around her head. It had been almost white when she was small but now it was blonde. She stood and smoothed her dress as she studied her reflection in the mirror.

The young lady looking back at her was petite and smiling. The dress she wore was not revealing, but it couldn't hide the curves of her small body. Her large blue eyes were friendly, and they sparkled when she smiled.

Grace was a contented young woman. Joseph and Kate Gallagher had adopted her after the death of her parents. She had been six years old at the time and was clinging to James, the only friend she had when she met them.

James Long had been like a big brother on their wagon train headed to Oregon. He was the one who had taken her to his parents' wagon when her family died.

Grace shuddered as she remembered the few details from that time in her life. James had carved her a small horse during that trip, and now it sat on her dressing table beside the picture of her parents. They were the only two items she had to remember her early days.

"I wonder what became of you, James. You were only ten, but you hunted for all seven families when the rest of the wagon train abandoned us. They left because we were sick. And when the last man died, you put me on your horse, and we rode for two days as we tried to find a town you had never been to nor even heard of."

Grace's face puckered into a frown.

"I don't remember much of that time. I know you made me sit in the tall grass away from the campsite so I couldn't see when you burned the wagons. I remember the smell though, and it was horrible."

She picked up the small horse and held it to her cheek.

"This was my favorite toy growing up. I even slept with it."

Grace set the small horse down gently and hurried toward the stairway.

"I'm coming, Mother!"

Kate Gallagher looked up the stairs as her daughter rushed down, and the smile on her face grew larger.

Aye, it was a good day when we found little Grace, Kate thought to herself. *She has filled our lives with joy and happiness.*

Joseph Gallagher had just stepped inside the door when Grace rushed down the stairs. He was a tall, distinguished-looking man with a groomed gray beard and short, neatly cut gray hair. His eyes were as blue as Grace's and most people commented on how much she resembled him.

He held open his arms to Grace and smiled as he hugged his only daughter.

"Gracie, you are as pretty as a sunset. How can you expect me to talk business with the men in Manhattan when you distract them so?" he teased.

Grace smiled up at him and pecked his cheek.

"Father, you know I like business as much as you do. I also know you are talking to these men about investing in a cattle venture in Wyoming Territory. I promise to listen quietly until I have a question, and if you make a trip west, I want to go along!"

Kate shook her head and smiled as the three of them hurried to the waiting buggy. Joseph helped both women up and sat down beside his wife.

CHAPTER 2

A Handsome Irishman

JOSEPH GALLAGHER WAS A TWENTY-TWO-YEAR-OLD Irish immigrant when he arrived in the United States in 1850. He was fresh of the boat from Ireland when he spied Kate Feeney. Their courtship was a quick one and to say Kate's father was not initially pleased would be an understatement.

Kate was a pretty girl with coal black hair and green eyes. Her ancestors were "Black Irish," and she had a temper that matched her fiery personality. Kate's father was angry when Joseph presented himself at their home in Altoona, Pennsylvania, to ask permission to court Kate. She was the youngest of his eight daughters, and he did not want twenty-year-old Katie to keep company with a common man with no means to support her should their relationship progress—and he certainly didn't trust the intentions of the handsome young Irishman.

Kate and her father had some loud discussions, but young Joseph was nothing but polite. He even encouraged Kate to be respectful and to let him try to win her father over.

Finally, Kate's mother put her foot down.

"John Feeney, my father didn't like you either," Mary said. "He told you, 'No man but a rich man is good enough for my daughter.'

And how did you respond? You promised him that you would always love his daughter. You said you would never let me lack for anything I needed to live. You said you planned to be a successful businessman someday, but until that time, you would work hard to be a son-in-law he could be proud of."

That was the beginning of a short courtship, and the wedding was just a few months later. John had his reservations at first, but he soon grew to love his son-in-law as much as his own daughters. The two men were close until John passed away. Now Mary was gone as well, but Joseph valued the love that both had shown him.

Joseph smiled as he patted Kate's hand and tucked it closer to him.

"Katie, I knew you were the woman for me the first time I saw you. You were buying meat at the market. All of the young men were trying to get your attention, and you ignored every one of them with a toss of your head," he whispered.

Kate laughed as she picked up the story.

"And then I saw you. You with your black hair and blue eyes. You smiled at me and offered to carry my packages. I knew Father would be furious that talked to a man I didn't know—even worse, let him walk me home—but I let you anyway."

Grace watched her parents and smiled. *They have been married twenty-nine years and are still so in love. I hope I have a love like that.*

Joseph was an engineer by trade but was a skilled stonemason and bricklayer as well. His ability to design and build helped him to develop an excellent reputation as he migrated west. By the time the Gallaghers arrived in Manhattan, Kansas, in 1872, Joseph had enough capital to start his own engineering firm. He had gone from a penniless Irish immigrant to a successful businessman, and Kate had been beside him all the way.

As a young couple, the Gallaghers had been unable to have children. Kate was devastated. She had always wanted a large family. Joseph wanted children as well. When it didn't happen, he threw himself into developing his career with more intensity.

Joseph was thirty-nine and Kate thirty-seven in 1867 when they passed through Manhattan, Kansas, on their way home to Kansas City. The Gallaghers were curious about the the large crowd that waited by the train station. When they heard the next train to arrive would be carrying abandoned children, they were shocked.

"I wonder how many there are. Do you suppose some are looking for homes?" Kate whispered to her husband.

Applications to adopt had been filled out and approved in advance. The Gallaghers could only watch from the side as one child after another was adopted.

CHAPTER 3

TWO DIRTY CHILDREN

WHEN THE TWO FILTHY, RAGGED CHILDREN RODE in on horseback later that day claiming to be part of a wagon train that had abandoned them, the Gallaghers were appalled. They immediately stepped forward and offered to adopt the small girl.

The boy who was holding her hand begged them to take him as well.

"Please take me too. I will help you do whatever you need me to do. I'm strong and I can work."

Kate had immediately wanted to adopt both children, but Joseph was a cautious man.

'Kate, one child is going to be a huge change for us. I don't know that we are ready for two children at one time.'

After discussing it in greater detail later that evening and watching little Grace cry for James, they rushed back to adopt the young man as well. They were devastated to find that he had been sent on west to Salina on another train. It was hoped that a farming family in the area would be willing to take the young man in.

Joseph wrote to the Children's Aid Society in New York. However, there was no record of a James Long since he was not actually part of the Orphan Train program.

That was when we decided to try to adopt again. Joseph smiled at his daughter and patted her hand.

Grace had been with them less than a year when a friend of theirs sent a telegram. Her niece was coming to spend some time with her in New Orleans. She was pregnant and the young woman's father insisted that she give up the child. The Gallaghers quickly took the train to New Orleans and rushed to the station with their friend to meet the little mother. However, the young woman never showed.

Another couple waited there as well. The Gallaghers never spoke to the stern man nor the severe-looking woman. When a young woman rushed off the train and embraced the couple, the Gallaghers' hearts broke even more. She was obviously their daughter and the delight on all of their faces was easy to see as they hurried away.

The Gallaghers had returned to Kansas City quite disappointed. Seven-year-old Grace was devastated.

"But where is our baby? We can't go home without our baby!" she cried as her parents lifted her onto the train.

Their friend wrote about year later. She said the young woman had married and moved to the Wyoming Territory. Her father had been frantic over her disappearance. He was relieved to know she was safe even though he feared he would never see her again.

Joseph looked out over the busy street as he remembered that hurried train ride to New Orleans. The young woman's name was Molly Brewster. *I hope you and your baby are happy, Molly Brewster. We have prayed often for you and your little one over the years. Your baby is six years younger than our Grace, so he or she would be twelve years old now.*

A year after their rushed train ride to New Orleans in 1868, a business colleague in Salina sent a note to tell them that he had found James. The young man had been adopted by a family in Cawker City, Kansas.

"The boy's new parents are both solid citizens, and James is treated well. The couple, Ike and Kathryn Eilert, have a small ranch close to

Waconda Springs. Ike loves to work with horses. They are a little older and were delighted to finally have a son."

Kate quickly sent a letter to the Eilerts and received a prompt reply. James was excited to hear from the Gallaghers and corresponded with them for three years. Grace had learned to write, and she included her own note each time a letter was sent. She was so excited when she could finally write and sign her name in cursive.

Sadly, their last letter to him in September of 1872 was returned. It was marked, "Non-deliverable. Recipient deceased." Grace was brokenhearted and sobbed for days. The puppy her parents gave her helped, but Grace never forgot James.

The Gallaghers moved to Manhattan, Kansas, shortly after that. Joseph knew it would be difficult for any mail sent to Kansas City to follow them. He comforted his daughter as best he could.

"Perhaps young James lived. We will keep searching, Grace. Once we are settled in Manhattan, I will see if I can find someone who knew the Eilerts. Perhaps James left after his parents died to start a new life for himself elsewhere."

Joseph never forgave himself for refusing to adopt James. He often thought about the young man and continued to try to find him. In his heart, he always believed James was still alive—that his parents had passed and young James had left, probably to go farther west. Joseph leaned back in his seat.

That was a long time ago and the West is a vast wilderness. I will continue to pray that he lived and that his life has been a good one. Maybe someday, I can apologize to him for not stepping forward as I should have.

CHAPTER 4

A Meeting with the Partners

THE DINING ROOM AT THE WOLF HOUSE WAS FULL, but John Frank greeted the Gallaghers.

"Welcome, Mr. and Mrs. Gallagher—and you too, Grace. I saved a table in the back for you. It is small but we are crowded this evening. It is the best we can do tonight."

Joseph thanked him, and John Frank hurried out to help with the rest of the guests. The Wolf House offered some of the best food in Manhattan.

Joseph smiled. Manhattan was growing and it seemed business was booming for everyone.

Grace looked around in surprise.

"Where are the men you wanted to present your business proposition to, Father? I thought you were going to discuss a cattle venture this evening with some potential partners."

Joseph smiled at the two women and took their hands.

"I have my two business partners right here. I do want to discuss a business venture, but the only partners that I need to discuss it with are sitting at this table. How would you two ladies like to jump into the cattle business?"

Grace stared at her father and Kate frowned.

"But Joseph, we know nothing of cattle. We promised ourselves a long time ago that we would invest in what we knew, and that is working well for us." Kate's concern showed on her face.

Joseph looked at both excitedly.

"I have been studying the numbers. I know I don't have the knowledge, but I have friends who do, and they can put me in contact with the people I need to talk to.

"I would like to purchase cattle in Texas and move a herd north. We could sell it in Dodge City and more than double our money. However, we would need to do it quickly. I have been told that lots of cattle will be moving north, and those in the lead will have the best grazing. The herds usually move eight to twelve miles per day. If you push them faster, I've read that they will lose weight. If they are moved slower, they might even gain a little weight as they are herded. It will take them nearly a month, maybe longer to travel north to Dodge City depending how far south in Texas they are purchased. Of course, if there are problems on the drive such as high water or other difficulties, I've been told it can take two or three months."

Joseph's eyes were bright with excitement as he looked at his wife.

"You remember Martha Shumaker? You met her several times when we visited Manhattan before we moved here."

Kate nodded. "Yes, she sent me a letter and told me that she had moved West to marry. That was June of 1868. I was surprised as she had been a widow for some time. She seemed quite settled here in Manhattan."

Joseph leaned forward eagerly.

"I knew Martha's second husband, Badger McCune, when he lived in Kansas City. We were business acquaintances and became quite good friends. I believe you even met him once or twice—a small man with a large personality. He raised mules."

Kate laughed and agreed as Joseph continued.

"I wrote to him last winter and shared my idea. We have been corresponding, and he would be willing to partner with us on the first herd.

"I put up the capital, and he will take care of the planning and the hiring. We will split the profits—ninety percent for me and ten percent for him."

Kate's brow was puckered as she studied her husband's face.

"You believe you can trust this man? I don't know how much money we are talking about, but I'm guessing it will be a sizable investment. Will it take all our savings?"

Joseph's blue eyes flashed as he laughed.

"Badger is an ornery old cuss, but he is as honest as the day is long. He was a wealthy man when he left Kansas City. He bought up all the land he could around there before Kansas City began to grow and sold it at a huge profit. Most folks thought he was just an old man who raised mules, but he is one of the most business-savvy men I have ever met.

"In fact, once those cattle are sold, I would like to venture up north and close out our deal in person. I told him that we would plan to be in Dodge City when the herd arrives.

"He lives outside Cheyenne in Wyoming Territory now. He invited us to come up and meet his family. Apparently, he has several sons in that area...although I didn't know Badger was married before Martha or had any children."

Grace watched her parents closely and laughed as she listened.

"Father, the West is calling you again, isn't it? First, we moved from Kansas City to Manhattan when I was eleven. Now I am eighteen and you are ready to move again!"

Her eyes were sparkling as she leaned forward. "I think it sounds like a grand adventure. I vote yes!"

Both parents looked at their daughter.

Joseph grinned as he leaned back in his chair.

Kate commented dryly, "He hasn't even told us how much it is going to cost or how much of our savings it will take."

Grace tossed her head. "Oh, Mother, you have always told me that Father is a wonderful provider and an astute businessman. We both know that he would never jump into anything he didn't study and analyze first. My question is—are we moving to Cheyenne this summer or are we just going to visit?"

Kate and Joseph both smiled at this young woman who had been their daughter since she was six years old.

Kate shook her head and Joseph laughed.

"We will visit first." His eyes twinkled as he added, "Actually, I have been invited to go even farther north. The town of Stevensville in Montana Territory is hiring engineers and builders. I was recommended by a friend, and the city fathers have asked me to come up. They will pay our way from Cheyenne and give me a consulting fee as well. Apparently, that little town is growing quickly. Both gold and sapphires have been discovered near there, and the population is climbing."

Kate looked from Joseph to Grace and laughed.

"We might not be moving right away, but I am going to start packing the house. Or maybe I should start selling things. Listening to the two of you, I am sure we will be moving north.

"Now, Joseph, tell us how much this adventure of yours is going to cost."

CHAPTER 5

Cattle Business

JOSEPH LAID A PIECE OF PAPER ON THE TABLE. Expenses were listed in neat columns, and he pointed at each as he explained it.

"The cost of the cattle should be around $22,500. Right now in Texas, cattle are selling for $8-$9 per head. At $9 per head, two thousand head will cost $18,000. When sold, they are bringing $25-$30 per head in Kansas and as much as $40 per head farther north, say in Wyoming Territory.

"Labor should run between $570 and $1140 depending on the amount of time it takes to move the herd. Drives require between ten and fifteen cowboys as well as a horse wrangler, the trail boss, and the cook. The drive will take one to two months. Weather and other factors can affect the length of the drive.

"The wrangler is usually paid less so I've calculated his wages around $25 per month. The cowboys are paid $30-$35 per month while the trail boss is paid $100-$150.

"The cook is considered second in importance. I don't really understand why but he is usually paid $60 per month. That puts the total labor around $570 per month. That would make labor $1140 for two months. I'm hoping two months will be the longest it will take them.

"Of course, there are food and supplies. I have them figured at—"

"Excuse me, sir. Would you be Mr. Gallagher? Mr. Badger McCune said that I should talk to you."

Joseph looked up in surprise.

The man who was speaking to them held a quiet but commanding presence. His eyes were dark with an intensity that made many people uncomfortable. He had a small smile on his face and held a well-worn cowboy hat in his hand.

"Excuse me? You say Badger? How did you know where to find me? Here, please pull up a chair. Sit down, Mr.?"

"Hawkins is the name. Gabe Hawkins. McCune said I needed to talk to you about the cattle drive you are planning. He said you would be needing some drovers. I can put together crew of men in Texas, and we'd be pleased to help you out."

Grace studied the cowboy. He was a tall man with dark hair. His face was browned from the weather, and the hands that turned his hat looked rough and strong. There were laugh wrinkles around his eyes, and his mouth turned up at the corners in what was almost a sardonic grin. He appeared to be in his twenties. The man's face was still, but his eyes sparkled with energy as he talked.

When Joseph and Kate continued to stare at the man in shock, Grace began to giggle.

"Father, it appears that your Mr. Badger McCune was quite sure you were going to forge ahead with this drive since he already hired your foreman."

Gabe turned his eyes on Grace and grinned.

"Why yes, ma'am. I was told to come to Manhattan as soon as I received his message. I was to talk to Mr. Gallagher here right away so's I could get back down to Texas in time for the spring gather. I'd like to head that herd north towards Dodge as soon as possible to be one of the first herds to hit the Texas Trail. The train leaves at ten tomorrow morning, and McCune said you would send a bank draft with me along with some cash."

As Joseph continued to stare at the man, Gabe took a telegram from his pocket.

"You can see here, Mr. Gallagher, that I am on the up and up. This telegram is from McCune. It was waiting for me in Dodge. You probably have one here as well. Mine came in yesterday and I headed right up."

Joseph nodded and then looked at the women. He blushed slightly.

"Mr. Hawkins, I beg your pardon. I didn't even introduce you to my family. My wife, Kate, and our daughter, Grace."

Gabe grinned and tipped his hat. "The pleasure is mine, ladies."

Joseph stood quickly.

"It appears that this meeting is over. Kate, Grace—I will see that John is waiting for you with the carriage. I believe I need to make haste with the final preparations."

As Joseph hurried out of the eating house, Gabe paused at the table before following his new boss.

He bowed slightly to the women and tipped his hat. "Ladies, it was plumb nice to meet you. I'll look forward to seeing you both again."

As he spoke, his dark eyes settled on Grace with such intensity that she blushed. She could feel the heat coming up on her neck, but she met his gaze directly.

"And you as well, Mr. Hawkins. May the drive be a prosperous one and may you all make it to Dodge City safely."

Grace watched Gabe as he strode away.

"Didn't he have a delightful accent, Mother? What an interesting man."

Kate frowned. She watched her daughter's eyes follow the cowboy as he worked his way through the crowded room.

Gabe looked back as he paused in the doorway. When he caught Grace's eyes, he nodded and tipped his hat before he ducked out the door.

Grace felt a little surge of excitement.

Surely, we will see him again. What an interesting man.

CHAPTER 6

QUICK PREPARATIONS

THE TELEGRAPH OPERATOR CALLED TO JOSEPH WHEN he saw him hurry by.

"Mr. Gallagher, I have a wire here for you from Cheyenne. Sender said it was important and to track you down."

Joseph hurriedly took it from the man. He glanced at hit briefly before he rushed on down the street toward the bank. He knew the bank president, Wilbur Higgenbottom, usually stayed at the bank until after six finishing up the business of the day.

He knocked loudly on the back door next to Wilbur's office as he whispered loudly. "Wilbur, I need to speak with you right away. Please let me in. It is Joseph Gallagher."

The door quickly opened and when Wilbur opened his mouth to speak, Joseph handed him the wire. "I need a bank draft for $18,000 and an additional cash withdrawal of $8,000."

Wilbur Higgenbottom sat down slowly in his chair as he studied Joseph. The two men had worked together for as long as Joseph had lived in Manhattan. During that time, Wilbur had never seen Joseph make a decision without pondering it over for several days or even weeks—and certainly never where money was concerned. He studied the telegram.

Joe, deals all lined up. Gabe Hawkins be yur trail boss. He had im a job over by Dodge an is headed back down ta Texas. He cin line his crew up down there. His cookie has his own chukwagen. Leve those thar details ta Gabe. He needs a bank draft fer $18,000. Hopin we cin git those 2000 cows fer $8 but if takes $9, he pay the rest in cash. Send im $8,000 cash, an he cin use the extry fer the hosses, food, an mebbie more cows. He be a good feller. Badger

Wilbur looked up at Joseph in surprise.

"Cattle? And he called you Joe!"

Joseph laughed ruefully.

"Well, we have known each other for a number of years. Badger lives in Cheyenne but was a friend of mine when I lived in Kansas City. This idea started percolating in my head last winter, and I wrote him. He has the contacts and I'll put up the capital. We will split the profit ninety and ten."

Wilbur slowly nodded his head. "I have thought about that as well. You are lucky to have a man who has connections in Texas. Your trail boss and drovers are a big part of making that work."

He paused and studied Joseph's face again. "This is going to take a large chunk of your available cash. Is Kate all right with this?"

Joseph laughed as he nodded.

"We haven't discussed it fully, but she trusts my judgment. I have faith in Badger, and he believes in the man who will oversee the herd. Lots of trusting. I hope it pays out as well as it looks on paper."

Wilbur quickly prepared the bank draft and handed Joseph the $8000. Joseph stared at the large wad of cash and Wilbur pulled out a money belt.

"Give this to your man. That is a lot of cash to be carrying around."

Joseph nodded. "I sure appreciate you helping me after hours, Wilbur. You're a fine banker and a good friend."

The two men shook hands and Joseph hurried outside to where Gabe was waiting.

"Why don't you come over to the house, Gabe. I would like to give you this money in private. I have some questions for you too.

"Did Badger tell you that I want a full accounting. I am a numbers man, and I will want a written list of expenditures."

Gabe grinned at Joseph as he stepped in beside him.

"Mr. Gallagher, I have brought six herds up from Texas, and all but one feller wanted an accounting."

When Joseph looked at him with a question on his face, Gabe's smile became larger.

"That sixth feller went along, and he held onto his own money so he could keep track himself."

Joseph laughed as his neck turned a little red.

"How about your train ticket? Do you have it already?"

Gabe patted his pocket. "Have it right here. I didn't want them to sell out, so I bought it today when I hit town. And after I bought it, I went to look for you."

CHAPTER 7

THE TRAIL BOSS

KATE HURRIED OUT OF THE KITCHEN WHEN SHE heard the men's voices.

"Do you like coffee, Mr. Hawkins? I just made some fresh and I can bring you a cup."

Gabe thanked her and then followed Joseph to the table.

The table was covered with a linen tablecloth. Gabe put his elbows on the table and then awkwardly removed them.

Grace hurried into the room and Gabe quickly stood. She sat down by her father and leaned forward excitedly as she rested her arms on the table.

"Tell us about your plans, Mr. Hawkins. This is new territory for us, and we are all very interested."

Gabe dropped into his chair. He set his hat on the table with the brim up and leaned forward. Tablecloths were confusing but cattle he knew.

"The spring gather will already be started when I get back to Texas. I contacted several ranchers I know around Eagle Flat. Between them and several other ranches, we can pick up the two thousand head you want. Ranches gather in the spring and as soon as that is done, we will start. We'll push harder for the first two or three days just to get them used to trailing. After that, we'll slow down and try to make eight to ten miles per day." He paused as he looked at the three of them.

"If you push cattle too hard, they will walk off the pounds. If the grass is good and we don't have much trouble, they may even put on some weight."

Grace's eyes were large as she listened. "But how do you know where to go? There aren't any roads to follow, are there?"

Gabe grinned at her and shook his head.

"Naw, but there are quite a few trail options. We'll take the Texas Trail. It has several names, but it goes up through Kerrville and Albany to Fort Griffin in Texas. Shoot, the main streets of some of those Texas towns even run north and south just to accommodate the herds that go through. We won't be that far south this time though. The herds we are picking up are within fifty miles of the Red River."

When the Gallaghers looked at him in confusion, Gabe added, "The Red is the dividing line between Texas and Indian Territory."

He frowned slightly as he looked at the three of them. "We have to trail the herds farther to the west because those Missouri and Kansas farmers don't like our Texas cattle going across their land. In fact, I think the days of trailing cattle north are coming to an end. Too many laws and too many fences. Besides, with the railroad putting out branches all over, before long you won't need to trail cattle for many miles at all. There will be railheads all over the place."

Grace watched the emotions flash across Gabe's face and then she asked, "And then what will you do, Mr. Hawkins? What will you do when progress takes your job away?"

Gabe grinned at her as he drawled, "Why I reckon I'll just have to find some rich gal and get married. Maybe I'll become a banker and get paid to spend other folks' money."

He winked at her and Grace laughed. Somehow though as she studied him, she couldn't envision Gabe as a banker.

Joseph handed Gabe a small ledger. "This book might help you to keep track of your expenditures." The first two lines were already filled in with notations beside the bank draft and the cash.

As Joseph pushed the money belt toward Gabe, the cowboy shook his head. He pulled his own belt out from around his waist and put the money inside. He handed the empty bank belt back to Joseph.

"Do you think $8000 will be adequate for the rest of your expenses? I have a little more cash here in the house if you think you will need more."

"This should be fine. One of the fellows I know is lining up the horses. Most cowboys have a favorite they like to ride, but we'll need five or six horses per rider for this long of a trip. One of your hires will be for a wrangler, and his job is to take care of the horses for all the men. We don't want to lose any of them along the way if we can help it. Our wrangler's not much more than a kid, but he's used to working. With the wrangler, the cook, and me, we'll have fourteen men."

Kate listened quietly and finally asked, "How will you get your meals, Mr. Hawkins? Meals for fourteen men is quite an undertaking."

Gabe laughed. "Cookie has done this for quite a few years. He used to cowboy, but he's kind of broken up now. 'Course, he makes double as a cook over what he did pushing cows. He's not too bad either. He has his own chuckwagon and team. He'll charge you for them but it's still cheaper and easier than buying an outfit like that just for the drive."

The smell of cookies wafted through the room and Grace could see that Gabe smelled them.

"Do you like cookies, Mr. Hawkins? I baked some fresh this afternoon."

Gabe grinned. "I reckon I haven't had a cookie in some time. I don't get to eat cookies much as a cowboy."

Grace quickly stacked several dozen on a plate and set them in front of him.

Gabe quit talking for a moment and chewed silently.

He finally looked at Grace and smiled. "My old ma used to make that same cookie. I do thank you, Miss Grace."

Joseph cleared his throat. "What kinds of problems do you anticipate on the drive, Mr. Hawkins? Anything you need to plan for?"

Gabe studied the cookie in his hand and then looked hard at Joseph.

"Lots of things can go wrong, Mr. Gallagher, and most certainly some will. We could run into bandits around the borders of all the states we pass through. 'Course, Indian Territory is always rough. We'll hit that when we cross the Red River and won't get out of it until we reach the Cimmaron River. And when we do meet bandits, they will want to cut the herd."

As the three listeners looked at him blankly, Gabe almost shook his head. *What are these people doing? They don't have a clue what they are buying into.*

"They will want part of the herd, or else they will threaten to attack and steal the entire herd—maybe stampede them. Longhorns are hardy animals, but they tend to be a little jumpy. We'll do our best to keep them calm, but they can stampede over just about any loud sound."

Grace and Kate both stared at him in shock and Joseph frowned.

"And how will you handle the bandits, Mr. Hawkins? It is my understanding that the trail boss is responsible for getting the herd through as safely as possible."

Gabe looked at them seriously. His eyes narrowed down and he stated softly, "Why I reckon we'll shoot them. Nobody cuts a herd I am trailing."

Kate's face turned white and Grace's eyes opened wide. Joseph reached over and patted their hands.

He nodded at Gabe. "Please go on, Mr. Hawkins."

"When we cross the Indian lands, they will want payment. I get along with most of their leaders though so that part shouldn't be too much of a problem…unless their chiefs have changed.

"Overall, we should lose around fifty head if all goes well. If things go sideways, we could lose five hundred head, maybe even more."

Joseph drummed his fingers on the table as he thought and then looked up at Gabe. "How will we know where you are? Will you send wires along the way?"

Gabe grinned at the man and then laughed as he shook his head. "Nope. Your best bet is to send a rider south from Dodge if we aren't there in forty-five days. He can see where we are and can tell you how long it will be before we expect to arrive.

"The gather has already started. It will take ten to fifteen days and then we'll head north. That should put us in Dodge City, Kansas, between May 15 and 20. Of course, you can always ride on south yourself and come in with your herd if you want. Herding cattle is business to me, but some folks think it's exciting and fun."

Joseph laughed and stated, "You mean greenhorns think that way!"

Gabe's grin became bigger. "Yep, that's shore enough what I meant. And I do believe you are a greenhorn when it comes to cattle, Mr. Gallagher."

Joseph looked at the man in surprise. He was used to more respect and not quite so much bluntness. Still, he liked this young man's honesty.

He grinned back at Gabe. "And perhaps after this drive, I won't be such a greenhorn—at least, not on paper.

"I believe I will do that. We will plan to be in Dodge City by May 15. If you have not arrived by May 20, I will begin to ride south to look for my herd."

Joseph stood and reached his hand toward Gabe.

As Gabe stood and took his hand, Joseph added, "Safe travels to you, young man. You bring that herd through safely along with all the cowboys who are in your charge."

Gabe nodded at the small group in front of him before letting his eyes rest on Grace.

"Good night, ladies. I look forward to seeing you at the end of the drive."

Both women watched him walk out the door. Grace turned quickly to her father and exclaimed excitedly, "Father, I want to ride with you! I want to meet the herd as well."

Joseph rarely told his daughter no, but he emphatically shook his head.

"No, Grace. The men won't need any distractions at the end of their drive. They will all be tired, lonesome, and anxious to get to town. You will not ride with me—it would not be appropriate."

Grace's face drew down in a scowl, but she knew better than to argue. When her father was emphatic, the issue was settled.

She stood and kissed both of her parents before she grumbled all the way upstairs and to her bed. *Men have all the fun. Why can't I ride where I want, when I want—like a man?* She glared at the mirror on her dresser.

Fine, but I will go riding tomorrow. At least Father hasn't told me that I can't ride by myself in the mornings.

Grace was still growling to herself when she closed her eyes. A strong face with intense eyes trailed through her mind as she dozed off. The frown lifted and she sighed in her sleep.

CHAPTER 8

A Morning Ride

GRACE WAS UP EARLY THE NEXT MORNING AND SLIPPED quietly through the front door. She hurried to the livery. Her riding skirt was new and almost touched the tops of her small western boots. She had braided her hair, and it hung down her back. The Stetson on her head was drawn tight with a stampede string.

The sun was just coming up when she stepped through the livery door.

"Cappy, I want to ride my horse this morning," she called as she hurried into the barn. Cappy Livingston was the hostler. He didn't answer, but she heard stirring in one of the stalls and almost screamed when a man appeared. She recognized Gabe and put her hand to her chest.

"Goodness, you frightened me. I like to ride early in the morning and Cappy usually saddles my horse for me. I guess he went for breakfast."

Gabe studied her for a moment and then asked, "You can't saddle your own horse?"

Pink colored Grace's cheeks and her chin jutted out slightly as she answered. "I can saddle Melba myself just fine. Cappy usually does it for me though and we visit awhile."

She turned her back on him but soon stopped and turned around. "Did you sleep in the livery last night? Why didn't you stay in the hotel?"

Gabe grinned at her as he brushed his clothes off. "Well," he drawled, "I am saving all my money for that little ranch I am going to buy. A dollar for a room is unnecessary when I can sleep with my horse."

Grace replied, "You could have stayed with us. We have extra rooms that are not used at all."

As Gabe continued to watch her and didn't reply, Grace could feel the color coming up the back of her neck. "I suppose that sounded inappropriate. I was only trying to be courteous."

Gabe laughed. "I know you were, Miss Grace. Would you like some company on your morning ride, or would you prefer to ride alone?"

This time the heat went quickly up to her face, but Grace replied calmly, "Your company would be welcome, Mr. Hawkins. I have lots more questions for you anyway...and I will saddle my horse myself."

She turned on her heel and hurried back to Melba's stall.

"Good morning, Melba. Are you ready to go for a run this morning? The sun is up, and the air is so clear that you can see for miles."

Gabe's eyes followed her as she walked away. Still grinning, he saddled his horse. His war bag was packed, and he set it inside the door of Cappy's small office. He wrote a quick note to the hostler and was waiting for Grace when she appeared with Melba.

He gave her a leg up and then mounted his stud. The horse blew several times at Grace's filly and tried to nip her.

Gabe pulled his horse's head away. "Now Buck, that's no way to treat a lady and certainly not one you just met. You be on good behavior today."

Grace giggled when the horse blew again.

"Your horse almost acts as if he understands you."

"Oh he understands, all right. He just doesn't agree."

Gabe put his hands on his saddle horn. "Which way are we riding today, Miss Grace?"

Grace looked over at Gabe excitedly. "Have you ever seen Pillsbury Crossing? The rock lays right on the floor of the creek so you can walk across. There is a small waterfall there that is beautiful. It is only about five feet high, but the water is so clean. In the mornings, it just sparkles."

Gabe smiled at her. "Lead the way, Miss Grace. I have heard of that crossing but never had cause to use it."

The dew was heavy on the grass as they rode and, true to her word, Grace began to ask Gabe questions.

"Is your family in Texas, Mr. Hawkins? You mentioned your mother. Do you have any brothers or sisters?"

Gabe looked ahead for a moment before he turned to look at Grace.

"My ma died four years ago, so it is just me and my little brother now. Nate is fourteen and he will be the wrangler on the drive this time even though he's just a kid." Gabe paused and then quietly added, "I left home when I was fourteen. Our pa was a no-account man, and we didn't get along. I sent most of my wages back home to Ma 'cause Pa didn't work much. He finally took off six years ago and left Nate and Ma alone. I didn't know until I went back home that he was taking the money from Ma and drinking it away."

Gabe was quiet a moment. Had he not been so tanned, Grace would have seen the red creep up his neck.

"I'm sorry, Miss Grace. I shouldn't have told you all that. This is supposed to be a fun ride."

Grace petted Melba's neck before she glanced sideways at Gabe. She had tears in her blue eyes.

"My parents died when I was six. We were on our way to Oregon from Missouri. Seven of the wagons had sick people and the rest of the wagon train went on. They left us there on the prairie with no way to care for ourselves. James Long was only ten, but he hunted meat every day for all of us. One by one, everyone died but James Long and me. The last man to die told James how to get to Manhattan, Kansas, and we rode in there several days later. Mother and Father—that is Joseph and

Kate—adopted me. I wanted them to take James too, but they didn't. I think he died but I'm not sure. My last letter to his family came back.

"I'm sorry about your family, Mr. Hawkins. I can't imagine having a father who didn't care about his family."

Gabe reached over and squeezed Grace's arm. "Do you know what your folks died of? Was it the cholera?"

Grace shrugged her shoulders. "We didn't know but before he died, the last old man told James to burn the wagons and everything." Grace's voice dropped to a whisper.

"It was the most horrible smell. James wouldn't let me watch, but that smell I will never forget. Neither of us became sick though. Some of the women in Manhattan scrubbed us with this terrible-smelling soap. They burned our clothes too. I guess they thought it was something bad."

Gabe had kept his hand on her arm, and he squeezed it a little tighter.

Grace smiled at him through her tears and added, "I have had a wonderful life. Mother and Father totally pamper me. Father rarely tells me no." She frowned as she thought of last night's conversation.

"Well, he did last night. I wanted to ride out with him to meet the herd south of Dodge City, and he absolutely refused."

Gabe laughed out loud and dropped his hand.

He looked somberly at Grace as his eyes twinkled. "Your father is a wise man, Miss Grace. Those men won't have seen a woman for nearly two months, maybe longer. You would have them all stirred up, and they wouldn't be able to focus on cattle at all. I am with your father on that decision."

Grace glanced at Gabe and then rolled her eyes. She looked ahead and squealed in excitement.

"There's Pillsbury Crossing. Race you!" She jabbed Melba with her spurs and the little filly sprang into a full run.

Buck quickly gained ground, and Gabe passed her before they reached the crossing.

The creek tinkled and chattered as the water ran over the rocks. The water was clear, and Gabe could see the limestone rocks that lined the bottom of the creek bed. Wheel ruts cut into the bank on both sides where the wagon trains had crossed.

"I can see why they would use this as a crossing area. That water is shallow here, and the bottom looks solid. Pretty place."

Grace nodded. "Come on, I'll show you the waterfall."

She guided her horse into the creek and followed the creek bed downstream for a quarter of a mile. The ledge began to break up, and a small waterfall appeared. It was nearly forty feet wide and dropped about five feet. Grace leaned over and caught some of the water in her mouth. "It's like a natural fountain and the water is so cool."

She caught more of the water in her hand and rubbed it on her face. Then she guided her horse to the small, flat clearing on the opposite side and slid to the ground.

"I love to come out here especially in the early mornings. No one will come by until later. I like to lie in the grass and watch the clouds."

Gabe sat on his horse and watched Grace. For the first time in his life, he realized that he had never had a childhood. *I spent my time at home working and protecting Ma from Pa. I never had time to play or just be a kid.*

Grace lay back on the grass and stared up at the sky, as she pointed toward the fluffy clouds. "Wouldn't you love to jump on the clouds? I think it would be so much fun. Sometimes, I pretend I am up there, running and jumping from cloud to cloud with all my friends." She looked up at Gabe and giggled as she added, "Actually, I don't have that many young friends. Most of them are Mother's age, and I doubt they would want to join me."

Gabe frowned and cleared his throat.

"Please sit up, Miss Grace. I don't think it is appropriate for me to be here when you are a layin' on the ground."

Grace sat up in surprise and then blushed a dark red.

"I'm sorry. I meant nothing—I—I meant nothing bad."

Gabe dismounted to sit beside her and looked down at her sincerely.

"I like your zest for life, Miss Grace, but I am a man grown. Besides, I work for your father. I would never want to be part of anything that might tarnish your reputation."

Grace was quiet a moment and then looked up at Gabe as her eyes sparkled. "Am I totally safe with you alone, Mr. Hawkins, or should I be worried?"

Gabe laughed softly as he pulled a piece of grass. "You are totally safe, Miss Grace, although I am struggling hard not to kiss you right now."

Grace stared up at him without answering, and Gabe stood quickly. He cursed silently.

"Come on, Miss Grace. Let's ride a little more and then I need to get you back home—unless you want to eat breakfast with me this morning. My train leaves at ten sharp and I need to eat a big meal this morning to tank up for the trip."

Gabe reached down his hand to pull Grace up, being careful not to pull her too close. He stood looking down at her for a moment as he held onto her hand. Then he led her to her horse and helped her up.

"You are a distracting woman, Miss Grace."

Grace was quiet as they rode. She finally looked over at Gabe and frowned.

"Mr. Hawkins, you said last night that you had taken six herds up the trail from Texas. You must have started driving cattle when you were quite young."

Gabe nodded. "I was horse wrangler on my first drive. That was the year I left home. I was fourteen and didn't know anyone but the cook. He was a tough old codger, but he took me under his wing. I learned a lot on that trip. I went two more times as a drover and then became trail boss at nineteen. This will be my tenth drive and my seventh as trail boss…and it will probably be my last."

Grace looked at him seriously.

"Isn't nineteen quite young to be the trail boss? Bosses are usually older. What did the owner of those cattle see in you that he gave you that responsibility so young?"

Gabe looked at Manhattan in the distance and then toward the prairie to the west. His eyes were bleak When he returned Grace's gaze.

"I'm good with a gun, Miss Grace, and I'm not hesitant about using it when necessary. I get the job done with luck or by force, but I take the herd through. No one cuts my herd, or he'll face some of the toughest cowboys on the trail. Several of the fellows who are trailing north on this trip have been with me on nearly every drive.

"Most of my drovers are from Texas although two are from Kansas and one is from Colorado."

He slapped his reins against his leg and muttered under his breath.

"I shouldn't have gone riding with you, Miss Grace. I like you and I want to spend time with you, but there is no future for us. You shouldn't see me again." His eyes glinted as he added seriously, "Even if I try to charm you into saying yes."

Grace studied the tall man beside her and then answered quietly, "Why don't you let me be the judge of who I spend time with, Mr. Hawkins. And yes, I would like to have breakfast with you."

CHAPTER 9

BREAKFAST WITH A PRETTY GIRL

CAPPY MET THEM AT THE DOOR OF THE LIVERY AND took Grace's horse.

"Good mornin', Miss Gracie. Did ya have a good ride? This here tall galoot didn't bother ya too much, did he?"

Grace laughed. "No, he was the perfect gentleman. Thank you for taking care of Melba. I'll bring you down some cookies later."

She kissed his cheek and Cappy's old eyes glinted. "Yore a special girl, Miss Gracie. I'm sure a goin' to miss ya when ya leave."

Gabe was startled. He looked quickly at Grace, but she was smiling.

"Have you met Mr. Hawkins? Mr. Hawkins, this is Cappy. Cappy was my first friend in Manhattan, and he is the one I pour my heart out to. He eats my cookies and I tell him all my troubles."

Cappy was grinning as he led Melba back to her stall. "Good to meet you, Mr. Hawkins. Good luck with that herd now."

Gabe hid a grin as he tied his war bag onto Buck's back. He had known Cappy for many years. They had first met back when Gabe was just a kid and Cappy was one of the older hands. In fact, Badger wrote Cappy when he was trying to track down Gabe because he knew the two men had stayed in contact over the years.

"Cappy is an ornery old fellow," Gabe commented as he grinned down at Grace and offered her his arm.

She nodded as she took it. She looked up at him.

"But he is so wise. I can tell him something that seems so complicated to me, and he can analyze it in just a few words and break through all the fogginess. He's been like a grandfather to me ever since I came here, and I am going to miss him."

Gabe frowned. *There that comment was again. Where was she going?*

"Going somewhere, Miss Grace? That is the second time this morning you have mentioned leaving."

Grace's eyes were full of humor when she answered. "Well, nothing solid, but Father has wandering feet. We are going up to the Wyoming Territory when the drive is over to settle our finances with Mr. McCune. Then, we are traveling on up to the Montana Territory. Several businessmen from Stevensville have asked Father to come up and consult with them on some building projects. Father is an engineer, but he is also a builder and a stone mason.

"He was penniless when he came to America from Ireland and swept my mother off her feet. I never met any of my grandparents, but Mother told me how unhappy her father was that she had 'taken up with that no-account Irishman'."

When Gabe grinned, Grace laughed. "It is even funnier when you know that my grandfather had the same kind of start. He also married when he was poor."

Gabe guided Grace to a table in the Wolf House. It was only eight so he was good on time. He frowned as he thought of Grace's parents.

"Miss Grace, will your parents be worried? How long are you usually gone when you ride? Maybe we should skip breakfast."

Grace shook her head. "I left them a note. When I am late, they check with Cappy because I am usually with him.

When their plates were set down, Grace smiled at Gabe.

"Nellie Frank is an excellent cook. Some people think that she is grumpy, but she is just busy and kind of gruff. She has a heart of gold if you take the time to know her."

Grace was still smiling as she began to eat, and Gabe studied her for a moment before he asked, "Many people take that time?"

Grace looked up, startled, and then laughed. "No, Nellie usually doesn't give them the time." Her eyes were sparkling as she looked at Gabe. "She is hardest on men, especially if she thinks they don't treat their women well." Grace added with a giggle, "Most of the men in here would be afraid to talk to her, not because they are impolite—just because she scares them."

Gabe and Grace talked all through their meal. Gabe finally checked his watch.

"It is nine-fifteen, Miss Grace. I will walk you home on my way to the train station. This morning has sure been a fun one. I'll have something to dream about now for the next month or so." Gabe was smiling but his eyes were intense.

Grace smiled up at him as she took his arm. "I will be in Dodge City when you bring the herd in," she whispered.

Gabe pulled her arm closer to him and they walked up the street. Buck fell in step behind them as Gabe walked by. He had pulled the slip knot loose with his teeth. He pushed up behind Gabe, dropping his head between the two people.

"Now don't you be acting that way, Buck. I guess I can walk a gal home if I want to. You get your big head out of here."

Buck snorted and then blew through his nose as he lifted his head.

Grace stared back at the horse and then up at Gabe. "He acts like a human—like he's your friend, not just your horse."

"Oh, he's my friend all right. Buck and I have been together for nigh on seven years. I bought his mother when he was just a colt, and I am his people. We have been up and down the creeks together. A better friend I have never had."

Grace was quiet. She had been around many men as business associates of her father but very few alone as her father was carefully protective. Still, this morning had been wonderful. The big man beside her hid a tender heart and an honest soul. She had never been so intrigued by a man in her life.

Gabe walked her to her gate and once again resisted the urge to kiss her.

"Goodbye, Miss Grace. Thank you for a wonderful morning. You have a good month and I will look forward to seeing you in Dodge City."

Gabe mounted Buck and headed down the street. He stopped and turned around to tip his hat to Grace.

She waved and then put her hand over her heart to slow it down.

"Goodness gracious. What is wrong with me?"

Grace's mother was standing in the doorway as Grace hurried toward the house. She frowned slightly as she looked from Grace's flushed face to Gabe's departing back.

"Did you have a nice ride, Grace?" she asked carefully.

Grace was a little breathless as she answered, "Oh Mother, it was a wonderful ride. Mr. Hawkins went with me and then took me out for breakfast. He is a fascinating man!"

Kate stepped aside to allow her daughter to enter and followed her quietly into the house. Grace chattered excitedly about her ride and Kate frowned again as she listened.

Cappy's Offer

GABE RODE HIS HORSE SLOWLY TO THE TRAIN STATION and dismounted. As he began to uncinch the saddle, Cappy appeared with a grin on his face.

"So ya found ya a gal, did ya? Pretty little thing an' a good heart too."

Gabe grinned at the older man. His hands slowly went still as he stared off into space.

"I don't have any business spending time with Grace, Cappy. I have nothing to offer her. I'm too rough a man for a girl like her."

Cappy's wise old eyes narrowed down, and he pulled Gabe around to face him.

"Now don't ya be discountin' yoreself. Yore one of the finest men I know. A gal could do a lot worse than to choose a man with a good heart even if his pockets is empty. Yore a hard worker an' you'll have that ranch someday. Shoot, maybe ya should take yore own herd over the trail. Add a thousand, mebbie fifteen hundred head to this one an' take 'em up at the same time."

Gabe stared at Cappy in surprise and then shook his head.

"I don't have the money to put a herd together. I have thought of it though. Gallagher wants two thousand head, and I've been offered more cattle than that. I haven't turned those fellows down, but my mind just can't come up with a way to get the money."

Cappy's old eyes twinkled.

"Well, mebbie ya jist need to think 'round that problem. What ya need is someone to bankroll ya, someone who believes ya cin be trusted an' who has the money to loan."

Gabe looked down at the small man beside him in surprise.

"Why, I don't know anyone like that, Cappy."

As the old man's grin became bigger, Gabe's face went pale.

"Are you offering to loan me money, Cappy? Money to buy a herd of my own?"

Cappy grinned at him.

"Ya know, fer such a smart feller, ya sure are slow to catch on. That's what I'm offerin', right here."

Cappy pulled a thick package out of his shirt and thrust it into Gabe's hands.

"There's $18,000 in that there envelope. Ya put a herd together an' take it up to Dodge City. Shoot, mebbie ya should take it all the way to Wyomin' Territory—beef is even higher up there. 'Course you'll have expenses on the way ya know. Part of the wages fer those boys 'ill be yore responsibility.

"Now ya write me outa note an' I'll drop it off to Gallagher so's he knows what yore doin'. Let's get ya in the cow business, boy!"

Gabe stared at the envelope in his hand and then at the small man beside him. For the first time in his adult life, Gabe's eyes felt watery.

"Shoot, Cappy. I—I don't know what to say."

Cappy put his gnarled hands on Gabe's shoulders and looked intently at the younger man.

"Ya jist say 'Thanks, Cappy.' Ya spent yore whole life tryin' to fix yore family an' it's time fer ya to work on a life of yore own. Now if things work out with that little gal, why I'd like to be a grandpappy. An' even if they don't, mebbie ya cin make a place fer me on yore ranch once ya git settled. Otherwise, this here loan is free an' clear."

Gabe's eyes were wet as he looked down at the old man. He reached out his hand and gripped Cappy's.

"Let me get Buck loaded and then I'll write that note. You're a good man, Cappy, and an even better friend."

The old man grinned at him.

"Let me load that hoss fer ya an' ya get started on that note." Cappy's old eyes twinkled as he added, "Maybe ya should add a second note fer Gracie while you's a writin'."

Cappy slid the saddle to the ground by Gabe and led Buck toward the open door of the livestock car.

Gabe dropped down on a hay bale. He stared at the envelope for a moment and then shoved it inside his coat. He took the little book from his pocket that Joseph had presented to him the night before and began to write.

Mr. Gallagher, I will be adding some cattle of my own to the drive. I'm not sure if I will be selling them in Dodge or taking them farther north. I will keep an accounting and will settle up with you for my share of the expenses when we meet next month. Yours truly,

Gabe Hawkins

Gabe folded the paper and then stared at the book. Finally, he penned a second note to Grace. He handed both notes to Cappy and gripped the old man's hand again.

"Cappy, I'll see you in a month or so."

The old man nodded as Gabe picked up his saddle and jumped onto the train.

The Katy was the train Gabe needed to ride south, and it would be a short trip west to Junction City to catch it there.

From Junction City, the Missouri, Kansas, and Texas Railroad headed southeast toward Council Grove and Chanute, Kansas, before crossing into Indian Territory. The train's abbreviation was the MK&T but most folks who rode the train called it the Katy. The final stop would be just across the Texas state line in Denison.

The whistle sounded as Gabe dropped the saddle by the open door and found a seat. He watched from the window as Cappy tipped his hat and lifted it to wave.

The small man strolled down the street whistling to himself as he tucked the notes into his pocket.

CHAPTER 11

MARY LOVING

SEVERAL LAUGHING COWBOYS JUMPED ONTO THE train as it pulled out. One was talking loudly about dancing with a girl the night before.

"Why that little old gal, she just offered..."

Gabe was out of his seat quickly and had the cowboy by his shirt front.

"There will be no loose talk in this car. There are ladies present, and the rest of us don't want to hear it either."

When the man started to protest, Gabe dragged him toward the door.

"This train isn't moving so fast that I can't toss you out right here. Now shut your mouth and sit down or get dumped out this door."

As the loud cowboy continued to argue, Gabe jerked the train door open. He held the man out while the cowboy's riding partner tried to pull the dangling man back in.

"Now, Preacher, he didn't mean nothin'. I'll make sure he ain't disrespectful. Don't drop my pard out this door."

Gabe dropped the man inside the door and jerked it shut. He pointed at the gasping man on the floor. "You keep it clean."

His eyes swung to the cowboy's partner. "And don't call me Preacher."

The car was quiet as Gabe sat down. Slowly, the talk began again.

An older woman in the same row as Gabe leaned toward him.

"Thank you for that, young man. I didn't want to see you drop that cowboy out the door, so I'm glad you were able to convince him to speak politely."

Her eyes were sparkling with merriment as she held out a can of cookies. "A cookie for your trouble?"

Gabe grinned at her and took one.

"Thank you, ma'am."

The first leg of Gabe's ride was hurried because the stop was brief, and he had to reboard his horse himself.

The same older woman was boarding as he finished. Gabe jumped up onto the platform. The woman smiled when he helped her with her bags.

"Your accent tells me you are a Texan. Are you headed home?"

Gabe nodded. "Not home but I am headed to Texas. I'm from Bandera and I'm putting a herd together north of Sherman. As soon as the spring gather is done, we'll take it up to Dodge City." Gabe paused and added, "I will be putting some of my own cattle together this year for the first time and driving them north as well."

The woman's blue eyes were warm as she listened.

The two visited for several hours about cattle, land, and ranching before they both dozed off. When the train pulled into the station in Chanute, Kansas, the woman stood.

"You have a safe drive now. I am stopping here to stay with my daughter for a while." She paused and softly added, "I lost my husband thirteen years ago. He was a cattleman too. He was never happier than when he was trailing cattle somewhere."

She smiled as she reached out her hand. "I didn't even introduce myself to you. My name is Mary Loving."

"Gabe Hawkins, Mrs. Loving. It was nice visiting with you."

Gabe grabbed Mary's bags. He carried them down the steps and into the rail station. He started to walk toward the train when he paused and looked back at her.

"Mrs. Loving, was your husband's name Oliver?"

Mary Loving smiled. "Yes, it was. We were married for thirty-four years when he passed."

Gabe smiled as he faced Mary.

"I was a fourteen-year-old kid and the wrangler on the first drive he made with Charlie Goodnight. Your husband was a fine man, and it was my pleasure to work for both him and Charlie."

Mary's blue eyes sparkled with tears as she smiled. "Thank you for that, Gabe. Now you remember what I said and be safe."

She turned around as happy little voices could be heard screaming, "Grandma!"

Gabe tipped his hat and jumped onto the train. He watched from the door as Mary's family encircled her and swept her away toward the waiting wagon. He quietly took his seat and pulled his hat down over his face.

Maybe someday I will have a greeting like that when I come home. It would sure be nice to have someone waiting for me. Gabe thought of his little brother and his face broke into a smile. *Well, Nate will be glad to see me and I him as well.*

Gabe settled back in his seat and stretched out his long legs. It was still another ten hours to Denison. He couldn't wait to get off the train and back in his saddle.

Denison, Texas
April 3, 1879

CHAPTER 12

THE SPRING GATHER

THE TRAIN ARRIVED IN DENISON, TEXAS, AT ONE IN the morning on the third of April. The townspeople of Denison were sleeping, but all the saloons were still open and busy.

Gabe grabbed his saddle and war bag. He dropped them on the ground while he collected Buck. He led his horse to the livery and climbed in beside him.

"Buck, we have a busy day tomorrow. You had better get some sleep too."

The sun was barely up when Gabe rode down the street. The small eating house opened early, and he was the first one through the door.

The list in his hand held the names of the ranches he wanted to talk to along with the number of cattle they had available, and it was a four-day ride from Denison to the nearest ranch. The owner of the eating house was used to riders asking to buy food to take with them, and she accommodated Gabe's request for a pack of food.

Buck was in a hurry and they covered forty-five miles the first day. Gabe turned the horse loose and built a small fire. He didn't expect any trouble, but he was still careful to pick a spot with protection.

By noon on the fourth day, Gabe was back in country he recognized. The cattle he rode by looked good. He helped a cowboy drag a cow out of a bog and they visited a little.

"Trailin' a herd north?"

Gabe nodded. "As soon as I have my herd together, I'm headed for Dodge."

The cowboy dropped one long leg over his saddle horn as he smoked a cigarette. "I always thought some on doin' that. Just didn't want to lose the good job I have. Afraid it won't be here waitin' when I get back."

The men talked a little more before Gabe rode on. The cowboy stared at his back for a moment and then hazed the cattle he had gathered toward the branding area. *Maybe I'll have to try that. The boss might even be interested in puttin' a herd together. Then I could trail cattle an' keep my job.*

On the fourth night, Gabe camped at one of the ranches he was buying cattle from. His mind was racing in circles and making plans. Finally, he forced himself to think of something other than the drive, and Grace's face trailed through his thoughts. He smiled as he thought of their ride and how much he enjoyed her company. She was the last thing he remembered when he finally went to sleep.

Gabe was up early on April 7. He helped round up some cattle and then talked to the foreman.

"Think you'll have everything branded and penned in three days?"

The foreman nodded. "I reckon that will work. Three of my boys said they are going with you. Old Swanson said he was sending some cattle too. With my boys and his two, they can trail the cattle that far."

By three that afternoon, Gabe had covered three roundups and had contracts for twenty-five hundred head. Two thousand were nearly four years old and the remaining five hundred were right at three.

Gabe handed the foreman of the last herd his road brand.

"Put this Lazy HB road brand on the last five hundred. Can you get them up to the pens at Doan's Crossing by the tenth? I'd like to leave at first light the next day."

The foreman nodded. "That'll work. Swanson's boys will trail within five miles of here an' we'll push them in with that herd."

Gabe looked over the cattle. The roundup was in full swing. There were no fences, so neighboring ranches worked together. It was a loud, messy process from the outside.

Calves were castrated and branded with the brand of the momma cow. The cattle were then sorted by owner and according to what was sold. One representative from each ranch was there to rep for that brand. Numbers were tallied and cattle were accounted for. When a group of cattle was processed, the unsold cattle would be gathered and pushed onto their home ranges. They wouldn't be worked again until the fall roundup.

Gabe patted Buck's neck. "One more stop, boy. I want to talk to Dan Waggoner and see if he is moving any cattle north this year. He usually takes his own herd, but just maybe he will have a few extra to sell."

Gabe smiled as he thought about the Waggoner Ranch. He rubbed his horse's neck as he talked softly to him.

"I worked for Dan Waggoner for seven years, Buck. He is the one who made me trail boss at nineteen. I took four herds north for him and was foreman the rest of the year along with his son, W.T. Then I heard that Pa had died and went back home to take care of Ma. I wanted to save our ranch, but the bank foreclosed the next month. I moved Ma to town and took a riding job close to her. The King Ranch offered me a job the next year as trail boss." He patted Buck's shoulder as he smiled.

"Dan Waggoner recommended me, and Richard King hired me sight unseen." Gabe out across the land and smiled. "King's method of making his trail bosses part owners of the herd worked well for him and for me too. I did that for two drives in '77 and '78. Now here we are sending our own herd."

CHAPTER 13

A Warm Welcome

DAN WAGGONER LOOKED UP FROM THE CALF HE WAS branding as Gabe rode up. He handed the iron to the cowboy next to him and walked towards the young cowboy. He wiped his hands on his pants before reaching up to shake Gabe's hand. A large smile creased his face.

"Afternoon, Gabe. What brings you this way? I thought you had contracted for all the cattle you needed."

Gabe grinned at the older man.

"I've spoken for twenty-five hundred head and need another thousand. I'm taking my own herd north this year.

"I have two thousand for a fellow back in Kansas plus five hundred for me. I need another thousand head of steers and thought you might have some ready to sell. I have a couple of other ranches I can talk to but thought I'd check with you first."

Dan Waggoner looked at Gabe in surprise and then gripped his hand hard before he released it.

"Well good for you, Gabe. About time you took some of your own cattle north. I have five hundred head I can sell you in addition to some cows if you want them. I know you like to take a few cows to trade in the Territory when you go through. Taking the Texas Trail I'm guessing?"

Gabe nodded, and the two men walked out to look over the cattle.

"Have any land picked out? Maybe you should take some breeding stock too."

The younger man shook his head.

"Naw. This is a cash drive. A friend in Kansas bankrolled me, so I need to make sure I have the funds to pay him back when I'm done. I am headed north though. Pa lost our little ranch down by Bandera so there is nothing for me in Texas. Nate is going along as wrangler so when we leave, we are gone."

Waggoner was quiet a moment as he looked down at the ground. *Gabe is one of the hardest working and most honest men I know. Hard to believe he had such a worthless pa.*

"I heard about your ma's passing and I'm plumb sorry. Your mother was a good woman. She was kin to my first wife you know."

Gabe looked at the man in surprise.

Waggoner nodded. "My Nancy was a Moore. Your ma and her were cousins."

Gabe stared at Dan for a moment and then looked away.

"I knew Ma's name was Moore, but she didn't talk much about her childhood." Gabe kicked at the dirt with his boot.

"I just can't figure out what she saw in our pa. Ma was a sharp businesswoman and was well-liked in our area. I saw her wedding picture and she was mighty pretty when she was young."

Gabe looked away and cursed quietly under his breath.

"My pa was no-account for as long as I can remember. After I left, I sent money home for Ma and Nate. Pa waited for those payments. He took each one of them and gambled them away. He left Ma with nothing to live on and no way to feed my little brother." Gabe's voice was hard when he added, "I despised him as a child for how he treated Ma, and I despise him more now that I'm a grown man."

Dan didn't answer. He just squeezed Gabe's shoulder and pointed toward the herd.

"You know, I'll just let you have a thousand head. I was saving some for another fellow, but he was supposed to be by two days ago. If he makes it, I can probably come up with five hundred for him." He grinned at Gabe and pointed toward the ranch headquarters.

"Now let's talk price over supper. Sicily Ann will skin me alive if she finds out you were here, and I didn't bring you by the house."

CHAPTER 14

A Surprise for an Old Friend

SICILY ANN WAGGONER SHADED HER EYES TO SEE WHO was riding up with her husband. When she recognized Gabe, she rushed to meet them.

"Gabe Hawkins, you come here and give me a hug. How is my favorite cowboy?"

Gabe grinned as he hugged her. These two people had taken him in as a young rider and helped him to become the man that he was.

Sicily took his arm and pulled him toward the house.

"And you are spending the night, no arguments. I know you plan to sleep on the ground to save money, but you will have several months of that. Tonight, you get a hot supper and a good bed."

Supper was a lively one with lots of laughing and sharing stories. When they finally finished with dessert, Gabe took a bank draft from his pocket and slid it across the table to the old rancher.

When Dan looked at him in surprise, Gabe grinned.

"Those fellows who cut your herd last spring were just plumb sorry and offered to pay you for the cattle they stole. "

Dan picked up the check and Sicily's face showed her surprise. She touched Gabe's arm.

"Gabe, it wasn't your responsibility to chase them down." She paused and then asked, "How did you find them?"

Gabe's grin became bigger as he patted Sicily's hand.

"When I heard what had happened, I took a winter riding job south of Dodge and kept my ears open. I showed your brand around and told a few people that I was looking for the fellows who might be riding horses with that brand. I also asked the hostler to keep an eye out for horses or cows with altered brands. Hostlers seem to have their fingers on the heartbeat of the town.

"Those rustlers tried to sell your cows the end of last month. I happened to be in town picking up supplies when that herd came in. We had a small altercation and they gave up the herd. 'Course, several of those boys didn't agree at all...and they aren't with us anymore."

Dan stared at Gabe for a moment.

"Gabe—"

Gabe put up his hand as he laughed.

"Apparently, there were some posters out on the two fellows I shot. I didn't know anything about that part, but the marshal paid me the bounty. I came away with a bank draft for your cattle, $500 in my pocket, and a trail boss job for this spring. Sometimes, the good guys do win!"

Dan Waggoner laughed along with Gabe and then he shook his head.

"Now Gabe, I know you well enough to know that you didn't plan all this to get my cattle cheaper, but I just don't see how I can charge you top price when you just gave me a check for $15,000. Those steers are yours at $8 a head and I'll throw in eight cows for $7 each."

Gabe blushed as he grinned bigger.

Dan added, "Now don't get too excited. Two of those old girls are mighty flighty. You make sure they are at the front of the herd. Once they get the idea that they can't go where they want, they'll lead that herd as far north as you want to go. You unload them there and we'll all be better off. They are both good cows, but they always have their heads up. They are just looking for a fence to jump or brush to hide in—and when their calves are born, we don't see either them or their calves until the fall gather—and that's after we look through the worse brush and brambles on the ranch."

Sicily cleared the table and came back with a large slice of apple pie for each man.

Gabe stared at the slab of pie.

"You know, Sicily, if I didn't already have a job, your cooking would sure tempt me to come back."

She laughed and patted his back.

"You come back whenever you want, and hopefully, someday you will bring a wife. You know little Mary Beamon is—"

Dan waved his hands.

"Sicily Ann, you have been trying to marry this boy off as long as we have known him. I reckon he will find a woman when he is good and ready."

Gabe laughed and Sicily was muttering as she began to wash dishes.

"Well, a man as fine as Gabe should be married, and he doesn't have a wife yet. Just maybe a little help *is* needed."

Dan laughed as he kissed his wife's cheek.

"We are going to write up that contract. How about making some of your good coffee? I'll want your name on the bill of sale too."

Sicily smiled at her husband and quickly started the coffee. When she joined the men, she had a plate of cookies along with the coffee. She set the plate in front of Gabe.

"Try these. I think they are the kind you used to love if I remember correctly. Now tell me about your new employer."

Gabe's neck turned red as he looked at Sicily, and her bright blue eyes began to shine.

"He has a daughter! How wonderful!"

When Gabe's neck became redder, Dan looked from one to the other and then shook his head.

"I sure set you up for that, Gabe, and I'm sorry. My wife is too sharp for me most of the time."

He was grinning as he looked at Sicily and winked.

"Sicily Ann, you leave that boy alone. You will have him so discombobulated that he won't be able to talk."

Gabe grinned as he looked at the two of them. Besides Nate and Cappy, these two people were more important to him than anyone else in the world.

"Her name is Grace. Joseph Gallagher is her father. He is a successful builder and engineer up in Kansas. This is his first venture into the cattle business and he's greener than grass.

"You remember Cappy, Dan? He rode for you for several years. Kind of took me under his wing. I met Cappy when I was wrangler on my first drive north. That was Goodnight and Loving's first drive together. I was fourteen and away from home for the first time. Cappy and I became tight." Dan nodded and Gabe continued.

"I followed him up here when he took a job with you.

"Cappy is hostler at one of the liveries in Manhattan, and we have stayed in contact. A man named Badger McCune met Cappy on one of his trips through Manhattan. It seems that Badger and Gallagher knew each other from when they both lived in Kansas City. Roundabout through Cappy, they tracked me down. I had just sold your cattle in Dodge, and I headed up to Manhattan right away. I had already been contacted by three ranches here in Texas wanting me to buy their cattle. I figured I could find a trail boss job without too much work, but this one found me."

Gabe's face became serious. "And Cappy is the one who bankrolled me. Probably took all he has, so I have to make this work...and work well."

He frowned slightly as he added, "I don't even know this McCune fellow, so I'm not sure why he wanted me for this job."

Dan was quiet but Sicily wasn't.

"And Grace?"

Gabe blushed again.

"I only just met her…she just has me all tangled up. She's a sweet little gal, so honest and trusting. I met her when her father gave me the job. We kind of met in the livery by accident the next morning. She wanted to go riding and I offered to go along."

Dan grinned and Gabe turned even redder.

"And when we were done, we ate breakfast together." He looked at the two of them.

Sicily's blue eyes were twinkling, and Dan was grinning.

"That's it. No promises or anything."

Sicily's eyes were wide and innocent as she leaned forward. "And she will be in Dodge when the herd arrives?"

Gabe's neck was a deep red even through his tan. "Well…yes. She is coming down with her parents."

Both Dan and Sicily began to laugh, and Gabe grinned back at them.

"Now don't make this into something it isn't. I have met her twice. Why, she doesn't even know me."

Sicily stood and collected their cups. She whispered in Gabe's ear, "And when she does get to know you, she will love you…just like we do." Sicily patted his shoulder and hurried into the kitchen.

Dan called it a night and Gabe headed to the creek with clean clothes. He didn't want to soil Sicily's clean bed with a sweaty body. The water was cool. He studied the range as he washed. The spring had been warm, and the grass was coming on nicely. *Grazing should be good all the way up.* He dressed quickly and headed back up to the house.

Sicily showed him to his bedroom and kissed his cheek.

"Gabe," she whispered, "I'm so glad you stopped by. I will pray that the Good Lord will send you the right woman. Maybe it will be your Grace, and if it is, we certainly hope to meet her someday." She smiled up at him and patted his arm as she hurried down the hall.

Gabe lay back on the bed and put his hands under his head as he stared up at the ceiling.

"This will be the last bed I sleep in for some time. Now I just need to decide how far north I am going to take my cows. Kansas or Nebraska? Or maybe even the Wyoming Territory."

Gabe fell asleep with a smile on his face. A pretty little blond waved at him from her horse, and he started to get up. When he realized it was a dream, he growled to himself and lay back down.

"Darn gal. She has me all tangled up."

The Waggoner's were up early. Sicily had breakfast ready for the men at five-thirty since Dan was headed back out to help with the gather. He offered to have his hands bring the cattle north to Doan's Crossing to join the rest of the cattle Gabe had purchased.

"That would be great, Dan. I want to leave by the eleventh. You know I like to be one of the first herds on the trail, so I sure appreciate that."

Gabe thanked these good friends again as he headed outside.

Dan shook his hand and Sicily hugged him. "Now you come and see us again. You know our home is always open to you." There were tears in her eyes when she kissed his cheek.

She thrust a package into his hands. "Just a few cookies for the ride." She kissed him again and hurried back into the house.

Gabe mounted and looked down at Dan. "I sure appreciate you selling me those cattle, Dan. I'll make it back down this way again sometime."

Dan nodded and waved as Gabe turned his horse down the lane. Had Gabe looked back, he would have seen pride in the older man's eyes.

Manhattan, Kansas
Thursday, April 3, 1879

CHAPTER 15

The Character of a Man

GRACE WAS AT THE LIVERY EARLY THE MORNING AFTER Gabe left. She was restless and wanted to clear her mind.

Cappy met her at the door. "Ready to go ridin', Miss Gracie? I'll have your horse ready in a shake."

Grace nodded distractedly. "Thanks, Cappy."

Cappy led Melba out. He brushed her back and laid the blanket on it. He was ready to put the saddle on when Grace sighed loudly.

Cappy turned around and studied her face for a moment. "Somethin' ya need to talk about, Gracie?" he asked softly. "Come over here an' sit down. Ya talk whilst I saddle yore hoss."

Grace was quiet for a moment before she asked softly, "Cappy, have you ever been in love?"

Cappy's hands went still, and he leaned his head into the horse's side before he turned around. He smiled at Grace and then looked over her head.

"I falled in love one time. Sweetest little ol' gal I ever did meet. Her Pappy didn't like me, but we was in love. I was jist a cowboy, an' he didn't think I could provide for his daughter. Said he didn't want 'er to be livin' in a shack somewhere." Cappy winked at Grace and added,

"He knowed we'd have a whole passel a kids an' she'd git old too soon. We both liked kids an' I reckon that part were right."

Grace's eyes were wide as she looked at Cappy. "What did you do? Did you marry her anyway?"

Cappy's old eyes had tears in them as he looked away. He slowly shook his head. "Naw, I rode away. Took a ridin' job up north an' tried to forget about 'er. It didn't work an' I decided to go back. I was goin' to ask her to run away with me if her pappy didn't say yes."

Grace's eyes sparkled as she leaned forward. "And did she say yes?"

Cappy's face crumpled and he rubbed one hand roughly across his eye before he answered. He squatted down in front of Grace and took her hands.

"Miss Grace, love don't care if a feller has money or not. It jist don't make no difference a'tall. Character is what counts. Character will take ya through the hard times an' let ya enjoy the good times. If the person ya love has character, he's probably good an' kind an' will treat ya right too, 'cause those things jist go hand in hand. If ya fall in love with someone like that, why ya jist let yore heart go."

Cappy squeezed her hands.

"Life ain't always easy an' it sure ain't fair, but the Good Lord gives us little moments to make things a bit easier. When I get sad, I think back on that little gal's smile an' the way she laughed, an' those memories make me happy again."

He looked intently at Grace.

"I shoulda married her, even if it meant scrapin' fer a time. When two folks work together in a harness, the load is easier to haul." Cappy paused and rubbed his eye again before he continued.

"After I worked fer that feller fer five years, he offered to bring me in as a partner on his little spread. It was small in comparison to those 'round 'im, but it was a nice little place with good grass an' a little water. I told 'im I didn't have the cash to buy in an' he jist laughed.

"That ol' boy said, 'Ya do the work an' I'll provide the capital.' His wife had died, an' they had no kids. He had got himself runned over by an old cow the winter before an' was kinda stoved up. I agreed.

"I give 'im my little stash a money to invest in cows. I had scrapped an' saved to put together $70. I handed it over to 'im an' I headed back down to Texas to get my Mary."

Cappy squeezed Grace's hands again before he let go of them. He rocked back on his heels and looked at her intently from his wise old eyes.

"My Mary died the year 'fore I come back. Folks said she waited fer me. Ever'one told 'er I wouldn't be back, but she jist knowed I would.

"A sickness come through, an' my Mary caught it. She died an' I lost my shot at love. Oh, there was other women along the way but no one so special as my Mary."

"I wrote that ol' man an' told him what happened. I told 'im I wasn't comin' back. After that, I jist worked an' worked hard. I put a little back when I could, an' over the years, I saved a little.

"In most folks' eyes, I'm jist a broke old man with nothin'. But I have what counts. I have a quiet life an' some good friends. I have a few men I'd lay my life down fer." He grinned at Grace and added, "An' one little gal."

Cappy put out his hand to help Grace up as he smiled at her. "So no, I never married. I jist couldn't get past my Mary."

Grace's eyes were large as she looked at him. "What happened to the old man in Wyoming? Did he write you back?"

Cappy grinned and winked at her before he responded.

"He did. Took in 'nother cowboy an' made 'im partner. That old man bought cows with my money an' ever' year, he reinvested that money in more cows. That went on till he died last year.

"The feller he took in paid me out. See, that there is character. That old man saw it in the youngster he took on, an' that young man proved 'im right. Now me, I took that little nest egg an' give it to a young feller I think a lot of fer 'im to buy cows. I'd like to see 'im catch a break."

Cappy's grin became bigger as he added, "After all, it is fer shore cow money.

"Now tell me jist what brung this conversation up anyhow."

CHAPTER 16

THE COWBOY'S NOTE

GRACE STUDIED CAPPY'S OLD FACE, AND A SLOW BLUSH began to climb up her neck.

"I met a cowboy, Cappy. I don't know him very well because...we... because we just met several days ago, but when I think about him, my chest hurts. And when he smiled at me, my heart beat all crazy. I have never been in love, and I just wondered if that is what love feels like."

Cappy grinned at her. He pulled the cinch tight as Grace continued.

"And then I think, it can't be love. People don't fall in love that fast. But if it isn't love, what is it?" Grace's brow was furrowed as she looked up at him.

Cappy's old blue eyes were bright with humor and he laughed. "I reckon that's what it is all right. 'Course, they's lotsa levels a love. I'd say ya have a first class, level one, all-fired beginners love.

"It starts with a little bitty ol' spark an' then it jist explodes into this giant fire that takes over yore soul. You cain't hardly focus 'cause your mind's all confused an' jumpin' all over the place." Cappy put his hands together and spread them apart dramatically as he talked.

"If ya's a lucky one, that feller 'ill feel the same way. If not, yore little ol' heart 'ill shore be broken."

Cappy's eyes twinkled as he watched Grace. "So are ya goin' to tell me who the feller is that has ya all tangled up? Mebbie I know 'im."

Grace's face turned a bright red. "I introduced you to him yesterday. His name is Gabe. Gabe Hawkins."

Cappy looked at Grace somberly and then laughed.

"Let me tell ya a secret, Gracie. Ya *introduced* me to Gabe yesterday, but I've *knowed* that boy since he was knee-high to a grasshopper."

Grace's eyes opened wide as she stared at Cappy.

His old eyes sparkled as he grinned at her.

"Shore now, I met 'im on his first drive back in '67. He was a serious fourteen-year-old kid, an' that was his first time away from home. He was responsible for the hosses, an' he worked hard to make sure ever' feller had a fresh hoss ever' day. Most cowboys have their favorite mounts, an' it's the wrangler's job to make sure each cowboy gets one outa his own string. It's an important thing to remember whose hoss is whose.

"'Bout halfway through that drive, we had us a stampede. Them ol' cows was scattered over at least twenty square miles if not farther. Gabe lost some a the hosses too. That boy tracked those hosses down an' he come back with ever' single one. Then he proceeded to curry 'em all out an' check 'em over to make sure they was sound. An' by the time that drive was over, he was doin' all the shoein' too." Cappy smiled down at Grace before he continued.

"See, Gabe's old man was a donkey's hind end, an' that boy spent his whole life tryin' to take care of his ma an' his little brother. Ya remember me talkin' 'bout character? Well, Gabe has so durn much character that sometimes he fergets to take care a hisself. He's spent his whole life tryin' to fix his family. The thing is, no matter how hard ya try, that jist cain't be done if the part that's broken don't want to be fixed.

"Gabe's all worried now 'cause he's twenty-six years old an' he ain't got nothin' set aside fer his future. But ya see, that ain't completely right. He ain't rich but that boy 'ill be successful someday 'cause he's a hard worker an' he's chuck full a character.

"That boy hides his heart, but it's a big one, an' he'll do anythin' fer those he loves. 'Course, his experience with family life has made 'im a little skittish 'round women most of the time, but a finer man you'll jist never meet."

Grace smiled at Cappy as tears sprang up in her eyes. "Cappy, you are one of the wisest men I have ever met. I just don't know what I'd do without you," she whispered as she hugged him.

Cappy grinned, but his old eyes became red for the second time that morning. He dug in his pocket and pulled out a folded piece of paper.

"This here note is from that feller we was jist speakin' of. Now ya read it out there in that little quiet spot ya like to go. And when ya get back, tell yore Pa that I'll be by tonight with a message from his trail boss."

Grace stared at the paper and then at Cappy.

Cappy waved his hands. "Now go on an' git outa here. Ya read that by yore own self an' I'll see ya afterwhile."

Grace nodded and jumped up on Melba.

Cappy grinned as he watched her race towards Pillsbury Crossing. His old eyes glinted with humor. "Now mebbie I shouldn't a read that there note, but I'm shore glad I did."

Grace's heart was beating quickly as she rode. The note was gripped tightly in her hand, and she finally pushed it into her pocket.

"I'd better let go of this paper or soon it will be so wet from my sweaty hands that I won't be able to read it."

They finally arrived at the crossing, and Grace slid to the ground. Melba was breathing hard, and Grace petted her.

"I'm sorry, Melba. I promise to be easier on you on the way back." She dropped down on a rock and opened the small note.

Miss Grace,
I take pencil in hand to write this to you. I am looking forward to seeing you in Dodge, and I would like very much if you would take a meal with me once I get the herd sold. I

may not be able to visit long. I added some of my own cattle to your father's herd and hope to take them on north. If I do, I will only be in Dodge a day, maybe two. I am pleased you are coming to Dodge to meet the herd and look forward to another visit.

Yours truly,
Gabe Hawkins

Grace read the note three times before she put it in her pocket. She patted her chest. "Heart, you had better slow down or my chest is going to explode!"

She pulled the note out and read it again before she fell back onto the grass.

"He wants to see me again, Melba. Gabe wants to spend time with me in Dodge. I just don't think May will come fast enough!"

Doan's Crossing, North Texas
Thursday, April 10, 1879

CHAPTER 17

ROUND 'EM UP!

THE HERDS BEGAN ARRIVING SOUTH OF DOAN'S Crossing on April 10. Gabe met the owners of the herds that morning in Eagle Flat and paid for his cattle. Cookie had his wagon stocked. He handed Gabe the ticket for his supplies.

"I told that feller you'd be in to pay an' he's expectin' ya."

Gabe nodded as he looked the herd over. Each animal carried the brand of the ranch where it was purchased as well as a road brand. Gabe used a Swinging J for Joseph's road brand and a Lazy HB for his. In addition, each animal had an ear notch that identified the ranch it came from. All male calves had been castrated when they were branded so unless something was missed, there were no bulls in the herd.

Gabe pulled out the bills of sale and studied them as he rode through the herd. He nodded at the cowboys as he rode. Some would be staying with the herd and trailing north with him while others were only there to help deliver for their boss. He spotted some men he recognized and rode towards them.

"Dink, Rufe—good to see you boys. Like Linc told you, the pay is $30 a month with a bonus of $10 each month if we bring the herd through without being cut. I'll handle the talking—you just back me up."

The two men grinned and spread out around the cattle.

The next herd he rode through was Dan Waggoner's. The foreman pulled a package out of his saddlebag and handed it to Gabe.

"Missus Waggoner wanted you to have this. Said I'd better not forget." The man's eyes were twinkling as he added, "Said she was plumb worried about that young man getting enough to eat." His face split into a grin when Gabe's neck turned red. The rider was chuckling as he wheeled his horse around.

"Come on, boys. We need to get back to the ranch. The 'youngster' will take them from here."

The other hands laughed as they waved, and Gabe grinned as he waved back. Gabe was considered a tough man, and the hands thought it was funny that Mrs. Waggoner looked at him as a youngster.

Dan's cattle looked good. He looked the herd over and quickly identified the two cows Dan had warned him about. He cut them out and pushed them north to join the first herd.

"You two troublemakers just go on up front since you think you are in charge. We'll just let you lead and see how you like it."

The last group of cattle was the largest and contained cattle from three different ranches. They were all in good condition.

Four riders separated from the herd and rode towards Gabe.

"Tobe, Bart, Red—good to see you boys again. Fluff—glad you were able to make it. Linc wasn't sure you and Rusty were coming when I last talked to him."

Gabe nodded toward the cattle. "The herd looks healthy. They came through the winter in good condition." He looked around. "Where are the rest of the boys?"

Rufe laughed. "Linc took them to town to get baths. He said they smelled too bad to start a drive, an' he sure didn't want to smell them in another couple a months. Took yore brother too. He left yore Indian friend with the horses."

Gabe nodded. "When they get back, you boys go on in and get a bath too. I don't want anyone drinking though. We are leaving at first light, and I don't intend to fish anyone out of jail before we leave."

A couple of the men scowled, and Gabe laughed. "You just focus on getting these cows to Dodge and then you can carouse as much as you want. And remember, a $10 bonus when we take them through without a cut."

The men who had been scowling perked up and grinned. They began discussing among themselves what they would do with their bonus.

Gabe shook his head. "Wouldn't hurt to try to hang onto to a little of your money so you have something to show for this drive when you get back home."

The men nodded somberly. They laughed after Gabe rode away.

"I like workin' with ol' Gabe. He's a no-nonsense sort of feller. He can be hard as nails, but he's always fair," Tobe commented as he watched Gabe ride off.

Rufe was short and wore a constant grin. He nodded and then remarked innocently, "Heard the boss had a girl."

The other men looked at him in surprise as Rufe nodded somberly. "Shore 'nuff. Fluff talked to one a Waggoner's hands, an' that feller heard Missus Waggoner givin' the boss a bad time 'bout some little gal up in Kansas."

The men discussed that possibility for a moment before they rode out to take their positions around the herd.

Gabe finally reached the area where the horses were penned. Stakes had been pounded in the ground and ropes attached to make a temporary corral. The horses were grazing outside the pen. Tall Eagle stood as Gabe rode up. The two men shook hands after Gabe stepped down.

"Good to see you, Tall Eagle."

Tall Eagle wore a simple buckskin shirt and the britches of a white man. His hair was in two sleek braids that hung long down his back. As a young man, he had been educated in the tribal schools in the Indian

Territory and was fluent in English. He had acclimated to the white man's world but refused to adopt all their ways.

"And you too, my friend.

"The horses look good, I think. Most of them are mustangs that I caught myself. Does the owner know anything about horses?"

Gabe pondered a moment before he shook his head.

"I don't believe so. He's a builder and an engineer but I don't think he has much experience or knowledge when it comes to livestock of any kind. He pretty much left all the buying up to me—and I delegated the horses to one of the best horsemen I know." Gabe grinned at his friend and the two men walked toward the horses.

A big gray nickered as they walked up, and Tall Eagle gave him a sugar cube. He put his arm around the horse's neck and the animal nuzzled him.

"This is Wind Dancer. He isn't for sale. When we are done, he will go with me to take your cattle farther north."

Gabe looked at the man in surprise. "Farther north? Who said I wasn't selling my cattle in Dodge when I sell Gallagher's?"

Tall Eagle's face was still, but his eyes glinted as he looked at his friend. "We both know you want to see the lands to the north where my brothers, the Arapaho, live. Perhaps you will go even farther—to the valley of the Salish?"

Gabe stared at Tall Eagle for a moment and finally laughed. "You know me too well, Tall Eagle."

The horses were calm as the men moved through them. Tall Eagle had done a fine job not only in his choice of horses but also in breaking them. Those who watched him work were amazed. He seemed to think just like the horses he loved. "We are one," he would say if asked how he broke them so easily.

Tall Eagle pointed to a large buckskin stallion.

"I chose him for you. His father is a great leader and has many mares. This horse is from his favorite mare. I call him Watie. He was very difficult to capture and even harder to break. He has a strong heart."

Gabe knew the story of Stand Watie. The Cherokee warrior was loyal to the Confederate cause and was a brigadier general by the end of the Civil War. He was also the last general in the Confederate army to surrender.

He walked slowly toward the buckskin stallion. Its dark eyes watched him, and the horse snuffled loudly when Gabe reached out his hand. "Watie. It is a fine name."

Gabe squeezed Tall Eagle's shoulder. "Thank you, my friend. I will ride him with pride. Now tell me how much this fine remuda is going to cost me so we can get you paid this evening."

Tall Eagle handed Gabe a bill of sale for sixty-seven horses. "Six horses for each of your men, six extra, plus Watie for you. I will keep my horses, so they are not on the sale bill." His dark eyes glinted as he added, "I may sell them myself for a large profit when we get to wherever you are going."

Gabe looked up from the bill of sale and laughed.

The two men had met on Gabe's first drive as a trail boss. Tall Eagle had supplied Gabe with horses for every drive since then and had even hired on as a drover for several of the drives.

Once again, he was joining Gabe on his drive north. Besides being an excellent rider, Tall Eagle was a sought-after drover as well. His ability to think like the animals he worked with allowed him to calm down many an anxious cow. He chose his riding jobs with discretion though.

When the Civil War broke out, Tall Eagle enlisted with Stand Watie as part of the Cherokee Mounted Rifles and left the Civil War as a major. However, his military career ended at the end of that war. He was well-liked then by the men he commanded and now by the men he worked with. Still, he preferred the company of animals over most people.

Gabe didn't haggle with Tall Eagle on the price of $60 per head or the additional $10 premium for Watie. Most trail horses were green broke, but Tall Eagle's mounts were solid animals and were broken slow. They were trail ready and sure-footed. Gabe counted out $4,030 and handed it to Tall Eagle.

"You are quite the businessman, Tall Eagle. If the other riders knew you were the one selling these horses, they would all be hitting you up for a loan."

Tall Eagle's face was expressionless as he accepted the cash, but again, his eyes glinted with humor. "Thank you, my friend. I always enjoy taking your money."

Gabe laughed but looked seriously at the man. "How is Nate working out? Think he will do all right on this drive as wrangler?"

Tall Eagle smiled and nodded. "Your brother will be a fine man someday. He has an eye for horses and knows how to calm them down. In fact, it is kind of like working with a younger, happier version of you."

Gabe snorted and Tall Eagle chuckled out loud.

CHAPTER 18

A Chivalrous Fool

GABE SPOTTED THE RIDERS RETURNING FROM TOWN and rode to meet them.

Nate's eyes sparkled with excitement as he rode up to his big brother. "Mr. Doan said that you told him to give me a new outfit, and Rusty helped me pick it out."

Gabe looked at the shotgun chaps with fringe down the side and the high-topped cowboy boots with fancy trim.

"I'm sure he did," Gabe answered dryly. Rusty was known for his enjoyment of flashy clothing, and the fancy boots were certainly something that he would have worn.

The red shirt, black vest, new Stetson and black neckerchief made Gabe's younger brother look older than his fourteen years.

Gabe looked over at the grinning Rusty. "Appreciate your help, Rusty. Now he looks just like you."

Rusty laughed wickedly and Nate looked from one to the other with confusion on his face.

Gabe pointed toward the horses. "Nate, get on down there and relieve Tall Eagle. I don't know if he wants to go into town, but those horses are in your care now."

Gabe watched his little brother a moment before he back turned back to the waiting men.

"Tab, you and Rusty relieve the rest of the crew. They can ride into town with me."

The arriving cowboys rode out to relieve the rest of the crew and the other cowhands joined Gabe as they all rode for town. Some of the cattle were penned so a light crew would work for a short time. Gabe still wanted nighthawks out all night though.

Gabe paid his bill at Doan's and wrote out a wire to send to Joseph. *I reckon I can tell him we are gathered and ready to leave. At least he will know we are on time.* He sent the wire and headed on down the street to take a bath himself.

The rest of his drovers were already in the bath area, and Gabe could hear their voices in front of him. He picked up the pace as he grinned.

Gabe had two sets of clothes and there was no time to wash the set he was wearing. He frowned and then shrugged. "It is going to be a dusty month, so I don't reckon it matters that much," he muttered.

The Cowboy Saloon was going full speed as Gabe passed by. A young woman stepped away from the outside wall. She walked to the edge of the street and called to Gabe as he walked by.

"Hey, cowboy. Want some company?"

Gabe didn't even slow down as he answered, "No thanks, ma'am."

She stepped into the street and fell in beside him.

"Headed north with a herd?"

Gabe looked down at her and frowned. "I am and I'm leaving early in the morning."

"Can you take me along, mister?"

Gabe stopped and stared at the woman in surprise. "Lady, I'm not interested in what you have for sale. Now you stop right here and quit following me. And before you ask me again, I don't allow any women on my drives."

120

Tears filled the eyes of the young woman. "Please, mister, I need to get out of here. I ran away from a place on Skiddy Street over in Denison, and I just want to go home. I'm from up by Dodge City and I know you're headed that way. Can I help you cook or something? I'll work—I'm not afraid of work."

Gabe cursed under his breath and turned away. He glanced back when he heard a noise. The young woman was on her knees, sobbing. Gabe stopped and slowly turned back.

He lifted her up by her shoulders and handed her $10.

"Go get yourself an outfit and make it look like you're a boy." He pointed at her long, curly hair falling out of a twist on top of her head. "That needs to come off. I'll pick you up in half an hour." He glared at her before he added, "And if you let on to any of my riders that you're a woman, I'll dump you out regardless of where we are." As Gabe stomped away, he turned and growled, "And if we come across any other method of travel, you will go that route with no arguing."

She called softly after him, "Thank you, mister. And my name's Laurel."

Gabe looked back. His voice was rough when he said, "Your name's Larry. Now get." He was still growling when he arrived at the bath area. He stepped into the tub and cursed himself for being a fool.

"What did you just do? You know you can't take a woman on a trail drive! If the boys figure out she's female, why I will have a wreck on my hands."

Gabe didn't even enjoy his bath. The cigar tasted bitter, and he finally threw it down. He scrubbed himself until he was raw and angrily stepped out of the tub.

Several of his riders passed by but disappeared quickly when he glared at them.

Gabe's mood was still foul when he headed back up the street. Buck was tied in front of Doan's, and he grabbed the reins as he stepped up.

A young boy stepped forward. "I'm ready, mister."

Gabe stared at the boy and finally realized it was Laurel. He swung her up behind him. "Now you hang onto those saddle strings and don't you talk to anyone but Cookie."

Laurel was so quiet that Gabe looked back once to make sure she was still there.

"Who is Cookie?" she whispered. "How will I know who he is?"

"Cookie is the cook—that is who you are helping. And you don't even tell him who you are, understand?"

Laurel nodded and then realized that the cranky man couldn't see her. "Yes, sir," she whispered.

The strings shook in Laurel's hands as she held on. The man she was riding with terrified her. *I hope this isn't a mistake.* Then she shuddered. *Nothing could be worse than Skiddy Street. I just need to be quiet and work. I can do that.*

Gabe grabbed her arm and swung her down beside the chuckwagon.

"This is Larry," he growled to Cookie. "He will be your cook's helper on the way to Dodge. We are giving him a ride as a favor." He glared around at the hands as he added, "The kid has a concussion so no horseplay with him. I want to get him home in one piece."

Gabe rode toward the horse herd without speaking to anyone else. Nate was in the middle of the horses. He talked to them as he brushed them and combed out their tails.

"Nate," he barked, "get saddles on twelve horses plus one for Tall Eagle. Switch my saddle to Watie. Every night, you keep thirteen horses saddled. If we have a stampede, those horses have to be ready."

Tall Eagle watched Gabe as he stomped away. He glided over to help Nate.

"Well, a bath didn't do much to improve his temperament, did it?" he asked as he grinned at Nate. He could see the tension ease out of Nate's shoulders as the young man shook his head.

"One of the things you will have to learn on this trip—and remember it well—is what horses each fellow likes to ride. They will all eventually get their favorites and there are enough for each to have six mounts. You will ride one when you wrangle the horses each day, and you will want to trade off. Don't ride two out of the same cowboy's string, and switch mounts when we stop to let them graze."

Nate nodded and Tall Eagle patted his shoulder.

"Your brother has a lot of responsibility as trail boss. Let's try to do our part to keep this drive as smooth as possible. He'll calm down once we get on the trail. Tomorrow, we'll cross that river in front of us, and she's a tricky one. You will bring the horses across when Gabe tells you. They should be fine—just push them in and let them take their time. Keep them moving and don't let anything mill around. Cookie will lead the way."

CHAPTER 19

MOVE 'EM OUT!

DAWN WAS BARELY BREAKING WHEN THE CAMP BEGAN to stir. The cattle had calmed down the night before and were now well-rested. They were the first herd up the trail. Gabe wanted to hold that position, for sure across the Red River. The spring rains had been light, and he knew the river was low. On one hand, that meant that the water would be running slower and shallower. On the other hand, it also meant that the sand bars and quicksand could be more of a danger.

Cookie handed him his plate, and Gabe gave the riding assignments.

"Linc and Tall Eagle, you are on point. Guide the herd toward Mount Tepee. You can see it in the distance." He pointed northwest. "Our crossing is there, just due south of that mountain. Fluff—you, Rusty, and Sandy are on drag today. We will trade that out each day. The rest of you are on flank and swing. You keep those cattle moving. I want to push them until we reach the water, and it is about a mile away.

"The grass is good on the other side of the river, so we'll let them graze some. Move them off the trail and keep them pointed north. If they start to get restless, we'll push them. I'm hoping all the grass will make them want to graze though. Keep your eyes open for other herds. We don't want other cows to mix in with ours if they overtake us.

"Our next river crossing will be the North Fork of the Red. We'll cross it again at Big Elk Crossing. There's a little grove of pecan trees to the northwest of the crossing. Those trees will make a good windbreak. We'll let them graze that out and bed them down there. Some of you boys will remember that crossing—it has rock on the bottom.

"Cookie, there's a ferry over the Red now. Cross your wagon on that and head north. Keep Mount TePee in front of you.

"Larry, you ride with Cookie and keep your eyes open for firewood and cow chips.

"Nate, bring those horses up to the front. When you reach the water, you hold the remuda back until the cattle catch up with you. You'll have those horses lead the cows into the water.

"Let's move out. There will be plenty of herds behind us."

The cattle were up and wanted to graze, but the cowboys pushed the large herd as they whooped and hollered at the animals to get them started.

Gabe smiled when he saw Dan Waggoner's two problem cows push to the front of the herd. They tried to cut out several times but Tall Eagle and Linc were ready for them.

The cows led off at a brisk walk. They didn't know where they were going, but they were in a hurry to get there.

Gabe led the way toward the river, and the herd slowly followed. After several days of trailing, they would be easier to manage. The first few days were always the hardest.

"And our first day includes crossing one of the worst rivers we'll cross," Gabe muttered.

The herd was moving and before long was strung out for nearly a mile. Gabe signaled for the drag riders to push those in back. He wanted them a little tighter when they hit the water. The riders waved back, and Gabe headed Watie towards the river at a lope. He needed to check the condition of the riverbed. "I sure wish this river had rock or gravel in the bottom. Too bad more of our crossings won't be like Big Elk."

Gabe could feel the power of Watie under him, and he patted the horse's neck. "You and I are going to get along just fine, old boy. I can tell you like to travel, and I don't like slackers. We think alike."

He reached the Red River about ten minutes later. He pulled up and studied the water. He could feel a chill go up his back when he looked at it. "Ol' Red, you and I don't like each other much, and I'm hoping this year will be the last time I have to cross you." He stared down at the red water that swirled and flowed over the sand bars scattered through the river.

The water was down but as he looked along the banks and the red bluffs, he could see the debris trapped in the tree branches. The spring floodwaters often rose to high levels. When the river was high, it smashed and surged as the water rushed downstream. When the flood waters receded, the sand bars and quicksand made the crossing treacherous. Gabe pushed the chill down and walked Watie along the riverbank.

CHAPTER 20

BRAND INSPECTORS

GABE LOOKED UP WHEN HE HEARD THE SOUND OF horses. The brand inspectors had arrived and would be checking his herd before it was crossed into Indian Territory. Each animal was to be inspected and had to carry a road brand. He waited for them to join him.

"Morning, fellows. My herd is right behind me. They should be arriving in an hour or so. I'd appreciate it if you would check them now. It is going to be hard enough to get them in the Red this morning since they aren't trail broke yet."

One of the inspectors looked down his nose at Gabe. "We will inspect them here as we always do. You will stop your herd so we can ride through them. My job does not require me to do as you wish."

Gabe's eyes narrowed down as he studied the man. "As I recall, your job is to inspect the herd where the most brands are visible. Now that time would have been yesterday or this morning when we started. Lack of ambition on your part does not require extra effort on mine. My cattle will not be stopped here. You are welcome to ride back and check them over as they come up the trail, or you can get out of the way because we are going to be pushing them when they hit this water."

The man tried to stare Gabe down, but the trail boss's hard blue eyes were unwavering. The second inspector rode forward and put his hand out.

"Good morning, Gabe. Good to see you again. You are the first herd across this year, and the grass in the Territory looks good."

Gabe nodded and shook the man's hand. "You too, Jack. I thought you had moved north. Did you change your mind or is this your last year?"

Jack laughed as he shook his head. "The wife doesn't want to move. Some drovers were in her store talking about the winters up north and now she refuses to leave." He grinned at Gabe and added, "I had the choice of heading north alone or a wife. I picked my wife."

Gabe laughed, "I think that was probably the right decision. Although, you never know—she may change her mind.

"I was just about to check this river. You are both welcome to wait or head on back towards the herd, whichever you'd rather."

Jack spoke before his companion could answer. "We will wait. I like to start at the back of the herd and work forward. Rupert here usually stays on the outside, but I work from inside."

Watie stepped tentatively into the water, snorting as he sniffed. Gabe leaned forward and talked to the horse. It took a few steps and then moved briskly to the other side. Watie avoided the sand bars in the middle and Gabe frowned. "You were smart enough to do that, but those cows won't be." He brought the horse back into the water and walked it back and forth to see where the soft spots were. He shook his head. "The water is low but there's plenty of mud and that means quicksand." Finally, he moved both up and downstream to do the same thing. When he finally brought the horse back to the south bank, he turned and studied the river again. He frowned as he thought about how deep the mud would be by the time the last cattle crossed.

Rupert spoke up irritably. "Must you keep us waiting? This is the start of a busy season, and I would like to be home for dinner today."

He rolled his eyes and sniffed. "Cowboys. Uncouth men with no proper manners or upbringing," he muttered.

Gabe studied the man a moment before he turned down the trail towards his cattle.

When they reached the herd, Rupert rode directly at the lead cows. The lead cows began to turn to the side while Tall Eagle and Linc fought to keep them headed toward the river. Gabe grabbed the reins of the man's horse and jerked him off the trail. He didn't let go until they were well off to the side.

Gabe looked at the man in disgust. "When you ride directly toward a cow, it is going to turn one way or the other. Now stay to the outside until we get to the back of the herd." He dropped the reins, and Rupert almost fell off his horse trying to retrieve them.

When they reached the back of the herd, Jack slowly rode into the cattle. He talked softly. They moved a little to the side, but he didn't seem to bother them. Rupert rode to the side of the herd where he fumed and muttered. Suddenly, he spotted a brand he wanted to check, and he charged into the herd. The cattle leaped out of the way. As they ran into each other, more cattle became frightened. The flank riders were trying to keep the herd from breaking to the outside. Several got through and riders rushed to bring them back into the herd.

Rupert's horse spun and lunged to get out of milling cattle. It was finally able to break free of the rattling horns. Its eyes were wild and frightened. As it spun to the outside, Gabe smacked its tail end hard with his rope. The horse began to buck and raced off toward the west as fast as it could run with Rupert flopping from side to side. He had lost the reins, and the horse held its head to the side as it raced away. The frightened man bounced wildly in the saddle and Gabe grinned. He was still grinning when he moved swiftly to push another animal back into the herd.

The cattle slowly calmed down. They were still strung out for nearly a half mile, and most of the cattle were unaffected.

Gabe pointed from the cattle to the drag riders and swung his arm in a circle as he hollered, "Bunch them up. We are almost to the river."

The drag riders began to whistle and holler to make the cattle move faster. Gabe rode back to the front of the herd. The lead cows were nearing the river. They began to pick up the pace on their own when they smelled the water.

Jack handed Gabe his inspection sheet.

"Everything looks good, Gabe. Now, if I can find Rupert, we will head back to the next herd."

Gabe's face was somber as he pointed toward the west. "Last I saw of him, he was headed that way. His horse spooked or something."

Jack studied Gabe's face. "Probably the 'something,'" he replied dryly.

Gabe's blue eyes twinkled as he shrugged his shoulders. "Some fellows just shouldn't be around cattle...and maybe not horses either." He folded up the inspection sheet, tucked it into his saddle bags, and headed for the front of the herd.

Nate was waiting with the horses and Gabe grinned at him. Nate smiled back. His eyes were bright with excitement.

"Nate, you ease those horses in. Be careful not to push too hard as we don't want one to go down. The water is not deep, and we should be all right. Stay back a little ways though so you don't get caught if there is a tangle." Gabe squeezed his brother's shoulder and began to push the cattle up.

The lead cattle surged toward the river and Gabe hollered, "Put them in the water, Nate!"

Nate herded the horses toward the river. The lead horses paused at the edge and sniffed, but the horses behind pushed them into the water. One horse tried to cross the sand bar and looked like it was going to bog down. Nate smacked it with his rope and turned his horse quickly to avoid the same bar as he charged through the water after the horses.

The lead cows didn't hesitate. They saw the grass on the other side and were quickly in the water. As more of the cattle arrived, bobbing horns filled the river. The cattle pushed and shoved as they tried to cross. One steer tripped and went down. Tall Eagle snaked a loop over its horns as he pulled from the other side. The animal lunged and was hit by another cow. T Wind Dancer dug in his feet and pulled the animal out of the mud. As the steer surged for the bank, Tall Eagle flipped his rope off and moved down to let it climb the bank.

It took nearly two hours for all the cattle to cross the Red River. As they pulled the last cow out, Gabe took off his hat and wiped his arm across his face. *No horses lost, no riders down and only one cow with a broken leg. It was a good crossing.*

Tall Eagle shot the injured cow. Broken legs in cattle or horses were death sentences, and he would not leave her to die slowly or to be pulled down by coyotes. He quickly cut out some of the choicer cuts of meat and slung them across his saddle. As he headed toward the chuckwagon, he thought to himself, *fresh beef tonight.*

The cattle spread out in the new grass and began to eat. Everyone was smiling, and the cowboys lounged in their saddles.

Linc waved his arm toward the grassy area where the cattle were grazing.

"Welcome to the Territory, boys. We have some good days of easy trailin' in front of us. Just look at all that grass."

Gabe pointed ahead. "Don't get too comfortable. We have to cross the North Fork of the Red several times to get around the mountains. The first crossing is about two miles ahead. It shouldn't be too hard. I do want to take it slow so the cattle water as they cross. The water in the North Fork is sweeter than the water of the Red."

The cattle grazed hungrily, and the men pushed them west a bit to the bank of the North Fork. They crossed with no trouble and spread out to graze.

Most of the cattle drank as they crossed the North Fork, and some wandered back down to the river to drink again. The cowboys hazed them north to keep them from grazing backwards.

Gabe watched the cattle and muttered a prayer of thanksgiving to himself.

"I sure am glad there is good water in the North Fork. The main part of the Red is always brackish. We would have some thirsty cattle if we couldn't water them today, especially after being gathered and moved yesterday. No cattle like the taste or the look of the Red's salty water."

The cattle were contented and bedded down for the night before sunset. The cowboys knew that well-watered, full cattle were less likely to startle into a stampede, and they had one more reason to be thankful that evening.

CHAPTER 21

Gabe's Secret

THE TEASING AND JESTING STARTED AT SUPPERTIME as the men picked first on one rider, then another.

Finally, Tab asked, "Ya fellers ever hear of a kid by the name of Billy Pickett?"

Several riders shook their heads. The rest turned toward the lanky cowboy to listen. Just maybe Tab had a story once that was worth listening to.

"I watched him throw a heifer one time. He was jist a littler feller. He bit that cow on the lip like a dog an' then threw himself backwards. Never seen the like. That ol' cow bellered but that kid brought 'er down."

The cowboys were quiet for a moment and then Rufe asked cautiously, "How old was he?"

"Don't really know. He was a little bitty black feller. Quit school as a little bugger 'cause he wanted to cowboy. Tried to hire on with several of the bigger outfits down by Bandera but nobody'd hire 'im 'cause he was too young.

"Heard he started puttin' on shows with his brothers shortly after I saw 'im pull down that cow. Called it bulldoggin'. Sure would like to

135

see that again." He leaned toward the other riders. "I think we should try that. It didn't look too hard."

Bart strolled up to the fire and dropped down on the ground. He looked around at the group of riders lounging there.

"What are y'all talkin' 'bout?"

Rufe nodded toward Tab.

"Tab there says he saw a little black feller bite the lip of an ol' cow an' lay 'er down. Thinks we should try it."

Bart looked toward Tab and snorted.

"Tab, ya couldn't catch a cow with a rope let alone pull 'er down with yore teeth. A calf mebbie. 'Course, when it bellered, its mama would come a runnin'. I'm a thinkin' when she looked at y'all, eyeball to eyeball, ya'd try to let loose. Then yore durn teeth would git stuck in all that hair an' that calf would drag ya all over with that mama a bangin' ya at ever' other bump. She'd be liftin' ya so high in the air that the durn ol' calf would fly ever' three feet or so." He paused and waited until the cowboys stopped laughing.

"But if ya ya want to try it, why I'll go rope one right now. Let's give it a go." His voice was soft, and he paused before he pulled off his boot.

Tab glared at him. "Well, I seen 'im do it. Someday, y'all are a gonna know I was right." He rolled up in his blanket and muttered to himself for a time.

The rest of the cowboys chuckled and then moved on to another topic.

Gabe grinned as he shook his head. *Poor old Tab. He gets picked on all the time. But then, a lot of it he brings on himself.* Gabe picked up his coffee. He walked outside the fire and stared toward the north.

Tomorrow should be a slow day. We probably won't make it to Big Elk Crossing for another day or even two if we let them graze. Regardless, it will be an easy crossing. The next day, the Indians will want their toll, and I am prepared for that as well.

Tall Eagle came to stand beside him. The two men were quiet as they listened to the sounds of the evening, and then Tall Eagle looked at his friend.

"Why is the young woman here, and why is she pretending to be a boy?"

Gabe choked on his coffee before he looked over at his friend. Tall Eagle's eyes were glittering in his still face as he tried not to smile.

"Yes, I could tell the first day. You are always surly when women are around because they interfere with your work. I don't think any of the men suspect yet...although Cookie will be the next to figure it out." He paused as he studied this man he knew well. "What is her story? I am guessing it is something to do with her honor or you wouldn't have taken her in."

Gabe looked over the tall grass and then back at his friend. A slow smile creased his face.

"I should have known you would be the first one to figure it out." Gabe's smile faded and he shook his head.

"She approached me in front of the saloon at Doan's as I was heading down to take a bath and asked me to take her with me. I refused and she fell down crying. Said she had run away from some place on Skiddy Street.

"Shoot, no young gal should be down there, let alone one who doesn't want to be." The frustration showed in Gabe's eyes as he looked at Tall Eagle.

"I couldn't leave her there, and I couldn't bring a girl along." He sighed and added, "So I told her we'd call her Larry. Her family is from around Dodge City, so we'll drop her there."

Tall Eagle stared at his friend and slowly nodded. He put his hand on Gabe's shoulder and squeezed. "You are a good man, my friend. I will do my best to help her keep her secret."

His face broke into a huge smile and Tall Eagle chuckled as he walked away. "Concussion...that was a good one."

Gabe dumped the coffee grains out of his cup and headed back to the chuckwagon. He dropped the cup in the wrecking pan with the rest of the dirty dishes.

Cookie looked up at him and winked. "Don't know exactly how Larry here come to be at Doan's, but I am likin' the extry help. Ya done spoilt me now. I'm a gonna 'spect this next time too."

Gabe grinned at him and nodded. "Well, he promised to work and he better. No freeloaders in my crews."

As Gabe walked toward the campfire, he heard Cookie say, "Larry, git over here. I'm a gonna trim up yore hair. Shoot. Looks like somebody jist hacked it off. I won't have a kid workin' with me what looks like a durn sheep when I cin help it."

Larry stopped scrubbing the dishes and sat down in front of Cookie. Her hands trembled a little as she pulled off her hat.

"Jerusalem crickets, boy, did ya cut this yerself? I ain't seen such a turrible job in all my days."

Cookie snipped and hacked until he was satisfied.

"There. Now ya look like a feller instead of jist a dirty little ol' gurl."

Larry slipped off the chair and dropped her head to brush the hair off her clothing and neck.

Cookie called after her, "Be easier jist to take off yore durn shirt." When Larry ignored him, he grumbled and went back to work getting things ready for breakfast.

When Larry had shaken off as much hair as she could, she began to wash dishes again. *My head feels lighter, and my hat even fits better.*

She looked over at Cookie and smiled. "Thanks, Cookie. Best haircut I ever had." She started to hum to herself but when Cookie looked over at her with surprise, she changed to a whistle. She wasn't very good, and the notes were off key or missing. Still, it fit better with who she was supposed to be.

CHAPTER 22

CATTLE THIEVES

COOKIE CLANGED THE BELL AS THE SUN WAS RISING. "Come an' git it 'fore I throw it out!"

Most of the cattle were already up and grazing. Others were still bedded down as they chewed their cuds.

The men shook out their boots before they pulled them on and dragged towards the wagon to grab their plates. Breakfast was always a little quieter than supper although the talking picked up as they ate.

One of the new hands stared north and then looked back at the eating men.

"Linc, you've been this way several times. How many days of this good grass do we have?"

Linc chewed on his biscuit for a moment as he thought. "I'd say fifteen to twenty days if all goes well. If we have a stampede, that could slow us down since we'd have to gather a day or two. Weather makes a difference as well—we won't make as good of time if it storms. Still, we should have at least fifteen good days of grazing." He waved his arm in an arch from the northwest to the northeast. "They call this stretch the Big Pasture and I reckon that is right."

The men were quiet as they thought about that.

Then Tobe commented, "Heard Tall Eagle talkin' to the boss about takin' cows farther north. He said anything to anybody 'bout that?"

One of the other hands commented, "I'd be up for that. Shoot, we started this drive so far north that we'll only be on the trail half as long if we pay out at Dodge. I've never been north, and I reckon summer is the best time to see the elephant."

Bart was the next to speak. "Ever been to Cheyenne? I always wanted to go there."

Several of the men started laughing and one jabbed him.

"Now Bart, you know that song ain't true." He looked around the fire at the rest of the riders. "Ol' Bart here heard a song about a Cheyenne Rose and now he wants to go there."

Rusty snorted, "Ya ain't even got yore song right, Bart. The song you's a thinkin' of is "The Yellow Rose of Texas."

The men all laughed and poked fun at Bart. They stood when Gabe walked up.

"Red, Rufe and Bart—you have drag today and be glad for it. More grass than dirt right now. We'll point them north. Don't push them but keep them moving forward."

He looked around at the group of men. "Keep your eyes open today. Tall Eagle saw some riders with glasses looking over the herd. The grass is good here but lots of fellows hide here who aren't."

The men pushed the rest of the herd towards the north and then slowed down to let them graze.

Gabe leaned forward to scratch Buck's neck and relaxed in the saddle. He was on a small hill and could look down on the cattle. "Now that is just a darn pretty sight. All those horns bobbing as they graze. Those mountains to our east are the Wichita Mountains. We'll follow this little valley until it widens out."

Movement to the east of the herd caught his eye, and he pulled out his glasses. Four riders were heading toward the herd from behind and eight more were in a grove of trees. He gave a sharp whistle, and all the men looked up.

Gabe lifted the rifle out of its scabbard and circled around the cattle. He arrived at the back of the herd just as the riders approached. His rifle rested across the top of his saddle and was pointed toward the midsection of the man who seemed to be in charge.

One of the oncoming riders leaned close to his boss. "I think we should ease on out of here. That there is the Preacher. This here deal ain't gonna work on him. Nobody cuts the Preacher's herds and lives to tell."

The boss pulled back a little. He finally shrugged and rode on up toward the herd.

"We're here to cut yore herd for strays. We have a list of brands we need to look for." The man smirked as he held out a piece of paper.

Gabe's drag riders spread out behind him. Those riding flank on the right side joined them quietly.

Gabe stared at the clustered outlaws for a moment and then asked, "So what ranch are you repping?"

The leader laughed sarcastically. "Oh, we have several."

Gabe nodded as his eyes became harder. "And I suppose they were through here earlier this week?"

The man's smirk became bigger as he agreed. "Sure were. We had a little problem with a stampede, and some were lost."

Gabe brought the rifle a little higher.

"You're a liar and I'm calling you out. Now you have one minute to bring those boys in the trees up here or I'm going to cut loose."

The herd-cutter's lips drew into a snarl. "You can't shoot me. You have no cause."

Gabe pulled the trigger, and the man fell from his horse as he held onto his stomach. The trail boss coolly looked over the rest of the outlaws.

"We are the first herd up the trail this year and nobody cuts my herd. Now you have two choices. Pick up your boss and go back to whatever hole you crawled out of or pull leather. Let's get this over with right now."

The men stared from Gabe to their leader. The man was curled up and no longer cared.

The rider closest to the center lifted his hands away from his guns. "I'm out of this. Ease back, Preacher." Several of the other men hesitated, and the rider with his hands up spoke again.

"Come on, fellows. Back off. Slade shoulda known better than to try to cut a herd that the Preacher was ramroddin'. Now back off!"

One of the outlaws dismounted and checked Slade. "Shoot. He's already dead." He started to remount, and Gabe's voice stopped him.

"Pick up that body and haul it out of here. Bury him down by the trees or roll some rocks over him. I don't rightly care, but you're not going to leave him laying on this trail."

The outlaw slung Slade's body over his horse and the outlaws rode away.

Tobe commented quietly, "We should have shot them all."

Gabe nodded in agreement, "Should have but all that shooting might have spooked the cattle. We'd better pay attention though. They may try to stampede our herd or one of those following us. Either way, they'll be back."

The riders slowly drifted back to their positions, and Gabe rode toward the front of the herd.

Red looked over at the other two men who had returned to the back of the herd.

"I heard of the Preacher before. I never knew his real name though. Word is he's faster than greased lightnin' an' he don't parley well."

The other men were quiet as they listened. They rode back to their positions, and all were more alert as they watched the cattle.

Gabe fell in beside Tall Eagle.

The man looked at Gabe. "Slade Knight. Bad man. His second in command is just as bad but more cautious. They'll be back." His dark eyes glinted as he added, "Maybe I should pay their camp a visit tonight. Scatter a few horses, maybe help a couple of them meet the Great White Spirit."

Gabe stared over at his somber-faced friend and laughed out loud. He slowly nodded, "You know, I doubt any of those horses have bills of sale. Why don't you take one of the boys and put those fellers on foot. Bring the horses back and we'll put them in our remuda. A large grin creased Gabe's face. "Kind of hard to be an outlaw if you're on foot."

Tall Eagle's eyes gleamed and he nodded. As Gabe rode ahead of the herd to check out the grass and water in front of them, Tall Eagle smiled. *Gabe is short on words and quick on action. Most trail bosses aren't quite so abrupt.*

As he sifted through which rider to take, he thought about each man. *I'll take Dink. He's doesn't talk much, and he grew up in the woods.*

CHAPTER 23

A Social Call

THE GRASS *WAS* GOOD. THE SPRING HAD BEEN WARM, and the grass came on fast. Gabe shook his head. "This is about the easiest start to a drive I have ever made. I know lots of things can go wrong, but it sure looks good so far."

There were several small creeks along the way, so the cattle had water and plenty of grass all day long. The men grabbed dinner in shifts. Cookie always made dinner from the breakfast leftovers, but the hash he served up wasn't half bad.

It was an easy day, and the men were relaxed when Cookie banged the supper bell around five-thirty.

Gabe usually let the men decide who was going to pull night watch. All would take their turn, and the discussion was loud as they decided who took what night. Dink volunteered for the first shift, but Tall Eagle shook his head.

"Dink is helping me tonight. We have a social call to make."

Immediately, all the men volunteered to help, but Tall Eagle just walked away.

Dink followed Tall Eagle over to the remuda with a hopeful smile on his face. "Social call? We collecting some horses?"

Tall Eagle's eyes gleamed. "Sure are. We'll leave around midnight." He looked over at Nate. "You have enough rope to build a second corral? We want to do this with as little disturbance as possible."

Nate nodded excitedly and put down his curry comb. He was about to head up to the chuckwagon to get more rope and boards when Tall Eagle called his name.

"And Nate, write down all the brands on those horses. We'll sell them if we can, but we may need to verify the brands first."

Nate thought about what Tall Eagle had said. *Tall Eagle is a smart man. No wonder Gabe and him are such good friends.*

Several of the riders came over to help Nate build the second corral. Wood was always scarce, so Cookie had thrown extra firewood under the wagon in the possum belly. The belly was just a piece of canvas slung beneath the wagon and tied in place. However, it worked well to toss firewood and cow chips into. Cookie gave some of the longer pieces of wood to Nate.

"Now ya be sure an' bring that wood back tomorry mornin'. We're a goin' to run outa firewood 'fore we get to Dodge, so ya fellers need to keep an eye out fer downed trees an' scrap wood. Dried cow chips too. We's a goin' to need 'em."

The men were excited that night to see the results of Tall Eagle's "social call," and most slept lightly as they waited for their two friends to return.

Gabe heard the horses coming around three in the morning. He joined Nate and several of the riders as they circled around and waited for the horses to be brought in. Fifteen horses rushed into the rope corral and Nate quickly tied it shut.

Dink was smiling, but Tall Eagle showed no emotion.

Gabe looked from one to the other.

"Any trouble?"

Dink looked over at Tall Eagle. When the man didn't answer, he shrugged. "We took every horse they had. They lost a few riders as well." Then he walked over to his bed, rolled up in his blanket, and was instantly asleep.

The men were irritated as they pulled their blankets over themselves.

"Now why couldn't the boss send at least one feller who talks? Shoot. We jist will never know what happened," Rusty commented irritably.

The nighthawks changed out and the sound of singing soon soothed the cowboys to sleep.

CHAPTER 24

THE GREENHORN

THE COWBOYS ALL GATHERED AROUND THE NEW horses in the morning to look them over. Several of the brands belonged to ranches they recognized. Nate had written down all the brands and now he added the names of the known ranches to his list.

Gabe looked on in approval. "That's good, Nate. Now that we have the Stock Association, we can turn that information over to them. They will make sure the money from their sale goes back to those ranches."

The riders were quiet as they listened. Rusty asked nonchalantly, "What about the rest of the horses?"

Gabe grinned at the him before he addressed all the men. "I reckon the proceeds from their sale will be a bonus for all of us. We'll have to have all of their brands verified but if they check out, they are ours."

Linc listened to Gabe and smiled to himself. *And that is why these men sign up to ride with him more than once. Gabe is a fair man.*

Their second day in Indian Territory was quiet again. The cattle were calm as they grazed the rich grass. That evening, as the cattle were starting to settle down for the night, they spotted a herd about two miles behind their own.

Gabe studied the second herd and turned to his men.

"I want some extra riders out tonight. Those outlaws are going to want some horses, and they might try to stampede one or both of our herds to capture some. In fact, I am going to ride back and talk to their trail boss to let him know what's going on.

"Linc, you ride with me. Let's head on out now."

Gabe and Linc rode slowly toward the herd bedded down behind them. It looked to be less than a thousand head, but the number of riders was too few. Gabe frowned as he studied the cattle.

An older man rode out to meet him.

Gabe put out his hand. "Howdy. I'm Gabe Hawkins, trail boss for that herd in front of you. This is Linc."

The man shook his hand. "Charles Cole. I own these cattle. I've never done a drive before and I wasn't expecting so many rivers."

Gabe stared at the man and then looked at the cattle. They were thin and some of the cows looked like they would drop calves any time.

"Headed to Dodge?"

Cole nodded his head. "I lost part of my herd before I crossed the Red River. Bandits attacked us and killed some of my men.

"We came up from Buffalo Gap down Texas way."

Gabe stared at the man and then looked out at the drovers gathered around the fire.

"How many men did you lose?"

"I lost two and then three more quit. I have five riders and my cook left. One of them has been over this trail before, so we should still be all right. After all, we don't have that many miles to go."

Gabe was quiet as he looked the outfit over. He finally commented, "None of your riders are carrying guns. A fellow should have his rifle with him all the time on a drive. You never know when a cat might attack. Even an old mossy horn steer could charge you. Not a good idea to send your drovers out without protection."

Cole stared at Gabe coolly. "I don't believe in violence. I had the men stack their guns in the chuckwagon. They will get them back when we reach Dodge."

Gabe's eyes narrowed down, and he asked dryly, "So how did that work for you when your herd was cut? You're lucky they didn't take all of them."

Cole's face turned red, and he pulled his shoulders in.

Gabe shook his head slightly as he looked at Cole. *This man is never going to finish this drive and he doesn't even know it.*

"How long have you been ranching, Mr. Cole?" When Cole didn't answer, Gabe shook his head.

"Tell you what. I'll buy you out right here for $6 a head. Cash. I'll pay your boys off or they can talk to me if they want a riding job. I'm particular about who I hire but they can ask."

Cole looked at Gabe in surprise and then glared at him. "You have a lot of nerve coming to me and telling me how to run my own cattle. Why if we were in Chicago, I could buy and sell you without blinking an eye."

Gabe grinned at the man. "Maybe, but we aren't in Chicago and at the rate you are going, you'll be lucky to see it again. You'd better take my offer." Gabe added quietly, "And was I you, I'd just head on north and catch the first train I could back home."

Cole's face turned a deep red and he began to sputter. "I could have gotten $7 a head from the Hashknife outfit, and I turned them down. I certainly am not going to take less."

Gabe leaned forward in his saddle and his eyes were hard as he stared at the man in front of him.

"Mr. Cole, you don't have enough riders to take this herd all the way through and you are going to lose more by not allowing them to protect themselves. You have a mixed herd and most of your cows haven't calved yet. The ones who have are slowing you down because their babies can't keep up.

"You need to figure out just what you are going to do because there are some outlaws who will probably spook your herd tonight to steal your horses. I recommend you move this herd farther north. Push it up in front of mine and do it now because if they stampede, you are going to lose a lot more than $1 per head. Move your cattle or you are going to have trouble tonight.

"You might have trouble anyway but at least you'll be farther away. They will have to work harder to steal your horses and your herd than they will now."

Cole glared at Gabe before he looked over his herd. He stubbornly shook his head. "My boys are tired, and the cattle are too. In fact, the cattle are already bedding down for the night. I'm not going to disturb them."

Gabe stared at the man in disgust. He snorted once before he rode toward the chuckwagon.

"You men get your rifles and six guns out of that wagon and strap them on. All of you need to be on nightguard for the next four or five nights. Move those horses up in front of your herd and put your sharpest man to work guarding them. Saddle a horse right now for each of you and do that every night. And get a rope corral around those horses."

As he looked closer at the horses, Gabe added, "And take off those hobbles. You might be attacked tonight, and a hobbled horse can't get out of the way of stampeding cattle—and you won't be able to get them off fast enough to get away."

Gabe stared hard from the riders to Cole. "Don't welcome any rider who comes riding up tonight and don't be afraid to use your guns if you see anyone trying to come in quiet. Anyone sneaking up on a herd is up to no good."

Gabe rode back out to where Cole sat on his horse glaring at him.

"Stay awake, Mr. Cole. This is going to be a long night. You are going to need God and luck to survive."

CHAPTER 25

TROUBLE'S COMING

GABE WAS WORRIED. HE STUDIED THE HERD BEHIND them and then studied his own.

His brow furrowed as he looked at Linc. "That herd is going to be stampeded tonight, and they could run right over ours. Let's get things ready for a run. I'll talk to Cookie and Nate. You roust all the men out. They are all going to ride nighthawk tonight. I want them heavy on the south and east side. We aren't going to be able to stop a run from behind, but I'd sure like to slow it down or push Cole's cows around ours. And tell the boys in the back to keep an eye behind them. I don't want anyone to get caught in a pileup."

Linc nodded as they rode towards the campfire. The men gathered around him and listened as he gave orders. They gobbled their food, dumped their plates in the wrecking pan, and were soon headed toward the remuda with their ropes.

Nate stared from Gabe to the group of men rushing toward the horses and then back to Gabe. He studied his brother's face. *Gabe is mad so that meeting didn't go well.*

Gabe pointed at the horses. "After the men pick their mounts, I want you to take the horses over west to that grove of trees. Be ready to run if you need to. I think that herd behind us will be stampeded, and when they are, those cows are going to run this way. We are going to need those horses, but I don't want you to get caught up in the herd.

"I hope no horses go down. If they do though, we need to have extra horses saddled and ready so try to keep an eye on the riders as they go by."

Nate's eyes were large as he nodded his head and listened to his brother.

"Cookie has a couple of extra rigs in the wagon. Put them on the two fastest horses that are left after the men pick their mounts. I'll ride Buck and I want you on Watie. And Nate, be careful. Let Watie take his head. He knows more about stampedes than you do so let him guide the horses."

Cookie was waiting for Gabe. He knew there was trouble from all the movement around camp, and he cursed under his breath. "Larry, start packin' things up. We're movin' an' movin' fast." He grabbed the traces for his mules and began to hitch them.

He looked up as Gabe rode toward him. "Trouble?"

Gabe nodded. "We have a durn fool behind us and outlaws who need horses. They'll stampede his cattle, and when they do, they could run right over the top of ours."

He cursed softly. "Some men just need to stay back East. Greenhorns think trailing cattle is such easy money. They just make a mess of everything."

Cookie handed Gabe a plate and a cup of coffee. "Better eat that. If yore right, she'll be a long night."

Gabe shoveled the food in and handed his plate back to Cookie. "Move your wagon over to the west. There's a hill there with trees around it. See how close to the top you can get. And if you see someplace that has more protection, take it."

His eyes moved to Larry. "You do whatever Cookie says and don't argue. He's been through stampedes before."

Tall Eagle rode up on Wind Dancer. "Should have killed all of them when you shot the first one."

Gabe grinned at him. "Well, you'll have your chance before the night is over if my guess is correct. If I'm wrong, we are moving out fast tomorrow. That herd behind us was cut once before they ever left Texas." He shook his head. "I offered to buy him out at $6 a head. He should have taken my offer."

Nate was struggling to saddle Watie, and Tall Eagle walked over to help him.

"Talk soft to him, Nate. A horse can tell you are worried so let it know that all is okay.

"Now get your ropes and posts in Cookie's wagon before he leaves, or you will be carrying all of them." Tall Eagle grinned at Nate and flicked his hat.

Nate smiled back as he pulled out the stakes and rushed toward the wagon.

Larry ran to the second corral and pulled out the stakes there. She dumped them in the wagon, and Nate followed with the ropes from both corrals.

Cookie had the mules hitched and was throwing in the last of the bedrolls.

"Get up here, boy. These mules is ready to go. Mules know when trouble's comin' an' they don't want no part of it. Shoot, sometimes I jist let 'em tell me where to go. No mule will put itself in harm's way. That's why some folks think they's stubborn. They ain't stubborn. They jist don't always agree with how we want to do things.

"Now ya hang on, boy, an' be ready to jump if I say jump. I like my sorry life better than this here chuckwagon."

CHAPTER 26

STAMPEDE!

THE MEN WERE TENSE, BUT THEY STILL SANG TO THE cattle. Rusty had a fine Irish voice, and his ballads echoed across the herd.

Somewhere around midnight, the cattle stood up to move around and then slowly lay back down. Some of the men had dozed a little in their saddles when a shot was heard behind them followed by a volley of shots. Crashing of horns and men screaming could also be heard.

Gabe's cattle surged to their feet and began to run. They scattered the remnants of the campfire as they raced into the night.

The sky was dark, and the men raced to turn the herd. They knew if they could get the cattle to turn, they could slow them down. Once the herd began to turn, the cowboys would make the circle smaller and smaller until the cattle stopped of their own accord.

As the herd raced into the night, the riders in front fired their guns in the faces of the front cattle. When the racing cattle veered away from the sound, the cowboys crowded closer and continued to push them. It was dangerous work at any time, but in the dark, it was deadly.

A horse stumbled and started to go down. The rider was thrown free and lurched to his feet. He turned to run with terror on his face as the cattle surged toward him. A strong hand grabbed him by the back of his shirt and lifted him off the ground. The cowboy gripped the rider's arm and threw his leg over the horse's back.

The cattle surged by and Tall Eagle dropped the man before he once again raced for the front of the herd. Nate appeared with a horse, and the cowboy was quickly back in the saddle, racing after the herd.

The cattle were milling in a tightening circle when Cole's herd charged down on them. The men in front of the herd began to yell and point. The cowboys at the back looked behind them. They tried to push their horses toward the edge of the cattle, but the second herd was moving too fast. They crashed into the milling animals. Horses, cowboys and cattle went down. As the smaller herd split around the back of Gabe's circling herd and continued to run, Gabe's herd broke again and ran with them.

The pileup wasn't far from where Nate held the horses, and he stared in horror at the tangled bodies lying on the ground. Cookie rushed his wagon down the hill. Larry jumped out and ran toward the mangled animals before the wagon stopped. She sank to her knees and began to sob.

Cookie jumped out with his rifle. He grabbed his medicine kit and dropped it on the ground beside the pile of cattle and horses. He shot the downed cattle that were still struggling and hollered for Nate.

"Git up here, boy! Let's pull these animals back and see if anyone is alive under there."

Nate left the herd of horses and raced Watie toward Cookie. He looped one end of his rope around the saddle horn and tossed the other end to Cookie. His stomach churned as he looked at the mass of bodies. Two of the men were trampled so badly that he couldn't tell who they were. Cookie gently moved them aside and hooked the rope over a dead horse. As he lifted the horse, a fine Irish voice drifted weakly up to them, "I'll take the highroad an' y'all take the low road…"

Rusty's leg was twisted, and he screamed as they moved the horse. Cookie quickly cut him free and laid him back.

"Tell me where ya hurt, boy."

Rusty gave him a weak smile. "It would be easier to tell ya where I don't."

Cookie felt the man's legs and arms. When he pressed on Rusty's ribs, the injured cowboy winced.

"How 'bout yore stomach. It feel all right?" Cookie was worried about internal injuries. Those he couldn't fix. *A broken leg I cin handle but if Rusty is all busted up inside...*

"My ribs an' my leg hurt the most. My chest feels like a wagon run over it, but it don't hurt so much as my leg."

Cookie took his knife and began to slit Rusty's britches.

The red-haired cowboy protested, "Now don't be cuttin' my durn britches. I bought 'em new 'fore we left, an' I ain't got another pair. I cain't ride into Dodge in short pants!"

Cookie grinned at him. "You cin wear pair a mine."

Rusty snorted and winced.

Cookie turned toward Nate. "You take some extry horses an' see if ya cin catch that herd. Might be one or two a those boys what needs a ride. You tell Gabe that Rusty here 'ill be fine." Cookie continued to cut Rusty's pants as he talked. When he finally had them cut high enough to see the break, he sat back on his haunches.

"Larry, ya git that bottle a whiskey out from under the wagon seat an' bring me the longest stake ya cin find. Bring me two if ya cin find 'em."

He looked down at Rusty.

"Boy, ya got a bad break an' it's gonna be a powerful hurt when I try to splint it. I want ya to drink some a that there whiskey an' git a quick drunk on. I'm gonna have to pull on that leg an' try to stick that piece a bone back in yore skin."

Rusty stared at Cookie for a moment and then tipped the bottle up. He took four long swigs and gave Larry a loose smile.

"Can ya sew, boy? I ain't so sure I want Cookie here to be sewin' on me. I've seen his sewin' an' it ain't purty."

Rusty chugged three more times. His face was flushed, and his words were slurred as he stared up at Cookie. "If I'd a knowed ya had this stashed in the chuckwagon, I'd a talked a little nicer 'bout yore vittles." He grinned loosely and Cookie grabbed the bottle.

"Now Larry, we're goin' to have to pull on that leg. That there broken bone has to go back through that gash an' line up with the other half or this boy 'ill be crippled. Think ya cin help me pull?"

Larry eyes were large and her bottom lip trembled, but she nodded.

"And we're gonna need to tie them splints on. Want to loan 'im yore shirt? I cin give ya one a mine ta wear later, but yores is newer an' won't rip when we pull on it to cinch that leg up tight."

Larry shook her head. "I can't," she whispered.

Cookie snorted as he looked up at her. "It's jist a shirt, boy. Ya cin git a new one when we git to Dodge. Now gimme yore durn shirt."

Larry shook her head again. "I can't. I'm a girl and yours is too thin," she whispered. Her face was slowly turning red as she tried not to look at the two men.

Cookie rocked back on his heels and stared at her while Rusty opened his eyes.

"Yore a gurl? An' I git to ride in the wagon!" He passed out again with a smile on his face. Larry stared first at Rusty and then at Cookie as her face turned a deep red.

Cookie peered at Larry in surprise. He snorted and stood when Nate rode up.

"They got the herd stopped and no one else was hurt."

Cookie's old, grizzled neck began to turn red. "Gimme yore shirt, Nate. I need the sleeves to tie this here splint on."

Nate quickly pulled his shirt off and handed it to Cookie.

"Now Larry, when we git this bone pulled back into place, I want ya to stitch that there gash shut. Leave a little hole fer it to drain. Ya cin sew, cain't ya?"

Larry nodded as she moved closer to Rusty.

"Ya ever stitched a feller up 'fore?" Cookie's eyes bored into Larry's face and she nodded again.

Cookie moved to Rusty's shoulders. "I'm a goin' to pull on his shoulders an' ya two fellers pull on that leg. Nate, ya get a good grip up there by the knee an' Larry, ya pull below him. We might have to twist that leg some but pull straight out till I say."

Fluff raced up on his horse and dropped to the ground beside Rusty. He stared in shock at the bodies of the other two men and then leaned forward holding his stomach as he retched.

"Fluff, yore pard is goin' to be jist fine, but we need to set this here leg. I was goin' have these here kids pull but a full-growed man cin pull harder. Cin ya pull?"

Fluff slowly sat up. He wiped his hand roughly across his mouth before he took hold of Rusty's leg.

"Nate, ya pull on the bottom, easy like. Larry, ya git a needle threaded up an' be ready to stitch."

Larry backed up and the men pulled. Rusty screamed as the two pieces of bone grated against each other. She ran to the wagon and grabbed a canteen as well as a rag. She poured some water on the rag and gently sponged Rusty's face.

Cookie carefully felt Rusty's leg, trying to keep his fingers away from the wound. He shook his head. "We gotta pull 'er again, boys. She's 'most there but she's crooked."

The three pulled again. Fluff's hands were shaking. A single tear leaked out of one eye when Rusty screamed a second time and passed out.

"Twist that leg a mite, Fluff."

Fluff twisted the leg and Cookie signaled for them to let go. "Now I'm gonin' to heat some water up. Larry, ya pour a little a that whiskey 'round that gash, an' we'll try to clean it up as best we cin."

Larry tipped the bottle and poured small amounts of the liquor onto and around the wound. Rusty moaned but he didn't wake up.

Cookie grabbed a handful of cow chips from the possum belly of the wagon and started a fire. He added a little wood and soon had water heating. He poured some into a bowl and handed Larry some soap. "Clean yore hands up an' let's git this boy stitched up."

Larry cleaned around the wound with the hot water and poured more whiskey on the edges of the gash. She pulled the sides of the skin together and began to take quick, short stitches. The men stared at her in surprise, and Cookie snorted as he backed away. He was muttering under his breath as he stomped back toward the chuckwagon. He was still muttering when Gabe rode up.

Gabe looked at the small group gathered around Rusty. "Everyone is accounted for except Red and Sandy." He stared at the bodies of the two men on the ground and cursed.

"Nate, let's swap horses. I need to go check on Cole and see if anyone is alive back there."

He kicked a rock as he turned away. *So unnecessary. If Cole had just done what I told him, these boys would be alive.*

Rufe and Tab rode up. They stared at the bodies of their friends, and Rufe cursed as he pulled a shovel out of the chuckwagon. He walked back toward the trees without speaking and began to dig two holes.

Gabe watched him for a moment before he turned to Tobe.

"Tobe, you come with me. Let's go check on Cole's men.

"Cookie, you want to camp here or move up closer to the cattle? There's a nice little hollow ahead that would give more shelter."

The cook nodded. *We are goin' to have to move Rusty anyway, so we jist as well do it while he's still out.*

162

"I'll move the wagon soon as we git these boys buried. Ya want us to wait so's ya cin say a word over 'em 'fore we cover 'em up?"

Gabe nodded and turned his horse to ride south. The sky was beginning to light in the east. It had been a long night, and it wasn't over yet. He fought to keep his face from showing the sorrow he felt at losing two of his men and cursed again under his breath.

CHAPTER 27

ONE HECK OF A WRECK

THE CATTLE HAD BEEN RUN RIGHT THROUGH COLE'S camp. The chuckwagon was turned on its side and the cooks' body was partly under the wagon. The rifles were scattered over the ground beside the wagon, stocks broken and barrels twisted. Gabe looked at them and cursed in disgust. "Dang tenderfoot. Didn't even let his men protect themselves."

They found the bodies of two more men. They looked like they had been in their bedrolls when the attack came.

Tobe looked in shock at the men. *Gabe warned them and they still didn't listen.*

Another rider and horse were close by the fire. The cowboy had one foot in the stirrup, and the horse was on top of him. Gabe shook his head. Another cowboy lay close by. A rope lay close to his hand, but no horse was anywhere to be seen.

Tobe muttered, "He was bucked off, fell off, or didn't have time to get on."

A man moaned and Gabe wheeled his horse toward the sound. It was Cole. His body was battered and broken. Gabe couldn't believe he was still alive.

"Any of my men make it?"

Gabe shook his head. "Not that I can see although we haven't found your last man yet."

Cole's face twisted into a smile. "That's probably Angel. He took his guns even when I told him to leave them. He called me a tenderfoot and threatened to join up with you." Cole gasped in pain as he added, "He was the only one who had ever been over this trail." The man looked up at Gabe. Pain showed in his eyes.

"You were right. I should have sold you the cattle and gone home. There's nothing left."

Gabe was quiet as he listened to the man. When Cole became quiet, Gabe asked, "You have any kin? Anyone we should send money to when we sell your cattle?"

Cole looked up at Gabe in surprise, and a brief smile creased his face. *Only a western man would ask that.*

"No, there is no one." He tried to lift his arm to reach inside his coat. He tried twice and then Gabe folded his coat back to expose some papers. He took the papers out and placed them in Cole's hand.

The man looked up at Gabe. "Write out a bill of sale—and—I'll sign—it. Put your name on it. Say I gave—gave them to you."

Gabe stared at the man a moment and then wrote on the back of the papers.

April 13, 1879
I, Charles Cole, gave my Circle C herd to Gabe Hawkins when I was dying.

Charles C. Cole

Cole looked at it and smiled. He scratched his name across the bottom before the pencil slipped from his hand.

"Would have liked to have known you better, Gabe. I could have learned..."

Charles Cole was dead. Gabe rocked back on his haunches as he stared at the mangled body of the man in front of him.

"Cole had no business trying to trail a herd. Shoot, he didn't know enough about cattle to even ranch. Given time, maybe he would have learned. Lessons can be harsh out here though."

A horse snuffled and both men wheeled with guns drawn to face whoever was riding up. A saddled horse walked slowly towards them. It had cuts on its legs and a gash on its hip. Its reins were trailing, and it trembled as Gabe slowly walked toward it.

"Easy now, boy. Let me look you over. You are banged up a little, but I think you'll be all right. This was a hard, old night for everyone."

He turned to the cowboy beside him. "Tobe, you take Cole back on this horse to where Rufe is digging graves. Have the boys dig six more and bring back five horses to carry the rest of these fellows." He paused and then added, "Go through Cole's pockets. Make sure you don't see anything personal that needs to be sent to someone before we lay him down."

As Tobe rode back towards their camp, Gabe called after him, "And have Cookie look at that horse. Those cuts should probably be treated."

Gabe bent down beside the cook. He searched through the man's pockets and found a picture of a young woman. He didn't find any name anywhere though. "I guess we'll bury you as Cookie."

The cowboy whose foot was caught in his stirrup had a stack of letters in his saddle bag. They were all from Mary Covington, Saint Louis, Missouri, and were addressed to Dusty Woods. Gabe pulled the saddle bags off the horse and put the letters back inside. "Dusty, your girl is going to cry when she gets word of your death, but I will make sure she knows."

The cowboy lying close to Dusty had a picture of a pretty young woman in his pocket. It said, "To Johnnie with love, Mandie" Gabe put the picture inside the young man's pocket and patted it. "At least we know your first name, Johnnie."

Not much was left of the two men by the campfire. Their clothing was scattered several feet around them. Part of a letter lay on the ground. The torn envelope showed Galveston, Texas, but the rest of the letter was gone. "Boys, I don't know who you were but I'm guessing someone will be missing you." He found a tarp in the wagon and wrapped both of their bodies in it.

He had just finished tying the ends when he heard a voice, "Hola, señor. May I come in?"

Gabe stood quickly. His hand was on his gun, but the man riding in kept his hands on his saddle horn as he smiled at Gabe.

"My name is Jorge, but my sainted mother calls me Angel. Angel Montero. I rode for señor Cole."

He looked around at the bodies of his comrades.

"Your advice was wise, señor. I was outside the herd when the banditos struck. They were on foot and wanted our horses. I think they did not care how many died as long as they had their caballos."

Gabe nodded. "How many were there?"

"Ten came, señor, but only seven left. I followed them back to their acampar. What is your gringo word? Camp, I believe. Three of them I killed with my small knife." He pulled a huge knife and wiped it on his pants before it disappeared again inside his jacket. "For the rest, I left gifts. I put my pet scorpions in their boots and told them to stay there. Scorpions do not like the grass so much, but they do like a nice boot... and a warm foot." Angel smiled at Gabe as he added, "Then I took our horses back and ran them through the camp. I think not all will wake up this day."

Gabe stared at the man a moment and finally chuckled.

"And your sainted mother calls you Angel!"

Angel grinned at him and his dark eyes twinkled. "Si, señor, but she doesn't always know what I do."

Gabe reached up his hand. "It's nice to meet you, Angel. I am short a few riders if you would like a job. Just know you can't bring your pet scorpions with you."

Angel looked mournful as he agreed. "Sadly, señor, all my pets were left as gifts. I will have to collect more, I think. Maybe this drive, maybe not." He pointed toward the bodies of the dead men as he named them.

"That one is Dusty Woods, and he is Johnnie Mississippi. I think that is not really his name but that is what he told us. The two who were sleeping were brothers, but they would not tell us their names. They went by Rip. If you said that name, both of them answered. I don't think they were so right in the head." Angel tapped his skull and rolled his dark eyes.

"What made you take a job with this outfit, Angel? Cole was lucky the herd made it this far."

Angel looked over the scattered remains of the riders and the wrecked camp. He answered quietly, "Si, but señor Cole was my friend. He was going to go with or without me. I tried to tell him that we needed more hombres, that we needed vaqueros, but he just laughed. 'It cannot be so difficult to drive cows in a straight line.'" Angel shook his head.

"Señor Cole was a good man, but he did not understand vacas. Of cows he knew nothing of. Perhaps he would have learned." Angel shrugged. "We will not know."

Gabe was quiet. He looked around at the scattered camp. His eyes rested on Cole and then at the bodies of young men who would never laugh again. Gabe shook his head. *Four riders dead and a cook who made his last meal...and all because of a kind man who liked cattle but knew nothing of what it took to be a rancher.*

Both men looked up as Gabe's riders rode into the camp area.

"Boys, this is Angel. He will be joining us. Bart, Tobe—let's get these fellows loaded up."

The men were buried under the trees. Some of the cowboys cut crosses and others carved names. The two brothers were buried together with R.I.P on their single cross.

Rusty had been moved into the back the chuckwagon while he was still passed out. Cookie drove it down to the little cove Gabe had suggested. Larry sat in the back and held Rusty's leg to keep it from bouncing.

The cattle were once again grazing calmly, and Tall Eagle offered to stay with the herd so the rest of the men could see their friends laid down.

Bart had a fine bass voice, and he led them in the song, "Shall We Gather at the River."

Gabe pulled a small bible from his saddlebag and read Psalm 23. When it was finished, he looked around at his men. "Anyone have anything else they want to say?"

Dink stepped forward. "Red and Sandy were fine men and good cowboys. They both went on this drive to make money to send home to their folks down by San Antone. They were my friends and my pards, and I am going to miss them." He stepped back into the little cluster of cowboys and squinted his eyes to keep tears from forming.

The rest of the men were silent. Dink rarely talked, and those were more words than the men had heard him say the entire drive.

Gabe nodded and then looked over at Angel.

"Would you like to add anything, Angel?"

The man nodded his head, "Si, señor.

"The hombres in my crew were not vaqueros. They were just niños who needed a job. Señor Cole was my friend, and he was a good man. He hired these niños, these—these boys because he was kind, not because they were vaqueros. Now all of them are dead and I think that our Dios, our God, will be happy to see them." He paused and added, "But I do not think he will put them in charge of his cattle."

Some of the cowboys looked up in surprise, but Angel's face looked so holy, so sincere, that they dropped their heads back down.

Gabe nodded at Angel and waited to see if anyone else had anything to add. When no one spoke up, Gabe stepped up to the graves. He dropped a handful of dirt into each one. "So long, boys. You ride high and you ride proud. You all did your best today."

The men were silent and Gabe looked them over quietly.

"Boys, we lost some good men today, and that is going to be hard for all of us. We can't do any more for them than we just did. You all mourn these fellows in your own way, but in the meantime, we still have a drive to complete." He nodded toward the cattle and looked back at the men.

"Some of you fill in those graves. The rest of you, head over to the chuckwagon. Cookie will have some breakfast ready before too long. You can all take turns sleeping and riding herd today—we'll let the cattle graze. The grass is good here and there are several creeks where they can water.

"Some of Cole's cows are dropping calves, and I would like to leave those calves with Quanah Parker when we meet up with him. We should see him in a day or two. Let's try to keep them alive until then. If we have to, we can load them in the chuckwagon. Just make sure you wrap a sack around each one so they keep their own scents.

"We can let them out at night to nurse." As he walked away, he added, "Or maybe sooner if they try to jump over the sides."

Angel grabbed a shovel and began to fill in graves. Dink and Tobe joined him. The rest of the men rode towards the chuckwagon. The horses moved slowly, and the men were even slower. Everyone was tired.

Cookie clanged the bell as they rode up. "Eat up, boys. This gravy an' biscuits should stick to yore ribs fer a while." Cookie was tough, but he loved his cowboys. *These boys have been up all night an' lost friends too. I'll fix 'em a dessert tonight. That should help cheer 'em up.*

Angel volunteered to ride herd and Dink raised his hand as he filled his mouth.

Tobe looked at the two riders and shrugged. "I'll take a turn first too. That means I can sleep longer when I get done," he drawled as he grinned at his friends.

Larry was quiet as she helped Cookie. He looked at her a couple of times and frowned. He said nothing until everything was cleaned and the wagon was loaded.

"Larry, you an' me need to talk."

CHAPTER 28

THE WHOLE STORY

LARRY TWISTED HER HANDS TOGETHER. AS COOKIE glared at her, she ducked her head.

"Now ya go ahead an' spit that story out, an' it better be a good one or I'm a sendin' ya down the road." He snorted and added, "Gabe must be gettin' soft."

Larry's face turned white, and she took a deep breath.

"I grew up south of Dodge City. My parents are hard-working farmers. My father is known as the animal doctor in our country community—that's how I learned to stitch up wounds." Larry looked toward the cattle and a blush moved up her neck as she continued.

"I met Dutch Dugan two years ago. He swept me off my feet with all kinds of promises, and I believed him.

"My parents were upset. My father told me he was a counterfeit, but I thought I was in love."

Larry's eyes filled with tears. "We were married in Kansas City, and Dutch gambled in every lousy saloon he could find. He was a bad gambler. The more he gambled, the more he lost, and the meaner he became.

"We ended up in Denison, Texas, down on Skiddy Street. Duke offered me as a dance partner to cover some of his expenses." Larry's looked away and added softly, "He wanted me to do more but I refused.

"I hated that dance hall. Some of the cowboys were just lonesome, but the words to the songs were bawdy." Her voice was barely a whisper when she added, "The dresses I had to wear were—were too revealing. I was always in trouble for not being 'friendly' enough.

"About two months after we arrived in Denison, Duke was shot for dealing cards from the bottom on the deck. I managed to get away and ended up at Doan's Crossing."

Larry's face was bleak as she looked at Cookie. "I can't believe I was so stupid."

Cookie studied her face for a bit. "Wahl, I reckon we cin all use a do-over from time to time.

"So how did ya end up with Gabe? Does he know yore a gurl? That feller's purty hard-nosed when it comes to breakin' rules on his drives."

Larry smiled and nodded. "I let a drunk cowboy take me outside during one of the dances. I hit him over the head with a piece of wood and then I ran away. I hid in the loft of the livery until the stage came in the next morning. I didn't have any money, but I begged the driver to take me." Larry's smile was soft as tears threatened to leak out of her eyes.

"The stage driver refused at first, but I guess I looked so scared that he finally agreed. He handed me his coat and put me on the stage headed for Doan's.

"I was hiding by the saloon when Mr. Hawkins walked by. I knew lots of herds went to Dodge because one of the cattle trails ran within ten miles of our house. I could tell Mr. Hawkins was a drover. I asked him to take me with him. I was at the end of my rope with nowhere to go. He refused of course. I fell down in the street and began to cry. I was so afraid and hopeless.

Larry's voice was barely audible as she added, "Mr. Hawkins turned around. He was so mad. I thought he was going to keep walking, but he gave me money for clothes and told me to cut my hair. He also said I was to go by the name of Larry."

Cookie studied Laurel's face. "So now what, Larry?"

Larry's face was determined when she looked at Cookie. Her eyes glinted as she stated, "I am going to get a job with old Doc Walters in Dodge, and I am going to learn animal medicine."

Cookie laughed and patted her hand. "Good. I reckon there's a need in Dodge fer animal docs. Now let's get back to work. We need to fix a good dinner fer these tuckered out boys. An' Miss Larry, yer secret's safe with me."

He waved his hand behind him. "There's a quiet little creek back there. Once we get these fellers fed, you go on an' take a bath. Otherwise, those rowdy cowboys 'ill be wantin' to toss ya in the water with 'em."

Larry smiled at Cookie. A huge weight had been lifted off her back. She nodded in agreement and hurried back to the chuckwagon.

Rusty was once again conscious, and Larry checked his leg. She felt his head and frowned.

"My leg hurts powerful. Cookie have any more whiskey? If I cin git drunk, I wouldn't feel it so much."

Larry studied his leg for a moment. "Let me talk to Cookie. He might have some medicine that would help."

Cookie looked up as he heard her talking to Rusty and waved his hand.

"Go ahead an' look fer what ya need in my medicine kit or go find it out there on the prairie if'n I don't have it. I reckon I cin handle the cookin'—done it fer lots a years on my own..." He continued to grumble but winked at Larry as she looked for a knife.

Cookie pulled his medicine kit from under the wagon seat and took out a small can. "I have some elk root here, but we cin use more if you's a diggin'."

Larry looked up in confusion. "Elk root?"

"Yeah, from coneflowers. Some folks has a fancier name, but I cain't even say that."

Larry smiled and nodded, "Yes, echinacea. That's what I was hoping to find. Thanks, Cookie."

CHAPTER 29

YORE MAMA A HEALER?

FLUFF WAS COMING UP TO CHECK ON RUSTY. HE stared from Larry to his friend. His face was worried as he asked, "So how is he? Infection comin' on?"

Larry nodded. "It is and that's why I want to collect some purple coneflowers. I want to make some tea, and I need some honey too."

Fluff stared at Larry. "Coneflowers? Why there's a passel of 'em jist outside a where we're camped. I cin show ya."

As they hurried to the area Fluff was talking about, he looked at Larry in surprise.

"A durned ol' flower cin help knock the infection? Never heard of it. Whatcha goin' do with it? Make a powder or drink it?"

Larry smiled up at him. "Both. How about honey? Do you know where I can find some of that?"

Several of the other cowboys wandered over to see what they were digging. They were as surprised as Fluff.

Angel rode up and peered into their group. "Ah, you dig for echinacea. Si, it is good for the leg. Perhaps you need a bigger knife?"

He dropped down beside them. He cut a circle of prairie sod out with his large knife and lifted the intact plant up. "How many more do you need, señor?"

Larry started laughing at the looks on the men's faces. "I think three will be plenty, but I'll take more if you want to dig them up. Now how about some honey?"

The conversation soon picked up on the possibility of biscuits with honey and where honey could be had.

Dink rode over and listened to them for a moment. He commented dryly, "Why don't ya jist follow those bees?"

He rode off whistling and soon a string of cowboys was headed into the little grove of trees.

Larry removed the roots of one plant. She chopped the flowers and the leaves. When the pieces were small, she poured boiling water over them and let them steep. The roots and the rest of the plants she wrapped in a damp towel and tucked down inside the wagon.

She seated herself beside Rusty. She gently unwrapped his leg.

"Rusty, this is going to hurt and I'm sorry. I am going clean your leg again and apply some medicine." Larry dabbed his leg with whiskey. She sprinkled the echinacea powder liberally over the wound.

Rusty studied the side of Larry's face as she worked on his leg.

"Where did ya learn about all this? Yore mama a healer?"

Larry looked up in surprise and then laughed. "No, my father treats animals and I help." She smiled at him and added, "I like animals. I especially like to treat them when they are wounded or sick. I am going to work with the animal doctor in Dodge when we get there."

Angel rode up on his horse and looked down at the leg. He nodded in approval. Lots of noise was coming from the trees and his eyes twinkled as he suggested somberly, "Perhaps I should assist them. I think your vaqueros know nothing of collecting honey." He grabbed a bucket and a spoon out of the chuckwagon and rode slowly toward the trees.

Rusty hadn't met Angel and looked after him in surprise. "New rider?"

Larry nodded as she applied more powder. "He was with the herd that ran you over. He is the only one who made it." She turned her head and added quietly. "Mr. Hawkins warned them, and he was the only one who listened."

She sat back on her heels and looked at the eight crosses under the trees before she looked back at Rusty.

"The outlaws spooked Mr. Cole's herd and stampeded it over his camp. Then the herd ran into the back of this herd and over the three of you. You were the lucky one. There are eight graves over there under the trees. Red and Sandy as well as four of their drovers plus their cook and the owner."

Rusty watched Larry closely and then asked, "How old are ya anyway? Yore plumb wise for a sprat of a fellow."

Larry shrugged. "Folks grow up fast when they have to."

She stood and looked down at him. "When the men get back, I am going to smear honey on that wound. It will draw the infection out." Her eyes scanned the wagon and the camp area as she added, "I just need a piece of light cloth to lay over it..." Larry's eyes settled on his neckerchief, and she put out her hand. "Give me your bandana. I'll wash it out and we'll put it over the honey to keep the flies and bugs off."

Rusty slowly took it off as he frowned at her. Larry rolled her eyes.

"Good grief, Rusty. It's just a bandanna, and it certainly won't be ruined. We can wash it out again when we're done."

The noise in the trees had subsided, and soon, cowboys began to trickle down to the camp.

Angel was the last to arrive. He carried a bucket about one fourth full of fresh honey and even some pieces of honeycomb. "It was a large hive. I politely asked and their boss lady said, 'Si, señor. We will be happy to share with those vaqueros.'" He grinned at the cowboys and sauntered away.

Cookie came over to look and then grunted. He grabbed his bowl and began to mix up biscuits.

Larry scooped out a little honey and poured it into a small bowl. She began to smear the honey on the wound. Her hands were gentle as she applied the honey and rubbed it into the stitches.

Rusty pulled himself up on his elbows to watch. "That feels good. Really cools it off."

Larry nodded. "We treated a fawn this way one time. Its leg was all torn up, and it could barely walk. Honey is a wonderful medicine."

She took the bandana and washed it out in the dish pan. She laid it over the wagon to dry and began to help Cookie with the meal.

He was quiet as he rolled out the biscuits. He finally looked up. "Ya better take all the honey ya want outa that there bucket. There likely won't be none left when those boys go through it." He pointed toward the wagon seat. "They's some cans under there. Fill a couple of 'em up so's ya have some on down the trail."

Cookie nodded at a blanket on the seat of the chuckwagon. "Now would be a good time to take that bath. And when ya come out, smear a little dirt on yore face so ya don't look so much like a durn gurl."

The water was cool, and Larry kept her bath short. She knew Cookie wouldn't let any of the men come down where she was, but their voices still made her nervous. As she put her dirty clothes back on, she whispered to herself, "Maybe I will come down tonight and wash my clothes. I can't wear a wet shirt during the day, but it should dry overnight."

She washed her hair and pulled the old hat on while it was still wet. Taking Cookie's advice, she smudged some dirt on her face before she returned to the wagon.

Cookie looked up and grinned at her. "Feel better? Now pull those biscuits off the fire and get ready to scoop out that honey." He clanged the dinner bell and the men came running.

Larry was careful to give each man the same amount of honey on his biscuit, and Cookie was right—they ate biscuits until the honey was gone.

CHAPTER 30

THAT LEG GLOWS IN THE DARK!

FLUFF MADE SURE THAT RUSTY RECEIVED BISCUITS and honey as well. He was sitting by his friend when Larry handed Rusty the tea to drink. She pressed the bandana over the honey as he tasted his tea.

Rusty wrinkled up his nose at the taste of the tea. He grinned at Larry as he stuck his finger in the honey on his leg and dipped it into his tea. He tasted it again and nodded happily.

Fluff looked at Larry and then pointed at the honey. "Reckon that will work?"

Larry nodded. "I've seen wounds like this heal. Moving is going to be the tricky part. That leg should be kept straight, and those stakes are too short." She started to ask Fluff to cut a splint, but he was already moving towards his horse.

He grinned back at her as he rode off toward the grove of trees. He was back shortly with four small saplings. All were slender and straight. He trimmed the branches and nubs off all four and cut a notch in the top of two of them. He fit a small piece of smooth wood horizontally in the notches and added a second horizontal piece around two feet from the top.

Fluff stood and lifted the crutches. He leaned his weight on them and then carried all four lengths of wood to Rusty.

"Made ya some crutches. Now ya need to git up off yore sorry tail an' quit layin' 'round."

Rusty grinned at his buddy. He held his face tight as Fluff untied the shirt and the stakes.

Fluff looked down at his friend and started laughing. When Rusty glared at him, he pointed toward Rusty's leg. Cookie had cut the britches apart from the bottom to above the cut. They were rolled up and exposed a long white leg.

"Ya look purty good in short pants but mebbie we should cut the other pant leg off too. That hairy thing is so white I swear it could glow in the dark!"

Rusty stared down at his leg and then at his friend. The contrast in color between Rusty's face and his bare leg was stark. The injured cowboy laughed too.

Fluff rolled the pant leg down and then placed one of the saplings on each side of Rusty's leg. He had cut some of the strings off his saddle, but he was struggling to keep everything in place as well as hold Rusty's leg straight. He turned toward the campfire and hollered at the cowboy reading there.

"Tab, come over here and help me tie this up."

The man complied quickly, and they soon had Rusty's leg secured.

"I put yore pant leg under those poles so's they don't rub yore leg so bad. We might have to cut that cloth again though if it rubs too hard on those stitches."

Rusty looked up at his partner. The cloth did rub on his leg, and he answered disgustedly, "Go ahead an' cut a piece out. My durn new britches are shot anyhow."

Larry was watching and stepped up. "Let me cut them. I will make it a flap. That way, it can provide a little protection but not be tight."

She cut the piece of cloth back and the two men helped Rusty up.

Rusty wobbled a little, but the crutches worked well. His buddies stacked some rocks and laid a blanket on the ground for him to sit on. They carefully helped him to stretch his leg out. Rusty's face was pale when they were done, but it did feel good to be up.

The men looked around as a wagon rattled up. Rufe was driving while Bart rode in the back. Tobe was on horseback and led the other men's mounts. The three men grinned at the surprised group.

"Gabe sent us out to look for strays, and Cole's wagon was just a layin' back there. We looked it over. Not much was broken and we figgered Rusty could ride in this easier than the chuckwagon." Tobe grinned again at the little group. "Him and the calves anyway."

The rest of the cowboys crowded around the wagon to look it over. The three cowboys had done a fine job of repairing it. None of the men could tell what had been fixed. A bed was made in the back out of bedrolls and blankets. It looked comfortable and Fluff offered to try it out.

Bart drawled, "I done tried it out already. Rode all the way back here in it. She's not too bad. 'Course, she'll smell bad by the time we get to Dodge since Rusty won't be takin' no bath till then."

Rusty swung a crutch at his friend, and the men laughed as they unhitched Cole's mules.

Rufe patted the mules. "Their cook had these mules hobbled back in some brush. Good thing we went lookin'. Some old coyotes was movin' in on 'em. Them mules was plumb glad to see us. The boss won't like it that we didn't find any cows but mebbie these here mules will improve his mood."

CHAPTER 31

BIG ELK CROSSING

GABE LET THE CATTLE GRAZE NORTH. BY FOUR THE next afternoon, they were close to Comanche Spring on the North Fork of the Red River. They pointed the cattle east to the crossing on Big Elk Creek.

Big Elk Crossing was almost ideal. When the herds came to the crossing from the south, a horseshoe bend helped the cowboys in front point the cattle toward the water. The rest of the cattle followed, and the natural corral made it easy for the cowboys riding drag to push their slower animals up. Once the cattle were in the water, they waded upstream, walking on a rock and gravel bed. Another natural rock formation was at the exit point, moving the cattle up the bank and out of the water.

Gabe watched as the cattle moved through the crossing. He said a small prayer to the Creator for making this natural corral. He was always thankful for this crossing and today was no different.

As the cattle climbed up the bank and back onto the prairie, the small valley ahead was covered in bluestem. It wasn't as tall as in would be in a month, but the grass was excellent. The cattle immediately spread out and began to graze.

Cookie had gone on ahead with his wagon. Larry followed Cookie into the water with the second wagon. Nate was the last to cross with the horses. It was a pretty sight to see the horses running through the water. They were spread out, and the water splashed around them as they ran. Watie led the herd through. He was the first to clamber up the bank.

Gabe's smile grew bigger as he watched the horses. Watie had been a leader in the wild, and he retained that role as he nipped the other horses that tried to get in front of him. They squealed as they fell back, and the rest of the band followed him as he led the way out onto the prairie.

Nate brought up the rear. His smile was visible to Gabe as he watched from the bluff. "This drive has been a good one for Nate. Of course, what about today has not been enjoyable."

Gabe looked south for strays before he rode down from the bluff. He had sent some of the men out to see if they could find any cattle left after the stampede. He grinned as he thought of their excitement at finding the mules. He was still chuckling as he crossed the water behind the horses. They hadn't found any cattle, but their horse herd had increased significantly.

The cattle scattered out, content to graze on the rich grass. Even Cole's cattle seemed to look a little better after some rest and good grazing. Gabe rode slowly beside the herd until he was at point. He stopped beside Linc. He waved, and Tall Eagle rode up beside them.

"I'm going to ride ahead to see Quanah Parker. We are now on Comanche land, and we need to negotiate a price for passage. The graze is good here so let them go as slow as they want. I will be back after supper."

Gabe rode west. He turned once in his saddle to wave at Nate before he urged Buck to a lope. He was looking forward to a visit with Quanah.

CHAPTER 32

QUANAH PARKER

GABE HAD MET QUANAH PARKER IN '77 ON HIS FIFTH drive as trail boss. It was two years after Quanah surrendered and moved his people to the reservation in Oklahoma. He was the last Comanche war chief to surrender. Quanah's mother was a white woman by the name of Cynthia Ann Parker. There was talk that maybe that helped him to adjust to reservation life because Quanah not only adjusted—he adjusted well and tried to lead his people to prosperity.

"Quanah was a great warrior and strategist. Now he has turned those qualities into business savvy. Throw in the fact that he is a knowledgeable cattle rancher, and he's becoming more successful every day." Gabe patted Buck's neck as he talked to him and the horse snorted as if he was listening.

Gabe laughed to himself as he remembered his last conversation with Quanah. The chief was tired of the great herds passing through his lands and refusing to pay for the reservation grasses that the cattle consumed during passage.

"I think I sell grazing rights to big ranchers. Then it be their problem to protect our lands—and they pay us to do it," Quanah told Gabe as his dark eyes glinted.

Quanah's braves met Gabe as he rode into their camp. Quanah still lived in a tipi, but he was talking more of building a house. He stood to greet his friend, Hawk, as he called Gabe.

"Hawk, I see you are the first herd this year. The grass is good, yes?"

Gabe grinned at Quanah as he put out his hand.

"If I say yes, my passage will cost me more. But...if I say no, you will know that I lie. You are a wise man, my friend."

Quanah's stern face broke into a grin. He pointed at the fire where a pot was cooking.

"Come, my friend. Join me in a meal. Then we will talk of how many cattle you will give me this year."

Their talk was varied and finally the topic of religion was breached.

Quanah snorted before he stated, "The White Man goes into his church house and talks *about* Jesus, but the Indian goes into his tipi and talks *to* Jesus."

Gabe laughed and shook his head. "I know better than to argue religion with my good friend. I have tried your peyote though, and I don't think I'm man enough for that."

Quanah grunted and his eyes glinted with humor. "I give Hawk peyote to carry with him. Peyote good medicine."

He leaned back and studied his tipi.

"I think I build a house. A big, fine house to welcome friends and to keep my wives happy. What do you think, Hawk? Should Quanah build house?"

Gabe studied the warrior in front of him. Quanah was a man of two worlds, one white and one Indian. Yet he didn't struggle with the differences. Instead, he navigated easily between the two.

"I reckon a house would be fine. You are no longer moving around, so a tipi isn't necessary anymore. Just was well be comfortable." Gabe's eyes twinkled as he added, "Might have to make it big with all those wives though. I'm not a married man, but I hear it's best to keep them happy."

Quanah laughed and then nodded. "Yes, sometimes, they don't like each other so much. Many wives is a difficult thing. I think big house with many rooms would be good. I put stars on roof, and it be a fine house."

It was late in the evening before the talk came around to the cattle.

Quanah's eyes glinted as he leaned back.

"Your herd is large since you mix it with another. Large herds mean more cows. Big herds eat more grass."

Gabe nodded and he told Quanah the story of Cole's herd.

Quanah's dark eyes penetrated Gabe as he listened and then he leaned forward.

"The dead man's herd has many cows with calves inside. Some will soon drop on ground. I take those cows and some whose calves now walk beside them. You keep steers. We create herd. We want breeding stock."

The two men agreed that Gabe would give Quanah seven cows, some with calves by their side and some that were close to calving. In return, Gabe could move his cattle slowly across the reservation lands, taking advantage of the abundance of nutritious grass. Most trail bosses gave fewer animals, but Gabe understood grazing. Besides, Quanah's braves would pick the cattle up and would give the herd safe passage across their lands. It was worth the price to Gabe.

The two men shook hands.

"Perhaps I see you next year, my friend. Maybe I have my house by then, and you be my guest.

Gabe shook his head. "I don't think I will be coming back this way, Quanah. I am going to sell my cattle in Dodge and maybe look at the land up north. I am ready to start my own ranch in Wyoming Territory or maybe even farther."

Quanah stared at Gabe. "You take wife. Maybe two. Wives be good for Hawk. They make him happy so he not so cranky maybe."

Gabe laughed out loud. "Maybe, but only one. I don't think I want to try to keep more than one happy."

Quanah's eyes sparkled as he gripped Gabe's shoulder.

"Be safe, my friend. My fire will always welcome you."

Gabe gripped Quanah's shoulder in return.

"You too, Quanah. You send your braves tomorrow, and we will cut out your cattle."

Quanah watched Gabe ride away before he turned back into his tipi. Gabe turned around once to wave. He knew the chief would not come the next day with his braves. It made him a little sad to think that this might be the last time that he would see his friend.

"Saying goodbye is always hard."

Buck snorted at him and Gabe laughed. "You always have an opinion, don't you, Buck. Well, let's get on back to the herd. Daylight is going to come early."

As Gabe rode back toward the herd, he pondered on what Quanah had said about wives.

"Cranky, huh? I guess I never thought of myself as cranky. Wonder if a wife does make a man happier." As Gabe thought on that a little longer, Grace's face passed through his mind and he smiled. "Maybe the right one."

Buck snorted at him again and Gabe chuckled.

CHAPTER 33

GOOD TRADE

GABE GATHERED THE MEN IN AT BREAKFAST TO discuss the day.

"Quanah's braves will be here this morning to pick up their cattle. He wants breeding animals, not steers. I want to cut out some of those cows that just calved along with some that are springing. Some of those cows will drop calves any time now and we just as well leave them here. We agreed on seven, but if we see more that are weak, we will throw a couple extra in.

"We will be entering the Cheyenne and Arapaho lands within a day or two so keep the cows that have longer to go for that trade."

"How much longer does this good grass last, boss?" Bart was looking ahead over the grassy land in front of them as he shaded his eyes.

Gabe shrugged as he followed Bart's eyes. "A day or two more in the Comanche and Apache lands, and then about the same to cross the Cheyenne and Arapaho reservations. The farther north we go, the shorter the grass will likely become." He pointed ahead toward a high rock bluff in front of them.

"The next good water will be Soldier Springs, so we'll point them toward that tall, sandstone bluff."

The men ate quickly and then began to sort off the cattle that Gabe wanted to send back to Quanah. Two cows kept trying to break out of the herd and go back down the trail.

Angel nodded at them, "I think those vacas have some bebés—some small ones maybe. Perhaps we let them go and follow." As the men stepped their horses apart, the cows headed down the trail.

Gabe watched them and nodded at Angel.

"Be careful. I heard cattle moving in the night last night so there is another herd close to us. We don't need spooked cattle to come charging up this trail."

Before long, the cowboys had sorted off six cows with calves and three more that looked like they were going to calve any time. As Gabe came back to look them over, a smiling Angel followed five pairs up to the herd.

"We picked up a few friends, señor. These belonged to Mr. Cole so I bring along." His eyes glinted briefly. "And what you hear last night—that herd is just two miles away. Many of Mr. Coles vacas are with them. Perhaps we should visit—you with your guns and me with my small knife."

Gabe frowned. He needed to be the one to present the cattle to Quanah's braves, but that herd needed to be checked as well.

"Tall Eagle, Angel, Tobe—you come with me. The rest of you, keep a close watch on this herd. And swap out those springers for some of the pairs Angel found. If riders other than Quanah's braves approach the herd, call out once and then shoot.

"Angel, show us the best way to come up on that herd."

The four men rode south and came on the herd from behind. Usually, the best drovers were at the front of the herd on point, and Gabe was hoping that would be the case. From where they stood in the small grove of trees, they could see that it was a smaller herd of mixed brands. Many of the closest ones were Cole cattle.

Gabe led the small group of cowboys down the hill and up to the herd.

"Morning, boys. Nice of you to catch our cows for us. We had a stampede several nights ago and lost some."

The two men riding drag stared at the men.

One shook his head and protested, "These are all our cattle. We don't have any strays in this herd."

Gabe's rifle was resting on his saddle and pointed at the cowboy closest to him. Tall Eagle had his rifle pointed at the other one. They slowly lifted their hands, and Tab quickly stripped their guns away.

Angel rode up to them with a dangerous smile on his face. "Perhaps, señors, you would like a little rest? I think your caballos would like to run, no?"

The two men slid off their horses, and Angel slapped their horses with his rope. He took out his knife and tested the edge as he looked at them. "I think you should take a little nap. Your amigos won't miss you...nor will my knife if you try to help."

Tall Eagle and Tobe went up the left side of the herd to the drover riding flank while Gabe and Angel took the right one.

Both riders were dozing in their saddles and were taken easily. Again, their horses were turned loose. This time, the men were tied and dropped off the trail.

Two men were talking to the cowboys riding point. They paused as Gabe's men rode toward them. When they realized the riders were not their own, one man went for his gun. Angel threw his knife, and the man slid from his saddle to the ground. The other three men threw up their hands.

Tobe again collected their guns and handed Angel's knife back to him.

Gabe glared at the three men.

"You boys have some of my cattle." His voice was hard as he added sarcastically, "I guess you knew that based on how your boss just acted."

Two of the men said nothing but the third one cursed quietly. He stared at one of the other men and spit on the ground.

"I should have known you would pull me into one of your dirty deals, Dick.

"I'm Zach Mitchum. That there is Whiskey Dick Jones and Slack Smith. The one you killed was Jack Sloan. He was the ramrod of this outfit."

Zach looked back at the cattle and cursed again under his breath. "My little brother is back there. Those boys all right?"

Gabe nodded slightly.

"What's the story with these cattle? You have quite the variety of brands, and I'm guessing there is no brand certification either."

Zack's neck turned red as he shook his head.

"We were hired to drive three hundred head of cattle from Fort Sill north to Fort Supply. We picked up a few cattle here and there. Then we came up on a herd wearing that Circle C brand. Sloan said we could just add them to our herd and sell them at the Fort."

Gabe stared coldly at him for a moment before he asked, "And you thought that would be the honest thing to do? And since it was honest, you were moving them at night."

Zack's neck became redder, and his Adam's apple bobbed as he tried to answer.

"I…we…well, Jack said that we would get a bonus if we could make it in fifteen days, but we would have to push them."

Linc stepped off his horse and pulled some papers out of Sloan's pocket. He studied them and then handed them to Gabe.

Gabe scanned the papers. Included in the packet was a bill of sale for three hundred head, all Double Diamond cattle.

He looked at the cowboys and pointed at the cattle.

"I suggest you fellows get busy sorting. The only thing you have a bill of sale for are cattle with a Double Diamond brand. Now you have a choice. You can cut out mine, drive the rest of them up to Fort

194

Supply, and hope the officer in charge there believes your story. Or you can cut out everything but Double Diamond and push them to our herd. I want an accounting of each brand and the number of cattle. The Stockgrowers's Association in Dodge will make sure the money goes back to the right ranches."

Zach stared at Gabe for a moment and then asked carefully, "You are going to let us go?"

Gabe smiled but his eyes were hard. "Why I sure am, boys. Colonel Grierson down at Fort Sill is a friend of mine so I'll just make a stop at Fort Supply to verify that you boys showed up. I might even have a little confab with old Phil Sheridan himself. Shoot, he's probably ready for a little skirmish now that he almost has the Indian' trouble quieted down."

Zack looked at the two men beside him who had been silent.

"Dick, you go catch those horses while Slack rounds up our boys. We have some sorting to do."

Angel and Linc already had some of Cole's cattle sorted out and were moving them slowly toward the bigger herd. Tab and Gabe cut out thirty more on the edge and pushed them up to join the smaller herd in front of them.

Once they were started, Gabe loped back to his herd.

Quanah's braves had just arrived, and Gabe pointed at eight pairs of cows with calves and one lame cow.

"You tell Quanah I sent extra so *all* his wives would be happy."

Most of the braves showed no expression, but one of the older braves grinned at Gabe. They quickly gathered the cattle and began to move them back to their camp.

Gabe sent Bart and Fluff back to take Linc and Tall Eagle's places and the herd was once again grazing north.

At supper that evening, Gabe outlined the next few days.

"We will reach Soldier's Spring tomorrow evening. You will be able to see it when we get closer. It is a red sandstone bluff that rises out of some rocks. There is good water there as well as a sheltered place to camp. There is only one lonely cottonwood tree by the spring so no whittling or carving on it.

"We'll let the cattle drink in the creeks we cross since that spring is too small for a herd this large. I want all the water barrels and canteens filled though. That is the best water we will have for a while.

"The next river will be the Washita. There hasn't been much for spring rains so it should be an easy crossing even though the banks are steep. We should be able to cross near Edwardsville Rock, but I'll ride ahead and check it out."

Gabe paused and then added quietly, "I expect we'll see either the Arapaho or the Cheyenne—or both—before the day is over. I'm not sure exactly where their southern boundary is but we're close.

"We may move a little faster through their lands. Some of their young men are still a little feisty, and I don't want to encourage them to stampede our cattle. That means you need to keep your eyes open too.

"If Little Raven is still principle chief of the Arapaho, we should be all right. I have worked with both him and White Shield of the Cheyenne. White Shield was on the Council of Chiefs and hopefully still is.

"Whatever you do, don't pick a fight with them or be goaded into one. We are on their lands, and we need to pass through."

As Gabe started to walk away, he turned back. His eyes were twinkling as he added, "You might want to take a bath and wash out your clothes this evening. There's a nice creek behind us that would accommodate all of you. This campsite would smell a site better."

Several of the men grabbed blankets and headed toward the creek. Bart and Rufe stopped by the wagon and offered to help Rusty. Larry was washing dishes and Rufe added, "Ya come along too, Larry. Ya jist as well get cleaned up."

Cookie swung his spoon at the cowboy and Rufe ducked as he grinned.

The old cook growled, "I have plenty a work fer Larry right here. He ain't a goin' down there now. 'Sides, he done took a bath t'other day. Now get outa here."

CHAPTER 34

A Bath and New Clothes

SOME OF THE COWBOYS STRIPPED AT THE CAMP AND had nothing on but their boots and their hats as they raced toward the creek. Larry didn't look up. She leaned over the washing pan as she scrubbed dishes that were already clean. Cookie snorted.

Angel and Dink were the first ones back, and they headed out to take the place of the cowboys watching the herd.

Larry looked up as they walked by. *Angel took a bath, but he always looks clean. How does he manage that? I want to take a bath too, but I'll wait until the men are bedded down. Then, I'll wash my clothes too.*

As the cowboys drifted up to the fire, they could hear Angel singing to the cattle in Spanish.

The men listened for a while and then Rusty asked, "What do you suppose he's a sayin'? It sounds durn sad, but those old cows settle right down."

Tobe grinned across the fire, "Why, he's a singin' 'em love songs. Shore now, I know a few words in Spanish lingo an' that 'more, 'more, he keeps a sayin', now that's love. He's a singin' love songs an' they like it."

Larry couldn't understand the words either, but the music was beautiful. She smiled as she cleaned up the cooking area and laid out what Cookie would need in the morning.

Gabe was one of the last ones to head for the creek. Nate rushed by the chuckwagon shortly after with a big smile.

"Tall Eagle is watching the horses if you want to come and take a bath, Larry. The boys said the water feels good. It's a little cool but not bad."

Larry shook her head, "No, I need to finish here but here's some soap if you need some." She tossed Nate her bar of soap. As he caught it on the run, she called after him, "Don't lose that. It has to last me until Dodge."

When they came back, Gabe had his arm over Nate's shoulders and was listening to his little brother with a smile on his face. He finally laughed and tousled the young man's hair. Nate smiled up at him and Larry smiled too.

She whispered to herself, "Nate adores his big brother. Mr. Hawkins is so different when it is just the two of them. He seems so happy and so… so…nice. Otherwise, I think he is scary…and grumpy."

Larry jumped when Nate called her name. He had the soap in his hand and was preparing to toss it to her.

"Thanks, Larry. Appreciate that. I sure do feel clean now!"

Slowly the camp settled down. Some nights, the men talked or argued, but the bath seemed to calm all of them down. Rufe and Bart headed out for nightguard. After the rest of the men were bedded down, Larry sneaked down to the creek.

She was humming to herself as she stood in the water and scrubbed her clothes. She heard a voice singing softly and dropped down in the water. A tree was close by, and Larry swam towards it. As the singing came closer, she slid into the roots of the tree, her heart beating quickly. Angel's voice was soft when he spoke.

"Señora, I leave some clothes here. The bambino inside you is beginning to show himself. I think something looser would feel better, yes?"

Larry gasped and held her stomach. The swell of the child inside was small, but Angel was right. Her britches were getting too tight.

She squeezed her eyes shut and tried not to cry as she hugged closer to the tree.

Angel's voice was gentle as he added, "Don't cry, señora. Bambinos are little gifts from Heaven, yes? It does not matter how they come to be. The seed is never bad because our Dios is the one who creates it."

His singing faded away and Larry quickly swam to the bank. The water in the middle was deep, but the sides of the creek were much shallower. She wrapped her blanket around herself and dried off quickly. The clothes that Angel had left were clean and larger than the ones she had been wearing. The shirt was long and dropped nearly halfway to her knees. She slipped a folded bandana under her shirt and tied it around her chest. As she struggled to tie the ends, tears leaked from her eyes. "Soon I won't be able to make these ends reach and then what will I do?"

Larry slipped quietly back into camp and lay down in her blankets. She stared up at the stars and once again tears leaked out of her eyes. Dutch had been drunk the last night they were together and that was nearly four months ago. She whispered softly, "You've left me with one more thing to make my life difficult, Duke. I hated you by the time you died. How will I ever love this child?" There was no stopping the tears that leaked out, and Larry sobbed softly as she cried herself to sleep.

CHAPTER 35

ANGEL

NGEL LISTENED AND SHOOK HIS HEAD. HE HAD recognized Larry as a girl he had danced with once in Denison, Texas. The first night he rode into Gabe's camp, he was surprised to see her. *If the señora wants to hide as a boy, I will help her do that. So small but so brave. And a lady too.* He frowned and shook his head again. The baby bump under her shirt was a new change though. *Soon her bambino will be hard to hide.*

He smiled as he thought of how carefully Laurel had danced. She would let none of the men hold her close and some complained to her boss.

Angel didn't complain. He liked how proud she was and how careful she was to be a lady even when the clothes she wore were so revealing. He laughed softly. *She is doing a good job of hiding a woman's body.* He frowned as he thought of her husband.

Duke Dugan had been a no-good man. He had treated Laurel like she was fodder that he could pass around. It made Angel angry when he thought of his last conversation with the man.

After Duke tried to sell his wife for a night to pay a gambling debt, Angel told him to get out. "Get a job or I will make sure you are no longer around to bother your wife."

Duke had sneered. "Leave me? Where would that little slut go? She was nothing when I married her, and she is nothing now."

Angel had pulled his knife, and if his friends hadn't interfered, he would have killed Duke that night. "Angel, the gringo has no knife, and his gun is tied down. They will hang you for murder."

His face tightened when he thought of how Duke had slapped Laurel around when she refused to go with the man he offered her to. Then he slowly relaxed. He had knocked Duke down that night. Duke was much larger than Angel's one hundred sixty-five pounds, but Angel was a scrapper and Duke was soft. Duke didn't get up because Angel's punch had knocked him out. *I almost wish I hadn't hit him so hard the first time. I would have liked to have beaten him.*

Angel had hung around Denison much longer than he intended to make sure that Laurel would be safe. When Angel left to meet Cole and move the cattle north, he had arranged with some friends to make sure that only respectful cowboys danced with her. If anyone became rude, they were to be promptly gotten rid of. When the herd arrived at Doan's Crossing, he heard that someone had killed Laurel's husband and that she had disappeared.

He muttered softly in Spanish, "Señora, you are a brave one. You are small but you are tough. I was going to kill Duke myself, but some gringo saved me the trouble."

Tobe opened one eye and glared at Angel. "Ya sing love songs to cows an' talk about women in your sleep. Now shut up, ya durn lover. The rest of us need our sleep."

Angel chuckled softly, "Si, señor, but my dreams will be sweet and what will yours be?"

Tobe snorted but was soon snoring.

Angel stayed awake until the quiet sobs coming from the chuckwagon stopped and then he went to sleep as well.

CHAPTER 36

GUESTS FOR DINNER

LITTLE RAVEN AND WHITE SHIELD APPEARED THE next morning around ten. They watched somberly as the cattle grazed and often turned their heads to stare at the cowboys. The men fidgeted in their saddles and tried not to make eye contact. They watched with concern for Gabe because these Indians did not look friendly.

Gabe came riding back from checking out Soldier Spring. He saw the warriors sitting off to one side watching the cattle and rode Watie toward them at a lope.

"Little Raven, White Shield. I greet my friends of the Southern Cheyenne and Arapaho."

Both chiefs nodded at Gabe and continued to watch the cattle trail by.

"Hawk brings many cattle this time. Many cattle each much grass." Little Raven's face was emotionless as he looked from the cattle to Gabe.

Gabe nodded somberly. "Yes, many cattle each much grass. Perhaps we can make a trade. Some of my healthy cattle for your good grass."

Little Raven's black eyes glistened, and the two chiefs nodded. "Perhaps," White Shield agreed.

Gabe pointed to where the chuckwagon was stopped.

"Would my Southern friends like to discuss this over food? Our cook will prepare a fine meal."

Each chief had brought five braves with him. As the Indians rode slowly up to the chuckwagon, Cookie cursed softly and turned to Larry. "Durn yore boss. He said to 'spect guests, but he didn't say there'd be twelve of 'em! Shoot, we'll be lucky to have any food left in this here wagon a'tall."

Gabe cut out a fat steer and one of the braves killed it. They quickly butchered the beef, and Cookie began to prepare a meal.

Larry made coffee and Gabe passed around tobacco to all the Indians. They smoked and drank the black Arbuckle coffee as the food was prepared.

Each chief wanted ten head but Gabe shook his head.

"Four cows for each of my friends. We give you cows with calves inside so you can build your herds." The men smoked and talked some more but Gabe wouldn't budge.

Finally, he added, "Four cows each plus tobacco and coffee. No more."

The chiefs grunted and both agreed. Larry quickly took some coffee from the wagon and began to measure it out. Gabe held up two fingers and she took that to mean two pounds each. The tobacco she was liberal with as she had no idea how much was expected, and she knew that Gabe didn't smoke.

Cookie had made a large stew, and as soon as it was ready, he began to dip it up for the Indians. Larry set out biscuits left from breakfast and Gabe took one. He dropped it into his stew and mashed it up. The braves watched him. Finally, two picked up a biscuit and did the same. The rest of the braves refused the biscuits and ate their stew in silence.

Gabe had signaled to Tall Eagle how many cattle he needed. The men cut out seven pregnant cows and one that had calved that morning. The rest of the herd had been pushed up the trail. Several straggler cows were limping behind the main herd, and Gabe somberly pushed them into the small herd of cows for the Indians.

Little Raven repressed a grin. *Hawk tough negotiator but he always fair.*

The stew was completely gone when the Indians stood. Gabe pointed at the fresh beef still on the ground.

"Take for your children. Let them eat well tonight."

The braves wrapped the beef in the hide and threw it over one of their horses. As they slowly rode out of camp with their cattle, White Shield looked back. Gabe lifted his hand, and the chief lifted his spear before he turned back around.

Cookie glared at Gabe as he began to clean up.

"Those durn braves ate that whole pot. Shoot. Should a been 'nough fer them *an'* the boys. Now what are yore cowboys goin' to eat fer dinner?"

Gabe grinned at the man. "Now, Cookie, I know you have been at this job long enough that you allowed for that. I'm guessing you stashed some food for the men somewhere."

Cookie continued to growl and then chuckled at Gabe's departing back. "That durn smart aleck. Thinks he knows me so well.

"Here, Larry. Pack up this here food so it cin be passed out to the fellers. They ought to be good an' hungry by now."

Gabe was pleased. The negotiations had gone well. *We'll be able to take our time on up the trail. Now, if only the rest of the river crossings are easy and the cattle stay calm.* Then he laughed out loud. "Shoot, I guess I can't ask for Heaven on earth. Let's just hope the cattle stay healthy and the boys stay safe."

CHAPTER 37

SOLDIER SPRING

THE HERD ARRIVED AT SOLDIER SPRING THAT EVENING. The campsite was excellent even though there was still just one cottonwood tree. The herd spread out on the bluestem grass. It was getting taller, and the cattle ate contentedly. The cowboys on nighthawk were able to ride the crests of the surrounding hills making it easy to guard the cattle in the moonlight.

The day had been an easy one, and the cowboys were looking for ways to expel their energy when supper was over.

Bart looked at his friends and shook his head mournfully.

"Sure too bad that some of you fellers cain't tell stories. Now if we had us a good storyteller here, why we could all jist lay back and listen."

Tab started to respond, and they all began yelling at him.

"Tab, yore stories is all sad. We don't want no durn stories 'bout cows dyin' or gettin' stuck in quicksand, or rivers that run over, or stampedes. We want us a nice, sweet story. Mebbie 'bout a gurl some feller has waitin' on 'im."

The men were silent for a moment and then as one accord, all heads turned to look at Angel.

Angel grinned at the cowboys staring at him hopefully and chuckled.

"Ah, señors, I have many love stories. Angel is a very loved vaquero. Many women wait for me in their homes, just hoping that I will ride up on my handsome caballo." He paused dramatically and added, "Ah, but I only have one true amour." He was quiet for a moment and the cowboys leaned forward to listen.

Angel leaned back on his blanket as he stared up at the stars. "She has the most beautiful hair. The color of a black horse but curly, so curly that the ringlets tickle the back of her neck when she walks. Her eyes are green, and when she smiles, little lights dance in them. I hold her in my arms when we dance, and she is so light. I just spin her in circles until neither of us can breathe. And her laugh…like a little bell tinkling through the night. And when she sees me, she rushes into my arms, and I pick her up. I hug her close to me and I kiss her cheeks—"

"What about her mouth? Why don't you kiss her mouth?" Rusty was leaning forward and frowning as he asked.

"Why, señors, Emilia is my sister and she is only four years old!"

The cowboys stared at Angel for a moment. Then one slapped his leg, and they all began to laugh.

Rusty grinned at him and nodded. "You really had us goin' there, Angel. I thought shore ya was goin' to tell us a real story."

Angel grinned at him and rolled his dark eyes.

"Señor, you know that a real man does not talk about his loves." He paused and frowned slightly. "Of course, there was this one time… perhaps I could share…"

Several of the men looked at him skeptically, but the rest once again leaned forward. Gabe walked up to the fire and squatted down as Angel began again.

"She had the most beautiful golden hair you ever did see, and she loved to toss her head. It would fall like silk on my face. Oh, the feeling of that hair on a moonlit night. Nothing can repeat that feeling. We would ride together through the night, racing for the pure love of it. We were one and we loved each other. Sometimes, she would let me braid her hair and I would weave beads and bits of ribbons into it."

Gabe grinned as he ducked his head, but the rest of the men were totally quiet as they listened.

Bart whispered incredulously, "She let you braid her hair?"

Angel smiled dramatically and rolled his dark eyes, "Si, señor... and her tail too. She was the most beautiful horse I have ever owned!"

The cowboys sat stunned for a moment before one threw his coffee cup at Angel.

"Yore durn horse! Boys, Angel cain't tell no more stories. My pore heart is all tangled up! An' all fer a durn horse an' a little bitty gurl."

The men began to laugh, and Angel chuckled with them as the mischievous lights flashed in his eyes.

Then he looked at them seriously, "But, señors, I did not lie. There is nothing like the love of a child or a good horse. Surely you know this yourselves. Perhaps one day I will have a child of my own, and she will look at me with those eyes. Now who of you would not want to be greeted like that by a child or by a horse. They are good dreams, señors."

The campfire was quiet that evening as the men thought about what Angel had said. Most of them hoped that someday they would have a girl and maybe even get married. Angel made the story so real though that they all needed to think on it for a while.

Gabe grinned as he lay back in his blankets. *Angel is a good addition to this crew. I'd like to take him on as a hand if I get anything bought up north.*

The men were quiet in their blankets until Tab asked, "Say, any a ya boys climb up on that big red rock? Why there's names carved all over it. Names an' dates an' everything. Bet some a those fellers is dead 'cause some a those dates is really old."

The men all began to yell, and Rusty threw his boot at the cowboy.

"Now why did ya have to go an' talk, Tab? I was jist havin' me a nice dream 'bout a girl, an' a little cabin an' mebbie a kid or two, an' ya have to go spoil the whole durn thing."

Tab ducked the boot and shut up, but Rufe chimed in.

"Shoot, Rusty, when we hit Dodge, those gurls is goin' to look at that big white hairy leg stickin' straight out from yore saddle an' they's all a goin' to skedaddle the other way."

The somber mood was broken. The men began arguing and laughing as they all discussed Rusty's leg and how the women of Dodge would react.

Talk picked up again and then moved back around to the tall bluff. Several had climbed to the top. They shared some of the names that they had read.

"We carved our names up there. Even saw the names of some fellers we met on our last drive to Dodge. Those boys was from Kansas, and here their names are on that big rock."

The men discussed that and then slowly the camp became quite again.

CHAPTER 38

ANOTHER RIVER CROSSING

THEY CROSSED THE WASHITA RIVER FIRST THING THE next morning. The water in the middle of the river was fairly deep, but the bottom didn't give them any trouble. Cattle and wagons both crossed without problems.

Then it began to rain. It rained all that day and most of the night. The men and the livestock were miserable, but the herd kept grazing north. Several times, they saw braves in the distance watching them.

The next morning, they saw more Indians.

"They don't like us tearing up their grass, so keep them moving, boys."

Gabe was already thinking ahead to the Canadian River. "With all this rain, I hope it's not high," he muttered to himself. "On the upside though, we have water and maybe the bottom won't be so boggy."

Once the herd was moving along, Gabe rode ahead to look at the Canadian. The water had been up but was back down. He rode Buck across in several places and then went downriver testing the river bottom every four hundred yards or so. The location he was happiest with was a half mile downstream from the usual crossing at Edwardsville Rock. He crossed it and rode up the bank to study the lay of the land on the other side.

As Gabe rode back towards the herd, he checked the creeks and streams. They were running with the recent rain, and finally, he had a plan in mind.

The herd was about three miles from the Canadian when Gabe met them.

"Let's water them as we go, boys. When we hit that water, I want those cattle moving and I want them to keep moving once they cross. I want to push the leaders straight in and keep the best crossing spot downstream for our weaker cattle. We'll break the herd into groups and move them as fast as we can.

"Cookie, you get those two wagons across first. Nate, you'll follow with the horses but wait for those lead cattle. As we push them in, three of you follow them right over the bank and out onto the flat. I don't want them coming back down to the water to drink so it's important that they water here as we go.

"When we get half of them over, five of you will stay with the herd and the rest of you, come back across to help push the next group." Gabe was pointing with his hands as he directed the crew where he wanted them to go.

Two cowboys hooked their ropes onto Cookie's chuckwagon, and he whipped the mules into the water. They charged through and up the other side.

Rusty was driving the second wagon. He was waiting for the men to come back when his mules took off on their own accord. Rusty lurched to his feet and whipped the lines. He hollered at the four mules, and they pulled the wagon with no trouble through the water and up the bank.

The lead mules stumbled a little as they topped the edge of the bank. The wagon jerked and threw Rusty's leg against the seat. He cussed as he fell and dropped the lines. Larry grabbed for the lines, lunging forward as she reached over the seat. The wagon hit a rock, and she was almost thrown out of the wagon. Rusty jerked on her shirt and then wrapped his arm around her hips to pull her back. When his arm encountered her baby bump, his eyes opened wide and he nearly dropped her. Then they were over the bank and Rusty sawed on the lines to slow the mules down.

Gabe was calm on the outside as he directed his crew, but his heart was pounding. He seemed to be everywhere.

About half of the herd was across when a steer bogged down. The cowboys behind hollered and pushed the animals to keep them from milling. If the cattle started milling, many more would bog down or pile on top of each other. The cattle broke around the bogged animal and slugged their way to the far shore. Angel dallied his long riata and dropped his loop over the horns of the struggling animal. He was able to finally pull it loose and it slogged its way to the far side where it stood trembling on the riverbank.

Another group appeared over the hill and the cowboys pushed them into the fresh crossing area. A few tried to turn back, but the men stayed close and kept them moving.

Finally, they were down to the tail end of the herd. This group was the weakest and the slowest-moving of all the cattle. Gabe rode Buck into the water. It was getting boggy and Buck struggled to get across. He turned the horse upstream and tried the same thing. The bottom was soft but not as soft as the previous location.

Gabe scanned the herd moving slowly down the riverbank and pointed upstream. "Push them in there and keep them moving!" He pushed Buck back into the water and toward the front of the herd. The cattle took the river in a rush and began to slog their way across, slowing down as they moved forward. Gabe moved to the side and began to whip the leaders. "Keep them moving—they are going too slow!"

The cowboys bringing up the drag rushed their horses forward, whipping the cattle with their ropes and hollering to move them faster. As the last cow crow hopped out of the mud and up the bank, the cowboys cheered. Even Gabe smiled. He signaled for someone to send Nate back with fresh horses because both horses and cowboys were worn out.

CHAPTER 39

SNAKEBITE!

SOME OF THE COWBOYS JUST DROPPED OFF THEIR horses and lay on the ground. Others pulled their saddles off first. One horse was favoring a leg and Gabe moved over to look at it. He leaned closer and touched the horse's leg.

"That looks like a snakebite. Any of you get bitten and don't know it?"

The cowboys stared at their boss a moment. Then boots came off quickly and pants came down. Fluff was pulling on his boot but couldn't get it off. His leg above his boot looked swollen. He stared in confusion and Gabe bent down. He tugged up Fluff's pant leg.

Two puncture marks showed on the calf of Fluff's leg. Gabe looked up at the cowboy and spoke quietly.

"Fluff, I want you to take off your belt. Don't make any fast movements. A couple of you fellers get over here and ease him down."

Two cowboys grabbed Fluff's shoulders and lowered him gently to the ground. He handed Gabe his belt and Gabe pulled it tight above the wound to create a tourniquet. He looked up to see who was still mounted. Rufe was on the top of the riverbank and just starting down on his horse.

"Rufe, get Cookie down here! Tell him to bring his medicine kit and some of that honey.

"Linc and Angel, pick me as many dandelions as you can find. Start mashing the leaves between those rocks. The rest of you look each other over and check your horses. See if any other horse has been bitten."

Tab was looking over his feet when he noticed that his boot had holes in the toe. He took off his sock and stared at his feet. The toes of his boots were pointed, and his feet were fine. He dipped his boot in the water to rinse it out and yellow water poured out of it. He rinsed it until the water was clear and then squatted down in front of Fluff and tried to take his boot off. Fluff's leg was so swollen that the boot would have to be cut off.

"Sorry, Fluff. We'll git you another pair of boots in Dodge." Tab slit the boot and slid it off Fluff's foot.

Cookie came racing down the bank followed by Larry. He quickly put an X cut on the bite. As the incision began to ooze, Gabe handed Cookie the crushed dandelion. Cookie dropped the weed in a can and added a small amount of water.

Larry was spreading honey directly on the bite as she talked softly to Fluff. His eyes were squeezed shut as the pain started to take over. When she finished, Cookie packed the poultice on top. Larry looked around at the men to see who had the cleanest bandana and Angel handed her his. She spread the bandana over the poultice. Cookie grabbed Tab's neckerchief and tied it around Fluff's leg.

Fluff's breathing was ragged, and his leg was swollen terribly. Cookie waved everyone away but Rusty and Gabe.

"Fluff, that there leg's gonna keep swellin' till the poison comes out. In fact, yore durn leg might bust open but don't ya give up 'cause I ain't lost no one to a snakebite yet. Now we's a goin' to have to carry ya up that there riverbank an' put ya in the wagon, an' I want ya to be as still as possible. The quieter ya lay, the slower the poison moves." Cookie winked at Fluff he added, "Looks like you an' Rusty is both a goin' to ride into Dodge in short pants." Cookie looked around at the cowboys.

"Fellers, I need three of ya to carry Fluff up the riverbank. He cain't be jolted 'round, so I need the steadiest of ya to keep 'im straight. Two of ya, git to pickin' more dandelions so's we cin make a poultice fer that snakebit horse if it ain't too late a'ready. Larry, ya take care a that there horse."

Tab, Tobe, and Dink carried Fluff up the bank and to the wagon. The bank was worn down some with all the cattle clambering over it, but it still was difficult to carry a man up.

Gabe sent Rufe to get Tall Eagle. He wanted to see if there was anything that should be done for the horse besides the honey and a poultice.

"The rest of you, as soon as you switch out horses, get around that herd. We don't need anything to spook them now."

As Gabe started to mount his horse, Cookie hollered back at him. "Ya best check yore own self over an' that brother a yores too."

Gabe quickly mounted and rode to where Nate was waiting with the horses.

"Drop your pants, Nate, and take off your boots and socks. I want to check you for any snakebites."

Nate's eyes were large, but he did as his brother told him. Gabe's chest was tight as he checked his brother. He let out a big sigh and nodded.

"You're good to go. Get dressed."

Nate stared up at Gabe. "How about you? Anyone check you over?"

Gabe grinned at this brother, but he dropped his britches and pulled off his socks. He didn't have any bite marks. His socks had a lot of holes though and Nate started laughing.

"Ma would sure have something to say about you not mending your socks."

Gabe chuckled as he agreed.

Nate eyes became large as he touched a bullet scar on Gabe's leg and another above his belt.

"You've been shot, Gabe…twice!"

Gabe shrugged as he pulled up his pants.

"Long time ago, Nate. Now you do whatever Tall Eagle says for that horse. We'll do our best, but snakebites on a horse can be bad. We may not be able to save him."

CHAPTER 40

FLUFF

R USTY'S LEG WAS BLEEDING WHERE IT HAD SLAMMED into the wagon seat, but he wouldn't let Larry look at it.

"It's nothin'. You make sure Fluff is all right. I cin still drive this wagon."

Larry glared at him and snapped, "When we catch up with Cookie, you are going to let one of us look at that leg. I will ride in the back with Fluff, but we can't take any chances on your leg either. I know you don't want to be a one-legged cowboy."

Larry climbed into the back of the wagon and sat down by Fluff. She poured water from her canteen onto a cloth and bathed his head.

"My leg hurts fierce, Larry. Do ya reckon I might die?"

Larry shook her head stubbornly.

"Cookie said he has never lost anyone to a snakebite and neither have I. I'll see if he has anything else we can give you for pain. I can make you some tea like I made Rusty when we get to the camp site, and that might help a little. For now, you just need to rest and stay as still as possible. We caught the bite fairly quickly, so that is a plus as well.

"Have you ever prayed, Fluff? I can say a prayer with you if you'd like me to."

Fluff was silent a moment.

"I'd like that. I ain't prayed in a fierce long time." He whispered, "My Ma used to sing a song about Jesus. I don't remember how it went, but it was somethin' about him lovin' me."

Larry nodded as she smiled at him. "I know that song. I can sing it to you.

"Jesus loves me, this I know,
for the Bible tells me so.
Little ones to him belong,
We are weak, but he is strong."

Fluff closed his eyes and smiled. "That's the one. My ma used to sing that ever' night to my kid brother an' I'd sit on the bed by him to listen." He relaxed and small smile hovered on his face. "Thanks, Larry. Yore a good kid."

Larry smiled at him and patted his arm. She looked over the side of the wagon and saw they were driving by a large patch of dandelions. She leaned forward and tapped Rusty's shoulder.

"Stop the wagon. I need to pick those dandelions. We are going to need to change that poultice twice a day, and that is going to take a lot of dandelions."

Rusty stopped the wagon and Larry jumped down. She dropped the flowers in the front of her long shirt and held it up as she put up one foot to climb into the wagon.

Rusty watched her and commented quietly, "I don't know what yore game is, but I know yore a gurl an' I know yore carryin' a kid. I ain't goin' to say nothin,' but the boss 'ill blow up if he's to find out."

Larry glared at him and then her face softened. She took a deep, ragged breath.

"Rusty, my husband is dead, and I need to get home. That is all that I am going to tell you. Now please, let's catch up with Cookie so he can look at your leg and I can make some tea for Fluff."

CHAPTER 41

A Lesson in Dying

THE MEN WERE WORN OUT AND GABE DECIDED TO take a day to rest. He was worried about Fluff as well. The cowboy's leg was swollen to nearly twice the size it should have been.

Tall Eagle checked the snakebitten horse and shook his head. "Bites in legs can be bad. I will check him tonight, but I don't like how he looks."

Nate called the horse Tex, and it was one of his favorites. He bathed the leg and talked to the horse as he applied honey and a new poultice.

By that evening, Tex had begun to kick at its stomach. Tall Eagle tied him short so he couldn't lay down, but the next morning, Tex was trembling and trying to roll. Tall Eagle showed Nate how to check the horse's pulse by holding his hand under its chin in front of the animal's cheekbone. Tex's pulse was racing. Then Tall Eagle lifted Tex's upper lip and studied the color. Where it should have been pink, the inside of the horse's upper lip was a dark, brick red.

"Those are both signs of a very sick horse, Nate. Tex is going to die. His body is full of poison. There is no way to bring him back, and we don't want him to suffer any longer." He paused, and his eyes were kind as he studied Nate.

Nate's eyes filled with tears, but he nodded.

Tall Eagle pointed over the hill as he added, "I will take him behind that hill into a grove of trees. The trees will deaden the sound.

"Say your goodbye, Nate. A horse can read your emotions. Talk to him and then send him away."

Tex looked back at Nate one time as Tall Eagle led him away. When Nate heard the shot, he folded his head over his knees and cried. He told himself that he was too big to cry, but the tears came anyway.

Tall Eagle smiled at Nate when he came back.

"He was a fine horse, Nate. He died as he lived—proudly." Tall Eagle added softly, "Never be afraid to share your heart, my friend. It may hurt, but the Great Spirit Father gives us many things. He gives us animals to work with, to love, and even to eat. We make ourselves better men when we respect those gifts and treat them as they deserve to be treated—and yes, even miss them when they are no longer here."

Nate watched Tall Eagle walk away.

"Someday, I am going to be as smart as Tall Eagle is when it comes to horses. Maybe I will get me a job on a horse ranch someday." He frowned slightly as he thought of that. "Shoot, I don't even know where we are headed. I'd better ask Gabe where we are going to settle."

Nate walked among the horses and talked to them. He rubbed their backs and checked them over. One horse had a few deep cuts on its front legs. Nate spread some honey on the wounds. His eyes watered when he thought about Tex, but he shook his head.

"I let you go, Tex. About now, you should be gathering cattle up in Heaven." He pondered on that a moment and then argued with himself, "Shoot, you don't even have to work at all anymore."

Nate was still thinking about Tex running free when he lay down, and the smile stayed on his face nearly all night.

CHAPTER 42

AN EASY DAY

LARRY CHANGED FLUFF'S POULTICE THAT EVENING and applied more honey. The wound was festering, and she made him some tea to drink.

"Do we have anything we can give him for pain, Cookie? His leg is so swollen."

Cookie shook his head. "I don't want him drinkin' whiskey an' that's all the pain medicine I have. The swellin' should start to come down here 'fore too long."

Larry got up during the night and repacked Fluff's leg. The flesh was rotting out around the wound, and she cleaned it as best she could. His face was warm and his breathing was shallow. She whispered a prayer for him as tears slid from her eyes. *Fluff's not even twenty-three years old. Please heal him, Lord.*

She scowled as she walked by Rusty's bed. He wouldn't let her look at his leg now that he knew she was a woman and it irritated her. Cookie said a couple of his stitches had broken loose, but Rusty refused to let her sew them back in.

"Stubborn, obstinate, irritating man," Larry muttered as she returned to her bed. She couldn't get back to sleep. After tossing for nearly an hour, she finally drifted off to sleep. It seemed like minutes later when Cookie shook her awake to help with breakfast.

Larry hurried to check on Fluff. He seemed to be the same although his breathing was maybe just a little easier.

The men dragged out of their bedrolls for breakfast. It was gray and cloudy. The dampness in the air made it chilly, and they were all complaining.

"Cows ain't movin' in this weather. We should jist sleep in today. Take the durn day off," Rufe commented sourly.

Gabe grinned at him.

"Why, I was actually thinking the same thing. I'm riding up ahead to look over Wolf Creek and Beaver River. I'll check in at Fort Supply while I'm there."

When all the men began to volunteer to go along, Gabe shook his head. "You can each give me a list of what you'd like me to pick up in Fort Supply. This is a provision trip—there won't be any drinking, so you're not missing much.

"Linc is in charge of the herd, and Cookie is in charge of the camp. If I'm not back by morning, push the herd north. Tall Eagle knows the route. This grass is short so the cattle will be getting restless. Wolf Creek isn't too far ahead, and it will be good water. If the weather clears, start moving these cows.

"Unless the water is up, we'll plan to cross the Beaver in a couple of days. After that we'll push on into Kansas, and we'll cross the Cimarron there." Gabe looked out over the grazing cattle and added quietly, "You probably shouldn't cuss the weather—be thankful that the rains have put a little water in these dry creek beds.

"And don't make Cookie mad—we don't need any more fellows riding in the wagon when we hit Dodge."

He noticed Rusty's leg and said, "Rusty, you let Larry stitch you back up. You're bleeding again."

Dink, Tall Eagle, Tobe, and Rufe ate quickly and headed out to the herd to relieve the night riders.

Angel and Bart rode in and filled their plates. When they saw their friends talking about what they wanted Gabe to pick up, Bart quickly handed him his list. Angel picked up his plate and walked over to where Tab and Rufe were studying Tab's boot.

"That snake shore did strike my boot. You cin see the bite marks. I had to dump the venom out or it mighta killed me." Tab was animated as he pulled off his boot and showed Rufe. "Why if I hadn't rinsed that boot out, my foot mighta jist sickened an' fallen clean off."

Bart stared at the boot for a moment before he snorted, "I swear, Tab. You are jist all doom and gloom. Them ain't bite marks. There's three pokes in that boot. Ain't no snake that I know of that has three fangs. Ya poked yore durn boot on some brambles an' the water was yellow 'cause yore durn socks is so dirty."

He snorted again and was still muttering as he lay down on his blanket. Angel began to laugh. He sauntered back to his blanket to eat.

Tab stared at his boot for a moment and then looked at his sock. "Well, durned if he ain't right. Guess I shouldn't be feelin' sickly no more now that I know I ain't dyin'."

Gabe dropped down beside Fluff. The rider's leg was still swollen, but his eyes were clearer.

"Fluff, I'm going to take your boot with me so I can pick up the right size at Fort Supply. I won't have any of my riders coming off a drive barefooted." He grinned at the man as he picked up the cut boot.

A smile crossed Fluff's lips and his eyes lit up.

"That would be jist fine, boss. Jist fine."

"How about you, Larry? Need anything from town?"

Larry nodded. "I'd like a large bandana like the one you wear if you don't mind. I have a little money and can pay you."

Gabe studied her face. Larry didn't wear bandanas. As the red began to climb up her neck, Gabe's neck turned red.

"I reckon I can find you one of those."

He squeezed Fluff's shoulder and moved to the horse herd. Nate already had Watie saddled and a pack saddle on another horse.

"You rode Buck yesterday, so I guessed you'd want Watie today." He smiled up at his brother, and Gabe flicked his brother's hat off.

"You're getting pretty good at this wrangler business, Nate. Anything you need from Fort Supply?"

Nate thought a moment and then nodded.

"I think you need to get some more bandanas. Larry is taking them to use on wounds." His eyes sparkled as he added, "And get you some new socks."

Gabe chuckled and mounted Watie. As he took the lead rope for the pack horse from Nate, Angel rode up.

"Señor, perhaps I can go with you. I need to wire my brother about señor Cole. He can tell our sisters. They must wait for me until I come for them."

Gabe looked out over the herd and slowly nodded.

"That will be fine. Let's get a move on. We'll be gone several days."

Fort Supply
Indian Territory
April 21, 1879

CHAPTER 43

A Letter for the Trail Boss

THE TWO MEN RODE SLOWLY AROUND THE CATTLE and then moved their horses to a lope. They had ridden about twenty-five miles when Wolf Creek came into view. Beaver River dropped southeast to join Wolf Creek and then dumped into the North Canadian. That would be the last good water they could count on before they crossed out of Indian Territory.

Gabe studied the water and the big sand bar that crossed it.

"We'll cross on that sand bar. We shouldn't have much trouble crossing here."

Angel nodded but didn't respond.

They turned their horses east and followed Wolf Creek toward Fort Supply. Gabe wasn't much for talking, but Angel had some things he needed to talk to the trail boss about.

"Señor Gabe, the señora is with child."

Gabe almost dropped his reins as he stared at Angel.

"Señora?"

"Señora Larry. She is carrying a child."

Gabe cursed under his breath and then looked hard at Angel.

"How many of the men know that Larry is a woman?"

Angel pushed back his hat and thought before he answered.

"There is Cookie, Tall Eagle, you, myself, and Rusty. Señor Rusty grabbed señora Larry when they were crossing the Canadian to keep her from falling. That is when he hurt his leg. His hand told him that she was a woman." His dark eyes glinted with humor. "That is why he does not want her to work on his leg." He paused and added, "I think Cookie has known for some time. No one is talking but more are thinking. I gave her my big shirt to help her hide her stomach."

Angel added quietly, "I knew of señora Laurel when she danced in Denison. She was always a lady, but her husband was a bad hombre. I was going back after this drive to use my small knife on him, but someone killed him already. He liked to play the cards, but he was not so good.

"I think the señora does not remember me as I only danced with her one time."

Angel looked hard at Gabe when the man didn't answer.

"Señora Laurel is a fine woman. I think it is good that you bring her north to her home, but I think the men will soon know that she is a woman. Her body changes quickly with the child inside."

Gabe released a deep breath and shook his head.

"My rules have always been no women and no alcohol. I'm the one who broke my own rule, but I just couldn't leave her crying on that street at Doan's." He stared over the sparse grass before he looked back at Angel. "We'll keep it a secret as long as we can. Her family lives south of Dodge, so we don't have many more days."

He grinned at the quiet vaquero beside him. "You keep me posted. You seem to know more about what is going on with the men than I do."

Angel laughed and agreed as he rolled his eyes dramatically. "Si, señor. You know the cows, but I know the ways of the heart." His eyes were twinkling as he added, "And mine is a very big heart, one that many women have tried to take."

Gabe grinned at the smiling man. He rubbed his chin and agreed.

"I don't know much about hearts. Sometimes I wish I did."

The two visited off and on as they rode the next ten miles. It was around five that afternoon when they arrived in Fort Supply. Gabe turned his horse toward the express office. The agent was just locking up when they dismounted in front of the building.

"I'm closed for the night, boys, but you can come back in the morning. I'll be open at eight."

Gabe frowned before he replied.

"Is there any way you can send a wire tonight? We have a herd headed north, and I'd like to be three hours out of town by that time tomorrow."

The man hesitated but slowly nodded.

"All right, but you need to hurry. And if you want any supplies, you had better be in the door of the supply house before five-thirty. The clerk locks up and won't let anyone in after that."

Gabe quickly wrote out a message to Joseph telling him where he was and that he expected to be in Dodge within fifteen days. When he signed his name, the clerk reached under his desk.

"If your name is Hawkins, this letter came for you today. Looks like some pretty girl is waiting for you to get back." The man winked at Gabe as he handed him the letter.

Gabe turned a deep red and shoved the letter inside his coat. He nodded over his shoulder at Angel.

"I'm headed over to the supply house. I'll meet you over there."

The air was cool when Gabe stepped outside, but it felt hot to him. The letter burned his skin, and the smell of Grace's perfume reached his nose. The heat came up in his face again and he crossed the street muttering to himself.

Gabe handed the clerk his list of items and wandered over to look at the socks. He picked up a pair for Nate and a pair for himself along with some hard candy for Nate.

The clerk was a gruff but efficient man. He filled Gabe's order quickly.

"You want these here girly things wrapped separate or just dump them in the bag with the rest?"

Gabe looked in surprise from the man to the stack and then shrugged.

"If you wrap them, I won't know who to give them to so just dump them in the bag."

Gabe laid the socks and the candy on the pile. He pulled a large red wild rag from a rack and threw it down. He studied it for a moment before he returned it for a pink one.

The clerk snorted as he looked up at the tall rider.

"Like pink bandanas, do you?"

When Gabe glared at him, the clerk chuckled. He added the purchases up and bagged them quickly. Gabe paid him silently. He shoved the wild rag in his pocket before he tied the bag shut.

Angel laid a few items on the counter and the two men were out of the store in just over five minutes.

Angel's eyes were twinkling as he looked up at his boss.

"I think perhaps señor, you should let me talk and buy for you. I think you are a cranky man sometimes."

Gabe looked at the man in surprise and then chuckled.

"You are the third person on this drive to tell me that I'm cranky. Of course, one suggested that I get married, and I'm just not sure how that would help."

Angel was laughing as they stepped off the boardwalk. They headed across to the eating house and Gabe grinned. He liked the slim man beside him. Angel was smart, savvy, and had a wise heart—he was also a tough man to have beside you in a fight.

The eating house was crowded, and they squeezed in on the end of a bench. As they waited for their food, an older gentleman in a coat and string tie stopped at the end of their table.

"Mr. Hawkins? My name is Charles Rutledge. I am a cattle buyer from Ogallala, Nebraska. I understand that you have a herd you are taking up the trail to Dodge City."

Gabe looked up with cool eyes and nodded his head as he continued to eat.

"I am interested in buying your herd, Mr. Hawkins. I will offer you $10 per head more than what you are going to get in Dodge City if you will drive them on north to Ogallala."

Gabe's hard eyes took in the man, and he stared for a moment before he answered.

"Mr. Rutledge, those beeves will bring $30 a head in Dodge and that is $20 more per head than I paid. Now Dodge to Ogallala is a longer drive than from Doan's Crossing to Dodge. Why would you think that I would be willing to do it for half the money more?"

Rutledge frowned and his face turned red.

"Now see here, cowboy, your beef ain't worth what you think it is. Why just while you've been driving up here, the price has dropped considerably."

Angel could feel the big man beside him go still and he stood.

"Perhaps señor, you would be more interested in the herds behind us. We only have a few cattle, surely not enough to fill your large order. Now if we may eat our supper...unless of course, you would perhaps like to buy our supper for us."

Rutledge's face turned deep red and several of the men at the table began to snicker.

Angel grinned at them before he addressed Rutledge again.

"Señor, time is money, and ours is very precious. This conversation cannot continue unless you would like to purchase our time. Until then, señor."

Charles Rutledge's face turned a mottled red and he strode away, muttering under his breath.

Gabe looked over at Angel and chuckled as he felt the tension run out of him.

"Angel, I believe I will let you do the talking. I don't like people as much as you do. In fact, I prefer my horses over just about everyone I know. You on the other hand are downright entertaining."

The two men ate quickly and headed outside. There would be no hotel room for them this evening, but they did want their horses to get some rest along with some good feed.

An older gentleman stopped in front of the hitching rail as they untied their horses.

"Evening. I heard that fellow inside the eating house offer to buy your cows and I wondered if you'd be interested in making that drive to Ogallala if the price was fair?"

Gabe looked hard at the man and then shrugged.

"I'd have to talk to my drovers. They signed on to go as far as Dodge, so I don't have cowboys lined up to go farther." Before the man could comment, he added, "And I'm particular with who I hire on."

The older man nodded. "Would you mind if I rode back to your camp with you and looked the cattle over? Maybe talk to your men? I have contacts up in Cheyenne and a fellow up there suggested that I talk to you when you stopped here at Fort Supply. Fellow by the name of Badger McCune. He seems to think quite a bit of you. Said you were a good cattleman."

Gabe frowned as he led his horse toward the livery. *There's that name again. I don't know who this Badger fellow is, but he seems to know me.*

The older man laughed as he put out his hand.

"I didn't even introduce myself. Name's Kirkham, John Kirkham. I am looking mostly for steers, but we'll take cows too if they're in good condition."

Gabe nodded as he put out his own hand. "Gabe Hawkins." He thought about the trail north of Dodge.

"I've never been over that part of the trail, Mr. Kirkham. How's the water and graze? I don't want to lose condition, and like I told Rutledge, it's farther up there than from the Red River to Dodge."

Kirkham shrugged. "The graze isn't as good as the Big Pasture, but parts will be good. As far as water is concerned, the farther northwest you get, the harder it is to find. Still, it's there if you know where to look. I'd even ride along if you want. I have to get back home anyway, and I prefer a horse to riding the cars even if my backside is bonier now than it used to be."

Gabe laughed and the older man grinned at him.

"Here's my offer to you, Hawkins. I want a thousand head. I'll pay you the same price that Dodge City's buyers are offering and then $20 more per head for each beef that leaves Dodge. The cattle will be mine so if the price goes up in Ogallala, I keep the difference. If the price goes down or we lose some between Dodge and Ogallala, that part of the risk is mine.

"We need beef, Mr. Hawkins, and yours is the first herd this year. I have buyers and they are chompin' at the bit to get healthy cattle. Your cattle are from north Texas and those fetch a better price than cattle from farther south. Not so much trouble with tick fever."

Gabe was quiet as he processed the man's offer. He slowly nodded.

"That sounds like a fair offer but let's see what the boys say." He put out his hand to Kirkham.

"We'll leave at five tomorrow morning. Bring some hardtack because we won't camp until we reach the herd."

Angel and Gabe led their horses into the livery, and Kirkham watched them go.

"Hawkin's is just as Badger said he'd be," Kirkham muttered to himself. "A man of few words, direct, and honest. I think we can do some business."

Gabe and Angel pulled the saddles off their horses and rubbed them down. Angel watched the big man beside him as he stashed the packsaddle and curried both horses.

"I know of this Kirkham. He owns many cows. He lives in what they call the Sandhills in Nebraska. Those hills are said to be good cow country. I have never seen these hills, but my brother has been up there. He said the hills are full of grass. Like oceans of grass. He also said there is sand beneath the grass. That would be something to see—grass that grows from sand."

"I've heard that too. Ever been farther north than Kansas, Angel? I'd like to look that country over."

"You never go back to Texas, señor?"

Gabe shook his head. "No, nothing for me there. Pa lost our little ranch, and Nate is my only family. I am going to start over some place new. I really liked the graze as we crossed the Big Pasture, but that is Indian land. Maybe I can find some good cow country farther north, something that isn't so settled. How about you?"

Angel smiled as he stopped currying his horse.

"My sainted mother died last year. I have a homely sister of nineteen and little Emilia as well as my younger brother. Miguel is much like me, but he likes his guns too much. I think I need to take my family away from Buffalo Gap. When señor Cole was alive, we worked for him. Now that he is gone, my brother will look for things to do, and trouble to cause." Angel shook his head, and his dark eyes twinkled.

"He is not so much an angel as I."

Gabe laughed out loud and Angel grinned at him.

"Homely sister, huh? I heard you describe Emilia, and if her older sister looks anything like that, you are going to have your hands full."

"Si, señor. It is a difficulty. Merina is…is not so meek. The young men like her, but she is very strong-willed. I fear for the man who marries her."

Gabe's grin was wide as he looked at the small man.

"Angel, I sure am glad you signed on with Cole. If we take that herd up north, I'd be proud to have you with me." He paused in the brushing and studied his friend. "What are you going to do with your family? Do you have a place to resettle?"

Angel shook his head. "No, but both my brother and I are good vaqueros. I think perhaps we can get riding jobs to support our sisters." He grinned over his shoulder. "Perhaps with you, señor, when you buy your ranch."

Gabe slapped Watie on the back and turned him loose in the stall. He lay down in the hay and pulled his blanket up as he put his hands behind his head.

"Know anything about mules, Angel? I always wanted to ride a mule. I've heard they are smart. Never do anything to put themselves in danger. They won't even founder if they find a bunch of grain. Always found that interesting."

Angel dropped down in the stall beside his horse.

"Si, señor. I have ridden a few mules. They are smart, yes, so the rider must be smarter. Mules have no—what do you say—tolerance—for a foolish man."

The two men were quiet as they drifted off to sleep. Gabe had forgotten about the letter in his pocket. Sometime during the night, a pretty girl waved at him in his dreams and then turned her horse the other way.

CHAPTER 44

It's the Little Things

THE MEN WERE UP EARLY. THE EATING HOUSE WAS JUST
opening, and Gabe bought some sandwiches to take with them.
Kirkham met them with three horses, and the men headed out of town.
Gabe was hoping that the cattle would be close to Wolf Creek, so once
again, they followed the river as it meandered southeast.

The morning was cool, and the sunrise was a pretty one. Gabe relaxed
on his horse. *These are the kinds of mornings I'm glad I live on my horse.*
He smiled to himself as Angel whistled softly.

Gabe finally looked over at Kirkham.

"This Badger McCune. How do you know him?"

Kirkham chuckled and shrugged.

"Badger seems to know folks everywhere. I met him in Julesburg in
'68. He was passing through with a young couple and he was getting
married. The lady was an older woman. You would have thought the
two of them had been married for years instead of just marrying. It's
rare to see a couple so well-matched.

"My missus had a sister who lived north of Julesburg, and we had
gone down to see her. While we were there, the missus helped her sister

at the little church to prepare the McCunes' wedding meal." Kirkham laughed and shook his head.

"I'm not sure how old Badger is, but that man has more energy than most young men. And ornery? Why the man just leaks orneriness.

"We visited awhile that afternoon and he told me he was resettling in the Wyoming Territory. Guess he'd lived around Kansas City for some time and was moving west. I didn't think he had ever been married before, but he called that young couple he was traveling with his kids so I'm not sure about that." Kirkham chuckled again and shook his head.

"Now you want to talk about mules. Badger knows his mules. He rides a big jack that he calls Mule, and I wouldn't go near that animal if Badger wasn't around. In fact, I wouldn't get close to him anyway.

"Badger bought a little place south of Cheyenne before he married, and that's where him and his missus settled.

"I ran into him in Ogallala this last year, and he told me he was thinking of selling if he could find the right fellow. Guess his missus started a dry goods store in Cheyenne, and they are living in town quite a bit now." Kirkham paused and added, "I'm guessing Badger would be pushing seventy or so, but it's hard to tell with him. He just always looks the same." Kirkham grinned as he looked over at Gabe.

"So, aren't you going to ask me how he knows you? He spoke highly of you, or I wouldn't have made this trip."

Gabe gave the older man a puzzled look and nodded.

"I've been pondering on that. I have sifted through my mind, and I just can't place him. I've been to Kansas City—rode the cars partway home after several drives, but most of my traveling outside Texas has been taking cattle north. The herds went first to Abilene, but most of them in the last five years have been to Dodge. I took one herd to Wichita." He frowned. "I just don't remember meeting a man by that name."

Kirkham's eyes twinkled and he laughed.

"Sometimes it's the little things, Gabe. Do you remember eating in a little joint in Kansas City one time in '73 or '74? You were on your way home after delivering a herd to Dodge. Fellow was rude to a woman, and you threw him out of the eating house. Hit him so hard you busted his jaw."

Gabe looked over at the man and grinned as he nodded.

"You didn't know the woman, but she was older. You apologized to her for the man's bad behavior. You said most men didn't act that way and you sure wouldn't tolerate it. I think folks started calling you Preacher after that."

Gabe chuckled as he looked ahead down the trail. "That's been a few years ago. She looked like someone's grandma, and that fellow had a foul mouth. I told him to shut up or I'd fix him so he wouldn't talk for a week." Gabe's grin became bigger as he looked over at Kirkham. "Heard he didn't talk for a month."

Kirkham nodded.

"Well, that lady was Badger's wife. He wasn't in there or the fellow probably wouldn't have lived. Ol' Betsy, as he calls his gun, would have left one more body behind. You took care of it for him though. He made it a point to eat breakfast with you the next morning. Didn't tell you he was the lady's husband though. You just talked cows, land, and cattle drives."

Gabe nodded as he listened to Kirkham. "Short fellow with bright blue eyes? Looked like he knew a joke that no one else did and carried a big buffalo gun. I remember that fellow.

"He said his name was Henry—never gave me a last name. We had a nice visit. We talked cows and land. He knew a lot about both. Said he'd recently moved to Cheyenne, and if I made it up that way to look him up. Just ask for the fellow around Cheyenne who raised mules.

"We visited for over an hour before I caught the train there and headed back to Texas.

"Haven't heard from him since. In fact, I'd forgotten all about that conversation until I bought cattle for this drive. I remembered what he'd said about the grass around Cheyenne. I've thought about taking a ride on up there to look that land over."

Gabe stared across at Kirkham as the connection finally came to him. "That Henry is this fellow Badger? Then he's responsible for getting me this drive too. He's the one who recommended me to Gallagher."

Kirkham laughed and winked at Gabe.

"Old Badger treasures his Martha. Why he thinks the sun rises up with her in the morning. Figures that he'd keep track of you."

Kirkham's eyes were somber as he added, "It's the little things, Gabe. Those times when you do the right thing just because it is right. Not because someone expects it of you or because folks are watching. Just because the goodness in your heart makes you act that way."

Gabe blushed and didn't answer as he looked across the land in front of them.

Angel's eyes were twinkling as he listened.

"Si, señor. It is the same reason that my sainted mother called me Angel."

Both men looked over at Angel and all three laughed.

CHAPTER 45

North Country

THERE WERE NO SIGNS THAT A LARGE HERD HAD crossed Wolf Creek, so the three men turned south. It was almost two that afternoon when they reached the herd about a mile south of Wolf Creek.

The cattle were thirsty. They had gone nearly two days with nothing but shallow creeks, and they wanted water. Suddenly the lead cows lifted their heads and smelled the air. They began to move faster. The cattle behind them picked up the pace as they also caught the scent of water. There was no time for introductions as every man worked to guide the cattle toward the crossing.

Cookie was already camped on the north side of Wolf Creek. The cowboys crossed the herd over the large sandy stream with no trouble and climbed out on the other side.

Wolf Creek was shallow, but it was cold, and the cattle watered well. It was nearly sixty feet wide, and the grass on the far side was thick. The cattle spread out and began to graze. Cookie had supper started, and the cowboys drifted in as the cattle settled down.

Gabe walked over to Fluff and squatted beside him. He had a new pair of boots in his hands, and he set them down beside the cowboy with a smile on his face.

"New boots, Fluff. Now I expect you to be up and back in these before too long."

Fluff grinned at him. "Feelin' better, boss. There is just something 'bout not havin' yore boots on though that makes a feller feel plumb naked."

Gabe grinned at him and squeezed his shoulder before he stood up.

The men stole sideways glances at the stranger standing by their trail boss but other than a nod, no one talked to him. As the men began to eat, Gabe gave them the items he had picked up at Fort Supply. The collection included everything from new socks and shaving supplies to new bandanas and even some perfume for Rusty.

Gabe handed the bottle to Rusty without saying anything. The red-haired cowboy blushed as he dropped it into his pocket.

The bag was finally empty when he strolled up to the chuckwagon. He pulled a pink wild rag out of his pocket. He handed it to Larry, and she took it as her face blushed. She started to pay him, but Gabe just waved her away. She quickly pushed it into her pocket and dropped her head over the pot she was stirring.

The men ate and then sat back. They wanted to know who the visitor was and why he was there. Gabe was lounging by the chuckwagon, and he walked back toward the campfire.

"Boys, this is John Kirkham from Ogallala, Nebraska. He would like to buy part of the herd and have us trail it north. I know none of you hired on for that long of a drive, so I need to know who is interested in going on past Dodge. And Cookie, that means you too. If we decide to do this, those who don't want to go on will be paid out in Dodge. The rest of you will get half of your pay in Dodge and will be paid out in Ogallala. Wages will be the same. You need to make a decision though because I don't want to hire a bunch of new drovers. Either enough of you continue on or we don't go at all."

The men looked from Gabe to Kirkham and talk picked up among them.

Finally, Tab asked, "Boss, you ever been over that trail? What if we run out of water or get lost or—"

Bart snorted at him, "Doggone it, Tab! Yore always a thinkin' of what cin go wrong. Just once, why don't you think of what cin go right.

"I'm in, boss. I've always wanted to see that north country. And mebbie I'll even go on up to Cheyenne an' see my little Cheyenne Rose."

Rusty rolled his eyes and some of the other men laughed.

Linc shook his head. "Not me, boss. I'm gettin' married next month, and I don't aim to miss my own weddin'."

The men all stared at Linc in surprise, and he grinned at them. The point rider was the oldest cowboy in their crew except for Cookie. He was nearly thirty, and all the hands but Gabe called him Old Man.

"When you boys grow up, mebbie you'll find ya a good woman. I met mine down in south Texas several years ago. Her daddy has a big ranch an' a pretty daughter. 'Course, I'd have tried to marry his pretty daughter even if he didn't need help on his ranch." Linc winked at his friends. "So get jealous, boys. I'm headed south to take a bride. Warm food, soft bed ever' night, and somebody waitin' for me at home."

The men all joshed him for a moment and then the talk turned back to the drive.

Gabe looked over at Cookie. "How about you, Cookie? I'd sure like to have you with us."

Cookie shrugged his shoulders. "I'm ready fer a change. Shoot, I know all these here trails. I jist as well learn some new ones. Besides, mebbie you'll take me on as yore cook when ya git yore ranch, so I cin finally settle down."

The discussion went up another notch at the idea of Gabe having his own ranch.

Tobe and Dink both raised their hands. "We're in, boss. This was a short drive, an' we'd like to see that country up north."

Rufe studied the ground for a moment before he looked up.

"I hear there's a lot more men than women up north. My luck ain't been so good here with *more* women. I'm feared if I go north, why I won't never get married."

Gabe grinned at him and laughed as he answered. "Well, the drive is just for a couple of months at the most, Rufe. You can always head south when you're done. And besides, I hear there's a real shortage of short, red-haired cowboys up north. Might be some momma just looking for a fellow like you."

Rufe grinned as he turned red, and the men began to laugh.

"All right. I'm in so long as I can drop south when those cows are delivered." Rufe's hair was bright red. He blushed easily and his coloring was light, so his face was red most of the time. He was short and looked skinny, but he was solid and tough as nails. His face was never seen without a smile, and his dry jokes kept the other men laughing.

Rusty and Fluff listened quietly. Injured riders couldn't hire on at the beginning of a drive, so they knew their chances of going on were slim.

Fluff pulled the bandage down and looked at the bite. Red streaks were going up his leg. He didn't remember seeing them the day before, and the sight of them made his stomach feel tight. Still, his leg looked smaller so the swelling was going down. The flesh around the bite had sluffed off and left a cavity in the muscle. He scowled at it and glanced towards the chuckwagon. Larry was finishing up and would be checking his leg soon.

He looked over at his partner. Rusty was leaning on his crutches with a smile on his face. The stitches had held this time, and he seemed to be healing fast. Still, it was only ten to fifteen days to Dodge. *We're both no good. I don't know how the two of us managed to get hurt on the same drive.*

CHAPTER 46

POINT THE TONGUE NORTH

LARRY SCRUBBED THE LAST PAN AND PUT IT AWAY. SHE watched as Cookie looked at the night sky and then pulled the tongue of his wagon to point it a certain way.

"Why do you do that, Cookie? Why do you turn the wagon tongue?"

Cookie pointed to the sky. "We's a followin' the North Star. Ain't no roads out here an' it's easy fer a feller to git turned 'round if it's cloudy or rainin' of a mornin'. I point that tongue to the north each night. 'Course, if the sky's dark or they's a storm, it's a little harder.

"Ol' Gabe now, he's like a durn coon dog. I don't believe that boy's been lost a day in his life. 'Sides, he's been over this trail a sight a times. Why I reckon he's been to Kansas six or seven times at least an' fer shore four or five by this here trail. I don't trail with jist any ol' Joe, but I'll go with Gabe. That boy knows his trails."

Larry listened with interest and then hurried to check on Fluff's leg. She stared at the red lines for a moment before she covered the wound liberally with echinacea powder. Angel had found three more plants on his trip to Fort Supply and had given her those as well. She had dried all the roots and now had adequate amounts of the root powder.

Once Fluff's wound was covered with the powder, she added liberal amounts of honey. There was now plenty of chickweed, so she mashed that and used it as a poultice.

His leg pained him, but Fluff was quiet as Larry worked on it. After she packed the last of the poultice, he looked up at her and asked casually, "Any cause to be concerned 'bout those red lines runnin' north?"

Larry's hands were still for a moment, but she looked at Fluff directly.

"Those lines are a sign of infection trying to take over in your blood. You need to drink lots of water in addition to all the tea you can stand. You are young and healthy, and you can fight back. So no, it's not good. Don't worry though. Cookie and I were expecting it." She smiled at Fluff and patted his shoulder.

"I will make you a big cup of tea, and I'll leave a canteen by you tonight. You need to drink as much as you can. And when you walk, remember to cinch your belt back above that wound.

"Now I am going to say a prayer for you," Larry whispered. "You can join if you want, but if you don't, it's all right."

She leaned over him and said the Lord's Prayer. Fluff stuttered along, adding words as he remembered them. When they finished, Larry added, "Lord, if it be Your will, please heal Fluff and give him many more years in the saddle. Amen."

Fluff smiled at her. He felt a sense of peace and fell asleep as soon as the tea was gone.

Larry was quiet as she washed Fluff's cup. She poured the rest of the tea into another cup for Rusty to drink. He had quit arguing with her and gulped it down. She rubbed her back as she made up her bed under the wagon.

Cookie watched and shook his head. He wanted to tell her to sleep in the wagon. He knew if he did the cowboys would call her a sissy, and she didn't need any extra attention.

"I hope that little gal can keep her secret fer a few more days," he muttered to himself. He grabbed an extra blanket out of his supply.

"Here," he said gruffly. "Put this here blanket on the ground an' lay on it. This ol' short grass ain't so soft as that bluestem was."

Larry looked up in surprise as she took the blanket.

"Thanks, Cookie. You're a good man."

Cookie sputtered and turned red as he climbed under his own blankets. He was growling to himself, and Larry smiled as she fell asleep.

CHAPTER 47

A Broken Heart

THE CAMP WAS QUIET FOR THE NIGHT WHEN GABE finally pulled out Grace's letter. He wanted to read it alone and this was his first opportunity.

He smelled the letter. The perfume smell was slight, but it was still there. Gabe smiled. He carefully opened the letter. His smile faded as he read the second paragraph.

Dear Gabe,

I'm not sure if you will receive this letter or not. Cappy sent it with a soldier friend of his who was being transferred to Fort Supply. That man promised to leave it at the express office when his company arrived. Cappy assured me that you would be stopping by Fort Supply, and the express agent would make sure that you received it.

Neither Father nor I will be able to meet you in Dodge City. Mother took ill shortly after you left. It wasn't cholera but she became very sick quickly. She passed away on April 6. Father is sick as well but seems to be doing better.

Mother's passing was so sudden. Both Father and I are brokenhearted. Father wants to leave Manhattan immediately. We will be taking the train to Cheyenne as soon as he is well enough to travel. He still wants to go to the Montana Territory, but we have no final plans for that. He has also mentioned going on to California where the weather is more temperate.

Cappy is going to meet you in Dodge City. He said if I was leaving then he was, in his words, "joining up with you." I don't know what your plans are, but I wish you well wherever you go. I will never forget our horseback ride and breakfast together the day you left.

Father asked that you please mail his bank draft to the First National Bank here in Manhattan along with an accounting of your expenses. Wilbur Higgenbottom is the bank president, and he will make sure that we receive it. We will be gone from Manhattan by the time you arrive in Dodge City.

Please be safe and know that I will remember with fondness my time with you. I only wish we could have known each other better.

Yours Truly,
Grace Gallagher

Gabe sat completely still as he read the letter twice. Then he folded it and placed it carefully in his pocket. His chest was tight, and he struggled to breathe. Finally, he stood and slipped out of camp.

Buck nickered as Gabe put his arm around his best friend's neck.

"She's gone, Buck. We'll never know what could have been."

Buck nuzzled Gabe's shoulder and pushed his soft nose into his friend's arm.

"I have never felt like this before. My heart has a hole in it." Gabe struggled to swallow, and his chest felt like someone was sitting on it. He roughly rubbed his face. "And that's why it is just best to keep your heart locked away. That's a lesson I won't forget for some time."

Gabe patted Buck again and walked quietly back to camp. He tried to sleep, but a pretty face kept popping up in his mind. When sleep finally came, it was filled with anxious dreams. He was chasing someone, but he could never catch them.

Angel rolled over. *Amor is sometimes cruel,* he thought.

CHAPTER 48

RIDERS IN NO MAN'S LAND

THE COWBOYS GRAZED THE CATTLE NORTH. A STORM was brewing, and the black clouds looked ominous.

Gabe watched the sky. Around noon, he had the point men guide the herd a little toward the west. The swing rider pushed on the right side and helped to turn the herd.

"If it starts to storm, we'll pull up here until the storm passes. If we get a stampede, I want them running toward the west and not into those steep hills to the east. Once everyone eats, let's put up double riders around the herd and be ready to run."

There were high, steep hills to their right and the running creek offered an adequate water supply for the herd. Gabe studied the grass and then shook his head as he muttered to himself, "This grass is short. It could use a good drink. I hope it isn't an indicator of what the graze is like as we move on north."

The storm moved to the south of them, and the cowboys once again began pushing the cattle north.

Gabe rode with Linc. He pointed to their east and then swung his arm to the north where a river wound its way south.

"That's the Beaver. It joins Wolf Creek to our east, and the two dump into the North Fork of the Canadian River. Fort Supply is right there at the confluence of Wolf Creek and Beaver River, but we need to keep the herd west. The army doesn't want any herds within ten miles of the fort." He added, "Some folks call all of this river the North Canadian, but I have always known this stretch as the Beaver. We will cross it this afternoon and then the Cimarron will be not long after that."

Linc was quiet. The Cimarron was known as one of the most dangerous streams in the southwest. It was filled to the brim with sand, and the quicksands that moved underneath were notorious. He felt a chill come over him.

He looked over at Gabe. "Call me a fool, but the Cimarron is one river that has always thrown the fear into me. I don't like quicksand."

Gabe nodded somberly. "When we get closer, keep your eye on the weather. If it starts to rain, we are going to push hard to get across. After a hard rain and high water, it's even more dangerous."

They were almost to Beaver River when Tall Eagle signaled to Gabe and pointed west. They were on the edge of the strip of grass known as No Man's Land and Tall Eagle had spotted riders.

Gabe cursed softly as he pulled his rifle from its boot. No Man's Land's official name was the Public Land Strip. The Strip was a large rectangular piece of land at the top of Texas that was not part of any state or Indian Territory. Of course, outlaws found this a welcoming refuge with no law and few people. The large cowherds meant money for the many bandits who hid there and used their guns wantonly. In that way, No Man's Land earned its name for a second reason.

The small group of riders was heading toward the herd. Gabe whistled to Tobe who was riding swing and pointed up to the front of the herd. Linc did the same thing on his side. Tall Eagle and Linc joined Gabe as he rode toward the group of riders.

Their leader was a swarthy man who sat heavy in the saddle. The four riders with him looked dangerous and tough.

Gabe's group was almost to them when Angel galloped up.

"Señor, that is Jack Cross. He is a bad outlaw from Texas. The Indians ran him out of the Territory and now he is here. Very bad hombre. You cannot let these men go. They will come back tonight and stampede your—your rabaño—your herd into the river." Angel pointed back at the herd as he struggled for the words in English.

Gabe didn't answer. His rifle was loosely pointed at the approaching men. Both Tall Eagle and Linc had their rifles across their saddle horns as well. He looked over at the two men and spoke softly.

"We are going to have to shoot our way out of this. Be ready and be quick."

Gabe stopped his horse, and the five approaching men continued on until they were about ten feet from where Gabe's riders waited.

Cross looked behind Gabe at the cattle.

"I see you have some of our cattle, señor. We are here to take them back."

The men behind him were laughing, and Gabe's gun moved slightly to cover their leader. His eyes were hard, and his voice was quiet when he spoke.

"You fellers picked the wrong outfit to rob, and now we can't let you go because you'll be back tonight. You just tried to cut your last herd."

The leader looked surprised, and then his hand streaked for his gun. Gabe's bullet knocked him off his horse and Angel's knife took out a second outlaw. Tall Eagle and Linc shot at the same time. The fifth outlaw was trying to draw his gun as he looked at the men in shock, but he was cut down by four guns.

Angel slipped out of his saddle and picked up his knife. A wave went through the herd as some of the steers shied to the side and snorted. The lead cows rolled their eyes but kept on heading north like nothing had happened. They smelled the water, and all the cattle were thirsty. The cowboys who rode beside the herd were singing, and the ripple that had started through the herd died away with no stampede.

Angel stripped the outlaws of their guns. Tall Eagle and Linc dragged their bodies away from the trail.

Gabe looked his men over. "Anyone take a bullet?"

Angel grinned at him. "I think, señor, you were so quick, perhaps they did not have time to draw their pistols." He patted his chest and added innocently, "I had little time to use my small knife." His smile became large as he pointed at the horses. "And now you have five fine caballos. Perhaps this was a good day."

Tall Eagle and Linc had already caught the outlaws' horses and were leading them toward the chuckwagon. They uncinched the saddles and dropped them into the bed. Nate appeared and led the horses toward his remuda. Larry's eyes were wide, but Cookie watched without speaking.

The cattle were moving faster toward Beaver River, and the cowboys moved into position to cross them. The crossing was going to be an easy one. They hazed the cattle toward the sand bar at the mouth of Clear Creek. The sand was coarse and white, but the water ran clear. The cattle dropped their heads to drink as they stepped into the clear water.

The cowboys spread out in the water and let the cattle drink as they came down the riverbank. Once the cattle lifted their heads, they were hazed across the river. The grass was short and coarse on the other side, but the cattle ate it hungrily.

The herd was spread out for nearly a mile, and it took almost two hours for all the cattle to drink and cross. Gabe had Nate wait until all the cattle had passed before he moved the horses into the water. When one of the new horses tried to cross before Watie, it was nipped hard. The horse squealed as the large stallion reminded the horses behind him of who was in charge.

Gabe grinned as he watched the herd of horses spread out in the water. Tall Eagle was standing to the side as the horses moved through, and once again, Gabe was reminded of what a pretty picture it was. Wind Dancer held his head proudly as the wind blew his long mane, and

Tall Eagle's black hair glistened in the sun. The water broke around the horses as they pawed, and it sparkled as it dripped from their mouths.

Nate looked around at Gabe and smiled as he waved. Gabe couldn't help but smile back as he rode toward his brother.

"Enjoying yourself, Nate?"

"I'm *loving* it! Tall Eagle showed me how to shoe the horses, and I shoed one by myself yesterday. He said I need to check their feet every day. I will probably need to shoe five or six each day as we get into rougher ground."

Gabe flicked his little brother's hat as he grinned at him. "You are getting to be quite the hand, Nate. I might have to hire you myself."

He followed the horses through the water and slowly rode past the cattle to where Cookie was waiting.

"We'll camp in this valley tonight. Pull your wagon to the west a mile or so and find a little shelter." He glanced at the mules and added, "And make sure your mules drink well. Water is going to be a little scarce for the next day or two.

"I want the herd moved west of this crossing. In fact, we'll move it west of you. We all need to keep our eyes open. Rufe saw three herds behind us, and we don't get any cattle mixed up."

There were unwritten rules on a trail drive, and one of them was that you didn't camp on the trail. You also didn't pass the herd in front of you unless there was a good reason to do so—and being in a hurry wasn't one.

Cookie nodded and Rusty pulled the second wagon in behind him. Gabe rode beside them and looked down at Fluff.

"How are you doing today, Fluff?"

The cowboy's face was flushed, and his eyes were red, but he smiled up at Gabe.

"Doin' jist fine, boss. This leg pains me when it gets jostled around though. I'm thinkin' that ridin' might almost be easier."

Gabe slowly nodded. "You talk to Cookie. If he says you can ride, we'll find you a calm horse."

Rusty grinned over his shoulder. "How 'bout me, boss? I reckon I can swing this leg over a horse now."

Gabe shook his head. "Naw, I want you in the wagon for a few more days. That was a nasty break, and we don't need that bone moving. Besides, I need a strong driver to get this wagon over the Cimarron in a few days.

He rode on to talk with Tall Eagle and Linc before he rode off at a gallop towards the north.

Larry watched Gabe and then asked, "Where is he going? He always rides off from the herd. Where does he go?"

Rusty moved the wagon in behind Cookie's and sat a moment before he answered.

"It's the trail boss' job to find water. He rides out ever' day an' double-checks the creeks an' the rivers in front of us to see what cin be crossed or if any routes need to be changed.

"Ol' Gabe knows his business. I cain't think of another feller I'd rather have leadin' me north."

Rusty hobbled out of the wagon and reached up to help Larry down. Then he realized he couldn't do that and turned a deep red.

"Miss Larry, I'll shore be glad when ya tell this here crew that yore a woman so's I cin treat ya like one." He hobbled off muttering to himself, and Larry looked after him in surprise.

She smiled to herself as she climbed down to help Cookie.

CHAPTER 49

LIGHTNING STRIKE!

GABE RODE NORTH AS HE SEARCHED FOR WATER AND a place to camp for the next night. He had gone about a mile when he came to a small creek in front of him. The bank dropped nearly straight down. He held Watie still as he peered down at the shallow creek over twenty below. He turned to look behind him. The creek looked benign from the south. Gabe frowned and studied the area around him. *If a running herd went over the edge here, you'd lose half of them.* He felt a chill go through him. "I sure hope we don't get a storm tonight. This would be a bad run."

Watie pulled to the west, and Gabe gave him his head. They topped a small rise about a half an hour later. A nice little valley lay below. A creek ran through it on the west end. Gabe sat on Watie and studied it for a time. He patted his horse and chuckled.

"I think I need to just send you ahead, Watie. You could check things out and then report back. You're a better trail boss than I am." He leaned on the saddle horn and looked around as he added, "You act like you grew up in this country. You for sure know all the little places with good graze around here."

Gabe turned back north. He didn't find much water other than a few small creeks. *There is some good grass here and only about ten miles ahead of that little valley. We could make it, but there is no water so we would be making a dry camp.* He frowned as he added the miles to the Cimarron in his head. "It is still another thirty miles from here to the Cimarron. We are going to need to find water before then." He rode another five miles north and found several nice creeks with good graze on both sides. They were close together and would provide sufficient water as well as protection to set up camp. "I think we will push tomorrow and camp here. It will be over a fifteen-mile day, but we should be able to make it. We'll turn west down that little valley back there to let them graze for a time before we push them back north."

Watie wasn't moving as fast on the way back to camp and Gabe patted his neck. "It's been a long old day, Watie, but we'll be back at camp in several hours and you can rest up tomorrow."

It was nearly midnight when Gabe rode into camp. Tall Eagle met him and took his horse without a word. Gabe nodded at him. He rolled out his blankets and was immediately asleep. He woke up several hours later. The sky was completely black, and lightning was flickering high above. Suddenly, a bolt of lightning streaked down from the sky and struck in the middle of the herd.

The sound of the thunder was deafening. Cattle bawled and horns crashed as the herd lurched to its feet and began to run.

Gabe raced for Buck and bellered, "Stampede!"

The men didn't speak as they jumped on their horses, saddled and waiting.

Gabe hollered at Link as they raced their horses, "You have flank. Don't try to mill them—let them run but push them west. Keep them as far left as you can. There's a deep creek to the right!"

Gabe, Tall Eagle, and Angel rushed to get around the herd. The cattle were running straight north. The three men strung out and rode their horses close to the lead cattle. They tried to turn them. The riders shot in the faces of the cattle that wouldn't swerve. The leaders finally pulled to the left. Gabe and Angel raced at the front of the herd while Link rode his horse along the side.

As the herd slowly swung to the left, Linc spun his horse and let more of the cattle surge by him. He once again raced his horse beside the herd and pressed them to follow the leaders.

A cow surged to the right and Linc followed her, pushing her back toward the mass of rattling horns. As he spun his horse towards the herd, it stepped in a hole. The horse landed on his leg when it went down. He jerked desperately to pull it free while the horse flailed and kicked to get up.

Linc was on the far-right side of the herd, but with no riders to keep them tight, the cattle began to spread out. He could see the last of the cattle charging down on him when Fluff dropped off his horse, grabbed the saddle horn, and heaved the horse off Linc's leg. Linc staggered to his feet.

Fluff pointed to his horse. "Ya git on first an' pull me up!"

Linc leaped into the saddle, and Fluff hit the horse on the back with his hat as he hopped away from the herd. A big mossy horned steer caught Fluff with one horn. It tossed him to the side as easily as a rag doll while the herd rushed by.

Fluff lay on his back and listened to the running of the herd as it drew further away. He couldn't see in the dark, but he knew the steer had hooked him deep.

"Ma, I'm comin'. I'm comin' home to see ya—you an' Joey."

As the yelling of the cowboys faded, the night became silent. Finally, he could hear faint singing in the distance, and he smiled.

"The boys got 'em millin' now. They have those dogies turnin' in a circle, an' soon they'll be back to grazin' like nothin' never even happened."

The clouds above him flitted over the moon and for a brief time it showed—big, golden, and bright. Fluff knew he was dying, but he wasn't afraid. Larry had talked with him while he rode in the wagon these last few days, and they'd had a lot of discussions about the hereafter.

"Dyin' ain't so hard if ya believe there's somethin' better."

He heard horses running and voices calling his name.

He answered weakly, "Over here."

Linc dropped beside him. His face was angry. It softened when Fluff smiled up at him.

"Now Linc, I ain't called Fluff 'cause I'm a skinny feller. Ya know we couldn't both ride that horse. Shoot, it'd taken me ten minutes to git up with this bum leg." He grinned at his friend. "Sides, ya have a bride to git home to."

Larry pulled her horse up and rushed to his side. Tears ran from her eyes as she pushed his hair back.

More cowboys dismounted and stood around him, hats in their hands, as Fluff looked at them.

"This here's my last ride, fellers. You tell Rusty I want him to have my saddle an' give Nate my fancy spurs. Give Rufe my new boots. You cin bury me in his old ones. His feet are 'bout the same size as mine. No point in wastin' a new pair a boots."

As Larry smiled at him and held his hand, he smiled.

"Larry, yore a gurl, ain't ya?"

Larry's heart stopped for a moment but she nodded. She leaned over and kissed his cheek.

"Yes, I am, Fluff."

Fluff stared up at her and his smile became bigger.

"I knowed ya was. Yore hands is gentle like my Ma's."

Rusty came racing up and almost fell trying to get off his horse. Linc grabbed him and helped him to sit by his partner.

Fluff smiled weakly at him.

"So long, Rusty. Ya find a new pard now an' don't ya be lonely. Ya was the best friend I ever..."

Fluff was gone and the men were quiet. It was hard to lose a friend, and Fluff had been well-liked by everyone.

Linc slapped his hat against his leg. His face was tight when he spoke.

"He saved my life. He pulled my horse off me an' gave me his. Fluff's dead 'cause a me, an' I'm alive." He turned away as his voice caught. None of the men looked at him or responded. Everyone was quiet.

Cookie pulled up in the extra wagon and hurried on his bowed legs to where Fluff lay. He was quiet a moment and then pointed to the wagon bed.

"Put 'im in the back, boys. We have the cattle grazin' in a nice little valley. Be a nice spot to lay 'im down.

"An' Rusty, ya drive this here wagon. I'll take yore horse."

Rusty's face was twisted in pain as the cowboys lifted Fluff's body and placed him in the wagon bed. He climbed up and took the lines without saying a word as he headed the wagon west toward the cattle.

Larry was sobbing, and the riders were awkwardly quiet. They had all heard what Fluff asked and Larry's answer as well.

Cookie helped her up on a horse. As she rode away, he turned and glared at the riders.

"Nothin' here has changed. That little ol' gal don't need to be pestered by a bunch a stinky, loud cowboys. Now ya cin be nice an' all, but ain't none a ya goin' to be courtin' 'er on this here drive. That clear?"

As the cowboys stared at him and slowly nodded, Cookie's voice softened and he added, "Now let's go lay Fluff down. That boy deserves a good goin' away."

The cowboys followed the wagon back to the herd and Gabe rode to meet them. He knew from the somber faces that someone didn't make it. Since Fluff was missing, he knew who that someone was. He cursed quietly under his breath as Rusty pulled up beside him. The cowboy's face was tight and he didn't speak.

Gabe's voice was soft. "Pick out a spot to lay him down, Rusty, and we'll dig the hole. You can make his marker if you want. And I want Larry to look at your leg when we're done. It looks like it's bleeding again."

Rusty nodded and roughly wiped his hand across his face. He drove the wagon to the far side of the valley. Several of the cowboys followed him with shovels. He pointed to the spot he wanted and then hobbled back in the trees to find some wood. He was struggling to hack down a tree when Nate found him.

"Let's use a couple of the stakes, Rusty. We can make some new stakes out of these trees. The stake wood will be easier to carve."

Rusty nodded and let Nate slip a shoulder under his arm. He stumbled once and almost fell, but Nate caught him. Rusty's curse was more of a sob as he jerked himself upright.

Nate was silent. He remembered how he had felt when his ma died, and he guessed Rusty felt the same way. He helped the cowboy find a place to sit and handed him the stakes.

CHAPTER 50

FLUFF'S LAST RIDE

NATE LOOKED UP IN SURPRISE AS LINC HANDED HIM Fluff's fancy spurs.

Link gestured toward Fluff. "He wanted you to have 'em." He handed Fluff's new boots to Rufe.

"Fluff wanted you to have his boots. He said he could be buried in your old ones."

Rufe stared at his boots and finally pulled them off. Both had holes in the bottom of the soles. He handed his old boots to Linc without speaking and pulled on the new boots.

Nate dropped the spurs on the ground. He walked over to where Rusty was carving the stakes. "Need any help, Rusty?"

The cowboy shook his head and pointed at the spurs. "Fluff ever tell you how he come by those?"

Nate shook his head and Rusty laughed softly.

"We had jist finished our first drive north. Fluff an' me was both purty young. We was barely fifteen, an' we looked as green as we was. There was an arm wrestlin' contest goin' on in the Long Branch in Dodge. The winner's name was Mort, an' he wanted to know if there was any more takers.

"Now Fluff looked soft, but that boy was always strong as an ox. He smiled at 'em an' raised his hand. 'I'll give 'er a try,' he says with a big ol' smile.

"The feller sittin' there laughed. 'Why yore jist a durn kid. What ya got to put up?'

"Now we was jist paid out an' Fluff had two months wages in his pocket. He was never one to waste 'round though. He said, 'I'll bet ya $10 against those there spurs ya have on.'

"The man looked down and laughed. 'Why those spurs is worth $25 at least.'

"Fluff give that feller his innocent boy smile an' shrugged his shoulders. 'It's all right. I didn't need 'em anyhow,' and then he turned 'round to face the bar.

"That feller let outa beller like an ol' bull. He hollered, 'Git over here, ya durn pup, an' let me bust yore arm! Ya Texans always think yore bigger, better, an' badder. I'm here to say ya ain't.'

"Fluff jist smiled. He sits down and looks across the table at the man. 'Left or right?' he asks.

"That big feller stared at Fluff an' his mouth falled open. He looked 'round the room at all the bystanders an' sneered, 'This kid don't even know which arm to use!'

"Fluff, he jist smiled and said, 'Didn't know there was a right or wrong arm. Don't rightly care. Y'all cin choose.'

"Now most fellers is right-handed but ol' Fluff, he were a leftie. Not that it mattered. One a his arms was as strong as the other.

"That loud-mouthed feller grinned at Fluff an' put his left arm up on the table. 'Let's do it with the wrong durn arm. I cin break yore left arm as easy as the right.'

"Fluff put his arm on the table, an' they gripped hands. The feller in charge hollered to go, an' Fluff laid that ol' boy's arm down backwards on the table easy as could be. Never broke a sweat. The feller that lost jist sat there an' stared at his arm. He couldn't believe that he'd been beat.

"Now the boys in that saloon didn't like that deal much so this big ox pushed the whupped feller outa the way an' sat down. He says, 'Ya durn little smart aleck. I'm a gonna lay yore hand over an' then I'm a gonna spank ya, right here in this saloon.'

"I was a little worried 'cause that feller was *huge,* but Fluff, he jist smiled. 'What y'all got to put up?'

"The big man hollered behind 'im, an' some feller led a hoss in. The big feller says, 'We'll bet this here fancy saddle. Brung it up from Ol' Mexico. Some general down there lost it in a card game. We'll bet this here saddle against Mort's spurs an' yore $10 that I cin take ya down.'

"The big feller, they called 'im Babe. He had his right arm up an' they locked hands. Now Babe, he started to move 'fore the ref said to go. He jerked Fluff's arm down partway but Fluff brung it back up an' laid 'im over. He smiled at the man as he stood up. He walked over to the hoss an' dropped the saddle on the floor. He pointed at the first feller's spurs. 'Shore was nice of ya boys to outfit me fer my ride back to Texas. I always wanted me a fancy saddle an' a pair a nice spurs.'

"He picked up his spurs an' his saddle, an' we sauntered on outa there like we didn't have a care. Now did he drop the old saddle an' put that fancy one on his hoss? Nope, he held that new saddle in one hand, mounted that ol' bay, an' laid that new saddle across in front of 'im. He hollered back as we rode down the street, 'If I'd a needed a hoss, I'd a stayed a little longer!' an' then we skedaddled it outa there an' back to camp."

Most of the cowboys had wandered up while Rusty was talking, and everyone was laughing when he finished. He grinned at his friends. His smile faded and he commented softly, "I'm shore goin' to miss Fluff. We been together since we was pups."

No one spoke for a moment and then Nate asked, "Does Fluff have any family?"

Rusty shook his head. "Naw, they was all killed in an Indian raid down by the Brazos. Some renegades went on a killin' spree. We both lost our folks in the same raid. That happened while we was on our second drive. We was both sixteen an' we was already as pards." Rusty added softly, "Fluff was like a brother to me. He's all I have fer family."

Linc had the fancy saddle in his hands. He set it down beside Rusty. "Fluff wanted you to have this. Told us before you got there today."

Rusty touched the smooth cantle of the saddle and then rubbed his eyes. He looked over at Nate.

"Help me up, kid. Let's git Fluff laid down."

Tall Eagle and Cookie offered to stay with the herd so the rest of the cowboys could say goodbye.

They buried Fluff just thirty miles south of the Kansas border in a nice little grove of trees. The water trickled over the rocks like hundreds of tiny bells, and the birds were singing happily.

Gabe looked over at his riders. He had to clear his throat twice before he spoke.

"This was Fluff's third drive with me. He had a gentle soul and a soft heart. We send him on to ride with more like him in the sky. We'll miss him here, but his riding days now will be easy ones."

He looked over at Rusty, but the cowboy shook his head.

"I said all I'm goin' to say."

Larry stepped forward. "I rode with Fluff these last few days in the wagon, and he considered every man on this drive his friend. He shared a story about each of you and said he felt privileged to be part of this group of cowhands.

"Fluff was a kind man with a big heart. He missed his family, and I'm sure they will all be glad to see him…and Rusty's family as well."

Rusty resisted the urge to look at Larry. Right then, he really wanted to hug her. Instead, he kept his eyes straight ahead and showed no emotion.

Larry looked at Rusty and Gabe as she offered softly, "I can sing his favorite song if you would like."

Gabe nodded and Larry sang "Jesus Loves Me." The music floated across the little valley and filled the hearts of the men standing there. Just as she finished singing, a hawk flew overhead. It floated on the wind and screamed as it soared away.

No one spoke after that until Gabe cleared his throat.

"When you get his grave filled in, Rusty, I want Larry to look at your leg."

Gabe glanced around at his riders. "Those of you who aren't helping here need to get back out to the herd. Cookie needs to be relieved or there won't be any breakfast." Gabe squeezed Rusty's shoulder as he walked away.

Angel was the only one who noticed how tight Gabe's shoulders were. He could tell his friend was crying inside, but Gabe would never show those emotions to his men. Angel shook his head. *It is a difficult thing to be strong all the time.*

CHAPTER 51

A Sad Bunch of Cowboys

GABE STUDIED THE MEN AS THEY ATE. HE WANTED TO push on so they could cross the Cimarron in three days. He was worried that spring rains would come and fill the river. It was a sad group that sat down to eat though, and he shook his head. *Maybe I should leave it up to them. Take another day here or push on to the next water.*

While the men were eating, Gabe explained where they were and what was ahead of them.

"Boys, I know it has been a short night and a sad one at that, but we have cattle to move. Right now, we are three to four days from the Cimarron. From there, it is another four days on into Dodge.

"Now we can stay here a day. The grass and water will hold, but I'd like to keep moving. The Cimarron is a nasty river and even nastier if it rains. There is good grass and water about twelve miles north. If we swing to the west the next day, we'll have water again. Now if it rains, there will be water in the small creeks everywhere, but I'm hoping the rains hold off for a time." He paused as he looked from man to man.

"I need you with me on this, so finish eating and let's vote. We'll do what the majority wants to do."

He walked toward the chuckwagon, and Cookie handed him a plate without speaking.

The men began talking among themselves and the consensus was leaning toward staying put for a day.

Angel looked around at the men.

"Señors, I think we should push on. I have been caught in the Cimarron after a rain, and she is an angry river. She eats anything that dares to stop. Perhaps if we cross before a rain, she will not be so hungry."

The men discussed it longer. Rufe finally asked Angel, "So is it true that lots of cowboys cross rivers like that in their birthday suits? Does that help keep a feller from boggin' down in the quicksand?"

Angel nodded somberly, "I have seen it done. If a man goes down, his ropa—his—his vestidos—can cause him to bog down. If a man is desnudo—if he has nothing on, the river cannot grab him so quickly."

The men thought about that and then began to discuss what all they would leave behind. When breakfast was over and Gabe took the vote, it was to move on.

He looked over at Angel in surprise, and the small vaquero winked at him as he shrugged.

"I think, señor, that you should let me do the talking." Angel's face was somber, but his eyes danced. Gabe grinned.

"I'm seeing that more and more," he agreed.

Gabe sent four riders and several pack horses back to pick up their bedrolls as well as to look for strays. The rest of the riders traded out their horses and began to graze the cattle north.

Gabe rode beside Angel for a bit before he went to the front.

"Think we lost many?"

Angel shook his head. "I do not think so, but the herd behind us was not so lucky."

Gabe looked at him in surprise.

Angel nodded, "They did not know of the steep bank above the small creek. Many of their vacas went over the edge. Very bad. Many cattle died and more had to be shot. They lost some of their vaqueros as well as their cook. Mucho bad."

Gabe felt a chill go through him. *That could have been us if I hadn't stopped to look at that creek.* He said a small prayer of thanksgiving for his drovers and a prayer for the other riders as well.

"You just play the odds with these drives. You never know how they are going to turn out."

Angel nodded, "Si, señor, but perhaps those who are most prepared come out in front. Maybe not always but many times."

Gabe remained silent at the discreet compliment and then rode ahead to talk with Linc and Tall Eagle. He explained again where they were going and then rode back to talk to the herd behind them.

"I have been up this trail many times and not once did I see that creek," Gabe muttered. "Prepared? I don't think so. I think the Good Lord rode with our herd."

CHAPTER 52

A Bad Pileup

GABE WAS ALMOST SICK IN HIS STOMACH AS HE looked at the cattle piled at the bottom of the embankment. Two men were still missing, and the other cowboys were working to pull dead or dying cattle aside to find their friends. Gabe helped them until noon.

They found one rider, but the cattle were piled so deep that they gave up on the other man. The cowboy that they found was dead. Their trail boss rode over to thank Gave. His face was bleak, and his eyes were red.

"I have brought three herds up this trail, and I never noticed that embankment before."

Gabe was quiet. There was nothing he could say that would make things better.

The trail boss studied his riders and then asked, "Think my boys could eat with your crew? We lost our cook and I'm mighty shorthanded. We have plenty of supplies if you want to work something out."

Gabe thought a moment before he answered. "I reckon that would work. I'll check with Cookie. How many riders do you have?"

The trail boss shook his head as he answered bitterly, "Five as well as me. I lost five good men last night. My cook was with me on every drive I've done. Two of those fellows who died were with me a number of years, and the other two were new riders. We have six cowboys to push two thousand head of cattle. Not enough riders. 'Course, we have fewer cattle now for sure."

Gabe listened quietly. He had adequate drovers, but he'd lost riders as well. He didn't have any to spare.

"You still have your chuckwagon and team or is it gone too?"

The man nodded. "We still have that. One of the boys must have gotten into some bad water. He had the squirts, and my cook offered to take his place as nighthawk last night. He was one of the first ones to go down."

"How are you on horses? We have some extras you can use if you need them. Rigging as well." The trail boss looked surprised, and Gabe grinned.

"We've had a few altercations with outlaws. They didn't need their horses when it was all over."

The trail boss laughed for the first time that day. "I did think it was a little quiet when we came up past No Man's Land."

He put out his hand to Gabe. "Amos is the name. Amos Winters. I own these cattle and I sure appreciate you clearing the way."

Gabe grinned as he shook the man's hand. "Gabe Hawkins. I'll send a couple of my boys back with some horses. How many do you need?"

Amos pushed back his hat as he looked over his tired riders. "Six would be good but if you have more, we'd take them. We lost horses in that run as well."

Gabe nodded. "I'll send back twelve horses and a couple of rigs. You use them and get them back to me when the drive is over.

"We'll pull your chuckwagon up with our herd, and I'll have my cook's helper drive it." He reached out his hand to Amos again.

"Luck to you and see you for supper tonight."

Gabe's riders were coming with the bedrolls, so he stopped to wait for them.

"See any of our cattle?"

The men shook their heads, "No, but those boys behind us had a heck of a night."

"Yeah, I talked to their boss. They are going to borrow some horses from us. When you boys get back, pick out twelve of those outlaw horses. Twelve that are solid and not so fancy. Trail them back to that herd. Those drovers are going to be worked to the bone and their horses as well." Gabe shook his head.

"They lost their cook, so they'll be eating with us. Tell Cookie to plan on six more for each meal. I don't know what they have for food supplies but Cookie can sort that part out.

"And bring their chuckwagon back after you drop off the horses. Head down there right away. Those riders need fresh horses."

Gabe headed north, and the four cowboys rode on toward the herd.

Finally, Bart spoke up. "The boss was back there helpin' those boys. Did you see the sweat on his horse?"

The other three men nodded. Rufe added, "And now he is loanin' 'em hosses. That's a right neighborly thing to do."

The men were quiet as they thought on that.

Tab's brow furrowed and finally, he spoke up. "So did ya boys know that Larry was a girl?"

Dink didn't answer, but Bart and Rufe shook their heads.

Tab continued, "I never guessed. I just thought he was a little sissy boy. He seemed to be a nice kid though, so I give it up."

"She."

"Who?"

"Larry. She's a she."

"I know she's a she." Tab thought for a moment. "So do we still call him Larry?"

Bart's face was getting dark from frustration. "Her! An' yes, we still call 'er Larry. Now quit talkin', Tab, or I'm goin' to punch ya."

Tab was quiet a moment and then he commented, "I don't know what you're so all-fired grumpy about. We all thought she was a he an' now she's a she. But, she still looks like a he an' we're s'posed to treat her like a he."

Bart's face turned purple, and he smacked Tab's horse with his hat.

The startled horse took off at a run and Tab grabbed for the reins as he fought to hold his seat.

Bart yelled after him, "An' ya jist keep on ridin'. When you get there, sort off those hosses."

He glared at Rufe and Dink when one of them snickered. Both men continued to grin.

Dink drawled, "Sure am glad none of the other boys heard that exchange. We'd be hearin' a repeat of that ever' night till we hit Dodge."

He mimicked the two men, "She? No, he. She's a he. No wait, he's a she."

Dink chuckled, and Bart's face lost some of his frustration as he laughed with them.

When they caught up with the herd, Tab had the horses wrangled and saddles on two of them. A scowl covered his face, and he refused to look at Bart.

Dink suggested they send Tab to deliver the horses and collect the chuckwagon. He looked at the other two cowboys and grinned.

"I think Bart and him should be separated. Poor ol' Tab might not live another day if we put those two together."

As Dink rode toward the front of the herd, he called back, "I'll okay that with Linc."

CHAPTER 53

JIST A LITTLE OL' BABY

RUSTY FINALLY GAVE IN AND LET LARRY LOOK AT HIS leg. He frowned and growled around until she leaned back with her hand on her hips.

"What is wrong with you, Rusty? I just need to look at the stitches."

Rusty was silent for a moment and then muttered, "Don't seem right, you bein' a woman an' all."

Larry's eyes glinted, and her voice was dangerously soft.

"A woman can't do doctoring?"

Rusty was sharp enough to catch her tone, and he blushed a dark red. "That ain't what I meant. I don't think it's right fer ya to be so close to my leg when I barely have any britches on is all."

Larry stared at him a moment and then laughed.

"Rusty, you are a mess. I am going to put some echinacea powder on your stitches. We'll put the honey pack on tonight, but it is healing nicely. You did rip a stitch at the bottom, but I am not going to replace it." She took one of the new bandanas that Gabe had given her and wrapped it around Rusty's leg.

She stood up and offered Rusty her hand. The splints were so long that he had a hard time standing unless he could pull himself up. Larry finally put her shoulder under Rusty's arm and pulled him up.

He staggered and fell against her before he caught himself. He caught her shoulders with his hands and stood there a moment before he let go. Once again, his face turned a deep red as he hobbled off.

Larry put the powder back in Cookie's medicine kit and the old man grinned at her.

"That boy has a bad case on ya."

It was Larry's turn to blush, and she didn't answer as Cookie laughed wickedly.

They quickly packed the wagons, and Larry was ready to climb in when Rusty appeared. He gave her a hand up with no comment and then climbed up himself. As he sat down on the seat beside her, she looked over at him. Rusty's face was still flushed, and Larry smiled.

"Thank you, Rusty. That was a welcome change."

As they followed Cookie's wagon, she asked, "What are you going to do when you get to Dodge?"

Rusty paused as he flicked the reins over the backs of the mules. "I don't rightly know. If Fluff was still here, I reckon we'd go back down to Texas since neither of us would be cowboyin'. Not that we have anything down there, but it's home." He paused and then added, "Now that I'm on my own, I jist don't know what to do. Fluff an' me been together for 'most nine years. I feel like part a me is missin'." Rusty's eyes were watery, and he looked away.

His eyes moved over the rough hills beside them. "If I didn't have this bum leg, I sign on with Gabe to go on north. I'd like to see that country."

Larry didn't respond, and Rusty looked over at her. "How 'bout you? What are ya goin' to do? Yore Pop let ya come back home now that y'all are carryin' a baby?"

Larry's face turned a deep red, and she glared at the man beside her.

"I was married, Rusty. My husband was as useful as a buffalo turd, but this child still has a father—even if he's dead."

Rusty was silent for a moment. He commented casually, "Even turds have lotsa uses. Why look at how many of 'em we burned—"

Larry slammed him in the ribs with her elbow, and Rusty started laughing.

He looked at her seriously. "Insinuatin' that yore baby didn't have no daddy ain't what I meant. Some folks don't want their kids back once they leave, an' they sure don't want no extra mouths to feed. I jist wondered if yore folks was like that."

Larry shook her head. "No, my parents are good people. My father didn't want me to marry Duke, but I thought I was in love." She added softly, "I knew it was a mistake a month into our marriage, but it was too late. I had already promised forever, and I took those vows seriously."

Rusty flicked the lines and they rode in silence for a time before he asked, "So what happened to yore man?"

Larry's body became stiff as she looked away, but her face was determined when she answered.

"He was shot. He loved to gamble, but he was terrible at cards. He began to cheat, but he wasn't even good at that. Someone caught him and shot him."

Larry's eyes were wide as she looked at Rusty. She whispered, "I was glad. I hated him by the time he died."

Rusty's jaw tightened, and he was silent for a time. He finally looked over at her.

"You goin' to use yore doctorin' skills? Yore purty good at patchin' folks up."

Larry gave him a quick smile. "I hope to. I want to work with old Doc Walters in Dodge. He's an animal doctor there. He wanted me to work with him before I married, so I'm hoping he will still take me on. That was two years ago. Except now I am having a baby by a man that I despised." Larry sucked in her breath.

"I don't want this child. I don't want to be reminded of Duke every day."

Rusty looked at Larry in surprise. "Why it's jist a little ol' baby. Don't matter none who the daddy is."

Larry stared at him and Rusty shrugged.

"I don't know much 'bout God an' Jesus an' all that religion stuff, but I know that babies ain't mistakes." He waved his hand around at the view before them. "Ain't no God that cin make this here country's a goin' to make the wrong baby on accident."

Rusty studied the traces on the mules for a time. He glanced at the quiet woman beside him before he looked ahead again. He added softly, "I know some folks grow up to be no-account, but I still don't reckon they was a mistake. Some good happened somewhere."

Larry's bottom lip began to tremble, and she started to cry.

Rusty looked at her and frowned. "Here now, don't cry. I didn't say those things to make ya cry now." He awkwardly put his arm around her, and Larry sobbed quietly.

She finally quit shaking, but Rusty left his arm where it was. "Angel told me the same thing. He figured out that I was a woman shortly after he joined us. He's a kind man too."

She smiled up at Rusty through her tears. "Why couldn't I have fallen in love with a man like you instead of the one I married?"

Rusty was silent for a moment. His blue eyes were intense when he looked down at Larry. "I don't reckon it's too late fer that. Not fer me anyhow."

Larry's green eyes opened wide, and she blushed as she sat up straight in the wagon. She was quiet, and Rusty let her think. She finally looked over at him.

"You shouldn't say things like that, Rusty. You have no idea the baggage that I carry around."

Rusty shrugged. "We all haul 'round things that weigh on us. Don't matter to me none 'bout what was. What matters is what is an' what's a comin'. An' I'd love yore little ol' baby even if he looked jist like that scallywag ya was married to 'cause—'cause—well 'cause he's a baby an' I like babies. An' 'sides, he'd be half y'all an' y'all I like a lot."

Larry stared at this man beside her and again her eyes filled with tears.

Rusty's clear blue eyes clouded up. "Now there ya go again with those tears. I ain't no hand with tears. They plumb tangle me up. Did I say somethin' that hurt ya 'cause that ain't what I intended."

Larry shook her head as she whispered, "No, that was just about the sweetest thing anyone has ever said to me, and if you keep saying sweet things, why I guess I will just keep crying because your words make me happy."

Rusty studied Larry's face with confusion all over his. She smiled at him as she scooted closer.

"Those were happy tears, Rusty. Women have lots of different kinds of tears. There are happy tears, sad ones, angry, scared, and even thankful tears—why, there are just too many reasons why women cry."

Rusty scowled at her. "Well, how's a feller to know what kind they are?"

Larry laughed up at him, "I guess if you stay around long enough, you will figure it out!"

Rusty still didn't understand, but Larry was smiling and that was good enough for him. He pulled her closer as he grinned. Then they talked and shared dreams for the next nine miles.

CHAPTER 54

A Soft Spot for Lost Causes

RUFE AND BART RODE UP TO COOKIE'S WAGON. "BOSS said to tell ya that we'd have six extry hands fer supper. One a the herds behind us lost their cook. Tab went to git their chuckwagon. Had a powerful bad pileup back yonder over a creek bank. Lost some riders an' their cook as well as a passel of cattle."

Cookie listened to Bart and nodded.

The two men headed out to the herd, and Cookie pulled his wagon into the area he chose to camp. He was jumping down from the chuckwagon when Rusty pulled the second wagon up behind him. He grinned at the two young people, and Larry blushed.

Cookie winked at Rusty. 'Bout time ya made use of all that time ya been spendin' in that there wagon. I was startin' to lose confidence in ya."

Rusty grinned as he helped Larry down. She hurried to the chuckwagon and busied herself pulling out items to prepare for supper. The men didn't get any dinner so supper would need to be a big meal.

"We got six more joinin' us this evenin' so when ya mix up them there biscuits, make plenty."

Cookie grumbled and growled under his breath. "Who knows what supplies that other cook had. Shoot, we might all starve to death on this here drive all on account of our boss havin' a soft spot fer lost causes."

Larry looked up at him and laughed out loud.

Cookie grinned at her despite himself and winked. "But I guess we knowed that, didn't we?

"Rusty, why don't ya wander 'round in those woods there an' see if ya cin find some berries or honey or both." He paused and glared at the smiling cowboy, "And don't be tryin' to sweet talk Larry here into joinin' ya. I got plenty fer her to do here. 'Sides, she's like my own daughter now, an' she sure ain't a goin' in the woods with no cowboy."

Cookie winked at Larry and once again she blushed. Rusty grinned and headed for the trees. Tab drove the third wagon up, and Cookie inspected it like a horse would a new foal. He opened boxes and cans as he grunted and growled. Finally, he pulled some cans out of the wagon and held them up.

"Canned peaches! Why I ain't seen canned peaches in a coon's age. We be havin' us some cobbler tonight. Mix up a little extry biscuit dough, Larry, an' throw some more sugar in that part."

Cookie dug a little further and held up dried beef, potatoes, and canned milk. "Those boys was eatin' good. We'll have us some chipped beef gravy tonight an' taters too." The old cook was soon whistling as he prepared his meal.

Larry looked at him a couple of times and then finally laughed.

"Cookie, I don't think I have ever seen you this happy when you cook. Are you that excited over the provisions in the new wagon?"

"I reckon it's 'cause a durn sad day turned into a happy one. Different vittles, a full stock a food, an' my favorite gurl has a beau that I 'prove of." Cookie grinned at Larry and began whistling again as she bent her face over the mixing bowl.

Cookie had Larry sort and combine the supplies in the two wagons. The staples were the same, but the new wagon definitely had some extra items not commonly seen on a drive.

Once the supplies were combined, they moved bedrolls to the second chuckwagon. Cookie spread out Larry's blankets in the wagon bed of the Cole wagon.

"Now that ever'body knows you's a gal, you cin sleep in the durn wagon."

Larry didn't answer but she appreciated it. Her hips were sore in the mornings from lying on the hard ground.

Cookie's cobbler smelled delicious, and soon the cowboys were strolling up to see what was cooking.

Rusty returned and handed the cook a small mess of wild strawberries.

Cookie looked from Rusty to the strawberries in disgust. "There ain't 'nough here to do nothin' with, an' lookin' at yore durn face, I reckon ya ate more'n ya picked."

Rusty grinned but said nothing as he hobbled away.

CHAPTER 55

ALMOST TO KANSAS

GABE WAS BACK BY EVENING. HE HAD FOLLOWED Buffalo Creek to the Cimarron.

"We'll camp on Buffalo Creek tomorrow night. It has water. We'll swing to the west and stop on Cowboy Creek the next night. We can trail the cattle from there right up to the Cimarron.

"I'd like everything watered before we reach the Cimmaron. That river is known for its underflow and it's chock-full of sand. In fact, it looks like it's dry. We'll cross at Deep Hole. I was over it today and it's not too bad." He paused and studied the faces of his riders.

"We will have some other drovers joining us for meals from here on into Dodge. Amos Winters is right behind us. He lost five boys yesterday including his cook. His brand is the Flying A. They'll trail behind us a ways." He frowned and shook his head as he added, "They're mighty short on hands. Heck of a spot to be in with the Cimmaron in front of us."

The men were quiet as they listened. Finally, Tab climbed to his feet.

"I just wanna be the first feller here to tell Miss Larry that we sure are glad to have her along with all the healin' an' cookin' she's done. And I'm glad she ain't no sissy boy."

Bart rolled his eyes and snorted. Several of the other hands grinned as they looked at her.

Larry blushed and smiled at them. "And you just treat me the same as when you thought I was a boy. Don't be all shy now."

The men looked down at their boots. Most were shy now and didn't know what to say.

Tab shifted his feet and looked over at Bart. He started to speak again but Bart stopped him.

"Whatever yore goin' to say, Tab, I don't wanna hear it."

Tab frowned and then muttered to himself, "I was jist wantin' to know how we's s'posed to cross the Cimarron in our birthday suits with a durn gurl along is all."

Bart glared at him moment and then frowned. *By George, ol' Tab has somethin' there. I ain't strippin' down in front of no gurl.*

Tobe looked over at Gabe. "How far are we from Kansas? I know Deep Hole Crossing is north of the border a piece."

Gabe nodded. "We'll cross into Kansas the day after tomorrow sometime. Nothing is marked, so it's hard to tell exactly where. Deep Hole Crossing is about five miles inside Kansas. We might hit the crossing tomorrow evening, but I think it will be the following morning."

The men began talking about Dodge and past drives. Finally, Tobe looked over at Gabe.

"So you goin' to let those of us trailin' on north go into town at all? Sure would like to wipe a little trail dust off 'fore I head out again."

Gabe grinned at the cowboy. "I've been pondering on that. Maybe I'll let a few of you boys go into town when we leave Bluff's Creek. John here is going to keep his herd moving north so we don't have to stop long outside of Dodge. I'll take care of business in town and meet him on the trail."

Bart muttered under his breath. "Durn Preacher. Probably won't even get drunk."

Gabe chuckled and agreed. "Sure won't, Bart. Can't afford to take the risk. Maybe you should think on that too."

Bart snorted and the rest of the men laughed. Discussion was soon hot on who would get to go into town first.

Dink grinned at them. "We could play a little cards. Winners go first an' losers go second—if they go at all."

Tab looked sorrowfully at Dink. "You would say that. You ain't lost at cards since this here drive started. I had a new pair a socks an' now yore wearin' 'em."

Dink continued to grin, and about that time, two of the Flying A Riders rode in. They looked a little nervous as they dismounted. Both groups just stared at each other until Angel stood.

"Señors, welcome to our casa. Please make yourselves comfortable—but don't expect us to let you vaqueros eat first." He gave them his innocent smile and all the cowboys laughed. It wasn't long before the two groups were talking and sharing stories.

The two cowboys looked over at Larry with surprise. She had washed her face and now was obviously female. They were surprised.

One of them leaned over to Bart and whispered, "Y'all trailin' with a gurl? Shoot, I'm likin' this here outfit better all the time."

Bart glared at the man as he snapped. "Her name's Larry an' don't ya be talkin' to 'er or we'll have us an altercation."

The rider sat back quietly and said nothing more.

Cookie clanged on the dinner bell, and the men were quick to fill their plates. The Flying A riders didn't stay long, and they took food back for their companions.

Gabe leaned against the chuckwagon. "How were they on provisions?"

Cookie grinned and winked at his boss as he drawled, "Let's jist say ya might have to dig a little deeper fer the next stretch. Those boys was eatin' good."

Gabe laughed and rolled his eyes. "Oh, I suppose." He looked at Cookie more seriously. "When we stop to sort the cattle, you just go on into Dodge and buy what you need. I'll send some cash along. I thought about having Rusty follow you with the second wagon. I want to sell it there. It was handy traveling with two wagons, but we won't have a driver for the next stretch." He added with a growl," And I'm sure not packing any more women along."

Cookie grinned at Gabe. "I reckon that will work *if* Rusty comes on into Dodge. He's been a spoonin' with Larry, an' I ain't so sure *he* even knows what he's doin."

Gabe scowled. "And that is why you never bring women on a drive."

Larry walked up just then. She heard Gabe's last comment and looked up at him with a smile. Gabe didn't scare her as much now that she had figured out that he was just all business.

"I do thank you, Mr. Hawkins. My Family lives west of Bluff Creek. If you can loan me a horse to ride there when we get closer, I can deliver it to Dodge the next day."

Gabe studied her face and shook his head. "No, I reckon we'll make sure you get on home. I think I'll have Rusty ride with you and he can bring the horse back. He's itching to get back in the saddle anyway. He's doing some nightguard tonight and we'll see how he gets along." His eyes twinkled as he looked at her seriously, "If that's all right with you."

Larry's face turned a deep red, but she looked Gabe in the eyes. "I would like that just fine, Mr. Hawkins, and thank you."

Gabe turned to walk away, but he paused and looked back. "Larry, you more than earned your keep this trip. I sure hope things work out for you."

Larry stared at Gabe's back as he walked away, and Cookie grinned at her.

"Now that's about the best durn compliment you'll ever git outa that hard boy." He began to laugh evilly. "Shoot, ya might even change his mind 'bout women on drives."

CHAPTER 56

BUFFALO CREEK

THEIR NEXT CROSSING WOULD BE BUFFALO CREEK. IT usually had water. Gabe wanted to cross it and then stop for the night there.

Buffalo Creek spurred off the Cimarron as the river dropped back into Oklahoma. It was a small creek with rough, high sides and arched from east to west. He had decided to take the cattle across it first and have the wagons follow. The animals would break the bank down some and make it easier to cross the wagons. Gabe looked at the three wagons driving end to end ahead of the herd, and he shook his head. *Sure never dreamed I'd be headed into Dodge with three wagons. Good thing we have Larry.*

Gabe's eyes twinkled as he thought of Rusty. The red-haired cowboy was ornery but had a heart of gold. *If he can handle riding, I just might let him trail along north. I'd like to have him as a drover. He's one of our best riders and works hard without complaining.*

He pondered on what Cookie had said about the two young people and frowned. "Tough to have nothing to show for yourself," Gabe muttered. "I will ask Rusty to come along. That will put a little more money in his pocket." He scowled and looked across Buck's head. "Hard to ask a gal to marry if you don't know where you'll live or what you'll do."

Buck snorted and Gabe grinned. He patted his horse. "You don't worry much about those things, do you, Buck? Pretty easy life you have."

The horse snorted again, and Gabe's smile became larger. The air was fresh, and it was going to be a good day.

He swung his arm at the drovers to start moving the cattle. His smile became bigger as he listened to the sounds coming from the herd. The cowboys whistled and called as they pushed the cattle, and the cattle bawled as they took their places in the herd.

Grace's face floated through his mind, and Gabe roughly shook his head. His mouth hardened down and then he smiled. *None of that was her fault. Who knows? Maybe I'll see her in Cheyenne.*

Gabe looked over as John Kirkham rode up beside him.

"So tell me about this trail north to Nebraska. Will we have water every day?"

John took a couple of puffs on his pipe before he answered and slowly nodded. "Mostly. There are creeks all the way across, but there might be a few times that we travel a day or two with no water.

"As we get farther north, the hardest thing will be fuel. Not much wood, and the cow chips have mostly been picked up. We'll want to pack as much wood as we can early on." He pointed north with his pipe.

"About halfway up, we'll hit some of the best grass of the trip. Then she thins out again."

Gabe listened and processed as John talked. He finally nodded. "I'm thinking it will take me a couple of days in Dodge to tie everything up once we get there. I figure that ought to put you about three days up the trail. Does that sound about right to you?"

John relaxed in his saddle and took another puff on his pipe. "Sounds about right. We ought to be somewhere between Buckner and Pawnee creeks." He drew a rough map in the in air in front of him as they rode. "The trail angles northwest. 'Course, we might not be the first herd

294

headed north. Either way, we'll spread out to find grass and water." He puffed on his pipe before he added, "Some folks think the herds follow along behind each other, but those of us who trail cows know different."

Kirkham grinned at Gabe. "The advantage that we have is that I know that trail, and I know where to find water if she gets dry. May not be much, and it might add a few days if we have to swing too far to the east or the west. Still, we'll bring the herd through in good shape." His smile became bigger. "Kind of like you have so far."

Gabe looked away and then looked back at the man with a grin. "Pays to know your business," he agreed.

They let the cattle cross Buffalo Creek slowly and drink as they crossed. The creek bottom was stirred up, and the cowboys filled their canteens upstream. The mules pulled the three wagons through with little trouble even though the mud in the creek was getting thick by the time they crossed.

Gabe rode up beside Rusty's wagon. "How did the leg do last night?"

Rusty grinned at him. "Well, other than I have to mount on the right side like a tinhorn 'stead of the left, it's all right. I have to swing that ol' leg mighty high to make it over the back with those durn trees hooked to it. My hosses are a little confused, but they're adjustin'. I let out the left stirrup so I cin git my foot in it."

Gabe nodded. "I want you to take Cole's wagon into town and sell it when we get closer to Dodge. It should bring at least $20, maybe $30 if we're lucky."

Rusty's eyes glinted. "I'd cin do that. My pa used to tell me that I had the gift when it come to dealin' an' sellin' things. 'Course, I was jist a short feller back then an' I smiled at those ol' ladies." His blue eyes were full of humor as he grinned again at Gabe. "Reckon a feller needs to use ever'thing available to 'im when he works a deal."

Gabe studied the grinning cowboy and laughed. "I'll just bet you do too.

"And another thing. If you think you would be up to it, I'd like to hire you to go on north with us. You're one of my best riders and that leg is healing fast. If you want to, that is."

Rusty stared at Gabe in surprise and excitement filled his face. "Why shore, boss. I'd like to do that. I jist didn't think you'd take on any riders with a bum leg."

Gabe chuckled as he rode away from the wagon. "Still won't, but I will hire a rider who works around a bum leg." He tapped the reins on Buck's neck and the horse moved ahead at a slow lope.

Rusty stared at Gabe as he rode off. His face was flushed, and he was smiling with excitement. "Well I'll be. Headed north with the herd. Cain't wait to tell Larry. An' me with a bum leg!"

CHAPTER 57

LAST NIGHT IN THE TERRITORY

THEY CAMPED THAT NIGHT ON COWBOY CREEK JUST south of the Kansas border. The riders were getting excited because Dodge City was getting closer. Those who were going on to Nebraska were looking forward to a new adventure as well.

The Flying A riders were slow in showing up that evening, and Gabe's cowboys discussed their planned trip to Dodge City as they waited to eat.

Tobe had been appointed as the designated speaker when their plan was presented to Gabe. The rest of the cowboys thought he was the best talker although they had lots of input. Tobe laughed at them as he nodded.

"I'll do it, but I git to pick the day I go to town. If I'm to do the talkin', why then that's like I'm the boss of this here lousy outfit. That means I'll do the decidin' of when I go."

Several of the cowboys growled and he waited for them to agree. Once it was decided, he wrote down their requests.

He looked them over somberly. "Probably cain't do nightguard tonight neither. This here list of wants is goin' to take me some time to gather together."

The riders glared and one of them threw a stick at him. Tobe grinned and relaxed against his saddle as he waited for Gabe to ride in.

The Flying A riders arrived about the same time as Gabe. Two different cowboys came to pick up their supper. They looked tired, and Gabe's cowboys felt sorry for them.

Cookie rang the bell and the men quickly lined up to eat. They even let the Flying A riders fill their plates first so they could get back to their herd. Gabe rode with them when they left.

Tobe looked around at the cowboys lounging around the fire. "So this is what I'm thinkin'.

"There's a little creek by the name of Bluff Creek that winds up from the Cimarron almost to Dodge. I think the first group of riders should ride in when we're 'bout twenty-five miles out on that creek. Those boys cin ride in, git cleaned up, hurrah the town that night, an' head back to the herd first thing the next mornin'. The second group will ride in soon as the first fellers is back. They will do the same thing. Ever'body has to be back at the herd by seven the next mornin'.

"We cain't none of us be late. The boss 'ill want all of us with the herd when it's time to cut out the cattle that are headed north...an' ya know ol' Gabe won't tolerate fellers who ain't where they's supposed to be. 'Sides, he probably has some buyers lined up, an' they'll start showin' up once we git closer to Dodge."

Tobe pulled some sticks of various sizes out of his pocket. "Now I have eight sticks here. Each feller cin draw him a stick, an' the short sticks git the second day."

Angel stepped forward. "Señors, I will go later. I am meeting my brother, and he is not always so quick."

Tobe grinned at Angel and tossed a short stick on the ground.

Rusty pointed a crutch at the wagon. "Boss wants me to sell Cole's wagon, so I'll go the second day too or whenever he tells me." He winked at the riders as more of them perked up. "Yore lucky day, boys. Ya know I always win at these short-stick games."

Tobe looked at the men. "That only leaves one short straw since Tall Eagle never goes in town until the drive is done."

The men quickly drew sticks and held them up. Dink was on nighthawk, and he received a short stick. He didn't care. He had no intention of getting drunk and losing all his money. He just wanted some new clothes and a couple of cold beers.

When he received his stick, he shook his head as he looked at the excited men. "One of ya had better be sober enough to git the rest back." He grinned at Tobe.

"Guess that's you since yore the designated boss of that outfit."

Tobe's face fell when he realized he had just set himself up, but he laughed with the rest of the riders. "Deal's a deal. I'll talk to the boss when he gets back."

Larry had finished helping Cookie and came over to the fire.

Bart looked up at her and asked, "So where do yore folks live, Larry? Shoot, we don't even know yore last name. We might want to look in on ya when we head back to Texas."

Larry laughed as she answered. "Evans. My pa's name is Harold. He was wounded in the army in '59 and mustered out. My folks liked the land by the Cimarron River and settled down in that area.

"Pa sold out to a rancher down there and moved up west of Bluff Creek when I was small. There were several big outfits on the Cimarron, and he just had a little spread. He told me it was easier to sell out and move than to argue with the big ranchers over grass since no one used any fences back then.

"We like our little place. It's a pretty area. Bluff Creek runs all year long. We have cattle and farm a little ground. Ma always had a big garden, and we did lots of canning. We kept some chickens around and a few pigs too. We had few neighbors when I was growing up, but people were moving in by the time I left.

"My father calls our place Basin Ranch, and our brand looks like a bowl. We don't live far from Jacob's Well and that is another place that always has water."

The men were quiet for a moment and then Tab asked cautiously, "You mean ya have eggs? I don't rightly recall the last time I ate an egg."

Larry nodded. "We did, but I haven't been home for two years. Lots of things could have changed since then."

Gabe rode up as Larry was talking. He handed Buck's reins to Nate and poured himself a cup of coffee.

He looked over at Larry in surprise. "Your folks run cattle in the Basin? I've seen your brand. In fact, we'll water at Jacob's Well on our way north. I may have even met your father before."

Tobe saw his opportunity and gave the best sales pitch he'd ever given. The cowboys watched him and nodded agreement.

Gabe tried not to smile. *They have obviously discussed this among themselves.* He glanced at the riders when Tobe finished and then back at the nonchalant cowboy.

"That was quite the presentation, Tobe," he commented dryly. He looked at the hopeful cowboys and slowly nodded his head.

"I'll go along with that except the riders in the second group have to help me trail the herd to Dodge before they cut out.

"Anyone who is late will have their pay docked…and if you don't show up, you're fired. And Tobe, you are responsible for getting the four of you back to the herd on time.

"Those who are headed on north will get two weeks wages when we hit Dodge. You'll be paid out the rest in Ogallala."

When Nate looked at him hopefully, Gabe shook his head. "You are not going to town, Nate. These fellas can't be trusted when they drink."

Gabe threw out his coffee grinds without waiting for a response. He tossed his cup in the wrecking pan and climbed into his blankets.

Before he lay down, he added, "Tonight is your last night in the Territory. We'll cross into Kansas tomorrow morning sometime."

CHAPTER 58

CROSSING THE CIMARRON

THE NEXT MORNING BROKE CLOUDY AND DAMP. GABE could feel his stomach tighten as he looked up at the sky.

"Let's get them moving, boys. It is only about five miles to the river, and I want to cross before it rains.

"I told the Flying A boys to bring their herd right up behind us. That's why you didn't see them at breakfast. Once we cross, you push our herd on for a couple more miles so those fellows can bring theirs across. I'll stay behind in case they need some help.

"And, Cookie, those riders behind us will be mighty hungry by the time they get across if you can save something for them.

"Let's go!"

The cattle started to move, and the drag cowboys pushed the slow ones as fast as they could. More of Cole's cows had calved and Gabe shook his head.

"Angel and Tobe, rope those babies and let's throw them in a wagon. Don't worry about blankets. This crossing will be too rough to keep them covered."

The two men quickly complied and had the calves roped quickly. The momma cows weren't happy as they dragged the bawling calves

301

toward the wagons. As a rope crossed over the top of the Cole wagon, Rusty grabbed it and hauled the calf into the wagon bed. That worked well and soon four baby calves were in the wagon. Gabe knew he should shoot them because new calves would never be able to complete the drive. Still, it pained him.

"Maybe some farmer will be waiting on the other side, and we can trade some calves for fresh eggs or greens," he muttered as he watched.

More of Cole's cows were springing and would be calving soon. Gabe frowned. "It's possible we might have to pay a fee to water as we get farther north. They might even be handy to trade for water."

By noon, the Cimarron was in front of them. The low banks looked innocent as the herd moved toward the sandy river. Gabe had placed stakes in the sand to mark the area he wanted the cattle to cross. Some of the stakes had almost sunk out of sight but there were enough showing to mark their way.

"Angel and Tall Eagle, keep your horses inside those stakes and try to keep any cattle from going beyond them. Linc, you and Bart fall in behind Angel and Tall Eagle. The rest of you, push those cows and push them hard."

Watie stepped into the river and quickly moved across the sand. Nate pushed the horses in behind his brother. The two lead cows followed, and the river was soon a mass of horns and hoses surging across the bed of sand. Once the first group of cattle crossed, Gabe rode back and took Bart's place while Bart helped push.

The rain came slowly at first and then in sheets of water. The river was getting boggy and Gabe yelled for them to push the laggers. The last of the cattle were finally across and now there were only the three heavy wagons.

Dink, Bart, Rufe, and Tab followed the herd to push them farther into the river valley while Linc, Tall Eagle, Angel, and Gabe each tied a rope onto Cookie's wagon and charged into the river. Cookie whipped his mules, and the heavy wagon pulled slowly across. The horses leaned into the ropes as the thick sand tried to suck the wheels down.

Rusty followed next with Cole's wagon full of baby calves. The wagon sank even deeper than Cookie's wagon had, and Larry's heart thumped in her chest. "Dear Lord, help them to get across and then help me to as well," she whispered.

Angel dropped to the ground and unhitched Cole's first two mules. He led them back across the river and quickly hitched them to Larry's wagon. The other three men followed with their ropes and attached them to her wagon.

Gabe looked over at Larry. "Ready?"

She nodded even though she was so afraid she could hardly breathe. The cowboys charged into the water and Larry whipped the lines. They hit the sand, and the wagon began to bog. She stood up and snapped the lines as she yelled. The lead mules surged forward, and the back mules lunged. Larry fell sideways. She staggered back to her feet still holding the lines. The wagon slowly pulled across the deep sand. When it drew closer to the edge, the mules increased in speed and jerked it up the riverbank. As the men loosened their ropes, the mules slowed and then drew to a stop.

Larry dropped down on the seat, breathing heavily. She looked back at the riverbed. The tracks of the cattle barely showed, and the wagon ruts were disappearing. She shivered. "I have always hated sand," she whispered as she said a silent prayer of thanksgiving.

Rusty climbed out of his wagon and limped over to her. His blue eyes were full of concern as he smiled up at her.

"Ya all right? That rough ol' ride didn't hurt ya none or the baby neither, did it?"

Larry stared at her cowboy and silent sobs shook her chest.

Rusty jumped into the wagon and put his arm around her. "Now, now. It's all over. Yore all done crossin' rivers. Yore next water will all be creeks an' then y'all be home."

Larry leaned against him, and Rusty held her until she quit shaking.

He hugged her tightly and kissed the top of her head as he smiled at her.

"Let's git on ahead a the herd an' git ya started on supper." He squeezed her again before he whispered, "An' then, I want ya to take a walk 'fore bed." His blue eyes were intense, and Larry let them swallow her up.

"I'd like that," she whispered.

Rusty squeezed her arm as he climbed down and limped toward his wagon.

Gabe watched the two of them and quick smile crossed his face. Somehow during a trail drive, two people had managed to fall in love. His mouth twisted as he shook his head. *Don't reckon that is ever going to happen for me. It will just be Nate and me. And then someday, he will leave, and it will just be me.*

"One more river before Dodge, señor. A few more arroyos—or as you say creeks—and then we will arrive." Angel's smile was huge as he gestured from the river to the trail in front of them.

Gabe's face relaxed as he listened to Angel. The small vaquero found joy wherever he was, and Gabe couldn't help but smile.

He nodded and pointed towards Cookie's disappearing wagon.

"You go up ahead and talk to Cookie. He should come to a little creek before too long. Tell him to make camp when he finds a spot. We'll bed the cattle down along the creek. I am going to trade horses and help Amos Winters cross his herd.

"We came about seven miles today. Tomorrow, we will water at Jacob's Well and maybe camp in the Big Basin."

Angel watched as Gabe cantered toward the horse herd. "Ah, señor, you have a good heart, but perhaps you try to do much by yourself," he muttered.

Gabe was almost done saddling Buck when he saw more of his riders joining him. Linc, Tall Eagle, Angel, and Tobe were switching out horses as well.

He watched them a moment before he asked quietly, "Where do you boys think you are going?"

Angel grinned at him.

"Señor, our patron thinks he will keep all the fun for himself, but we join him."

Gabe stared at his best men for a moment and his throat felt tight. He shook his head as he looked at Linc.

"Not you, Linc. I need someone in charge here."

Linc started to protest and Gabe grinned at him. "Now, Linc, you are the only one in this crew with prospects of getting married. We don't want to do anything that will put a damper on that wedding."

He added more seriously, "Besides, you know where to find the water. Make sure the herd makes it to that jog in that creek before you bed them down."

Gabe mounted and the four men headed back toward the Cimarron to help the Flying A drovers.

CHAPTER 59

Across the Cimarron
One More Time

THE RAIN HAD LET UP, BUT THERE WERE PUDDLES OF water among the sand bars now. Gabe put Buck into the water, and the horse picked his way carefully across. Gabe looked back at the other riders.

"Tall Eagle, you and Tobe spread out—go each direction. See if there is a better spot to cross than here. You shouldn't need to go much farther than two hundred yards in either direction. If nothing is better, come on back.

"Angel, you pull out those stakes. I don't want to run them into one of our horses and they can barely be seen now."

The Flying A herd was about a mile away, and Gabe rode slowly to meet them. Amos Winter's face was hopeful as the trail boss rode up.

Gabe pointed behind him. "My riders are looking the river over to see if another spot would be better to cross than the one we used. Deep Hole Crossing is usually the best, but rain always moves the sand around some."

Amos slowly nodded as he studied Gabe's profile.

"You know, you and your boys don't need to do this. I sure appreciate it and I know my riders do too, but our difficulties sure ain't your problem."

Gabe's eyes twinkled. "And I didn't tell my riders they had to help. They just didn't want me to have all the fun."

The cattle moved up to the water slowly. Their lead steer was a huge brindle. He stopped at the edge of the water and snorted. Then he stepped in and began to slog his way across.

Gabe's riders were spread out on the water to form an alley, and Gabe signaled the Flying A drovers to push the cattle hard.

He charged into the water with the first group, hollering and snapping his rope. The leaders pushed forward, and the rest of the cattle followed. The sand was getting deeper, and as the last of the cattle jumped in, some of those partway across tried to turn around. The cattle in the middle of the river began to mill, turning in circles. The crossing quickly clogged, and the cattle behind tried to jump over each other. The cowboys charged toward the struggling cattle, trying to break up the jam.

Angel jumped from his horse and hopped across the tops of the milling cattle until he was on the steer in front. He dropped down and dug in with his spurs as he whipped the cattle around him. The mill broke and the steer charged out of the water. Tall Eagle followed, and Angel grabbed Tall Eagle's arm as the steer climbed out of the water.

The huge steer's dignity was insulted, and it charged the first thing it saw. Wind Dancer easily dodged the angry animal's horns and raced downriver with the steer in pursuit.

The cowboys laughed as they watched the horse and the angry steer draw out of sight. All the cattle had crossed when the steer came tearing back down the same path with Tall Eagle chasing it and Angel hanging onto the saddle.

Gabe turned the steer into the herd, and the angry animal spun around. It swiped its horns back and forth across the ground and snorted.

Four cowboys charged it, and the steer swerved away. The riders followed and the steer turned back into the herd.

The Flying A riders made it a point to thank each of the men who helped. They were all talking about Angel's ride with amazement.

"So where did ya learn to dance on cows?"

Angel grinned at the men. "Ah, señors, my family was so poor that we rode the longhorns since we had no dinero to buy horses. Their backs are not so bony as they look, and their horns are easy to hang onto."

The riders stared at him in amazement while Gabe laughed.

"Angel, you are quite the storyteller, but that was a pretty picture." He added, "You'd better thank Tall Eagle though. I'm not sure how you would have gotten off that steer if he hadn't been right there."

Angel's face was somber, but his dark eyes twinkled as he nodded.

"Si, señor. Tall Eagle and I—we discussed just that. It was all part of the plan." Tall Eagle was usually quiet, but even he chuckled at that statement.

Angel grinned at him and winked. "Señor, you were where you needed to be. Gracias."

Tobe led Angel's horse up to him as he drawled, "Well, it ain't a longhorn, but mebbie y'all can ride this horse a while now."

The riders were all smiling as Gabe's drovers rode forward to their own herd. Gabe looked over at Angel and shook his head.

"I have never seen a man jump across cows like that to break up a mill. I've heard of it being done but was always a little skeptical."

Angel shrugged. "Some vaqueros call it dancing on cows. I have seen it done many times when cattle crossed the Brazos. Often that river is low, but it can flood too." He looked over at Gabe and winked as he added, "I much prefer to dance with beautiful women."

The riders all laughed, and Angel chuckled with them.

CHAPTER 60

A Walk in the Moonlight

IT WAS A RELAXED GROUP OF RIDERS AROUND THE FIRE that night. None of Gabe's men said anything about Angel's trick riding, but the Flying A riders shared the story with a few enhancements.

"Why he rode that ol' steer right up the riverbank, jist a buckin' an' a snortin'. That tall Indian plucked him off the back of that mad mossy horn easy as could be an' then the Indian's horse did a little dance with that steer. They all went a hightailin' it up the river an' then that ol' steer come a hightailin' it back. That ol' horse had its mouth open jist tryin' to take a bite, an' those boys was a whoopin' an' a hollerin'."

"Shoot, I think Angel there was a tryin' to git back on as close as they was to the hind end of that cow."

Gabe's riders listened in amazement and then stared at Angel suspiciously.

Bart shook his head. "I don't know. Angel here tells some tall tales. I think he put ya fellers up to this."

They all looked over at Gabe and he shrugged. "That was mostly the truth. Old Lightfoot there can dance with cows. Might be fun to watch him dance with women."

The mention of women took the conversation off in that direction, and the Flying A cowboys left with their food.

John Kirkham listened to the stories quietly. When Gabe sat down beside him, he commented, "I've seen riders jump on cows in a mill before. Dangerous thing to do." He took a couple of puffs on his pipe and added quietly, "Especially if the cows are not even part of the brand he's riding for."

"Angel was a drover for Charles Cole and was the only survivor in their last stampede. He's a good man and fits well with my crew. He will be going on north with us."

Kirkham tamped out his pipe. "Never was too fond of Mexicans," he stated quietly.

Gabe could feel anger rising from deep within him as he looked hard at the man. He forced himself to keep his voice calm, but fury grated out of him when he spoke.

"Where I grew up down by Bandera, Texas, there were more Mexicans than there were Anglos. Most of my friends were Mexican, and they were some of the best vaqueros and finest men I have ever ridden with. Angel is an exceptional man and a good friend to all of us." His eyes were angry and his face was tight as he growled, "And I won't do business with a man who says otherwise."

Kirkham looked at Gabe in surprise and slowly turned red. His neck became even darker as he looked away.

"I reckon I was out of line, Gabe. I didn't know you felt that strongly."

"Well, I do. This conversation is over, or our business deal is off."

Gabe stood and stalked out of the camp. He walked over to where the horses were penned. The night sky sparkled with stars, and the moon was bright. It was a beautiful evening. He cursed under his breath. "Why did he have to go and ruin a fine day with talk like that."

His growling was interrupted by the sound of voices. Gabe slipped into the rope corral with the horses and watched as Rusty and Larry stopped near him.

Rusty turned the young woman toward him.

"Larry, when we git to yore house, I want to have a talk with yore Pop. I ain't never asked a gurl to marry before, but I'd shore like to ask y'all."

Larry's breath caught in her throat and tears sparkled in the corners of her eyes.

Rusty barely breathed until she smiled.

"And?"

He pulled her close and kissed her tears. "An' I'd like to know if y'all will be my wife when I git back from Ogallala."

Larry looked up at him and shook her head. "No. No, I won't."

Rusty's happy face paled and his breath caught.

Larry smiled up at him. "I'd like to be your wife *before* you go north. Maybe I'll just go with you."

Rusty's smile was so big it looked like his face might break in two. He grabbed Larry and swung her around.

"Well, I reckon that will work. I'll talk to the boss tomorrow. He's not much fer women on drives, but he likes ya an' ya shore done yore share a work." He paused and asked cautiously, "This mean ya might be all right with movin' up north if I was to take a ridin' job with Gabe on his ranch?"

Larry nodded happily, and Rusty squeezed her.

"We won't have much to live on at first, but I reckon we cin run a few cows an' git by. Mebbie we cin even save up a little an' buy our own place down the road."

The young couple walked farther out on the prairie. Gabe stood for a moment as he thought about what Rusty had said. *Will I be willing to let Larry come along as Rusty's wife?* He scowled and shook his head. *Can't think of any reason not to.*

Gabe snorted as he walked back toward camp. "Shoot. Before long, there won't be a darn rule left that I follow."

Rusty couldn't get to sleep. He finally saddled his horse and went out to relieve Linc.

"I cain't sleep. Ya jist as well catch ya some shut-eye."

Linc grinned at the younger man. "What's the matter? Larry have ya all tangled up?"

Rusty grinned as he shook his head. "Naw. I asked her to marry me when I git back from Ogallala, but she wants to marry in Dodge an' go with me."

Linc chuckled as he listened to he happy cowboy.

"Well, I reckon that is what ya should do then. Mebbie the boss 'ill give ya a day off to go to yore own weddin'."

Rusty nodded and grinned.

As Linc rode back toward camp, he could hear Rusty's fine tenor voice singing an Irish ballad to the cattle. Gabe opened one eye as Linc climbed into his blankets and the cowboy chuckled.

"Things are gettin' more interestin' 'round here all the time."

Gabe grunted and Linc went to sleep with a smile on his face.

CHAPTER 61

BIG BASIN

THE NEXT DAY WAS RAINY AND COLD. THE MEN ALL put on their slickers, and Rusty gave Larry Fluff's to wear. It was huge on her, but at least she wasn't as wet. Breakfast was quick and Gabe lined out the day.

"We'll head northwest today. The cattle might be able to find a little water with this rain, but I want to camp in Big Basin tonight. Jacob's Well is a water hole close to it. No one knows how deep it is, but the water is cold. It's never been known to go dry either.

"It's about fifteen miles from here, so it will be a full day's drive. Of course, if this rain gets heavier, we aren't going to make it that far. If that happens, we'll make a dry camp tonight.

"Larry lives close by, and Rusty is going to take her home today. You fellows might want to tell her goodbye since this is the last we'll see of her."

Gabe's eyes were twinkling as he looked at Rusty, and the cowboy's neck turned red. *I swear, it's like the boss knows already what I want to ask 'im. That's uncanny, jist plumb uncanny.*

Rusty stepped forward. He had planned to talk to Gabe in private, but he decided to take the bull by the horns. He cleared his throat.

"Actually, boss, that ain't entirely right. Larry an' me, we'd like to marry in Dodge an' then both go with ya on the drive to Ogallala."

While some of the cowboys stared at Rusty in surprise, others started to grin. All of them turned their heads to see what Gabe said.

Gabe kept his face still and Bart spoke up.

"Boss, we liked Larry when we thought she was a boy, an' her bein' a gurl ain't caused no problems. The rest of us fellers is fine with 'er comin' along on the drive.

"'Sides, she sews way better'n Cookie any day." He looked around at the rest of the riders. Some nodded and others just grinned.

Tall Eagle was watching the scene play out with a small smile on his face, and Angel was grinning.

Gabe shrugged his shoulders and stretched out his hand to Rusty.

"Heck, Rusty. I have no reason to disagree. You go ahead and get married when you sell the wagon. I can't give you any time off now, so you'll have to take your honeymoon at the end of the drive." He waved at Larry.

"Come on over here, Larry, and stand by this wild cowboy who stole yore heart. I sure didn't see this coming when I picked you up at Doan's Crossing."

Larry shyly came over to stand by Rusty, and their friends cheered. They all clapped Rusty on the back and tried to shake Larry's hand. She hugged each of them instead. Once again, her eyes were full of tears.

Cookie watched them and finally came over to give his blessing.

"Boss, I reckon I better git the makin's of a cake. Looks like we need to have us a party here real soon."

Everyone was in a pleasant mood that day. Even the wet, rainy weather couldn't put a damper on their spirits that day. The cows cooperated, and they made Big Basin by six that evening.

The men who had never been there before stared at the circular depression. It was about a mile wide and was a huge sink hole in the middle of the prairie. A smaller, less-visible basin to the east was called

Little Basin. It was just under a half-mile across. Jacob's Well was located there. The well was about fifty feet across and was spring-fed.

The cowboys brought the cattle up to the well in small groups. They didn't want cattle pushing each other since it was so deep. It was a long and tedious job to water all of them. Cookie and Larry started on supper, and the men ate in shifts as they traded off. The watering took nearly four hours. Once the cattle were watered, they were pushed over to the large basin. The men were tired as they crawled into their blankets.

Rufe groaned as he lay down. "I sure hope the boss lets us stay at here a day. This is easy grazing and a good place to hold cattle, maybe the best for the whole drive."

Gabe put two extra men on nightguard since the Flying A herd would be grazing in the Little Basin. He didn't want the herds mixed, especially this close to Dodge. *I have two buyers coming out to look at cattle when we reach our camp site on Buck's Creek, and I sure don't want to be sorting when buyers are here.*

It took the Flying A riders most of the night to water their cattle. In the morning, they pushed them out of Little Basin to let them graze on the surrounding grass.

The herd was now within five miles of Larry's ranch. Gabe sent Rusty with the excited young woman to see her home. He looked at the happy cowboy and shook his head as he chuckled.

"Load up all those baby calves and take them with you. Give them to Larry's folks, and be back by supper. We are going to stay here one more day, so I reckon we can get along without you that long."

He looked over at the other riders. "We'll plan to hold the herd in the Basin until the grass runs out. After that, we'll let them trail north. We are headed to Bluff Creek next, and our camping spot is about ten miles away. We are almost to Dodge City, boys!"

Gabe rode ahead to check Bluff Creek. He had never seen it without water, but he checked every year anyway. Kirkham rode with him and the two men didn't talk for the first five miles.

Finally, John looked over at Gabe.

"Hawkins, I'm sorry about last night. I haven't known a lot of Mexicans, and the ones I have…Well, let's just say my experiences haven't been good ones."

Gabe's shoulders were tight as he looked straight ahead. He finally replied quietly, "I don't think you can hold an entire group of folks responsible for the actions of a few any more than you can hold all horses responsible for the poor behavior of a few knotheads."

Kirkham looked over at him and laughed. He nodded his head slowly as he grinned.

"I reckon that's right. We good?"

Gabe nodded. "Good."

The two men talked the rest of the way and Gabe pointed out the route they would be taking.

"We'll want to pick up kindling and cow chips these next two days. We'll have nothing for fuel once we leave Bluff Creek. None on the Arkansas River either, not even cow chips. You'd think cow chips would be plentiful with all the herds, but the townsfolk use them for fuel too."

CHAPTER 62

RUSTY MEETS THE FOLKS

RUSTY AND LARRY DROVE THE WAGONFUL OF BAWLING baby calves towards Larry's home. On the way, they drove by a dugout cut in a small hill and a corral of nice horses.

An old man came out to meet them. He squinted his eyes, and a large smile lit up his face.

"Well, I'll be. Little Laurel done come back home, an' brought a feller too!"

His sly old eyes looked Rusty and the wagon over. "I reckon you be needin' a hoss once ya leave here. As ya cin see, I have plenty."

Larry laughed and shook her head.

"Now, Dutch, we had a deal. You never sell horses to any of my friends, and I don't turn you in to the sheriff."

The old man grinned and shrugged.

"I want you to meet my fiancé, Rusty O'Brian. Rusty, this is Dutch Henry. He has been our neighbor for many years. He trains his horses to always come back home." A smile covered her face as she tried not to laugh. "Dutch has been accused of selling the same horse numerous time."

Dutch grinned at her and winked at Rusty. His twinkling eyes sparkled as he looked from Larry to Rusty.

"Accused but ain't been caught. They's a difference." He looked back over at Larry.

"You an' yore man stayin' long? Mebbie I'll come over fer supper."

Larry laughed and nodded. "You come on over, but Rusty has to get back to his herd before dark. I would love for you to come to the wedding though. We are going to be married in Dodge and then head up the trail to Ogallala with his drovers."

Dutch rubbed his bristly jaw and slowly nodded. "I reckon I cin mebbie do that. You jist tell me when an' I'll be there." Rusty clucked to the mules, and Dutch waved as they drove away.

"Little Laurel's gettin' married. Guess that no-account feller what took 'er away musta died. An' good riddance to 'im. That little gal deserves to be happy." Dutch grinned. "Well, I reckon I'd better mosey on over to the neighbors an' do me a little visitin'. I want to go to that weddin'."

Rusty looked back at the pen of horses and then over at Larry.

"Sounds like a fine arrangement to me," he commented with a grin. "Looks mighty profitable. I don't believe I'll do it though. It might be a quick way to earn a rope necktie."

Larry laughed and took hold of Rusty's arm as they continued down the road.

A small boy of around five shaded his eyes as they drove up to Larry's house. He slowly walked toward the wagon. When he recognized his sister, he ran toward her hollering behind him.

"Ma, Laurel's home! She brung some feller an' it ain't that no-account she runned off with!"

Larry blushed and Rusty grinned as he lifted her down. Her little brother raced to meet her and jumped into her arms. Larry laughed as she kissed him.

"Noah, this is my beau, Rusty.

"Rusty, meet my little brother, Noah."

Noah looked Rusty up and down. "What did ya do to yer leg?"

Rusty grinned at him. "Why a couple a old cows tried to sit on me an' I didn't move fast 'nough. They done broke my leg an' then left. Didn't even stick 'round to apologize or nothin'."

As Noah stared up at him, Rusty pointed in the back of the wagon. "How would ya like to have some baby calves? My boss sent 'em along. Maybe y'all cin bottle-feed 'em. What do ya think?"

Noah's eyes became large. "Say, that would be fine. I can start my own herd an' be a real cowboy."

Rusty boosted Noah up into the wagon. The calves surrounded him, trying to suck on anything they could.

The little boy's eyes were delighted as he patted and talked to each one.

"Only one thing," Rusty stated seriously. "Ya have to clean out this here wagon when we're done unloadin' 'cause I have to sell it in Dodge. No durn woman is goin' to want a wagonful a cow dung, is she?"

Larry's mother came to the door of the house. When she saw her daughter, she put her hand over her heart and then held out her arms. Larry ran to her mother and they both cried.

When they finally dried their eyes, Larry pulled her mother toward Rusty.

"Mother, this is Rusty O'Brian. I met him on a trail drive up from Texas. Rusty, my mother, Mary Evans."

Rusty put out his hand. "Pleasure, Mrs. Evans."

Mary Evans looked from Larry to Rusty in confusion, and Larry blushed.

"Duke died about two months ago. Mr. Hawkins, Rusty's boss, gave me a job on the drive as cook's helper. That's where I met Rusty."

Mrs. Evans frowned and Rusty added softly, "Mrs. Evans, I love yore daughter an' I want to speak to yore husband 'bout marryin' her.

Larry's a fine woman, an' I'd be proud if y'all think I'd be good enough to be her man."

Just then, Larry's father rode up. He spied her and dropped to the ground.

"My little girl is back home. Ah, Laurel. The missus and I prayed for this." Tears filled his eyes as he hugged his only daughter.

"Pa, this is Rusty O'Brian. I came up from Texas with a cattle herd, and he was one of the drovers.

"Rusty, this is my father, Harold Evans."

Harold frowned at Rusty. His eyes moved to Larry.

"Where's that scallywag of a man you run off with? Take off and leave you, did he?" He glared at Rusty as he pointed a finger toward Larry's stomach.

"That kid yours?"

Rusty's face tightened and he took a step forward as he glared at Larry's father.

Larry blushed and put her hand on Rusty's arm. She held her head high and looked directly at her father before she responded, "Dutch was shot...but not before he gave me this child." She defiantly pointed at her stomach and her father's glare became bigger.

"Laurel—"

"Mr. Evans," Rusty interrupted, "Mebbie y'all an' me cin talk. My leg is painin' me so if we cin lean on yore fence over there, I'd be mighty appreciatin'."

Larry's father looked from his daughter to the tall young man standing before him and slowly nodded his head.

When they reached the fence, Harold turned to Rusty and growled, "I don't know where you fit into this here deal, but that kid she's carryin' better not be yours."

Rusty's blue eyes hardened down, but his voice was soft as he looked at his future father-in-law.

"Mr. Evans, that baby ain't mine yet, but I'm a goin' to marry yore daughter. She's a fine woman an' I love 'er. That little ol' baby is goin' to have a happy home, an' I'm a goin' to love both it an' its little momma. I wanted to ask ya fer yore daughter's hand, but ya done pushed me into jist a sayin' it."

Harold Evans stared at the young man in front of him. Rusty's eyes were angry, and his mouth was tight. Still, the young man had been courteous and polite.

Harold's face slowly relaxed into a smile, and he put out his hand.

"I reckon that speech just won you the hand of my daughter. I'm just sorry you didn't show up here several years ago. Would have maybe saved Laurel some heartache, and us too."

Rusty nodded his head. "Me too, Mr. Evans, though I reckon time don't matter much to me." He added, "We'll be married in Dodge in a few days, an' then we'll head on up north with the herd. I've hired on to work for the brand when the boss gits his ranch up in Wyomin' somewhere."

Harold looked down at Rusty's leg with surprise. "Your boss must think a lot of you if he hired you for a drive—and you with a bum leg."

Rusty shrugged. "I broke it in a stampede, but it's comin' along. Larry's got a way with healin' an' we all liked havin' 'er along."

"Larry?"

Rusty grinned and nodded. "That's what we all called yore daughter when she first joined up as cook's helper. 'Course we all thought she was a feller too.

"I reckon all of us is pleased she's a gal." Rusty's grin became bigger and he added, "'Specially me."

Harold studied the young man before him and chuckled.

"Rusty, I think I like you. Let's go on up to the house, and the missus will fix us some dinner. You can tell me all about yourself and your family too. And how in Sam Hill is a Texas cowboy going to survive winter in up north?"

Larry looked up with concern when the two men came through the door. Rusty winked at her and her father smiled. She felt a huge surge of relief and hurried to help her mother prepare the meal.

Little Noah had scrubbed the wagon and even the manure smell was slight. Rusty swung the little boy up on his shoulders as he walked out of the house.

"Now that's a fine job, Noah. Why the boss 'ill be jist plumb pleased when he sees how clean that is." Rusty set the small boy on the ground and pulled off his bandana. He tied it around Noah's neck as he looked seriously at him.

"Ever' cowboy ought to have his own bandana. Now ya have yore ma wash that out fer ya, an' mebbie she'll let y'all wear it to the weddin'." He winked at Noah and kissed Larry's cheek before he climbed onto the wagon seat.

"I'll see y'all in two days." He pinched Larry's cheek and clucked to the horses. Rusty waved his hat at the four of them as he turned the wagon around.

"Two days till my weddin'. My ol' ma would be plumb happy."

Larry smiled happily at her mother. "Isn't Rusty wonderful? I think he's just wonderful." Larry's voice was soft and her mother smiled.

"Come, Laurel. Let's see what dress we can make fit over your stomach so you have something pretty to wear to your wedding."

CHAPTER 63

BIG PLANS

THE NEXT CAMP SITE HAD ALWAYS BEEN ONE OF GABE'S favorites. Hackberry Creek met Bluff Creek to form Horse Shoe Canyon. The grass and water were plentiful, and the canyon provided a natural corral to contain the cattle.

The herd was settling in for the evening when Rusty pulled up in the Cole wagon.

Gabe looked at the clean wagon and grinned.

"What kid did you get to clean that out, Rusty? Looks pretty good."

Rusty's eyes twinkled as he agreed. "I traded a good bandana an' a wagonload a baby calves fer that cleanin' job. Now I'm ready to take it to Dodge an' sell it fer some cash money." He winked at Gabe as he added, "Mebbie even $40."

Gabe shook his head and sat down by the fire. He wrote in his tally book each night so he could give Joseph an accurate accounting of the drive. His pencil paused a moment as he thought of Grace. Her pretty face was a little hazy in his mind now, and he didn't know if he was irritated by that or relieved. He scowled and pushed away his thoughts of her as he made his notations.

Mulberry Creek was north of them, so water wouldn't be a problem. He had checked it today and it was running. Gabe shook his head slightly. *We've had water all the way and good water most days. Hope that continues as we go north.*

His men were busy making plans. The four who planned to go into town the next day were doing their best to get out of nighthawk.

"Come on, Rusty. Ya been goofin' off all day. Y'all cin take my turn ridin' herd tonight. Why, I'll be too tuckered out to even hurrah the town much if I don't git some sleep tonight."

Rusty grinned at Bart. "Shore, Bart. I'll take yore turn tonight. You take mine Saturday *an'* Sunday as I'll be at my weddin'."

Gabe listened to their talk and smiled. He finally looked up and asked, "So when is the wedding, Rusty?"

"Day after tomorrow. That's May 3. We plan to git hitched at some little church there in Dodge at six in the evenin', an' all ya fellers who'll be in town cin come. There might even be some single gals there. Larry said she'd invite some a her girlfriends."

Bart snorted with disgust. "Well that's jist fine. Single women an' the only ones goin' in town Saturday are the boss who barely drinks *an'* avoids women, Linc who's gettin' married, an' Rusty who's goin' to his own weddin'. That leaves all the women to Dink. We been had, boys."

Angel chuckled and they looked over at him. "You forget about me, señors. I like the ladies very much and those kinds of numbers, I think you say odds—those are numbers I can work with. I thank you for your generosity, señors."

Rufe threw his cup at Angel who dodged it easily, and the talk turned back again to their trip to Dodge.

Gabe handed each of the four going to Dodge the next day $15.

"That is half of your pay so far, boys. You can leave tomorrow once we get the cattle moving up the trail unless the buyers show up early."

Tab was pulling his boots off when he looked up around the group of relaxed riders. "Say, did you fellers see that rock back yonder a piece that that Buffalo Bill carved his name in? Says 'Bill Cody 1861.'"

Rufe looked over at him. "Cain't be. What would Buffalo Bill been doin' in these here parts in '61? He was ridin' fer the Pony Express, an' those riders shore didn't come this way. Their route was way north a here, 'most clean outa Kansas."

Tab shrugged. "Mebbie he was runnin' from the Indians an' got hisself lost. Man could do that out here with no markers. Why he might never find his way back home."

The men all began to laugh, and Bart threw his boot at Tab.

"Tab, ya shut yore durn mouth. If y'all keep puttin' confusin' thoughts in my head at night, I'm a goin' to put snakes in yore boots ever' night till we git to Ogallala."

Tab frowned as he looked around at the men. "That were a true story," he muttered as he rolled up in his blanket.

Bart started to growl again, and Tobe laughed.

"I saw that rock on the last drive, so Tab ain't seein' things. Don't know what he was doin', but Buffalo Bill was here all right."

Angel listened to the men and then grinned.

"Or perhaps, amigos, *someone* carved this señor Cody's name into that rock. Perhaps he was never there—some vaquero just pretended he was."

The men stared at Angel, and Bart threw out his coffee in disgust. "Now that's jist a turrible thought, Angel. Why did ya have to go an' say that, right 'fore I go to bed?"

Angel's grin became bigger, and the men watched him suspiciously.

"Why, señors, I have done it myself. Sometimes, I write little love messages. I address them to whatever nombre—I think you say name—that comes to my head. I sign them with my name of course." His dark eyes were sparkling as he added, "And what vaqueros such as yourselves would not want to get a love message from such a woman? And with the name of Angel too!"

The men started at Angel in shock. They slowly lay back in their blankets. They were not talking but they were all thinking. Gabe had to work hard to keep his face straight and hold back his laugh.

Bart cursed to himself, and the men became quiet. All was silent for a time as the men lay back in their blankets.

Tab's voice came to them from the other side of the fire.

"If we go on up to Cheyenne, I'm a goin' to catch me some cats. Then I'll haul 'em up to Deadwood. Mebbie farther north. Cats is a sellin' prospect in them minin' towns."

Several of the men sat up to stare at him. Bart snorted but didn't move.

Tab sat up. He leaned forward excitedly and added, "I hear tell some a those cathouses is payin' good money fer a wagonload a cats. One a those Flyin' A riders told me there's a madam up north who's offerin' cash fer cats—$5 each, even up to $25 a head. Be a sight easier to haul cats than herd cattle." His eyes opened wide as he looked around at the sleepy men.

"Say, mebbie that's how those cathouses got their names!"

Bart came out of his blanket with a roar, and Tab raced for his horse carrying his boots.

Gabe was chuckling as he shoved his tally book into his pocket. He dropped down on his blankets and was almost instantly asleep. Grace's face floated through his mind again, waving as she rode away, and Gabe frowned in his sleep.

Bart was still muttering and calling Tab names, but Gabe didn't hear him. Finally, even Bart was quiet. The campfire burned low, and the men dreamed of what they would do in Dodge.

CHAPTER 64

Just a Few More Miles

BREAKFAST WAS EARLY AND THE MEN MOVED SLOWLY as they drug themselves to the chuckwagon.

"We'll push them a little today, boys. We can take a break around noon if we need to, but I want to make it to Mulberry Creek by tonight. That is the next water."

Tobe, Bart, Rufe, and Tab were waiting for their signal from Gabe. When he waved, they took off for Dodge like something was chasing them.

The grass was good, and the day's drive was easy. The cowboys let the herd rest for a few hours around noon but didn't stop for the night until nearly seven that evening. They camped on the north side of Mulberry Creek. The cattle had moved nearly fifteen miles that day. They were now fifteen miles from Dodge City.

"Nate, go ahead and pin those outlaw horses separately. The buyers will start showing up tomorrow and our remuda isn't for sale. Check their feet too. If we sell them, who knows how far they will go or when they will be shoed again."

Nate nodded and quickly began to sort the horses.

Tall Eagle stopped his horse beside Gabe. "Nate is a good wrangler. He has learned a lot on this drive. He will be a fine horseman."

Gabe nodded as he watched his brother. "Kind of hard to watch him though. It seems like he should still be small."

Tall Eagle laughed, "And we should be younger." Gabe grinned and the two men headed to supper.

Two buyers showed up at seven the next morning, and Gabe grinned as he watched them ride up. "That's a good sign. When the buyers are willing to come out before nine, that means the market is hot.

"Morning, fellows. Nice day for a ride."

It was a nice day. The sun was low in the east, dew was still on the grass, and the morning was cool.

The first man nodded, "Gabe. Good to see you. What do you have this year?" His eyes were already studying the cattle.

Gabe pointed towards the herd. "Anything you see with a Circle C or Swinging J is available. The Lazy HB has already been sold and will go on north."

Gallagher's Swinging J cattle were a mix of three- and four-year-old steers. All were carrying some meat. The buyer offered $20 per head and Gabe refused. He grinned at the man.

"I left Texas nearly a month ago, but prices have held or you wouldn't be out here this early. Besides, these are cattle from north Texas, and I am one of the first herds to reach Dodge this year. Better up that offer or these cattle will go to someone else."

The man hemmed and hawed around some, but eventually, Gabe was offered $36 per head for Gallagher's cattle.

"You said there were around two thousand head?"

Gabe nodded. "We lost a few on the way up here. Stampedes and a lightning strike but I don't think we are more than forty head short. When do you want them?"

"Bring them on in this evening if you can. We can load them on the nine o'clock train tomorrow morning. And just go ahead and fill that order on up to a full two thousand head."

Tall Eagle passed the word, and the men quickly began to sort the cattle. Tobe and his crew had ridden in ahead of the slower-moving buyers and soon had their new clothes dusty as they sorted and pushed cattle. There was little time to grumble though since the sorting required the attention of riders and horses.

Angel, Tall Eagle, Gabe, and Linc cut out cattle while Tobe, Rufe, Rusty, and Bart hazed them out to where Tab held them.

The buyer rode slowly around the herd. He held his horse to the outside as the cowboys worked. It was an impressive sight to watch that number of cattle sorted and moved in an open area. The buyer was always amazed at the riding skills and agility of the cowboys and their horses.

The second buyer was interested in horses. Gabe was surprised as they didn't have that many for sale. Usually when buyers rode out to a herd, they were looking for a hundred or more. He nodded at the horses Nate had sorted off.

"We have the brands written down on those horses and we need to verify them, but they are for sale."

Gabe waved at Rusty. "Dicker with Morris Johnson here. I have cattle to sort."

Johnson studied Rusty. He'd been at this business a long time, and he believed he knew how to get the best deal.

"How much are you asking?"

"$150 apiece."

The horse trader nearly choked.

"Why I can't make a profit on those. Besides, there are two in that bunch that have some scarring on their legs."

Rusty leaned an elbow on his saddle horn and chewed on a piece of grass as he studied the horse trader.

"Mister, eight a those hosses are Morgans, four are Appaloosa, two are Arabian-cross, an' ten be long-legged thoroughbreds. The last two hosses be Palominos an' the ladies do like those yeller hosses.

"Y'all an' me both know ya ain't buyin' no cow ponies. Nope. Y'all want hosses to sell to folks that want fancy ridin' hosses, not used up ponies that was rode by a bunch a cowboys."

As the horse trader looked at him in surprise, Rusty grinned.

"Those hosses was prize stock from some outlaws down in Oklahoma. Now outlaws don't ride no run-down cow ponies. No sir. They want fast hosses so's they cin outrun the law.

"Ya don't have to pay $150 fer hosses. There will be more comin' north…but there won't be many so fancy as these.

"Now ya go ahead an' tell me what ya *don't* want an' I'll cut it out, but the price is $150 firm."

Rusty threw the grass he was chewing on the ground and added seriously, "Or I'm a goin' into Dodge tomorrow an' I cin jist sell 'em my own self."

The horse trader stared at Rusty and shook his head. "Most cowboys aren't nearly as proud of their horses as you are," he muttered.

Rusty chuckled. "An' that's why the boss put me in charge a the dealin'. Now make up yore mind—I have cattle to sort."

Morris Johnson finally agreed. "I'll take all but that bay with the scarred-up legs. And I want them delivered to Dodge today. Have your wrangler clean them up. I have folks who want to look at them right away."

Rusty grinned and shook the man's hand. "It was a pleasure, Mr. Johnson, an' we look forward to doin' more hoss business with ya."

Nate watched quietly. After Johnson left, he commented. "Gabe thought we would get around $60 apiece out of them."

Rusty winked at him. "Pays to know yore stock when yore workin' with a buyer of any kind. Yore brother knows his horseflesh, but he ain't much on dickerin'. Now me, I like to dicker. Ya have to think it through."

Do ya want to sell worse than they want to buy or is it the other way 'round? Whoever wants to less is goin' to win.

"'Sides, these was the first buyers an' we're one a the first herds. Things is in our favor.

"Now ya git those hosses curried an' combed. Wash their legs down an' clean their hooves. We want Mr. Johnson to feel good 'bout this here deal. He'll make his money back an' he'll be lookin' fer us again to deal with."

The sorting went on all morning. By noon, Gallagher's cattle had been sorted out of the herd. They were short eighteen head, so Gabe added some of the Cole cattle to bring the number up to two thousand.

Horses were changed out, and two thousand head of cattle were pushed slowly toward Dodge. They would be allowed to graze along the way.

Cookie, Kirkham, Tobe, and Rusty stayed with the rest of the herd at Mulberry Creek. Gabe gave orders to the remaining cowboys as he left with the Dodge City herd.

"Try to keep them on the Mulberry until you run out of grass. Then let them graze north. There won't be much water between here and the Arkansas though, so you may need to make a dry camp tonight if you move. Whatever you do, don't cross the river. The land to the north is all settled and no cows are allowed.

"I'll stay in town to look for a buyer Cole's cattle. Most of the crew will be back as soon as we deliver the herd though.

"Nate, you and Tall Eagle can take those horses into Dodge. Tall Eagle knows where to cross and where to pen them. Then get on back here and keep on eye on the rest of the remuda."

Dodge City, Kansas
Friday, May 2, 1879

CHAPTER 65

JUST A FEW MISSING LETTERS

THE TALL COWBOY STRODE ALONGSIDE THE TRAIN AS he looked from his shipping ticket to the numbers on the cars. He as almost to the end when he found the car he wanted. He pulled the door open to his livestock car, and a large stallion snorted at him as it rolled its eyes.

"Easy, boy. They call you El Diablo and you are a beauty. Let's get you out of there and get you watered. It won't be long now before you are back on grass. Then you and your mares will be at your new home on our ranch in Wyoming Territory." The man ran his hand softly over the stallion's neck and the animal trembled.

The large stallion was black with a long mane and tail. The blaze of white on his forehead and two white front feet stood out against his glossy black coat. Arabian blood was obvious in the horse's size and conformation as well as in the proud way it held its head.

Rowdy Rankin talked soothingly to the horse as he led it out of the rail car. The northbound train had just arrived in the Dodge City station, and he wanted to get the animal unloaded quickly. He turned to walk down the street when he heard a quiet stirring behind him. He looked back with a frown on his face.

A beautiful young woman and a small girl stood in the doorway of the livestock car staring at him.

"Por favor, señor. Can you tell me what town this is?"

Rowdy stared at the young woman for a moment before he answered.

"Dodge City, ma'am. And what are you doing in there? They say this horse is unpredictable. You could have been killed!"

The woman took the small girl by the hand and smiled at him as she lifted the child down.

"Unpredictable? Perhaps. I believe horses are much like women. They like to be treated kindly and they don't take to a whip well."

The horse nickered softly and nuzzled the woman's arm as Rowdy watched in surprise.

"I was told this horse had one owner, and that señor Montero was the only one he trusted."

Lights flashed in the woman's eyes as smiled.

"That was mostly true, señor. Perhaps just a few missing letters in a name. I am señorita Montero. I raised this horse from a colt and broke him." A smile lit her face as she added, "You must be señor Rankin?"

Rowdy nodded and laughed.

"Señorita! It is nice to meet you, señorita Montero. Perhaps you will do me the honor of walking you to the Dodge House. It is not good for a woman or a small girl to walk alone on the south side of such a rough town although it is said that women are completely safe in Dodge City." He was still chuckling as he offered the young woman his arm.

The rail conductor came alongside the open door and began to pull it shut. When he saw hay in the small girl's hair, he pointed at her angrily.

"You can't be catchin' no ride on this here train. You two women, come with me."

Rowdy's blue eyes pierced the man as he growled, "This lady is my guest, and if you think she rode in that car with El Diablo here, then you go ahead and lead him back to where you need to go." He thrust the stallion's rope toward the conductor.

The horse snorted and reared as it pawed the air. As its front feet came down, it lunged at the conductor with an open mouth.

The man stepped back so quickly that he stumbled and nearly fell. He gave the horse a wide birth as he shut the door. He muttered angrily as he walked away.

"Darn cowboys. They think they own this town."

The woman looked up at Rowdy innocently as she commented, "Perhaps that wasn't completely true, señor."

Rowdy grinned at her, "It was mostly correct. Just a few extra words is all."

As the woman took his arm, he said, "My name is Rowdy Rankin. Tell me your names. And why in the world did you ride all the way from Texas in a livestock car?"

The woman laughed. "I am Merina and my little sister is Emilia. Our brothers are riders. Angel is bringing a herd up from Texas. Miguel left his riding job, and we are all meeting here."

She added softly, "Our employer died and there was nothing for us in Texas." She shrugged one shoulder. "One of the hombres who hung around señor Cole's ranchero thought I should go walking with him. I did not choose to so I left."

Merina looked away and then back at Rowdy. "Angel does not know that Emilia and I are coming to Dodge. He will not be so happy with me."

Rowdy was quiet for a moment as they walked.

"Where is the herd going? Maybe you could meet them there."

"No, señor. I do not think so. They go to Ogallala and maybe farther north. It would take much money to stay in a town for so long. And what would I do? I will try to persuade their patron to take me on as his horse wrangler."

Rowdy listened in surprise and then chuckled.

"Miss Merina, I believe that you would be very distracting on a cattle drive. I'm not sure that trail boss or any trail boss for that matter would be in favor of a beautiful young woman on his drive."

He frowned as he studied her face. "What happened to Charles Cole? I was to wire him the money for these horses when I took delivery in Dodge."

Merina's face became sad. "Señor Cole died in a stampede. He was a good man, but he did not know vacas. Angel told him that taking a herd to Kansas would be a difficult job, but señor Cole was a—a novato—a tenderfoot I think. He believed it would be easy and now he is dead."

Rowdy looked from the horse to Merina and scowled. "Then who do I pay for these animals?"

"There is no one to pay, señor. The caballos are yours for the taking. Señor Cole had no family. We worked for him, but he had no one. Now he is gone."

Her eyes sparkled as she looked up at Rowdy.

"I wrote up a bill of sale before I came so there would be no questions. I often signed for señor Cole, and I can write his name as he did." She pulled a paper from her pocket and handed it to Rowdy.

He stared at it and frowned again. "This isn't right. He surely has a brother or someone."

Merina shook her head. "There is no one. That is why we came to join our brothers. Your mares are on another train. They did not have room for all of them, and Diablo would not allow any other horses in his car. They were short on cars with all of the vacas going north, and there were no cars available for your ten mares."

"Did you break all of them?"

"Si. Señor Cole was to pay me when he returned from Dodge." She looked up at Rowdy, and for the first time, he saw fear in her eyes.

"Perhaps, señor, you could give me my fee. Señor Cole pays me $30 per horse. That would be $330."

Rowdy slowly shook his head and Merina's face blanched white before she looked away. She had always worked for Charles Cole with only a verbal agreement. With Cole dead, she had nothing and no way

340

to collect. She tried to hide her desperation as she straightened her back and squeezed Emilia's hand more tightly.

Rowdy grinned down at her. "No, I reckon if you are the one who broke them and Cole is dead, then those horses belong to you. I'll pay you what I was going to pay Cole. That was $400 for Diablo and $250 for each mare. I'll pay you $2900."

Merina stopped so suddenly that Rowdy almost tripped.

"Señor?"

Before he could answer, Merina heard someone call Rowdy's name. The cowboy led Merina and Diablo toward a small, wizened man with a big smile on his face.

"Badger, this is Merina Montero and her little sister, Emilia. Miss Montero, my friend and neighbor, Badger McCune.

"Merina and Emilia rode the cars up from Texas with Diablo here to meet their brothers. They are going on north with a herd to Ogallala."

Badger's blue eyes snapped as he shook Merina's hand, and she smiled at him.

"I am pleased to meet you, señor Badger."

The small man cocked his head as he studied her. "I reckon you'ins plan to go on north with the herd, Miss Merina. An' I'm a guessin' ya won't be a ridin' in the wagon."

Merina's eyes opened wide and sparkled as she laughed softly.

Rowdy laughed. He stopped Diablo in front of the Dodge House.

"Yes, it appears that señor Montero should have been señorita Montero." He grinned down at Merina. "Just a matter of some missing letters."

"Miss Montero, would you like to settle up now in the hotel or join Badger and me this evening for supper? I would like to pay you today since we will be leaving as soon as I collect my mares."

Merina hesitated as she looked at the two men. She pulled herself a little taller.

"Supper would be fine, señors. Please tell me what time and where you would like me to meet you."

Badger was watching her with his bright blue eyes. "Maybe you'ins should jist come on up ta Cheyenne an' take a job with me a workin' with my mules. I'm a gittin' ta be an ol' feller an' could use a little help now an' again."

Rowdy snorted, "Getting to be? You haven't aged a day since I met you almost ten years ago, and I thought you were old then." He smiled at Merina. "We'll meet you in the lobby in an hour."

Badger offered Merina his arm and led her quickly up the steps into the Dodge House. He stepped up to the counter.

"Now you'ins make sure these here little gals gits a good bath, an' treat 'im right. They's friends a Rowdy Rankin, an' that means they's friends a mine." He winked at Merina and bounced back down the steps. He spoke quickly to Rowdy and then headed to the hotel's saloon.

The hotel clerk smiled at Merina. "Friends of Mr. McCune get his special rate. Welcome to the Dodge House."

Merina's eyes opened wide in surprise, and she turned around to look at Badger's quickly departing back. *He doesn't look like someone important. He must be though to have a special rate.*

Rowdy watched them with a grin before he led Diablo to the watering trough. The horse drank deeply, and Rowdy talked softly to him.

"Diablo, I think you and I are going to be fine friends." The horse looked over its shoulder at him before it pushed its nose deep into the tank and blew.

Rowdy grinned and led the horse down to the livery. He put him in a stall, gave him grain, and began to brush him as he talked softly. Diablo looked back at the man working with him several times but calmed down and ate contentedly.

Rowdy strolled back up to the Dodge House and walked into the saloon. Badger was waiting for him, and the two men settled down at a table over beers.

Badger's wise eyes bored into Rowdy. "So what's the story with those two little gals. Long ways ta ride with a horse."

Rowdy frowned and nodded. "I think there was trouble when she left. Her employer died on the way up here with his herd. She put the horses on the train and left with them. She's a little spunky gal to do all that by herself."

Badger nodded his head. The two men drank their beer slowly and had a second. An hour later, they strolled into the lobby to meet Merina.

Merina looked up when the two men walked in. She almost smiled at the contrast. One was young, clean-cut, and tall while the other was short, quite old, and had a scruffy beard. Both had blue eyes that didn't miss a thing. Merina was thoughtful as she studied them. She had a feeling that both men could be quite dangerous if necessary.

CHAPTER 66

NEW FRIENDS

ROWDY OFFERED MERINA HIS ARM AND LED HER INTO the restaurant. Both the young woman and the child had dusky skin and black hair that gleamed when the light caught it. Merina wore hers twisted around her head, but Emilia's hung down her back. It was curly, and Merina had pulled it back from her sister's face with a ribbon. Both wore traditional Mexican blouses and full, bright-colored skirts. Merina's slender figure was not disguised by her loose clothing, and she turned the heads of many men when she walked into the dining area. She carried her head high and didn't make eye contact with any of the staring men as she walked between the crowded tables.

Rowdy shook his head. "One pretty gal is hard enough to get through this dining room but two of you is just downright difficult."

Merina was startled but smiled to herself. *Señor Rankin is a gentleman. He is kind to horses as well. Diablo will have a good home.*

Badger's bright eyes were snapping with internal secrets as he grinned at Merina and slipped Emilia some candy.

"So ya rode all the way up here in a livestock car, did ya? Long ride fer two little gals."

Merina's eyes were cool when she looked at Badger.

"We were not alone, señor. I have my knife."

Badger's blue eyes opened wide, and he laughed wickedly.

"Miss Merina, I think you'ins should jist mosey on up ta Cheyenne. I think ya'd be a good fit in our little town." His face became more somber. "So you'ins folks is gone? Rowdy said ya had a couple a brother's meetin' ya here."

Merina nodded. "Papá died before Emilia was born.

"He was pushing cattle across the Brazos in a flood. He made my two brothers learn to swim, but Papá was not so good. After he died, Mamá took in sewing. She also cooked for people to help us to get by.

"After he died, both Angel and Miguel took riding jobs with other ranchos. It was easier with our brothers sending money home even though it meant we were alone much. When señor Cole came, he hired my mother to be his cook and housekeeper. He offered me a job taking care of his books, but I also broke and rode all his horses." Merina's dark eyes sparkled.

"At first, he did not know. When he found out, he did not mind so much. Señor Cole did not think that a woman needed to stay in the house.

"Our little shack was not so nice, and the señor, he begged us to move in with him. He said he could be out earlier in the mornings if Mamá was there to cook his breakfast sooner.

"Señor Cole was a lonely man. I do not think he was so happy to be much alone. His house was large, and we had our own quarters." Merina lifted one shoulder in a shrug.

"He lived five miles from us, and it was easier for Mamá.

"When Mamá grew sick, señor Cole brought a doctor in, but it was no good. She died. I took over the cooking and cleaning of his house in addition to my other work." Merina looked down briefly before she added softly. "Señor Cole was like a father to me." She looked across at the two men, and tears sparkled in the corners of her eyes.

"Señor Cole was a kind man, but he should have stayed in his big city. He knew little about vacas or running a rancho.

"Angel tried to talk him out of going on the drive, but señor Cole, he showed us Dodge City on the map. He said, 'We just drive straight north. How hard can that be?' Angel went along because señor Cole was our friend, but it was a bad drive.

"He didn't want the men to use pistols, so he stacked them in the chuckwagon. When the banditos came, his men could not fight back."

Her dark eyes sparkled with pride as she added, "Angel did not put his guns away. He told señor Cole it was a mistake." She shrugged her shoulders again. "Angel lived and the other men died.

"Now señor Cole is dead, banditos took over his little rancho on the Brazos, his cattle herd belongs to another man, and Angel works for that man to bring the cattle here."

She looked at Rowdy and smiled. "I am glad you buy the horses. Now they have a kind master with a gentle hand. I did not want the banditos to take them."

Rowdy was quiet as he listened to her. Then he pushed a stack of greenbacks across the table. "There is $2900. And Badger is right. You come on up and see us any time…for anything."

His blue eyes were friendly, and Merina smiled back at both men. She stared at the money for a moment before she dropped it quickly into her bag. Her hands were shaking as she placed them back on the table. She had never seen that much cash money in her life, and she could barely breathe.

They visited more through the meal. When Emilia began to fall asleep, Merina excused herself. As she reached for her bag to pay, Rowdy waved his hand and shook his head.

"Nope, I invited you to supper. I will pay."

Merina hesitated but thanked the two men. She took Emilia's hand and walked quickly out of the restaurant.

Badger rubbed his whiskery face as he watched the Monteros leave. "I'm a thinkin' that little ol' gal would know how to use a toad sticker. I reckon she's had ta take care a her own self a mighty long time."

The Arkansas River
South of Dodge City, Kansas
Friday, May 2, 1879

CHAPTER 67

A NIGHT DRIVE

THE CATTLE ARRIVED AT THE ARKANSAS RIVER AROUND nine in the evening. The moon was shining brightly, and Gabe frowned as it cast silver ribbons of light across the water. The ribbons moved with the waves and glistened in the cattle's eyes. Some of those in front tried to turn around and Gabe muttered, "I might have to get Deacon Cox's milk cow to lead these cows across. If they break back, we won't get them across until daylight."

Angel looked at his boss in surprise, and Gabe grinned. "Cox has an old Jersey cow that he rents out to lead herds across the Arkansas. They take her to the south side across that bridge and she pilots the herd right back across."

The men crowded the cattle forward. Several large steers pushed through to the front of the herd and walked into the river to drink. As they wandered farther into the water, more cattle followed. Soon the entire herd was crossing the Arkansas. Several places were deep enough to swim, but the crossing was still an easy one.

The cowboys kept the back cattle bunched but let them work their way across. Linc pointed downriver. "Look there, boys. This river looks to be a mile wide in places."

Gabe followed Linc's arm with his eyes. "I sure am glad that someone before me figured out all these river crossings," he muttered to himself as the last of the cattle climbed up the bank and began to graze.

It was nearly ten-thirty that night when the cowboys finally penned the last of Gallagher's cattle in the corrals by the tracks.

Dink, Angel, and Linc turned their horses toward Front Street with its wide selection of saloons. As they rode away, Angel turned around in his saddle and waved at the four cowboys who remained with Gabe.

"So long, señors. I will dance with a señorita for each of you. And drink a little whiskey too!"

Bart, Rufe, Tobe, and Tab watched them go with mournful faces. Finally, Bart cleared his throat and casually commented, "Boss, ya know it shore is late to go back to the herd. Mebbie we should jist stay in town tonight. Awful dark to be ridin'—our horses could step in a hole or somethin'."

Gabe grinned at the men. "Now Bart, I've seen you ride fifty miles to go to a dance and ride back home when it was over! Nope, you get on back to the herd. You can have a nice moonlight ride. Just pretend these fellows are pretty gals."

He added more seriously, "You tell Tall Eagle to graze those cattle along the river. Graze them on that nice patch of grass we passed tonight just outside town. I would like to find a buyer for some of those Cole cows, so hold them for one day. I'll be out as soon as they are sold to help sort. Then Kirkham can start the rest for Ogallala."

The four men turned back south, away from the lights and music of a loud Dodge City. None of them spoke for the first several miles. Then Tab pointed at the moon. Clouds were gathering, and the moon was disappearing.

"I hope we cin find our way back. I'd sure hate to git lost out here at night."

Bart snorted and spurred his horse. The rest of the horses leaped to keep up with him as they rode swiftly back to the herd.

CHAPTER 68

QUEEN OF THE COWTOWNS

GABE STUDIED THE TOWN AS THEY RODE IN. DODGE City in 1879 was rough. While there were laws against carrying a gun, those laws were not enforced south of the railroad tracks. The railroad tracks were considered the "deadline." South of the deadline, the businesses catered to the wild cowboys with lots of rough saloons, fights, dance halls, and "soiled doves" to fill every man's taste. Gabe shook his head.

The saloons north of the deadline were considered respectable. There, gunplay and carrying weapons was discouraged. The saloons along the main drag or Front Street as it was called were even named and renamed to attract the throngs of cowboys moving the herds north from Texas. Names designed to draw the southern cowboys in were boldly displayed: the Alamo, the Nueces, the Lone Star, and the Long Branch were just a few. *Lots of places available to take a man's money,* Gabe thought dryly. "Those boys won't have a dime left when they get back to the herd tomorrow."

Gabe's night ride toward the north side of Dodge City took him by the wash area, and he was hoping to take a quick bath.

He gave the older woman who was cleaning up his best smile as he asked, "Any chance of getting a bath? I'd sure like to be clean when I sleep in a bed tonight. First bed in over a month."

She glared at him and Gabe's smile became larger. She finally growled and pointed at a tub in the corner. "Aye, since ye smile reminds me of me Liam's. Now don't ye be dilly dallyin' or I'll dump yer tub over and ye with it. I 'ave work yet to do an' an early morn on the morrow."

Gabe thanked her and asked cautiously, "If I pay double, can I sit for just a bit and enjoy it?"

The ruddy-faced woman stared at him and then chuckled. "Aye, go 'head. I guess the lassies should be glad ye want to clean up first 'fore ye go a courtin'. And ye keep that horse back. If he leaves any cac, I'll douse ya with cold water or my name tisn't Maggie Maloney."

When the tub was nearly full, Gabe stripped quickly and climbed in. He lathered up and dropped his shirt into the water to soak.

Maggie brought one last bucket of water. "And don't ye be a smokin'. I like my air clean at night, laddie."

Gabe smiled as he leaned back in the tub. He squeezed the water from his shirt and dropped it on the ground beside the tub. Maggie came by and grabbed the wet shirt along with his longhandles and his socks.

"Always there's work to be done. Still, I just won't walk by such a stinkin' pile of clothes an' do naught."

She brought back his wet clothes just as Gabe pulled on his britches and boots. She shoved the clean clothes into his hands with a grin. He handed her some money.

"Thank you, Maggie Maloney. And if I see your young Liam, I will tell him that his mother is an angel."

Maggie smiled softly and whispered to Gabe's back as he strode toward his horse, "Aye, but ye won't be seein' 'im any time soon, maybe. At least not on this side of eternity." Tears trickled down her red cheeks and she brushed at them roughly. "Me Liam was found in the river two years today." She blew her nose in her apron and wiped her eyes.

"He was not always such a good boy, but I loved 'im anyway. Aye, he was a cheeky one and I'm thinkin' that mouth of his did 'im in—that and the knife he liked to play with." Maggie shook her head. "Enough talkin' to myself. I'm knackered out now, and I still have me plenty of manky work to do before mornin'."

Maggie watched the cowboy talk to his horse before he mounted. She smiled as she dumped the tub and walked back to her laundry area. Even though she was tired, she wasn't looking forward to going home to a silent house.

Gabe tied the wet clothes behind his saddle. He shrugged into the dirty shirt he had tied there and mounted, his wet feet squishing in his boots. He was looking forward to a bed and a good night's sleep.

As he lay back on his bed in the Dodge House, he could hear a woman singing softly in the room next to him through the thin wall. Her song was in Spanish, and he smiled as he recognized some of the words to the old lullaby. 'Hush little baby, don't you cry...'

Gabe's smile was a little melancholy as he thought about his own mother. *She sang that to me when I was little and to Nate as well. I haven't thought of that song in years.* From time to time, a child's voice would interrupt, and then the woman would sing softly again. Gabe had intended to plan out the next day in his head, but he let the woman's soothing voice lull him to sleep.

CHAPTER 69

ANGEL'S LITTLE SISTERS

GABE AWOKE TO THE SOUND OF CRYING. THE LITTLE girl next door was unhappy about something, and she was letting it be known. He grinned to himself and climbed out of bed. He shaved, dressed quickly, and was soon headed down the stairs.

He was partway down when a door flew open behind him and a small girl rushed toward the stairs. Gabe lunged and caught her just as she started to tumble down the stairs.

He lifted back the mess of black curls and peered at the sorrowful face underneath.

"Well, what do we have under all this pretty hair? And why all the tears?"

The small girl's lips trembled as she responded, "Nina chases the rats in my hair. They don't want to be caught and they bite me."

Gabe tried to keep from grinning as he listened. He chuckled as a young woman lifted the child quickly from his arms.

"I am sorry, señor. My sister doesn't like to have her hair brushed." She set the child down and took her hand. "Come, Emilia, we must get ready. We need to find Angel today."

Gabe stared at the woman's departing back in surprise before he bounded up the stairs.

"Wait. Are you Merina? Are the two of you Angel Montero's sisters?"

The woman slowly turned around as she nodded.

Gabe's smile became large and he extended his hand. "My name is Gabe Hawkins. Angel rides for me."

Merina stared up at the tall man in front of her. *This American is very young to be a trail boss.*

Merina accepted his hand but quickly let it go. "I am Merina, and this is our little sister, Emilia."

Gabe stared at Merina as she spoke. Her hair hung in a long braid down her back, and her eyes sparkled with a secret humor just as Angel's did. She was small but carried herself proudly. He almost laughed when he thought of Angel calling her homely.

When Gabe realized that he was staring, he shook his head and grinned. "Begging your pardon, ma'am. Your resemblance to Angel is uncanny." His smile became bigger as he added, "You are much prettier though."

Merina was startled but her face showed little expression as she replied, "I think, señor, that you are quite charming."

It was Gabe's turn to be startled. He laughed and shook his head. "No one has told me that before. Usually, I'm told that I'm cranky. I don't know that I agree with you but thank you, Miss Merina."

He started to move down the stairs but turned back. "Would you ladies like to join us for breakfast? Angel will probably be in to eat before long." He paused as he frowned slightly. "Angel didn't tell me he was expecting you. He said Miguel would be here, but he didn't mention you or Emilia."

Merina shrugged and her dark eyes sparkled. "Perhaps because he does not know, señor. Si, we will join you as soon as I finish Emilia's hair."

She hurried her sister back into the room as she scolded her in Spanish. "Emilia, you cannot run out of the room like that. You would have fallen down the stairs had señor Hawkins not caught you."

Emilia was quiet. Before the door closed, she answered softly, "Can I sit by the big señor? He is a nice man."

When the two came down the stairs, Emilia's hair was in loose ringlets down her back, and a red ribbon kept her hair out of her face. Her eyes were red from crying and Gabe squatted down in front of her.

"My, you sure look pretty, Emilia. I like your hair better when I can see your face. Now if that face just had a smile." Gabe's blue eyes twinkled as he watched her, and the little girl slowly smiled. She reached up her small hand and Gabe took it in surprise. He offered his other arm to Merina.

"I just don't know that I have ever escorted two such pretty ladies to breakfast before."

Emilia smiled up at him and Merina took his arm without speaking. *Another smooth-talking gringo*, she thought to herself as she resisted the urge to roll her eyes.

CHAPTER 70

A Hagglin' Man

GABE'S HANDS WERE MEETING FOR BREAKFAST AT Beatty & Kelley's. The restaurant and Opera House Saloon were on the first floor along with a barber shop. The second floor held a theater and meeting hall. The locals were now calling it Kelley's Opera House.

He frowned as he guided Merina that direction. *There are going to be lots of rowdy cowboys in there this morning. Probably not the best place for a lady early on a Saturday.*

Angel waved as Gabe came through the door. He stood when he saw Merina.

Emilia tugged loose from Gabe and ran toward her brother squealing in Spanish, "Angel! Nina said you'd find us!"

Gabe approached with a grin as he led Merina forward.

"I met your sister, Angel. She is just as you described."

Angel looked from Gabe to Merina. He frowned and his words were abrupt as he spoke.

"How did you come to be here, Merina? You were to wait until I sent for you."

Merina tossed her head and replied in a torrent of Spanish, "One of the gringos from Buffalo Gap began to hang around señor Cole's ranch.

He would not leave when I asked him to go. One night, he tried to force his way into the house, and I pricked him with my knife." Her eyes glinted with a touch of a smile, "He did not get up." She shrugged and added, "I did not think the law would be so understanding, so Emilia and I rode north in the car with Diablo. Now here we are."

Angel stared at her and replied in Spanish. "But what will you do? You cannot go with the herd! Where will you stay?"

Merina's eyes flashed. "I can ride horses and trail cattle every bit as well as you. I will ask your patron to take me on. If he will not, Emilia and I will follow behind as you trail the herd north."

Gabe listened to the exchange between brother and sister and tried not to laugh. He had grown up in south Texas and many of his friends spoke Spanish. He was almost as fluent in Spanish as English although he rarely told anyone. His eyes glinted with humor and he chuckled. *Angel is right—Merina is very stubborn.*

He looked down at the little girl beside him. "Emilia, how would you like to have a piece of hard candy before breakfast? Let's go see if we can find you some while your sister and brother argue out whatever it is that they are discussing."

Emilia's eyes sparkled and Gabe lifted her up. Merina paused long enough to glare at him. Gabe winked at her and then worked his way between the busy tables to the door. He paused at the street to wait for the horses and wagons to cross. He stared when he saw Rusty driving a gleaming team of mules and a flashy wagon into town. Rusty winked at Gabe but made no motion to wave.

Gabe hid a grin. He crossed the street and only nodded at the cowboy as he walked by.

"Nice wagon and team. Selling them today?"

Rusty pulled his team to a stop in front of Wright, Beverley & Co. It was just one of the large mercantile houses in Dodge City. Rusty shook his head somberly in disagreement. "Naw. The boss told me to pick up supplies."

Cookie also had his wagon tied there. When he heard Rusty speak, he turned around with a frown on his face. He opened his mouth to yell at the ornery cowboy, but Gabe stepped in front of him.

Gabe pointed at the cantankerous cook and then at Emilia.

"Cookie, this is Angel's little sister, the one he was telling us about." He winked at Cookie and then smiled at Emilia.

"Say hello to Cookie, Emilia. He is the one who fixes all our meals. If you smile nice at him, he might stash some candy in his wagon."

Cookie tried to look around his trail boss, but Gabe shifted his feet. Cookie glared at him. Finally, he looked up at Emilia and a smile creased his old face.

"Howdy there, little missy. Now ain't ya a cute one. Kinda put that there brother a yores to shame."

Emilia smiled shyly and Gabe pointed toward the door of the mercantile. "Let's go over that list, Cookie. I want to add a few things to it."

Cookie growled as he followed his boss into the store. He looked over his shoulder one more time to glare at Rusty.

Rusty had climbed off the wagon and was working over the traces to the mules when a large man walked up.

He wore a white Stetson with a tall crown and a wide brim. The man nodded brusquely to Rusty as he looked the wagon over.

"How much for your wagon, cowboy?"

Rusty barely looked up as he fiddled with the traces.

"Ain't for sale. Just here pickin' up supplies to head on north."

"I'll give you $50 for the wagon."

Rusty looked up in shock. "$50? This here's a Studebaker, mister. Now that's the top a the line in wagons." He pointed toward the wagon as he talked, "Steel skeins and tire rivets, a rack bed with a raised seat and a chuck box as well. Why the boss paid near $300 fer this here wagon. 'Sides, she ain't fer sale."

The large man's eyes narrowed, and he pulled some bills out of his pocket. "I'll give you $250 and nothing more. I need a wagon and I need one now." He stared at the puncher whose pant leg was cut nearly up to this thigh. A small sapling was tied on each side of his leg as a splint.

"Take this money and buy your boss another wagon." He added, "And get yourself a new pair of britches while you're at it," as he pushed another $5 toward Rusty.

Rusty studied the money closely and finally nodded. He put the bills in his pocket and began to unhitch the mules.

The man's face turned red, and he jerked Rusty's shoulder to spin the smaller man around. "What are you doing with those mules?" he demanded. "I just bought your outfit."

Rusty's blue eyes were hard as he stared up at the larger man.

"Mister, ya bought the wagon. We didn't talk nothin' 'bout these here mules. If ya want the mules, two of 'em are $350 an' two would be enough to pull this here wagon. The harness will cost ya another $25. Now ya cin hitch hosses to yore chuckwagon but mules is more sure-footed an' cin stand harder drivin'. That's why they's more expensive than hosses or oxen."

Rusty pointed behind him at some broken-down horses.

"That feller would sell ya those glue bags fer $50 each, but they'll break down 'fore ya cross the first river. These here mules is five years old as y'all cin see by their teeth, an' if I sell ya two of 'em, I'll have to do some explainin' to my boss."

Rusty looked toward the door of the mercantile where Gabe stood watching and added, "Now he ain't a very understandin' feller so ya have to pay what they's worth."

The large man glared at Rusty for a moment and then cursed as he counted out more money. He paused his counting and asked, "If two is enough, why did your boss bring four mules north on that wagon?"

Rusty grinned at the man, "'Cause the boss ain't much of a mule man an' he figgered he needed four. Now if ya have some boys who know how to handle mules, why two is a plenty. If yore boys ain't much good, then ya might need four dependin' on what rivers ya'll be crossin'."

"Then I get my choice of mules."

Rusty nodded somberly, "I reckon ya shore cin do that…but I would take one from each side. See mules, they git used to workin' on one side or t'other."

The big man stared at Rusty and a slow smile crossed his face.

He drawled, "So if you were buying these mules, which ones would you buy?"

Rusty grinned at the man and pointed at the mules. "Suzie there, she likes to kick but she pulls the hardest if she likes ya. Belle's up front an' she's the quickest. Pete there, he likes Belle an' does what she tells him. Jasper back here on the right, he's the slowest but he's the most gentle. Now I won't tell a man what hoss or mule to buy jist like I won't tell 'im what gal to walk out with 'cause they all have their own good an' bad parts. But now ya know so's y'all cin decide yore own self."

The big man chuckled and counted out another $375. "Give me those two front mules.

"Young man, do you want a job? Bum leg or not, I think I would like to have you as a rider."

Rusty's grin became bigger as he pocketed the money and shook his head.

"Nope, I already have me a ridin' job headin' on north to Ogallala. Today is my weddin' day though an' I am goin' to buy me a new pair a britches." His grin remained on his face as he looked toward Gabe and then back at the man beside him. "An' I thank ya fer that $5."

Rusty unhitched Susie and Jasper. He moved Belle and Pete back before he looked at the man seriously. "Yore cook know anythin' 'bout mules? They's different from drivin' hosses."

The large man nodded. "My cook does. He is coming in on the train, and I wanted to get this rig bought to save us a little time." His eyes twinkled as he added somberly, "I'd hoped to pick up a solid wagon cheap. I just didn't know I would have to deal with such a shyster cow puncher."

Rusty grinned at him as he tied the two extra mules to the hitching rail. "I'm a hagglin' man, mister, an' that's why the boss sent me to town with this here wagon…to pick up supplies. I do thank ya though."

The happy cowboy tipped his hat at the man before he swung his bum leg up the steps and through the door of Wright, Beverley and Co. He winked at Gabe as he pushed by and hobbled over to the britches.

The large man stared at Rusty's departing back. He finally shook his head and frowned. He led the team down the street toward the livery as he muttered under his breath, pausing to look back several times.

Gabe strolled over to the britches and paused beside Rusty.

The red-haired cowboy pulled the $625 out of his pocket and handed it to Gabe with a grin.

Gabe stared from the money to Rusty and shook his head. "Remind me to never try to do business with you. I don't believe I have ever seen such a slick job in all my days."

Rusty laughed. "Well, Cole had him a Studebaker an' that's a fancy wagon. What do you want me to do with those other two mules?"

Gabe frowned as he looked out the door. He handed Rusty $100. "We are going to need a second wagon after all. Angel's sisters will be going north with us. With Larry, that is three women. We'll have Larry drive the second wagon." He had set Emilia down in front of of the candy. He lifted her up again. "Say hello to Rusty, Emilia. You'll get to know him better on the drive."

Rusty winked at the little girl and thought a moment. He looked up at Gabe. "Mebbie we should try an' buy Amos Winters' wagon. He is sellin' his herd in Dodge, ain't he? I saw 'im at the livery as I drove through town." His face looked overly innocent as he added, "We don't need the chuck box, but I cin probably sell that."

Gabe laughed as Rusty talked. His eyes twinkled as he shrugged. "I'll just leave that up to you. You have $100. I want a solid wagon, but it doesn't have to be fancy since we'll probably sell it in Ogallala. Whatever you have left after you buy it is yours to keep."

Rusty was quiet when he looked at Gabe. He started to respond, and Gabe waved as he spoke softly, "You earned it, Rusty. I would have sold that wagon for $50. Consider it a wedding gift." He handed Rusty $30 more, "And here are your wages for this part of the drive in case you need to buy anything else before your wedding.

"Now pay for those britches and meet us over at Beatty's for some breakfast."

CHAPTER 71

MERINA

ANGEL LOOKED DEFEATED AND MERINA'S DARK EYES were flashing when Gabe and Emilia arrived at their table.

Gabe looked from Angel to his sister and back again as he grinned at his friend.

"I take it you lost the argument?"

Angel looked at Gabe sorrowfully and shrugged. Merina touched Gabe's arm.

"Señor, I would like you to hire me on as a rider or as your wrangler. I can ride and shoot as well as either of my brothers."

Gabe looked down at Merina and held his face still to keep from laughing. Her eyes were bright with defiance as she waited for his answer.

"And if I say no?"

Merina tossed her head. "Then Emilia and I will follow the herd." Her dark eyes sparkled as she added softly, "Of course, Emilia will be lonesome for her nice gringo and will cry at night since she can't see her brothers."

Gabe stared at Merina and laughed out loud. He winked at Angel and the frustrated vaquero glared at his sister.

"This battle was won before it was ever fought," Gabe stated.

"Merina, I will make you wrangler and move Nate up to drover. Emilia can ride in the wagon with Larry during the day and the three of you women can use the second wagon as yours." Gabe's smile became larger as he added, "Rusty is already looking for a second wagon. I told him we would need one since there would be three women going with us."

Merina frowned at him. "You knew that I would want to go along?"

Gabe grinned at her. "Merina, I don't know much about women, but I know horses and cattle.

"When a cow makes up her mind to do something, you either have to rope her and tie her up or figure a way to let her think she won. The second way is better than arguing with her because that argument will be long and hard...and you rarely win."

Merina's dark eyes flashed, and she let go a torrent of words in Spanish at Gabe. She leaned back calmly in her seat and studied the menu.

Angel glared at Merina. He shook his head as he muttered.

Gabe grinned and Angel looked at his boss with irritation. "Si and this is why Merina will never marry. Always, I will have her in my house because she is a difficult woman."

Merina's eyes flashed and she was leaning forward in her chair to unload on Angel when the waitress arrived at their table.

"We are terribly busy this morning. The cook is only making griddle cakes, bacon, and sausage. You may have one egg if you'd like, but you get all the griddle cakes you want."

Gabe nodded at her. "That sounds fine. We'll need a couple more plates for some fellows who will be arriving. Bring us a pot of coffee and keep the griddle cakes coming."

Rusty arrived at their table. He grinned at Merina as he put out his hand.

"You must be Angel's sister. He described you to us." Rusty's blue eyes were sparkling with humor as Merina took his hand. He looked sideways at Angel and added, "Well, at least part of what you said was true."

Merina glared from Rusty to Angel, and Rusty laughed again as he sat down. He looked over at Gabe and his eyes became more serious.

"I talked to Amos in the mercantile. He said you can keep the wagon and the rest of the food stuff. He wants to pay you for helping him and he didn't want to mess with trying to get the wagon to town."

Gabe was quiet as he listened. He finally grinned at Rusty. "Well, I guess you had better find someone to buy some mules. We don't need four of them." He paused and frowned slightly before he added, "Think you have time to get that wagon in town before your wedding? Cookie will be over in a little bit, and we'll see what he wants to take out of it before you sell the chuck box.

"I need to talk to some buyers today about Cole's cattle. I'll have to prove my ownership first, and I want to get all that done quickly since Kirkham wants to leave as soon as possible.

"You hang onto Amos' wagon. You can take an extra day here if you want or head out on Sunday and take it slower. You should be able to catch the herd in several days even if you wait.

"I want to take some oats along. Throw six bags in before you leave, and I'll settle up at the livery before I head out." Gabe's frown became deeper. "I'm worried about feed on this next part of the drive. It sure isn't going to be like the Big Pasture down in the Territory."

Gabe looked over at Merina. "Emilia will have to ride with you or Cookie until Rusty catches up with the second wagon. I'm hoping to have Kirkham on the trail by tomorrow sometime." He cautiously cleared his throat before he added, "Do you need an advance on your wages to get an outfit? I don't think you want to wrangle in a dress."

Merina smiled sweetly as she looked up, but her eyes glittered as she replied, "I have money, señor. I will buy my own clothes."

Gabe almost shrank back in his chair. *I really don't understand women at all,* he thought as he gulped his hot coffee. He almost cursed when he burned his tongue. Rusty laughed out loud and Angel grinned while Gabe glared at both of them.

Cookie sat down just as the food arrived. He scowled at Rusty. "What was the deal with ya tryin' to pick up provisions? That's my job."

Rusty's blue eyes began to twinkle and Gabe laughed.

"Just part of his sales pitch, Cookie. He negotiated $275 for that wagon, and I would have sold it for $50."

Cookie studied Rusty for a moment and then grinned. "I'll remember that next time I need to haggle."

Rusty's smile became bigger, and the talking died down as the men ate.

Gabe spoke to Rusty between bites. "When you get back to the herd, tell Nate to bring in the rest of those horses that didn't sell. I think those left are mostly Cole's horses. Decide which mules you want to sell too."

Merina stood when Emilia finished, and the men all rose quickly. She looked at them in surprise. "I-I am going to take Emilia with me to get some riding clothes."

Gabe nodded. "You be ready to head out by tomorrow morning." He paused and added, "In fact, if you'd like, we can all go to Rusty's wedding this evening."

A tall man stopped by their table. "Well, Miss Merina, I see that you found your brother and his boss. I am headed back to Cheyenne on the afternoon train, but I sure hope to see you again."

Merina smiled and thanked him. She left quickly and the men sat down again. The stranger started to turn away. He hesitated as he looked back at Gabe.

"Did I hear you say that you are going to be selling some horses in Ogallala?"

Gabe nodded. "We are cutting a few out today, and the rest of the remuda will go north with us."

Rowdy turned around. "I am in the market for horses if they are good quality. Mind if I ride out and look them over?"

Gabe grinned and nodded. "Be my guest. You can deal with Rusty here. He is headed back out to the herd this morning. Don't keep him too long though. He has a wedding to get to this afternoon!"

The man put out his hand to Gabe just as a short man joined him. "I'm Rowdy Rankin. This is my neighbor and good friend, Badger McCune."

Gabe's eyes opened wide in surprise. He rose to his feet as he shook Rowdy's hand. He reached for Badger's and shook it too.

"Gabe Hawkins, and I believe I owe you a thank you, Mr. McCune. You seem to have opened some doors for me."

Badger studied the tall man standing in front of him and grinned as he nodded. "Mebbie we cin talk over dinner today? Say around eleven? Our train goes out at two this afternoon."

Gabe shook his head, "No, I am hoping to sell some cattle this morning. I could meet you at noon though. Twelve at the Dodge House?"

Badger nodded. Rusty shoved in another bite before he joined the two men. As they entered the livery, Badger commented to Rusty, "I hear ya sold a Studebaker wagon. The feller what bought it thinks he's a sharp one. He were kinda quiet on that there deal so I'm a thinkin' he ain't quite so good as he thought."

Rusty's blue eyes twinkled, but his face was innocent as he shrugged. "It was a fancy wagon an' brought a fancy price. Now I jist need to sell a couple a mules."

Badger grinned at him, and the three men turned their mounts south to find the herd.

Merina watched the men ride out of town. *I am so tired of being penned up in a hotel. I can hardly wait to be on horseback again.* She frowned slightly before she led Emilia into the dry goods store.

CHAPTER 72

COLE'S CATTLE

MORE CATTLE BUYERS WERE ARRIVING IN TOWN EVERY day, and Gabe was anxious to get his claim to Charles Cole's cattle cleared. He caught the new sheriff, Bat Masterson, as the man was walking down the street and followed him to the jail. Gabe explained what had happened and then handed him Cole's last will.

"I have some buyers who want to look this herd over, but they want to make sure that my ownership claim is clean."

Masterson read the scrawled will and looked hard at Gabe. "Any witnesses who can verify this?"

Gabe's neck turned red as he stared back at the man.

"One of Cole's riders as well as one of mine were there at the time. The rest of my riders were holding our cattle. They were stampeded when Cole's cattle ran through them."

Masterson nodded. "I will ride out and look the herd over, but it won't be today."

Gabe's neck turned a darker red. "Sheriff, part of that herd needs to move on north and I need to complete this sale today. I can't hold those cattle another day. Other herds are piling up behind me and I worked hard to be one of the first herds up the trail. If you need to look things over, I would like you to do it this morning so I can finalize my sale this afternoon."

Masterson stared at Gabe with his cold eyes. He was just about to speak when Marshal Deger stepped through the door. His face lit up when he saw Gabe.

"Hello there, Preacher!"

Marshal Deger stared from Gabe to Masterson. He could feel the tension between the two men. Then noticed the paper that Gabe held.

"That Cole's last will? I heard from John Kirkham that he had been killed by some outlaws and left you his herd. Need me to verify that will for you?"

Masterson looked from one to the other and then shrugged. "Work it out with Deger," and he walked out the door.

Marshal Deger grinned. "Don't pay any attention to Masterson. He isn't getting enough sleep. Besides, he is still trying to get to know everyone. Lucky for all of us, I don't need much sleep and know most everyone in my town." He took the paper from Gabe's hand. "I can vouch for you." The marshal scribbled his name on the bottom of the will and wrote "Verified" above it.

"I haven't seen many of your riders. You headed on north?"

Gabe nodded. "I want to sell Cole's Circle C cattle here. There should be around eight hundred, maybe a few more. They are a mixed herd. The rest of my herd will go on north to Ogallala."

Deger nodded. "You know, you should talk to Chalk Beeson. He is increasing his herd and might be interested in some of those cows that are ready to calve. The pairs too. He usually takes his dinner in the Dodge House on Saturday's so you might be able to catch him there. John Mueller and Herman Fringer are buying too, so you shouldn't have any trouble selling. In fact, I will be seeing Mueller and Fringer in an hour or so. I will see if either is interested."

Gabe shook the marshal's hand and thanked him. He stopped in the doorway and looked down the street. He saw Chalk Beeson walking towards Front Street and strode toward him. Both men were grinning as they met.

"Good to see you, Gabe! I hear there's a wedding today. You aren't getting married, are you? I'd sure come down and sing you a song if you are!"

Gabe's grin became bigger. "Not me, but one of my hands is. Come on down and sing him a song if you want but keep it proper. He is still trying to impress the new in-laws."

Chalk laughed and Gabe's face became more serious.

"I hear you are buying cows. I have about eight hundred head of mixed cattle I am going to be selling today if you are interested."

Chalk studied Gabe's face and slowly nodded. "I am if they are from northern Texas. I don't want any from the southern part. I don't need any tick fever in my herd."

"These are all from north of the Brazos. Fellow by the name of Charles Cole trailed them partway. He was killed by outlaws in the Territory, and I brought them on up.

"Some have already calved, but there are quite a few springing. They should calve soon. We were dropping a few calves all the way up here, and now they are getting down to business. I am going to talk to Mueller and Fringer too. Since I saw you first, you get first chance."

Chalk turned toward Gabe.

"Let's just go look at them now. I need about five hundred head. We are going to run them along Sand Creek, so they wouldn't be too far to drive either. You are probably on the Mulberry?"

Gabe nodded and the two men visited more as they headed for the livery. They weren't too far south of Dodge when they met Nate and Tall Eagle. The two were driving eleven horses. Nate's eyes were shining with excitement. Gabe stopped his horse when Nate rode up.

"Tall Eagle sorted off this eleven head. Mr. Rankin is interested in the rest when you get to Ogallala. He said he will talk to you at the Dodge House at noon today."

Gabe smiled. He was always relieved when the buyers started lining up. "Nate, this is Chalk Beeson. We have known each other for quite some time. Chalk, this is my brother, Nate."

Chalk grinned as he looked at the two brothers. "He is a younger, happier version of you, Gabe. Hope he's not as ugly when he grows up."

Gabe chuckled and waved his hand toward Nate. "Take the horses on in and I'll see you in an hour or so. You can pick out some new clothes at Wright, Beverley & Co. You stay with Tall Eagle until I get back in town, and then we'll take a bath."

Nate nodded and galloped away to follow the horses. Tall Eagle waved at Gabe, and the horses splashed into the water of the Arkansas.

Chalk bought five hundred fifty head at $35 per head. Three hundred ninety-two were carrying calves and the other one hundred fifty-eight had calves by their side.

"I'll ride out to my place and send five of my hands back to move these cattle. I can meet you in town around eleven to settle up. Let's meet at the Long Branch."

The cowboys were soon busy sorting, and Gabe rode slowly toward the rest of the herd.

CHAPTER 73

A Stubborn Woman

GABE PULLED HIS HORSE TO A STOP AND STUDIED THE remaining cattle. They were strung out for nearly a mile. There were over fifteen hundred head of cattle, and they ate a lot of grass. The thick graze was disappearing. Gabe rode through the remaining cattle and studied the animals as he counted them.

John Kirkham joined him. "The cattle look good, Gabe. We've grazed this down though and I'd sure like to get on up the trail."

Gabe nodded. "Let's plan to move them out tomorrow morning. If I don't sell those last two hundred fifty head of cows, I can always move them in Ogallala.

"I hope to see Cookie before you leave. If I don't, you tell him where to go." Gabe frowned and then added, "Point out the route you will be taking, and I will catch you tomorrow some time."

The two men visited a while before Gabe headed back into Dodge. Finalizing the drive was almost more stressful to him than the drive itself. He muttered to himself, "I'll talk to Chalk about who handles money. There isn't a bank in town yet, but so much money changes hands here that there has to be a way to get Gallagher's money to him." Gabe heard a wagon behind him, and Rusty grinned as he pulled up beside his boss.

"Need some help sellin' those hosses?" Rusty nodded toward the corral where Tall Eagle and Nate had penned the eleven horses they brought in.

"I seen some fellers gathered 'round the corral lookin' at 'em."

Gabe's eyes twinkled and he laughed. "You just take care of that, Rusty. I am going to leave the selling of everything but the cows to you from now on."

Both men turned when they heard a loud commotion coming from the direction of the corral. The gate flew open and a horse charged through the opening. Nate was able to slam the gate before the other horses followed, but the loose horse raced around the corrals and headed north toward Dodge.

Gabe cursed under his breath and spurred Buck toward the Arkansas River. The running horse suddenly slowed down and began to nicker as it trotted toward Front Street. A woman walked toward the animal and reached out her hand. The horse pushed its nose into her shoulder and face as it nickered softly.

Buck climbed up on the riverbank and Gabe guided him toward the loose horse. "My apologies, ma'am." He started to explain when he recognized Merina.

"Merina! You could have been hurt!"

The young woman laughed softly. "Not by Mascota. He is a big pet. Señor Cole rode him when he left for the drive. He was the first horse I raised from a colt, and he has always been a baby. He didn't want to leave me when they headed north. He must have smelled me. Otherwise, he would never have broken loose."

She smiled up at Gabe. "Perhaps my patron will let me buy this horse?"

Gabe locked his hands around the saddle horn and stared down at the small woman. Her eyes were sparkling, and again he noticed how many mannerisms she had the same as Angel.

He chuckled and shook his head. "No, you don't have to buy him. We will add him to the remuda," Emilia was peeking out from behind her sister and smiling. Gabe winked at her and asked, "How about Emilia? Do we need a short horse for her? She surely doesn't ride a full-sized one, does she?"

Merina was quiet as she studied her sister. "She can, but I don't want her on that big of a horse every day. There are several ponies in the livery. I will talk to the hostler about purchasing one."

Gabe nodded and then pointed toward the wagon that was just pulling out of the river. "Talk to Rusty. We ended up with several extra rigs, and I don't think he sold them yet. You can pick a saddle and bridle for you and one for Emilia if any of them will work for her. Otherwise, you'll need that as well. Just put it on my tab at the livery and I will settle up in the morning before I leave."

Merina pulled herself straighter, and her eyes glistened as she looked up at Gabe. "I will buy my own horse, señor, and that of my sister as well. I do not accept favors from men."

Gabe stared at her and then grinned. "It is not a favor. You are an employee and that means until we get to Ogallala, like it or not, you get to take orders from me.

"My riders don't have to buy their own horses. They ride horses from the remuda, and we sell them when we are done." He gestured toward the livery as he added, "Ham Bell will set you up."

Merina looked away. When she looked back, her face was tight, and something that looked like tears were glistening in the corners of her eyes. She held herself very straight and spoke softly, "Señor, I would like to buy Mascota because I don't want you to sell him at the end of the drive. He is my amigo—my—I think you say—friend."

Gabe stared at the determined young woman and his grin faded. *Angel is right. Merina is very stubborn.* Still, Mascota was not his horse. It was Cole's, and Merina had more right to it than anyone.

"I reckon we can work something out," he growled. "Meet me at the Dodge House at noon and I will have a bill of sale for you." He was frowning as he rode away, and he resisted the urge to look back at her.

Merina watched Gabe ride away. She tossed her head and almost snorted. She turned to Emilia.

"Come, Emilia, you may ride Mascota." She lifted her sister onto the horse's back. Mascota followed her as she walked north past Front Street and to Ham Bell's livery stable. She muttered to herself in Spanish as she walked. "That big gringo is a difficult man. He thinks he can run everything…but he will not run me, even if he is my patron."

CHAPTER 74

FREE STEAK!

ABE FOUND NATE WITH TALL EAGLE. THE THREE OF them took a quick bath and were back in the Long Branch by eleven.

Chalk arrived just as they sat down, and the two men settled up quickly. Gabe ordered beers for the three of them and a root beer for Nate. As they visited, Chalk slapped his leg.

"Say, there is a fellow in town looking for you. Said to tell you his name was Cappy."

Gabe looked surprised but nodded. "I heard he might be headed this way. He owns a livery up in Manhattan but was thinking about making a change. He is sure I will be relocating up north and said he might join me."

Chalk studied the younger man and slowly nodded. "I've heard there is some fine cow country up in Nebraska. Farther north in Wyoming and Montana Territories too.

"I have never been there myself. There are lots of freighters through here though, and some of them are familiar with that country." Chalk frowned as he added, "Too many folks moving in here. Most of the land north of Dodge has already seen a plow. Those sodbusters tear up the grass and plant all kinds of crops. I hate to see land torn up. They will be the end of the cattleman, and that is for sure."

Gabe laughed. "It is all perspective, Chalk. You need to look at those settlers as opportunities and clients instead of interlopers. The farmers raise products you don't, and they have lots of kids. Shoot, in five or ten years, you won't have to leave Dodge to put hands together. You'll have young men knocking on your door just looking for a job. Besides, they are north of Dodge. You have the better grass south of town."

Chalk visited a while longer. As he was leaving, Rusty strolled in. His blue eyes were sparkling, and his walk was cocky as he sauntered back to their table.

Gabe looked at him and grinned. "Chuck box sold?"

Rusty's face was overly innocent as he nodded somberly. "Met a feller in town a while ago with a busted-up wagon. He rolled it durin' a stampede. The wagon was fixable, but the chuck box was gone." He grinned at Nate and winked as he added, "I felt compelled to help 'im out.

"Sold those hosses too. I saw Angel's sister leadin' the one that got loose up to the livery. I figgered that one warn't fer sale, so I didn't mention it. Same feller with the busted chuck box needed more hosses fer his remuda. Since they was all there an' handy-like, he bought 'em." Rusty pushed the money across the table to Gabe. "$50 each fer the ten hosses an' $40 fer the chuck box."

Gabe looked at the ornery puncher and shook his head. He laughed as he looked at the group around the table. "Boys, if you need to sell something, talk to Rusty here—just don't buy anything from him or I guarantee you will pay too much!" He stood and pointed toward the Dodge House.

"If you fellers want a steak dinner today, meet me at the Dodge House at noon. I am going to go find Cappy and see if he is headed north with us. Kirkham is starting the herd north tomorrow morning.

"Tall Eagle, I'd like you to let the rest of the riders know I'm buying steak today. I want them sober too if they are planning to go to Rusty's wedding." He grinned at Rusty and added, "Rusty will meet up with us on the trail in a day or two with his new bride."

Gabe started for the door. "Nate, you can come with me or stay with Tall Eagle. I trust him to keep you out of trouble."

Nate stood. "I think I would like to come with you," and he hurried to follow his brother out of the Long Branch.

"Who is Cappy? I don't think I have ever met him, have I?"

Gabe shook his head, "No, Cappy is an old friend. I hadn't seen him in quite a while until I met up with him in Manhattan last month. He is the one who bankrolled me for our cattle on this drive." He grinned down at his younger brother. "And I have enough already to repay him.

"Cappy is a rascal of a man, but his heart is big. A good fellow to have on your side wherever you go." Gabe checked his pocket watch and frowned.

"Nate, go over to the Dodge house. Find Merina and her little sister. They are eating dinner with us, and I don't want them waiting around in the hotel lobby. Lots of rough men around town right now. You go on into the restaurant and get a big table as soon as she comes down. I'll find Cappy and join you as soon as I can."

Nate nodded and walked quickly toward the Dodge House. The streets were full of dusty cowboys and cattle buyers of all types. He could feel the excitement and energy of the town, and he was proud to be part of it.

A young woman and a small girl came down the stairs as Nate walked through the door. The woman's eyes were searching the busy lobby. They rested on him for a moment before she continued to scan the room. Nate pushed through the crowd until he was in front of her.

"Miss Merina? I'm Nate Hawkins. Gabe asked me to escort you to a table in the restaurant. He said he will join us as soon as he can."

Merina smiled at the young man. *Nate is a younger, sweeter version of his grumpy brother.* She took the arm he offered and let him lead her into the busy restaurant.

A waitress met them. When Nate told her his name, she nodded.

"Please come this way, Mr. Hawkins. Mr. McCune said you would be along, and he is waiting for you."

Nate looked at the woman in surprise. She was already walking away. He followed her to a private room in the back of the restaurant.

A small old man with bright blue eyes stood as they walked in. He bowed deeply to Merina and pulled out a chair for her.

"Go ahead an' sit yerself down, missy. That cranky cowpoke 'ill be along shortly." His sharp eyes settled on Nate. "You'ins must be the younger brother. You's a shorter copy a yore brother, but ya look like ya smile more." Badger put out his hand.

"Badger McCune. Pleased ta meet ya. This here tall feller is Rowdy Rankin. He used to be 'most as grumpy as ol' Gabe. Now that he has 'im a happy wife ta home, he smiles a little more."

Rowdy grinned and shook Nate's hand. He tipped his hat to Merina. "Miss Merina and Emilia, good to see both of you. Our train leaves this afternoon, but Badger wanted to visit with Gabe some before we left." He sat down beside Emilia and smiled at her. "You sure do look pretty today, Emilia. Are you hungry?"

Before long, Angel and a young man who looked a lot like him sauntered through the door. They were followed by Dink. Emilia squealed and almost tipped her chair over as she rushed to greet her brothers. The younger one scooped her up with a huge smile and swung her around.

"Hello, Emmie. I guess you missed me," he whispered to her. She nodded excitedly and squeezed his neck. Miguel laughed again and kissed his little sister. He walked around the table and put an arm around Merina. "Hello, Nina." He kissed her cheek, He tried to untangle Emilia's arms, but the little girl refused to let go. She hugged his neck so tightly that he could barely see around her.

Angel laughed as he looked at the full table. "I am Angel. This is my brother, Miguel, and my sisters, Emilia and Merina." He looked around the table in surprise.

"Señor Gabe is not here?" Angel was surprised.

Linc wandered in about five minutes later.

"I heard this was the place to come for a free steak!" Linc shook hands and introductions were quickly made. Gabe was rarely late for anything, and his friends kept an eye on the door as everyone visited.

CHAPTER 75

BADGER'S OFFER

GABE FINALLY ARRIVED. HE WAS FOLLOWED BY AN OLD man. He looked around the room in surprise. "I guess when I offer a free steak, you boys don't waste any time showing up.

"And how did we get this room? I asked earlier but was told it was already taken."

Badger grinned at him and winked. "Ya never want ta leave nothin' ta chance, boy. I reserved this here room yesterday. Now come on over here an' sit down so's we'uns cin eat. Rowdy here eats 'nough fer three already, an' if'n we go much longer, it'll be fer four." He pointed at the chair across from him.

Gabe sat down with Cappy on one side and Nate on the other. Rusty and Tall Eagle soon joined them. The room was full and loud as everyone found a chair.

Merina studied Gabe's face. He seemed quieter than he had been earlier that morning. He was busy then, but now he almost seemed a little sad. He looked up, and she was surprised at the pain she saw in his eyes before he looked away. The pain was hidden when his eyes met hers again, and she looked down.

Large plates of food arrived, and the table became quieter as the men ate. Emilia chattered to her brothers and smiled often at Gabe.

"Are we all going on the cattle drive? Nina bought me a horse so I can ride too. And she is going to ride Mascota. He broke out of a pen and found her. Now Nina is happy again."

Gabe smiled at the little girl and slid a paper across the table. "You give this to Nina. It says that Mascota is her horse now."

Emilia's eyes were large as she handed the paper to her sister. "Señor Gabe says Mascota is your horse. Now you can ride him whenever you want!"

Merina smiled at her sister and then at Gabe. "Thank you, señor. It is good to have him back."

Rowdy and Gabe talked horses and settled on a price. They agreed the horses would be delivered to Cheyenne at the end of the drive.

"Shoot me a wire when you reach Ogallala. I can have payment sent there once I hear from you and know the number you ended the drive with. Let me know what train they are on, and I'll make sure to have a rider in town to pick them up."

Rowdy's grin was friendly as he added, "Of course, if you come on up to Cheyenne, we can take of our business in person."

Gabe laughed and the two men visited more as they ate.

Linc was the first to leave. He was headed back to Texas in an hour and had some last-minute details to take care of. Gabe stood and handed him a packet of money before the two men shook hands. Gabe gripped Linc's shoulder

"Best of wishes with the new wife and your ranch. I hope to hear about some little ones someday."

His foreman grinned and nodded. He shook hands with his friends and headed out the door. He knew he wouldn't see many of the men in that room again, and it made him a little sad.

"Life just keeps moving and changing. Gabe is headed north tomorrow, and I may never see him again either. It's a long way from south Texas to the north country if he decides to settle up there."

Linc patted his pocket where his money was. He could tell that Gabe had given him a nice bonus. "Gabe is a good man and a fair one."

Tall Eagle followed Linc out the door. His eyes glinted when Linc look at him in surprise.

"Too many people in there. I prefer livestock. I am headed back out to the herd." The two men shook hands again and strode in opposite directions.

Angel offered to take Nate down to get a bath, but Nate shook his head.

"I just took one this morning. Besides, I'd rather go fishing than go to a wedding." He caught Rusty's eye and turned a dark red. "Sorry, Rusty. I didn't mean—"

Rusty grinned at the young man. "Me too if it warn't my own. I do need a bath to be all clean fer my bride though." He winked at Nate and followed Angel out of the room. He stopped at the door, "Thanks fer the steak, boss. Hope to have lots more of those when ya git to be a cattle baron!" Rusty looked around the table and his eyes settled on Dink.

"Ya jist as well come too, Dink. I know y'all cin use a bath an' I sure don't want to be smellin' ya tonight."

Dink looked up in surprise. He scowled as he followed Rusty. He was muttering about baths being overrated as he followed his friends out the door. Cappy grinned and looked over at Nate.

"Nate, I'm a fishin' man myself, an' I would sure like to try that river. Want to come with me? I rustled up a few poles an' ol' Ham is holdin' onto 'em down to the livery."

Nate nodded excitedly, and Gabe laughed as he agreed. "Be back here by five so we can change and head out for the wedding. I don't want to be late."

Emilia looked up at Merina hopefully, "Can we go fishing, Nina?"

Cappy winked at the little girl. "Come along. If ya don't catch any fish, at least ya cin git all muddy."

Merina studied her little sister's face and laughed. "Si, you can go, but we are going to change. I won't have you getting your vestido all dirty."

Rowdy stood. "I'll walk down to the livery with you. I need to get my horses watered and ready to load." He turned to Gabe and put out his hand. "Gabe, it was nice to meet you. Stop in if you make it up to Cheyenne."

Gabe stood as the men left and he gripped Rowdy's hand. "I'll do that. I'd like to see that country."

He sat down and glanced around at the nearly empty room. Badger and he were the only ones left, and the room was quiet.

"Badger, I haven't thanked you properly for recommending me to Gallagher."

The old man chuckled and waved his hands. "No need fer that, boy. I come down with Rowdy 'cause I wanted ta talk with ya. See, ya did my Martha a good turn an' I figger I owe ya."

Gabe's neck turned red and he shook his head. "Your wife is a fine woman, and I just won't tolerate rudeness. I didn't do anything special though—most fellows in that situation would have done the same thing."

Badger nodded his head and leaned toward Gabe. "I been a checkin' ya out, boy. I'm always a lookin' fer men what has character. I like what I see in front a me as well as what I heard.

"How'd ya like ta come on up ta Cheyenne an' buy my little ranch? My Martha wants ta spend the winters in town, an' we been a thinkin' on sellin'. I'm a particular feller though, so I won't sell ta jist any ol' boy. They has ta be the kind a feller I want 'round my fam'ly."

Gabe stared at the small man in front of him in surprise. His neck once again turned red.

"Badger, I'm honored that you would offer me your place, but I'm not in the position to buy. This was my first drive with my own cattle, and Cappy bankrolled me. I will have a little nest egg when I'm done.

In fact, I'll have more money than I've ever had. It still won't be enough to buy a place and stock it though."

Badger's bright blue eyes were serious. "Gabe, I'm offerin' it ta ya. Ya don't have ta have all the money up front. Ya cin buy 'er from me a little at a time. I have six thousand acres mostly in one piece. I'll sell it fer $7 an acre. The water's good an' ya cin buy my mules too if'n ya want. 'Course, Rowdy likes mules an' I know he'd buy 'em up fast too.

"I been talkin' this here idea over with my Martha, an' we done decided that we'd like ya ta have our place.

"Rowdy's brother, Lance, 'ill be yore closest neighbor, an' you'ins 'ill be 'bout twenty miles south a Cheyenne. There's goin' ta be more land comin' up fer sale close to ya in the next year or so if yore a buyin' feller." His eyes glinted as he grinned, "'Course, you'ins 'ill have ta bid against Lance. He wants ta own the whole durn country."

Gabe stared across the table at the man in front of him. He had no idea how old Badger was, but he was guessing the little man was older than he looked. He seemed to know people everywhere. Gabe was overcome with emotion. He cleared his throat and ducked his head.

Badger had looked away. He turned his eyes on Gabe once again when the younger man looked up.

"Gabe, they's lotsa good men out there an' I cain't help ever' one. But I cin give you'ins a leg up. Now Dan Waggoner's a good friend a mine, an' we had us some talks 'bout you'ins. He wired me 'bout what ya did fer 'im 'fore you'ins left on this here drive. That's the kind a men we need ta build this here country with.

"Now ya come on up ta Wyomin' an' see me when this drive's over. Rowdy wants ta buy yore horses anyhow. Ya jist as well finalize that there deal in person. I know my Martha would like ta see ya again too. Shoot, we'll jist have us a fam'ly gatherin' so's you'ins cin meet the whole clan."

Badger stood and put out his hand. "I have a train ta catch, but I hope you'ins 'ill take me up on my offer. 'Course, if'n ya don't show up or write me in a couple a months, I'll know ya ain't comin'."

Gabe was quiet as he stood. He wasn't used to people helping him. He was always the one who helped other people, and it was a new experience for him. He gripped Badger's hand.

"That is a fine offer, Badger. I will see you in a few months and we'll talk more. I'm honored you would offer me your ranch. I'll do what I can to make that deal happen."

Badger winked at Gabe and rushed out of the room. He did a little jig as he reached the door and bounded down the steps of the hotel. He rushed to the livery to see if Rowdy needed any help, and the two men were soon headed south with Rowdy's horses.

Gabe paid his bill. He hesitated before he walked outside. *I need to clear my head.* He walked slowly up the stairs to his room and sat down on the bed. He lifted the packet of letters Cappy had given him from his vest pocket, but he couldn't bring himself to open them. He dropped them on the floor, lay back on the bed, and drifted off to sleep.

Grace's face was sad as she waved at him and rode away. He tried to follow her. She stopped and turned around in her saddle. Her face slowly changed until she was glowing with excitement. She smiled as she spurred her horse and raced away. He called to her, but she didn't turn around. Gabe awoke with a start and a heavy sadness overcame him.

Cappy hadn't said much when he handed Gabe the letters. His face was sad though, and his eyes were red. Gabe didn't want to read the letters around people. *I'll just go for a ride. Buck is the best listener that I know. I will read them and talk things over with him.* He rose and walked down to the livery. It was three in the afternoon, so he had two hours before he needed to be back.

CHAPTER 76

GRACE'S LAST LETTER

THE AFTERNOON WAS WARM, AND GABE RODE BUCK slowly across Front Street toward the river. He found a quiet spot with some brush and stepped off. He turned Buck loose and found a big rock to lean against.

He opened the packet of letters and took out the one with Grace's name. He smelled it. There was no perfume smell and his heart pinched. He took a deep breath and opened the letter.

The handwriting was not Grace's, and he frowned as he started to read.

April 30, 1879

My Dearest Gabe,

Sister Rose is writing this letter for me as I am now too weak to write. When Mother became ill, we thought it was fast pneumonia. She had attended a funeral in Clay County, Kansas (just west of Manhattan) shortly after you left. It was for her good friend Mary Sterrett's little son, Harry. He drowned in a well. Mother took the train out to his funeral.

Four children in the Mussellman family in that community died shortly after the funeral. The doctor here believes that Mother contracted diphtheria while she was at the funeral. It is very contagious. He diagnosed my illness as diphtheria when both Father and I became ill. I haven't seen Father, but Sister Rose told me that he was improving. He misses mother so. We both do.

Gabe, I am dying. By the time you receive this letter, I will be gone. Please don't be sad. I am not sending this to you to make you sad. I am sending it to thank you for allowing me to dream about you and to fall in love with you.

When I became ill, Cappy sat with me and told me stories. He told me all about your childhood and your life in South Texas. He told me about your first drive as a wrangler for Charlie Goodnight and Oliver Loving and how he became your friend. He described Dan and Sicily Ann Waggoner, and he shared the entire story of how you helped them get their money back. He told me how you worked so hard to take care of your mother and little Nate. How I wish I could have met them.

Cappy loves you so much. Just being with him these last few days was a wonderful gift. You didn't know it, but we had a talk about you the morning after you left. Cappy has been a wonderful friend to me.

Gabe, I will never forget our horseback ride. How I wanted you to kiss me before you left that day, but you were such a gentleman. I was so sure that I would see you again—that we would fall madly in love like they do in the fairy tales. I guess it just wasn't to be.

Please don't be sad, Gabe. You allowed me to experience love, and it has been a wonderful month of dreaming about you. Now that Cappy has shared so many stories, I know that love would have been even deeper if we had been given the chance to know each other better. Perhaps it was just my dreamings, but I believe you felt something too.

I hope your drive went well and that you will someday have that ranch you want so badly. In my dreams, you call it the Diamond H Ranch. I wanted to be the woman who would put that sparkle in your eye, but I know now it will be someone else. I hope she will love you deeply and make you smile.

May you think of me sometimes when the sun is shining, and it is a perfect day for a horseback ride. Thank you for coming into my life and for letting me taste just a little of what love must be.

Yours forever,
Grace

Gabe stared at the letter in his hand and then dropped it to the ground. He put his head in his hands and cried silently. He cried for Grace and for the love that would never be. Great sobs shook his shoulders, but no sound came out. Finally, he wiped his eyes and picked up the letter. He stared at it for a moment and then held it up in the air. He let the wind take it away. "Yep, it's gone just like Grace."

Buck nuzzled his shoulder and nickered softly. Gabe wrapped his hand in the horse's mane and buried his face in Buck's neck. "She was a good one, Buck. I think we might have made it together." Quietly, Gabe mounted Buck and started slowly back to Dodge. He was in no mood to go to a wedding or a party, but he owed it to Rusty and Larry. Grace's words came back to him.

"Diamond H Ranch. That is what we will call our ranch, Buck. It will be my gift to Grace." Buck didn't respond and Gabe urged him to a lope. He left his horse at the livery and walked down to take another bath.

CHAPTER 77

RUSTY'S WEDDING

RUSTY ARRIVED AT THE CHURCH EARLY. HE WAS nervous and excited. He had purchased a green shirt and black vest to go with his black britches. His leg was healing well. He had hoped to leave the splint off for the ceremony but when he put a little weight on it, his leg almost gave out. Reluctantly, he tied the splint back on. He grinned as he looked at the sticks on either side of his leg.

"That boot black worked. Those sticks just durn near blend in with my britches."

At five-thirty, the guests began to arrive. Rusty watched anxiously for Larry and her family. Finally, he saw their wagon coming down the street.

Larry's short hair was curled around her head and tied back with a small bow. Her dress was blue, and the swell of the child growing inside her showed beneath the gathered skirt that draped over her stomach.

Rusty caught his breath. For just a moment, he couldn't move. When he was able to breathe again, he hurried to help his bride down. He offered his hand to Mrs. Evans first and swung Larry around before he set her on the ground. He was grinning, and Larry laughed at the excitement and happiness on his face.

Harold Evans slapped him on the back. "Let's get this deal started. Some of these folks have driven quite a ways to come. The church ladies will feed everyone afterwards, and that will make it a long evening.

"Now you get up to the front of that church, young man. I am walking my own daughter up the aisle."

Gabe chuckled at Rusty's surprised look. "Ever been to a wedding, Rusty?"

The cowboy's eyebrows drew together. "Cain't say that I have. Ain't even been in a church since I left home."

Gabe nodded somberly. "Who did you ask to stand up with you?"

Rusty looked confused and Gabe laughed.

He grabbed the younger man by the arm and led him inside. "Do you have any kind of a ring? If you don't, you might tell the pastor so he leaves that part out."

Rusty nodded and patted his pocket. "I have one. My ol' ma give me hers. It was passed down from her Ma. She handed it to me when I left home." He added softly, "She would sure have liked to be here today. She always wanted me to marry a nice gurl, an' I know she'd a liked little Larry."

Gabe was quiet. *Larry is a nice girl. I guess sometimes it is all right to change your rules up. It sure worked out for Rusty and Larry.*

He looked back to where Emilia and Merina were sitting. They had returned from fishing after him. Merina had been quiet on the walk to the church, but Gabe didn't mind. It had been an emotional day. He thought about Badger's offer and then about Grace. *My mind is too full to even concentrate,* he thought to himself.

The young man next to him began to fidget, and Gabe brought his mind back to the moment. Larry was walking up the aisle, and she looked beautiful. Her smile was for Rusty alone, and for one of the few times in his life, Gabe was envious. His heart pinched and then he smiled.

They both deserve this. Rusty will be the best father and husband he can be for little Larry, and we will all get to see that little baby grow up. His smile grew bigger.

Tears filled Larry's eyes as her father kissed her cheek and placed her hand in Rusty's. She smiled up at Rusty before she looked over at Gabe. She whispered, "Thank you," and the pastor began the ceremony.

Larry's hands were shaking, and Rusty kissed one of them. He squeezed it and smiled at her. Larry slowly relaxed, and the ceremony went off without a hitch. When Rusty kissed his bride, Emilia laughed out loud.

"Look, Nina. They are kissing in front of everyone. You always said that girls should only kiss where people can't see them!"

Merina's blush rushed up her neck to her face, and Gabe laughed along with the rest of the guests.

Rusty led his bride down the aisle. When they reached the doors, he scooped her up and carried her through them.

"We won't have a house fer a time, so I reckon I will jist carry ya through this here doorway into our new life," he whispered as he kissed her. Larry smiled at him, and he kissed her again before he stood her on her feet. They greeted each guest as people left the church and then joined their friends for the wedding reception.

The church ladies had outdone themselves. Gabe looked at all the food in amazement. "How did they get all this planned and cooked in such a short time?" he wondered out loud.

Angel joined him and nodded his head. "Si, women will run the world if we let them. We must be firm or they will take over." His dark eyes were twinkling, and Gabe laughed at his friend.

"Shoot, Angel. That hasn't even worked in your own family!"

Angel watched Merina as she walked toward them talking to Emilia. He nodded and his face was mournful. "I will never find a husband for Merina. She is a difficult woman."

Merina looked up just then, and Gabe grinned at her. She looked from him to her brother. Gabe's grin became larger when she frowned at them.

"Ladies, allow me to escort you to your seats," he drawled as he offered Merina his arm. Emilia grabbed his hand, and he swung her up to carry her.

"You sure look pretty today, Emilia. Did any of those old rats bite you in your hair today?"

The little girl looked at him somberly and nodded. Then she whispered, "Nina offered me candy if I didn't cry when she brushed my hair."

Gabe grinned at her and gave her a hug. "Well I reckon that was a good trade. I think your sister is a pretty wise woman."

He grinned at Merina and was rewarded with a quick smile before she looked away.

The food was delicious, but the guests didn't stay long once they had eaten. Most wanted to be home before dark to do chores.

Dink left early too. Gabe watched him go with surprise, and Angel chuckled.

"Señor Dink found a girl at the Lady Gay Dance Hall. He is sure she loves him. I'm thinking he might not make the drive north."

Gabe stared at the slim rider beside him in surprise before he shrugged. "Well, he had better make up his mind tonight or he will have to come north to get the other half of his wages."

Larry dragged Gabe over to her parents. "Mother, Father—I want you to meet Gabe Hawkins. He is the trail boss who rescued me at Doan's Crossing. Had it not been for him, I would never have met Rusty. Gabe, these are my parents, Harold and Mary Evans."

Harold Evans held out his hand. He studied the face of the tall young man in front of him and then squeezed his hand.

"Mr. Hawkins, I know trail bosses rarely take women along on cattle drives. My wife and I sure thank you for breaking your rules and helping our daughter. Even though we are sorry to see her leave again, we wish all of you the best on the drive up north. Best of luck in locating your new spread as well. Any idea where you will be settling?"

Gabe looked around at the small group waiting for his answer. Nate had come to the wedding with Merina's brothers, and he was watching Gabe hopefully. Even Merina seemed to be waiting for an answer.

He nodded his head and his smile became wide. "I was offered a spread south of Cheyenne this afternoon, a place called the Diamond H Ranch. So yes, we do have a place to settle now." His eyes moved from the Monteros to Nate and then on to the O'Briens. "We might have to add on though. I don't know that all these people will fit into one small house."

Harold Evans' brows raised before he laughed. "I guess you will at that."

The wedding party broke up, and their friends all waved as Rusty and Larry drove off in their wagon. Rusty waved his hat and hollered back at the riders, "See y'all in a few days." He headed the wagon north and Gabe chuckled.

"I guess he opted to sleep on the ground for his first night of married life."

Mary Evans shook her head, "No, John's sister lives north of town a piece. She and her husband are visiting family in Manhattan. They offered to let Laurel and Rusty stay in their home since they will be gone." She blushed slightly as she added, "It will be a little quieter there for the two of them."

Gabe nodded and shook hands again with both of Larry's parents. He looked at them directly as he stated, "Mr. and Mrs. Evans, you raised a fine girl. Larry found herself a good man, and they are going to be happy. I'm glad I broke my rules and let her come along. She was nothing but an asset to our drive."

John said nothing, but Mary Evans hugged Gabe and whispered, "Thank you. I have been so worried about her. I just knew she was in some kind of trouble, but I had no idea how to find her." She smiled at Gabe as she released him.

"You have a kind heart, Gabe Hawkins."

Gabe blushed and turned to the small party waiting on him. "We had better get back to the Dodge House. I want to be headed up the trail by six tomorrow morning."

CHAPTER 78

A Walk with a Friend

EMILIA RAN AHEAD CALLING BACK TO HER BROTHERS. Angel and Miguel laughed as they followed her and Nate ran after them.

The evening was cool, and Gabe slowed down. "It is a pleasant evening for a walk."

Merina was quiet. She finally stopped and turned toward Gabe. She carefully lifted a smudged paper from her pocket.

"Emilia found your letter. It was stuck in a bush by the trail when we came back from fishing." Her eyes were dark with emotion as she whispered, "I am so sorry."

Gabe took the letter. He stared at it a moment before he shoved it into his pocket. "I threw it away after I read it this afternoon, but I regretted that later. Thank you for finding it."

Merina stared up at him. Her eyes were soft, and her face was serious.

"Señor, I owe you an apologia—a—I believe you say apology. I have treated you rudely. I thought you were just a bold gringo who was used to many women. I know now that you are not that person."

Gabe shook his head and laughed dryly. "No, I can assure you that I know little about women. Kids I like—women I don't understand at all." His face slowly broke into a grin as they continued their walk, "Although I don't think that you are as difficult as Angel claims you are."

Merina looked up at him. "Did Grace's father die?"

Gabe frowned. "I don't know. There were several letters in the pack that Cappy gave me, but I didn't read any of the others. I guess I had better so I know what to do with Gallagher's share of the herd money."

He looked down at Merina and cautiously asked, "Would you like to walk with me and read the other letters? I can get them from my room and we could maybe go someplace quiet." He looked away. He could feel the heat climb up his neck.

"I don't mean to be forward. I know you don't like to walk out with men, but maybe as friends?"

Merina studied his face and nodded. "I would like that, señor. I will ask Angel to see to Emilia."

After they entered the Dodge House, Gabe waited until Merina was in her room. He took the stairs two at a time. Nate was pulling off his boots, and Gabe nodded toward the bed.

"I have some paperwork to tend to. I will be back in an hour or so. You go ahead and take the bed. I can bunk on the floor. If Cappy comes by, he can sleep here too."

Gabe grabbed the packet of papers and loped back down the stairs. He was waiting in the lobby when Merina joined him. Angel poked his head out of their door and grinned at him. Gabe promptly blushed, and the ornery cowpuncher laughed as he shut the door.

Merina looked behind her and then muttered under her breath in Spanish. She looked up in surprise when Gabe laughed and rolled her eyes. "Hermanos."

Gabe's grin remained, "Brothers?" he asked.

She nodded, "Si, they are always trying to run my life."

Gabe chuckled as he offered her his arm. "I reckon if I had two sisters or even one as pretty as you and Emilia, I would be trying to keep an eye on you too."

Merina rolled her eyes and pointed to the east. "This way, señor. I know a little spot that is quiet. Last night, I slipped out when I could not sleep. It is close and quieter than the street." She led him to a small cluster of trees. They were small, but their trunks were straight. The two young people sat down.

Gabe laid the packet of letters on the ground without speaking, and Merina asked quietly, "Would you like me to read them to you?"

He nodded. "If you don't mind. I will just listen and think as you read."

Merina opened the packet. A small wooden horse fell out along with a tin type of a happy family. She set them on the ground and pulled out the first letter. She studied the name on the front of the envelope.

"This is from Sister Rose." Merina opened the letter and quickly scanned it. She looked up and whispered, "Her father died. The doctor said it was his heart. He seemed to be getting well. Then he became weak and died." She studied the letter again and then looked at Gabe. "All of them are gone. That is very sad."

Gabe was quiet. He thought about Joseph Gallagher and the evening he had spent at their house. "They were fine people, Joseph and Kate. They adopted Grace as a child and gave her a wonderful life.

"Joseph wanted to go West. He was an engineer and a stone mason. He loved to work with his hands. I think I would have liked him had we known each other better."

Merina carefully laid the letter down and reached back into the packet. There were three envelopes left. She chose the one that was the most wrinkled. Her face showed surprise as she read it. "This one is to Grace from someone called James. He seemed to know her as a child."

Gabe looked up in surprise and took the letter from Merina. He was smiling as he read it, but his face became tight as he looked at Merina. "James and Grace were on the same wagon train. James took care of her after her folks died. She loved him like a brother." He pointed at the small wooden horse on the ground. "I am guessing he carved that horse for her.

"The Gallaghers adopted Grace, but they didn't adopt James. Her family lost contact with him and they all hoped to find him one day." He added softly, "I will need to tell him about Grace."

Merina lifted the last two envelopes from the packet. One was large and looked like it contained many papers. The smaller one was another letter. She opened it and surprise filled her face as she read it. She handed the letter to Gabe.

"Señor Gallagher left his cattle to you!"

Gabe took the note and read it quickly. His expression was stunned as he looked at Merina. "I barely knew him."

Merina touched his hand, "But you knew Grace and he could see how much you meant to her." Her lower lip trembled as she added, "What a sad thing for a father—to have lost his entire family and know that he too was dying."

She handed the large envelope to Gabe without speaking.

As he opened it and flipped through the documents, he looked up. His face was pale. "He asked me to try to find James. He has left James all his land and business holdings. There is a note here apologizing for not adopting him. Evidentially, James begged them to take him too when they adopted Grace. The Gallaghers had regrets later, and Joseph always wanted to apologize to James."

He handed the note back to Merina, and she read it carefully before she looked up at Gabe.

"It asks that you try to find him. If he doesn't want the investments, or if you can't locate him, after five years everything is yours."

Gabe leaned back against the tree and stared up at the sky. "I would have rather had Grace," he whispered softly.

Merina was quiet as she put the envelopes back into the packet. She closed it and pulled her knees up to her chest. She wrapped her arms around them as she watched Gabe. *Grace saw Gabe's heart. I didn't see it until she showed it to me. He carries so much weight on his shoulders, and I don't know how to make his load lighter.*

Gabe finally looked up and smiled at Merina. "Thank you, Merina, for helping me to read these. I didn't want to read them alone." The sun was nearly to the horizon and Gabe stood. He held out his hand to Merina. "We had better get back. Tomorrow will come early, and I am tired already."

He offered her his arm, and they walked slowly back to the Dodge House.

Dink was waiting in front of the Dodge House when Merina and Gabe returned. He stared from his boss to the young woman on Gabe's arm before he spoke.

"Boss, I want my time. I have decided to stay in Dodge. I found me a ridin' job with a feller south of town for the winter. I'll give it a year an' see how it goes."

Gabe was quiet as he pulled his tally book from inside his vest. He checked some numbers and pulled cash out of the money belt around his waist. He counted it out to Dink and offered him his hand.

"I hope it works out for you, Dink. You're a good hand, and any ranch would be lucky to have you."

Dink blushed slightly as he shook Gabe's hand. "Thanks, boss." He grinned as he added, "Ya never know—I might show up on your spread someday. Life seems to have a few twists." He turned to walk away but looked back. "'Luck, boss. Ma'am," and he tipped his hat to Merina.

Gabe growled under his breath. "Love and women. They just keep fellers all stirred up."

Merina looked up at him and laughed. "Of course, señor, but the men, perhaps it makes them happy."

He grinned down at her. "Some of them. *Some* of them it makes happy. And call me Gabe." His eyes twinkled as he studied her face, "Or boss. I think I would like to hear you call me boss."

Merina's brows drew together in a slight frown and Gabe chuckled. *I am her boss, but Merina refuses to buckle down for any man. This could be an interesting drive.*

Gabe watched as she walked up the stairs to her room. She turned around at the top of the stairs. "Thank you for the nice evening, señor Gabe." The sparkle was back in her eyes, and she smiled as she opened the door to her room.

Gabe walked slowly up the stairs. Nate was asleep on the floor, and Cappy was there as well. He pushed the packet of letters into his war bag and pulled off his boots. As he lay back on the bed, he could hear Merina talking to her brothers.

Angel's voice was clear as he spoke in Spanish, "So you walked out with the boss? Ah, little sister, I didn't think that you liked men so much."

Gabe grinned. He could hear the humor in Angel's voice as he teased Merina.

Merina spoke quickly, "We walked as friends. The señor needed a friend tonight."

"And how about Merina? Did my sister need a friend tonight as well?"

"The señor is a good man with a sad heart. I think maybe I would like to be his friend."

Her brothers were quiet, and Gabe put his hands under his head as he closed his eyes. A small woman with dark eyes and hair as black as that of a raven smiled at him in his sleep. He looked around for Grace, but she was gone. When he looked back toward the small woman, she smiled at him again. Gabe frowned. Slowly the frown faded and a smile crossed his face.

Cappy was awake but he said nothing. When Gabe was ready to talk, he would be there to listen. He was pleased that Merina had been there for Gabe.

A tear ran down the side of Cappy's cheek. He wiped at it but slowly smiled. *Merina. Mebbie Gabe will find happiness after all.* He closed his eyes and pinched them shut to keep more tears from leaking out.

"Aw, Gracie. Ya was such a sweet little gal. Gabe misses ya an' I shore do too."

CHAPTER 79

NORTH TO OGALLALA

GABE, NATE, AND CAPPY WERE IN BEATTY'S WHEN IT opened at five the next morning. The restaurant catered to the working cowboy and opened earlier in the mornings than some of the other eating houses. They were nearly finished when Angel entered followed by the rest of his family.

"The horses are in front, señor. The hostler said you had paid him already, so we will be ready to leave as soon as we eat."

Gabe looked up in surprise and laughed. "Angel, your mother was correct. You are an angel...sometimes."

The lean cowboy winked at him, and they all sat down. Emilia pushed Nate out of his chair and climbed up beside Gabe. She smiled at him, and Gabe's heart melted.

"Good morning, Emilia. Are you ready to ride your pony today? I guess I don't know what his name is. Every good cow pony should have a name, you know."

Her small face broke into a huge smile. "I call him Hawk. I name him after you, señor. He is very smart and very quick. He is much like you."

Gabe looked over her shoulder at the small, scruffy Shetland tied in front. Cappy started laughing, and Gabe slowly turned red. He grinned down at the small girl and patted her head.

"Well, I reckon I am pleased to have a horse named after me even if he is a short one. Now you eat those griddlecakes so we can get on up the trail."

He looked from Merina to her brothers before he studied Cappy and Nate.

"Fellers, I think the good looks of this outfit just went up a couple of notches. Compared to the Moneros, we look mighty shabby."

Cappy grinned and winked at Merina. "I reckon I'll jist settle on the lowest rung of that there ladder an' stay there. I ain't too worried 'bout lookin' sharp fer no one." He pushed back his old hat and rubbed his nearly bald head. His scruffy face was rough—somewhere between needing a shave and barely a beard. His eyes were bright blue, and his face was friendly as he looked around the table.

"'Course Gabe on the other hand, he thinks he's a hand with the ladies. He's always a tryin' to look good fer some little gal."

Gabe almost choked on his coffee, and Cappy laughed wickedly. The breakfast conversation was lively, but they were soon finished.

Gabe offered Merina his hand as she mounted. He almost commented on how pretty she looked. Instead, he turned away to mount Buck.

Merina *was* striking. She sat her horse proudly. Her dark britches were tucked into tall, western boots, and her hair hung in a long braid down her back. The Stetson she wore was tan, and the stampede string was pulled tight under her chin. Her long-sleeved shirt was dark blue, and she wore a leather belt at her waist with a silver buckle. Emilia wore britches and a bright pink shirt with embroidery on the yoke. Her pants were tied at her small waist with a piece of leather.

Gabe led the way out of Dodge. The air was clear, and the sun was just rising as they turned their horses to the north. He grinned as he looked over his crew. They were an interesting group, but he would put them up against any drovers out there. He patted his horse's neck and muttered, "This is going to be a fine ride, Buck. Just downright enjoyable."

Gabe glanced behind as they drew away from Dodge. His chest tightened and he took a deep breath. *I'll leave you there, Grace. You are just a memory now.*

He urged Buck to a lope, and Merina's horse moved up beside him. He looked over at the young woman. Merina was smiling. She rode Mascota like she was one with him while Emilia chattered happily with Cappy. Nate and Miguel were laughing at something Angel had said. Gabe slowly relaxed.

His heart lost some of its tightness as they crossed the small stream in front of them and headed for Buckner Creek. He settled back in his saddle. They should reach the herd in several hours.

Gabe slowly smiled. *Seven riders and seven lives. It will be a new start for all of us.*